Dedalus European Antho
General Editor: Mike M

C000247308

The Dedalus Book of Flemish Fantasy

The Dedalus Book
of
Flemish Fantasy

Edited by Eric Dickens
and
Translated by Paul Vincent

Dedalus

Dedalus would like to thank The Flemish Literature Fund (Vlaams Fonds voor de Letteren) in Belgium and Grants for the Arts in Cambridge for their assistance in producing this book.

Published in the UK by Dedalus Limited,
24-26, St Judith's Lane, Sawtry, Cambs, PE28 5XE
email: info@dedalusbooks.com   www.dedalusbooks.com

ISBN 978 1 903517 93 2

Dedalus is distributed in the USA by SCB Distributors,
15608 South New Century Drive, Gardena, CA 90248
email: info@scbdistributors.com   www.scbdistributors.com

Dedalus is distributed in Australia by Peribo Pty Ltd.
58, Beaumont Road, Mount Kuring-gai, N.S.W. 2080
email: info@peribo.com.au

Dedalus is distributed in Canada by Disticor Direct-Book Division
695, Westney Road South, Suite 14, Ajax, Ontario, LI6 6M9
email: ndalton@disticor.com   www.disticordirect.com

First published by Dedalus in 2010

Introduction, Notes and Selection copyright © Eric Dickens 2010
Translations copyright © Paul Vincent 2010

The right of Eric Dickens to be identified as the editor and of Paul Vincent to be identified as the translator of this work has been asserted by them in accordance with the Copyright, Designs and Patents Act, 1988

Printed in Finland by Bookwell
Typeset by Marie Lane

The Editor

Eric Dickens (born 1953) is a literary translator who takes an interest in the literature of some of the smaller countries of Europe. These include that of the Estonians, the Finland-Swedes, the speakers of Nynorsk in Norway, and the Flemings. For him Flemish literature is more experimental, avant garde and groundbreaking than that of the Netherlands; he attributes this to its minority status. Eric is from an Anglo-Dutch family. He grew up in England and went to the University of East Anglia, where he studied Swedish and European Literature. He now lives in Sweden. He is also the translator of the texts for *The Dedalus Book of Estonian Literature.*

The Translator

Paul Vincent taught Dutch at London University for many years, and since 1989 has been a freelance translator from Dutch and German. In fiction he has translated numerous modern classics from the Low Countries, including work by Couperus, Elsschot, Mulisch, Boon and Van den Brink. In addition he specialises in non-fiction, and has translated a wide range of poetry from the seventeenth century onwards. In 2007 he co-edited an anthology of twentieth-century stories: *In Praise of Navigation* (Seren Books).

He is a member of the Society of Dutch Literature.

Acknowledgements

The editor would like to thank, first of all, Greet Ramael of the Flemish Literature Fund for her support and especially for identifying some of the contemporary Flemish authors for this anthology. Secondly, I would like to thank all the copyright holders for allowing the works to be published here, and for their prompt responses. And last, but certainly not least, Paul Vincent for translating what is a very broad range of styles of works written between the early 20th century and the present day.

Eric Dickens, Uppsala, December 2010

Contents

Introduction

Belgium came into being as recently as 1830, an amalgamation of a Dutch-speaking north, Flanders, and a French-speaking south, Wallonia, with bilingual Brussels right in the middle. Belgium became a nation state owing to a complex, centuries-long search for identity as the region broke away, first from Spanish-Austrian rule, then from Napoleonic France, and finally from the Protestant Netherlands. This volume will therefore deal with literature written in the northern half of Belgium. The adjective "Flemish" can be used about the Dutch-speaking part, but while the dialects are Flemish, the standard language is Dutch, which is also spoken in the Netherlands.

Within Flanders, there are several different provinces and regions, each with its own character. While the French-speaking south of Belgium is hilly, rural and, around Charleroi, the Borinage and Liège, once supported a now largely extinct coal-mining and steel industry, Flanders is much more urbanised, though even today there are surprisingly many havens of rural peace. The open countryside is usually flatter, cut through by rivers. And it is Flanders that has Belgium's short stretch of coastline, including the once chic seaside resort Ostend, visited by many famous authors from all over Europe, including Zweig, Couperus, Roth, Joyce and Proust.

The cities of Flanders emerged commercially and politically in the Middle Ages and flourished during the Flemish golden age of the 17th century. A traditional Flemish city will have a beautifully ornate town hall on the main square, e.g. Brussels, Brugge (Bruges), Antwerp, Ghent, Mechelen (Malines) and Leuven (Louvain). But in later centuries, and with the advent of the industrial revolution, industrial towns sprang up with their cités, i.e. grim housing estates for factory workers. Several of the authors here are associated in some way with the larger cities of Ghent or Antwerp where they were born or have lived.

The spoken Dutch of Flanders has many dialects, some very broad indeed, incomprehensible even to those from the next town or village. But most authors write in standard Dutch, with a few regional expressions strewn through the text. Apart from these expressions and idioms, the language is basically the same as that spoken and written in Amsterdam, The Hague, and Groningen in the neighbouring Netherlands. The language was standardised and brought closer to northern Dutch especially during the 19th century, when there was a surge of Flemish national awareness and local patriotism. Currently, spelling and terminology are being standardised throughout the Dutch language-area under the auspices of the Dutch Language Union.

Belgium is largely Roman Catholic, but especially since industrialisation in the 19th century there has been tension between religion and secularism, mainly the Socialist brand. Catholicism informs most of earlier Belgian, and especially Flemish, literature. As the century wore on there were far more allusions to the struggle for workers rights in this literature than that of the Netherlands.

*

Like the country itself, Flemish literature is young. From 1830 until about the turn of the 20th century, most modern literature of any value was written in the French language. So, with notable exceptions like the novelist Hendrik Conscience (1812-1883) and the poet Guido Gezelle (1830-1899), there are few significant authors in Flanders writing in Dutch until the beginning of the 20th century. This does not mean that Flemings were not writing literature before that. Several famous Belgian authors, such as Nobel prizewinner Maurice Maeterlinck, and the famous poet Emile Verhaeren, were in fact Flemings who wrote in French. Even during the 20th century, several notable Flemish authors, such as realist Marie Gevers and fantasy author Jean Ray, continued to write in French. But French-speaking Flemish authors have been excluded from this volume on language grounds.

Nevertheless, the influence of the French language and literary style can be seen in the works of early Flemish authors, some of whom consciously chose to change from writing in French to writing in their native Flemish brand of Dutch.

Once Flemish literature was established in the Dutch language, things took off. Karel van de Woestijne, a major poet, also wrote Symbolist stories, and Felix Timmermans, evolved from writing morbid and ghostly horror tales to become the author of a kind of affirmative, joyous poetic prose, praising the joys of life. Only the first aspect of his work is represented here.

Some stories clearly echo the two poles of Flemish society, religiosity and secularism. Authors such as Karel van de Woestijne and Felix Timmermans have been deeply affected by the Catholic brand of Christianity with its piety, monasteries and devotion to the Virgin Mary. By contrast, secularism and social comment is reflected in the works of, for instance, Paul van Ostaijen, Louis Paul Boon and Kristien Hemmerechts. But some of the authors here have written fantasy that is not especially linked to either clericalism or secularism, especially those writing horror stories or magical realism such as Hugo Raes and Hubert Lampo.

Flanders was devastated by the Second World War as it had been in the Great War, when many of the key battles were fought on Flemish soil. But by the late 1940s, Belgian literature on both sides of the language divide was recovering and some of the greatest works of Flemish literature, especially in the genre magical realism, were written in the 1940s and 1950s.

Flemish authors have, on average, a more experimental tendency, compared with those from the Netherlands. This may be due in part to the tensions emerging from the clash, as mentioned above, between clericalism and Socialism, a tension which actually produced some of the best Flemish literature. But whatever their background, Flemings tend to be very conscious of language. The fact that the Dutch language is safe in the Netherlands, but is never entirely free of outside cultural pressure from the French language in Flanders means that Flemish authors have become very conscious of the social, as well as linguistic aspects of their use of language. The author of many novels, Ivo Michiels, has continued to write in Dutch even though he has lived for thirty years in the south of France.

Apart from the true experimentalists, there are several other genres represented here. The early works are nearer to poetic Symbolism, the later ones introduce horror and magical realism. All of the texts here see reality through a prism that somehow distorts. And some recent works have anti-utopian or apocalyptic traits associated with science fiction.

The horror stories begin with Felix Timmermans. Early Flemish horror was of the spooky kind with crypts, ghosts and Death ever present. Later horror, by such authors as Ruyslinck and Raes is more linked to contemporary society. Though Hugo Claus does a kind of semi-parody on life in the Middle Ages.

Magic realism is represented by Johan Daisne and Hubert Lampo. Magic realism was furthered, if not actually invented, by these two authors, although it is of a gentler, less weird, exotic or narcotic, brand than works of say Márquez or Rushdie. The realism is of a mostly urban, Belgian kind, while the fantasy involves mysterious women, people who disappear under mysterious circumstances, dream landscapes, even a hint of Atlantis and the Holy Grail.

Louis Paul Boon is perhaps one of the best known Flemish authors in international terms. He came closest to winning the Nobel Prize for Literature than any other Flanders author writing in Dutch. And he would have been a worthy winner. His two most experimental novels, almost postmodernist before the term was widely used, i.e. *Chapel Road* and *Summer in Termuren* have appeared in English translation in the United States. Boon jumps from topic to topic in what are usually short sections, but he always maintains a main theme, as here with five spoof micro-fairy-tales.

Satire is represented by two authors. Paul van Ostaijen is the nearest thing to a Flemish Dadaist that could be imagined, but his weird and nervous tales have a satirical bent, lodged in that curious limbo between committed literature and experimental narration that often makes Flemish literature so fascinating. Paul Snoek was equally politically critical of society as a whole and there is a pacifist streak in the story here. Both Van Ostaijen and Snoek were innovative poets.

The most experimental writers represented here are J. M. H. Berkmans, Ivo Michiels and Walter van den Broeck. The first of these wrote manic-zany descriptions of a fairly sleazy brand of everyday life, while Michiels has done things in a more leisurely manner. His story is a self-standing excerpt from his ten-volume novel cycle *Journal Brut*. Walter van den Broeck has also written mildly Kafkaesque novels, including the one from which the excerpt here has been taken. Its principal themes are the futility of work and family tensions. Walter van den Broeck situates his characters, mostly of working-class origin, in unusual environments or situations.

In Flanders, women authors have not written as much non-realist prose as have men. There are only four represented here out of a total of 23, and all four stories are in some degree rooted in realism. The perception of what are basically plausible events can be interwoven with a distortion of perceived reality to a greater or lesser extent.

*

An anthology can be no more than a sampler of any national literature, but the authors represented here give something of a cross-section of those writing in Dutch in Belgium. I hope this anthology will encourage readers to seek out more works of those authors featured here where they are already available in English. It is to be hoped that Flemish literature, produced in cities which as the crow flies are nearer to London than Edinburgh is, can gain an identity of its own in the minds of British readers. The Flemish coast faces England, yet nowadays all we hear about Belgium is Brussels, not as a literary city, but as the seat of many of the institutions of the European Union. I hope that this anthology will increase the awareness that Flanders has a proud literature of its own and has, over the past century or so,

Introduction

built up a literary profile worth examining.

Just Like Rasputin, We Plod Through Mud And Piss In Search Of Kellogg's Cornflakes

J.M.H. Berckmans

When gigolos speak

From my right knee shoot shit-coloured titanium roses, on my left side silver warts on my prick, warts with long iron hairs, three metres long, no, longer still, four or five metres.
The lights are now going out all over Europe and we emerge from our lairs in the browned, scorched wood, we, kings of the earth spirits, and Greta is our queen.
(While all that shoots from granddad and granny is nasal and moustache hair respectively. Christ.)

The man who knew too much got totally pissed and as a result suddenly knew much more than Fons was happy about.
There ensued an initially minimal scuffle which however became faster and faster and was cranked up with increasing intensity to the maximum by the public, between the man who knew too much (and suddenly turned out to know everything much better) on the one hand and Fons on the other.
I can't remember the rest and will have to ask Szukalski or Leon some time, since de Brees probably won't remember either. And Fons is still in hospital.

Every day, again and again, whatever the weather, in pouring rain or boiling sun, Leon and Szukalski and de Brees and Raimundo van Bedaf and Doctor Bang the Wormbonker together with thirty-seven other Greeks, stand waiting at the bus stop at five in the afternoon

15

for the girls from the shit factories. Leon particularly has a virtually infallible nose for them.

Of course not here and now, you idiots, in the Grey Zone, but in 1967, on the island of Papathanassiou, right, you idiots, like Vangelis, I can tell from your mugs that you know something about it.

200398123246

Up to now the day had not posed any unanswerable questions or any problems to speak of but it can still all get fucked up, of course.

Yeah yeah. Life is beautiful and we're cheerful chums. Of course. I read it in New Gazette. So it's bound to be true. After the discovery of fire, yesterday, today Leon has invented hot water. It took quite a while. He now drinks rose hip tea instead of beer. He thinks that's better for his bladder, which was recently diagnosed as clapped out.

Fire and hot water, though, are only some of the tens of thousands of patents he has taken out at the Paris patent office, which some malicious people are occasionally inclined to confuse deliberately with Gilbert's Original Electronic Shithouse Bureaux (since he already has two, the old guy is earning money, give him another five bagsful).

Christ's new plane is finished. Next week, if atmospheric conditions are at all favourable, he's going to fly it , he's going to fly it with Szukalski on the Left Bank (oh Le Corbusier, dead too now), if it doesn't, like his previous one (all his previous ones, that means) crash and disintegrate in a fraction of a second.

153221 wish my baby were here.

Rien de brûlé, except for the mashed potatoes in the old potatoes' home. And the bacon next to it.

I can still hear the lard melting, then Szukalski's voice, harsh as always, that razor-sharp intonation.

But I don't understand what he's saying.

Hier ist Radio Grauzone, Hallo, Hallo.

Ausgangsverbot von 00.00 Uhr bis 00.00 Uhr.

(Doctor Bang the Wormbonker never said this.)

220398195812
I descend from sweatbox to bog and have a shit.
After only a few moments I leave the bog, I mean after only a few sheets of bog paper later I leave the bog, I've washed my hands with Christian Dior liquid soap and I leave the bog. Where to? What for?

230398035645
With a big display of weaponry a bailiff, whom I also know, enters Leon's place.
Like a speaking condom dispenser he reads, as a kind of litany, Leon's personalia essentialia substantialia paraphernalia, which take up many volumes, so that the light of dawn eventually breaks through the gloom of what else is new.
Then he casts a cursory eye over Leon's Scant Possessions and leaves. As long as he doesn't call the police.

Went on the bus and through cartoon figures like Suske Prinz Fritske and other interesting brain pathways started to grasp Kamelia's affairs.

It seems that the Butcher of Bekkevoort has arrived in the Grey Zone, the brother of the Killer of Kaggevinne. The whole Grey Zone is plastered with his identikit photo. Everyone must be on their guard, the area around all shithouses is being cordoned off. Because the Butcher of Bekkevoort, the brother of the Killer of Kaggevinne is coming. So it's better if you all stay indoors, in your huts and caravans. In the Grey Zone. Because it seems he's not only been sighted but sighted in the Grey Zone. Then the flippos show up with their Zippos and their BMWs and their Mercedes Benzes and their brains hanging down from their fat guts.

Piss is a corrosive flesh-eating flesh-devouring acid.
If you pee in your pants three nights running, like Dr Bang the Wormbonker and Marcel van den Dorpel, who yesterday asked me with his last remnant of lucidity whether I thought he might be

eligible for subsidies, you'll be in agony with the pain and the itching and the eczema on the inside of your buttocks. Then you must rub on Nivea or Olaz. Or else you just go to Bulcke Nathalie, a gangsteress of a generalist who peed in all the beer vats at Interbrew, for a piss puncture, though preceded by a shit-rectoscopy.

So that from today on you're going to sit there gleaming until you start stinking. And nowadays in the Grey Zone from stinking comes gleaming like blablabla from patati patata.

(Patachou. Those were the days. Ages and ages before the times of Dr Bang the Wormbonker. Memory back to Zero.)

230398204500

At a quarter to nine, on his way in the rain in his underpants and his yellow tailcoat the man who knew too much after all bumps unexpectedly into Jeannine.

Stiffer than a stick grows his big Grey Prick.

An empty taxi drives past, somewhere a misanthropic stray cat barks, and somewhere a lonely dog meows.

Nothing changes. Ostensibly nothing changes.

Professor Fussbett wonders aloud what it would be like with Greta.

I say that I can't make any binding assertions regarding her present situation but that an hour ago at any rate she was completely rat-arsed.

Next Kamelia inquires in a rather rarefied way whether Dr Bang the Wormbonker has gone mad and then Greta comes in stone cold sober and in this and in no other way everything just continues and so on and so forth and so forth until no one understands a thing about it and no more questions are asked anymore.

Amen. Station Disconnected.

Just as you have the many lepers and the many people ravaged by Creutzfeldt-Jacob, you also have the deaf-mutes and the garrulous. Marcinelle is garrulous so she rattles and she prattles and she fiddles and she shits and she does things that are quite simply not exactly normal. We had all, except for Fons who had staked a whole pile, bet 100 francs that Marcinelle was deaf and dumb. Fons takes everything, Losers of the Grey Zone take nothing.

300398113456
Out of pure rage Szukalski beat Pittooke to death and grabbed Liliane by the scruff of the neck and threw her out.
What kinds of salons are these nowadays for Christ's sake, what kind of conditions are these in the Grey Zone nowadays.
(Suck the apple because it's Golden Delicious.)

Perhaps different times will come.
Perhaps new love will come.
When the spoon is once again stuck where it should be stuck.
In the fuckin' porridge.

Grim Fairy Tales

Louis Paul Boon

The Sad Blackbird

Not long ago I met a blackbird in the silent forest. It sat singing to itself. When I stopped it began the story of its life.

The forest was just a forest, said the blackbird. Suitors came and hid in it and were free to make lots and lots of chicks. Old women gleaned and gathered wood too. Shady shirkers trapped hares, sometimes a gnome, but never a fairy they could sleep with.

It was known that somewhere there was a main road that led to the heart of the forest, where the owner of all this had a fairy-tale castle. They didn't know him in the village, but around the hearth he was spoken of like the werewolf. Yet they had already seen quite a lot of him. They did not know it but he was the wolf that came among them disguised as a passing traveller. He cured the sick, foretold the future and exchanged foreign coins that were not valid in this world. Whenever he had been through the village, someone or other would be missing a burgeoning young daughter, although he had warned: 'I've just caught a glimpse of the werewolf!'

Every year too he dropped in to see the carpenter, where there was not much to cure or change, but where ripening young girls romped across the floor. And the squire, disguised as a passing traveller, always thought: I'm curious to know whether one of the three young daughters will be ready for plucking this year.

One Saturday morning he came by, when the eldest was about to wash in the tub in the lean-to. She had pitch-black hair, eyes that glowed like hot coals, and deep-brown folds of flesh.

Shrill birds screeched in the squire's blood when he saw her creep into the tub. The memory of the lonely nights in his castle, where his only entertainment was to watch the blocks of wood in the

20

hearth collapsing into ash, was more terrifying than ever. He took her from the tub and stuffed her, wet and naked as she was, in his big haversack.

Taking a detour he returned to the heart of the forest, and only when darkness had fallen and the shutters were closed did he retrieve her from the haversack.

'Dance like the flames in the hearth, screech like the birds in my blood, and stay naked as there in the tub,' he said.

She obeyed, having expected worse.

For a long time she remained his playmate, and he intoxicated himself looking at the deep folds in her flesh, which were tanned so dark brown. It was like a nicely roasted chicken. He had to swallow his spittle when he saw her in his imagination sitting on a dish. But she never gave him cause to be angry, so that he could say in fury: 'I'm going to put you on the spit!'

He crept around pondering his plans, and one day he gave her a silver key and a newly-laid blackbird's egg.

'Carry this always in your hands, but do not insert the key in the wrong lock, or break the egg!' he said.

Then he sat down by the hearth and pretended to sleep. With her key she was dying to know what lock it would fit. She crept off quietly and tried it on all the doors. Eventually she reached the tower room, which she had never entered. And lo, the key fitted. When she went in even the darkest fold in her flesh paled. A large tub was full to the brim with blood, and in it floated the girls who had disappeared from the village.

The fright made her drop the egg, which broke.

When she returned he saw at once what happened and that it was too late. However much he had played with her, it was now time to roast her and eat her up. She would look so wonderful on a dish browned and garnished with parsley. With a melancholy heart he ate the last morsel – it was a kidney – and then collected up the bones and took them to the tower room.

Again his evenings became very lonely, and soon he longed for the carpenter's second daughter, who must now be ripe.

Evening was falling when he dropped by, and he hurried to see her as she was going to bed. His eyes were glued to the low window, and he saw her peeling off the petticoat that had become one with her body. Her head was a blazing torch of red hair, her eyes were green like a cat's.

He hastily stuffed her into his haversack, so he could savour the cream of her skin in his castle, and to warm his hands at the red flame that licked playfully at her belly.

But when he tired of the taste of cream, and he discovered that the tongue of fire between her thighs was all too immobile, he gnawed his fingernails to the quick as before.

Again he fetched the silver key and the newly-laid blackbird's egg, and thrust them into her hands. And he crept silently after her as she climbed the tower stairs. As he looked up from the bottom of the stairs at the swaying of her hips and thighs – in the deep there was now an almost blue shadow, as milk can have – his regret became even greater and even hornier.

The key turned in the lock, the egg went thwack and smashed. It did him good to know that he could now punish her with impunity: he hung her up by the red flame of her hair. The great clamp on the wall soon began to rust.

Then he rushed back to the carpenter's house, as he had an intense longing for the youngest daughter, the most beautiful of all, whom he had saved for last.

She was more playful than her sisters, and liked nothing better than pranks. If she couldn't play pranks she would go and look at her reflection in the water of the brook. Her blonde hair hung around her and her little breasts played blind man's buff among it.

She laughed when she found out that the passing traveller was back, and was ogling her from behind the bushes. She herself asked if she could go with him and whether he knew any nice games.

But by the third evening in the castle she had tired of his games.

'You're far too sad a bird for me,' she said. 'And your song is already making me sad. Don't you know anything else?'

Then he gave her the silver key too and the blackbird's egg, and said: 'Look, the object of this game is to open the right lock and not to break the egg.'

She looked for longer than was necessary, simply because she enjoyed looking so much. Each time she inserted the silver key into the wrong lock, she laughed so much that her little breasts started in the undergrowth of her blonde hair.

At a certain moment she laughed so much that the egg slipped from her grasp, but halfway to the floor she was able to catch it.

The next evening she discovered the tower room. Curious, she bent over the tub and its contents. She looked at her sister's gnawed bones in one corner and at her sister on the nail in the other corner. And when she saw the sad old bird of a squire standing on the threshold, she sad: 'That's a joke I can't laugh at.'

He couldn't kill her. She had opened the tower room and yet had not broken the egg.

'I have no power over you,' he said. 'I give you the heart of the forest and the castle, my fortune, my silver key and my egg. Let us live more or less happily ever after.'

In answer she threw the blackbird's egg in his face. It broke, and the yellow yolk made a big stain. And lo, the squire shrivelled away and became very small and black, but kept the yellow stain of the yolk.

I turned into a sad blackbird. What happened to her afterwards, I don't know. Perhaps she still lives in the heart of the forest in the castle. But I sit here lonely and sing in the rain.

The Three Quacks

They were three comrades but had nothing in common. The war brought them together. And the many and various acts of violence they had committed together weighed on their backs like a common ballast of memories. They looked down with contempt on the petty-minded bourgeois among whom they appeared again, who regarded rapes and the cutting off of bollocks as criminal acts. They could no longer talk to those kinds of people.

When night fell they arrived at an inn, but unfortunately had little ready money left. It was another of those damned things that that they had to cope with from now on, having to pay for everything with money, and not being able to get anything they wanted with it.

Still they went in. The landlord was a worn-out drooling creature, the barmaid on the other had was a bitch, wearing a blouse with not a single button done up. The point of one breast then the other ogled a country bumpkin sitting and sweating by the stove.

The three comrades, rather awkward now they were no longer bursting in with weapons cocked in their hands, sat down sulkily but meekly at the pub table.

'We've got no money,' said the youngest of the three. 'But we can cure all diseases. Look, I'll cut my hand off and leave it on a table tonight and only put it back on again tomorrow morning.'

The senile landlord dribbled heavily. The country bumpkin by the stove goggled. The barmaid leant full of curiosity over the hand that had been severed. She cooed a little, as the limb lay there on the table like the amputated claw of a bird of prey.

'And I,' said the second, 'shall cut off the magic flute and only replace it tomorrow morning.'

Neither the senile landlord nor the country bumpkin could see a thing, so deeply was the barmaid hanging over the second quack, as he flicked open the knife.

'Oh,' she said.

'And what can you do?' she asked the oldest of the three quacks.

'I can cut off one of your breasts and put it back in its place tomorrow morning,' said the oldest.

And he immediately took hold of the knife. But the barmaid hastily withdrew and held her hands protectively in her open blouse. The country bumpkin scrambled to his feet by the stove.

'Not that,' he said. 'Cut off everything thing you've got, but leave her breasts alone.'

A vicious flame smouldered in the eyes of the three quacks, but they already knew that this was a world in which bumpkins had a right to speak. And angered by this fact the oldest gouged out one of his own eyes. They now lay there so strangely on the scrubbed tabletop: the hand like the claw of a bird of prey, the magic flute that had been through so much, and the eye that still glared at the bumpkin with bitter regret.

In return for their performances they were given a not too lavish evening meal, bread with minced brawn and beer – although the larder was full to bursting with braised rabbit and thick pork sausages. But they were hungry, wolfed down everything and went to bed. The oldest without an eye slept next to the youngest without a hand, as they had always done in the war, but the quack without a magic flute slept by himself.

Downstairs the senile landlord had fallen asleep behind the bar, as he was counting the receipts for the previous day. The barmaid on the other hand rode up and down on the bumpkin's knee. They looked towards the table on which the hand, the magic flute and the eye had been left lying – which the cat now came padding around – but she did not see it, because her eyes were full of visions. Much later, when she had sat down quietly, she realised that the cat had gobbled up everything that had been lying on the table.

'What's going to happen tomorrow morning?' she asked.

'Keep calm,' said the bumpkin. 'My old father died yesterday, I'll cut a hand off him and put it there on the table.'
When that was dealt with, the barmaid got a pork sausage from the larder and put it next to the hand. 'Now all we need is an eye!' she said.

She looked round, with her blouse hanging completely open again, grabbed the cat and took out one of its eyes. And when the three quacks appeared in the bar the following morning, they rubbed some magic ointment on what was lying on the table and put everything back in its place. The senile landlord clapped his hands in amazement.

But scarcely had everything started growing back together when the youngest kept putting his hand in his pocket to distribute alms, because the bumpkin's father had been a compassionate man. The second had to resist the repeated impulse to cut off a piece of the sausage and eat it. As for the youngest, he crawled round the floor, sniffing for a possible mouse under the cupboard or the barmaid's skirts.

Then they realised that they had been deceived during the night. And in their rage they battered the old man and the barmaid to death. And they learned the lesson that you must not leave body parts unattended that you happened to have cut off.

The Cyclopses of Schellebelle

Long ago in the bogs of Schellebelle there lived a woman who had only one eye. It was in the middle of her face, just above the base of the nose. It wasn't ugly, but it was fairly unusual – especially since people had never heard about Cyclopses in those parts.

Consequently she withdrew further and further into the bogs, and lived on moorhens and balm bread, which were sufficiently abundant. When she met the waterfowl hunter unexpectedly, she quickly pulled a hood over her head.

One day something strange occurred that had never happened to her before: like the apple tree bears a ripe fruit so she gave birth to a child. It landed with a slight thud in the sodden bog grass. She tiptoed around it as if it were too hot a chestnut. When she finally looked into its face, she saw a single eye staring at her, in the middle of the forehead.

She cried out with joy.

She was so foolish and so happy that in the very first days of the new spring (it was still the beginning of February) she again became pregnant. Perhaps her unconscious aim was to populate the whole bog with Cyclopses. But as the last days of autumn drew near, and the time had come for her to give birth, she became very troubled.

26

She withdrew by herself deep into the salt marshes and gave birth there. Again she scarcely dared look. She was prepared for almost anything – and yet the outcome was even harsher than what she had imagined: the baby had two eyes in its head like farmers and their pigs and in addition, like her sister, a Cyclops' eye, just above the base of her nose.

She looked at this second child, not knowing what to do. Was it of greater or lesser quality than the first? She did not allow herself to be impregnated so stupidly and wildly as before. She picked her balm bread with slower movements, and often sat staring into space.

And when a third child appeared, for God's sake, it quite simply had two eyes. She called the first girl Cyclops and the second Tryclops, but she didn't give the third any name at all, but always said 'That One'. Cyclops and Tryclops eventually thought her name was 'That One'. They stole the balm bread out of her mouth, and kept pulling her dress of woven grass to pieces. So That One went around naked and with her stomach rumbling with hunger.

All day she hunted in the salt marshes for something edible, and one day she managed to get hold of a gnome. It had a fat tummy, which was unfortunately covered by a long dense beard. She first had to pluck it out, before putting him to her mouth. She started when she heard him strike up a conversation…

'It may be an impertinent question,' said the gnome, 'but I'd like to know if you are about to devour me from voluptuousness or from hunger?'

That One had never given the matter any thought. She said it was just because her stomach was completely empty. This disappointed the gnome greatly.

'Then I know of something much better for you,' he said. 'A tree of life that appears at the slightest magic word and has the most wonderful fruit growing on it.'

That One said the magic word, and indeed she saw the tree of life swelling and growing ever larger in the midst of the salt marshes. She climbed into it and ate till she was so full, that she fell back to earth fat and blubbery.

Cyclops and Tryclops noticed that something about her had changed. Her two hungry eyes used to wander into every nook and cranny, in search of a few scraps. Now she was always lying on her back somewhere dozing with a languid look, happy in her nakedness, her lazy legs open, and a smile of contentment round her gleaming navel.

The mother gave That One a bitter look with her one eye. She herself had never lain so nakedly and pleasurably with her arms and legs open wide, like someone who no longer gives two hoots about God or the world.

What was going on with her? And she ordered Cyclops to follow her on one of her trips.

When That One woke, she felt like a cup of chocolate. She quickly hurried into the salt marshes, in order to be alone and say her magic word. But she looked round suspiciously now and then, and discovered that Cyclops had followed her. Instead of making the tree appear, she lay down in the wet grass, and kept singing 'Go to bye-byes – go to bye-byes.' And Cyclops fell asleep.

Only then did the tree of life appear, now with cups of chocolate growing on it. She climbed into it and filled her tummy with the wonderful drink, occasionally plucking a raisin cake. She ate and drank her fill, until she fell, bare bottom and a little more into Cyclops' face.

When she came home Cyclops had nothing to tell.

'I couldn't see a thing,' she said by way of apology, 'That One sat with her derrière in my face.'

Her furious mother now ordered Tryclops to follow That One. And when on this afternoon she felt like pasta with lettuce, Tryclops crept after her. That One again started singing 'Go to bye-byes – go to bye-byes.' However, she didn't know when tryclopses are asleep they shut two eyes but leave the third eye open. And when she was stuffed full of pasta, and returned home with her sister, her sister was able to tell them everything that had happened.

That One was beaten black and blue to make her reveal the

magic word, and when that didn't help they wrenched her legs apart and released a big cross spider. In her terror she blurted out the magic word, and lo, the tree of life appeared. It had no sooner materialised than the three were perched in it. They stuffed everything going into their mouths.

That One hurriedly spoke the word that made the tree disappear again. It quickly shrank, and with it her mother and sisters too. She had a glimpse of the shrivelling Cyclops, with almost ridiculously small legs and a *mons Veneris* without a split, like a doll's.

The last thing she saw was Tryclops, who had tried to drop out of the tree. She was hanging upside down by her feet, with a strange, terrified, goggle-eyed stare.

When everything had disappeared, That One resolved to mend her ways and never again to summon up the tree of life. She squatted down in the very place where her family had disappeared.

As she washed herself, she laughed, and the sound was like a bell. And she roamed the bogs, slapping her buttocks with pleasure. She acquired the name Schellebelle. And as before she fed on balm bread and moorhens. Gnomes were welcome too but she no longer gave them the chance to sweet-talk her.

And if a man spoke to her about the tree of life, she swallowed him whole.

The Disobedient Girl

There was once a girl who was very disobedient, stubborn and, what's more, inquisitive. She didn't even believe that children are found in cauliflowers, and so caused her parents, who were good people, a great deal of unhappiness. One day she said: 'They say in the village that deep in the forest there's a witch who does all kinds of strange things. I'd really like to know if there's any truth in all those tales…'

'My child, please don't ever go into the forest,' said her father. 'I'm much more experienced than you, and know that besides witches there are other dangers lurking too.'

'I'd like to know what they are!' said the disobedient girl.

And her scepticism became even greater when her father remained silent. One Sunday afternoon when everyone was having a nap, she crept off deep into the forest without a word. She had never been there and soon lost her way. She didn't know where the witch lived, and she couldn't find her way back home.

After looking in vain she heard the report of a rifle and the barking of dogs. That must be the hunter. Perhaps he could put her back on the right road! She crawled through the bushes, tearing her dress on the hawthorn and cutting herself on the brambles, but eventually found the hunter.

But as soon as the hunter saw her – young and desirable as she was – he took aim. You didn't shoot a very young girl in the forest every day!

He missed by only a hair's breadth, but his dog came trotting towards her, jaws open and sporting an array of yellow fangs.

She hurriedly retreated. Now it was already her petticoat that tore on the thorns. But she didn't notice, she heard only the panting of the dog behind her, and the hunter's cries of encouragement.

'Get her… I'm going to let her have it!'

The hunter's dog sank its great yellow teeth in her, but she was able to tear herself free, though she left a large part of her petticoat and a piece of her bottom behind. The smell of the blood gradually left a trail that was easy to follow. Fortunately she was able to cross a brook, and so escape. It was none too soon.

Exhausted, she sat down. There was nothing left of her dress but a few shreds, which she had to throw away. But she could scarcely cover her nakedness with her petticoat either. She carefully took it off, and started to wash her wounds in the water of the stream.

However, in the reflection of the water she noticed some movement in the bushes on the other side. Had the hunter found her after all? Her little bare breasts bobbed up and down, and in her fright she put her hands on them. But it wasn't the hunter, it was the butcher. He laughed ferociously, and from behind his back produced his sharp knife.

'And now we're going to prepare a delicious cut of meat!' he said… 'Young girl's flesh is delicious, you know.'

She raised her hands towards him in supplication, and told him how she had just managed to escape the hunter by the skin of her teeth. But she noticed that, eyes gleaming, he was already consuming what she was trying to hide from his eyes with her hands.

'This left breast is delightful. And it's a fraction bigger than the right one… Oh, just a tiny bit, and really, it suits you very well.'

And while the girl burst into bitter tears, he took from his knapsack his well-thumb cookery book, and opened it.

'Girl's breast… Brown a small quantity of finely chopped onion in a little butter, then sprinkle the washed breast with breadcrumbs, and fry until a nice crust is produced. Be sure to avoid pricking the breast with a fork; instead turn over using the nipple.'

The girl now wept even more abundantly.

'I shan't dare to go back home if I'm all battered and chopped about,' she said.

'Come on!' said the butcher. 'All on account of one little breast! They'll get used to it at home.'

And holding the breast in one hand, he sliced into it with the other. Once it was cut off he put it carefully away in his knapsack.

Fortunately he paid no further attention to the girl. She had inched her way forward towards a thick tree, where she hid. When the time was ripe she started running. She didn't even think about the witch anymore, and that had been the reason she had come to the forest in the first place!

And at that same instant she discovered the hut…

'Let me rest here for a moment,' she begged the woman who seemed to be standing waiting for her in the lop-sided doorway. 'I've suffered so terribly!' And she showed her wounds, and also the breast she no longer had.

'Oh, I see!' said the woman, who had an ugly hooked nose with a wart on it…. 'I can see you're the disobedient girl!'

'And who are you?' asked the girl.

'I'm the witch. And because you wouldn't listen to your parents, I'm going to punish you.'

And she turned the girl into a tree stump, threw it into the fire, and stretched out her hand to the warming flames.

That'll teach young girls to be disobedient!

The Bird of Paradise

For years the boy had whetted the knife with which he planned to sever family ties. They were very tough, but when the last fibre gave way he fell with a bump into the middle of his freedom. It was very different from what he had imagined. By the third day all he felt was his hunger.

He roamed the forest for hours, looking for something edible, and towards evening he managed to catch a bird of paradise. He felt like someone forced to swallow his dreams, and he knew he would eat the bird with the sauce of his tears. The eager wood fire stretched out a thousand fingers towards the marvellous feathers. He discovered that they were made of pure gold.

He had the strangest feeling, as they say. He had become a wealthy man, and was dying of hunger. All kinds of plans blossomed profusely in his mind, but immediately fell apart like dead roses.

Whatever ideas he came up with, they could not deceive his plaintive stomach.

He clutched the bird to his chest, and went in search of someone who might be prepared to give bread and cheese for a glimpse of the golden bird.

It was already late when the reached the big motorway through the forest, and 'The Twelve Buttocks Inn'. A trollop lived there with her five daughters. He had to knock, since the door and the buttocks too were already closed. 'Open up,' he shouted. 'I've got a golden bird of paradise to show you.'

The landlady couldn't help having come into the world as a trollop (it's said that some women are born as virgins) and so she pulled open the upstairs window and screamed down that he should show his dicky-bird by day, as befitted a respectable man. 'It's all gold,' said the boy, close to tears.

The youngest and most curious of the daughters let him in. She was immediately excited and went to prod her sisters awake who had gone to sleep around the crackling hearth. They were like molluscs which when near the fire lose all sense of propriety and start opening up.

Rubbing the sleep from their eyes they scrambled to their feet, one dribbling as she did at night, the other scratching herself to make her fire fleas move. They hung over the bird, and weighed it on the scales of their desires.

They totted up what they could give in exchange – something insignificant, a view of some wind and water, the momentary retention of some dreams, which leave behind only the memory and perhaps a disease.

Greatly saddened by this the boy stammered that in exchange for the view he thought he deserved at least something like a supper. But behind their backs stood the trollop and winked meaningfully at her ten buttocks. She spoke with the honey-drenched words of one capable of murder. 'A good agreement,' she said... 'As long as you eat and sleep here the bird is ours, but if you want to leave, it will become your property again.'

'Done!' said the boy.

He was allowed to drop a few sausages into the bottomless pit of his stomach, and some sauerkraut that had gone off. He was also given the milk of the eldest daughter to drink which flowed sweet and warm from her breasts. His eyelids grew heavy and closed. The purple teat slipped from his mouth. He snored and dreamed of breasts of paradise with gold feathers.

The landlady held a council of war with her daughters on how they could gain possession of the bird. She groped in her memory for a possible nugget of wisdom, and found: feathers make the bird. But one of the daughters was able to make the equally true riposte, that on the other hand it is the bird that makes the feathers...

'So let's pluck the bird, and it will constantly grow new

gold feathers.'

Perhaps there was an even better solution – night brings council for those who can sleep on it – but they had little time and could at least start at the beginning.

They plucked the bird expertly. It turned out to be subject to the same laws as a barn owl, for example, or a common or garden cockerel. It even got goose pimples, since it was cold in its nakedness. And something neither the trollop nor the other buttocks had taken into account: it almost died. Fortunately it rallied a little with their warm breath. They decided to take turns in letting it live in the incubator under their skirts, until it had grown new feathers. The mother would accommodate him first, then the eldest, then the second eldest... Since there were unfortunately only six of them, they didn't know what to do about Sundays.

But there was another, more urgent problem: what story must the boy be told when he woke up?

The second eldest, who was the cleverest and cruellest, suggested implanting the old feathers in a scrawny chicken for soup-making. The middle one of the six, however, who was the least pretty and the most jealous – it made her go cross-eyed – came up with the idea of sticking the feathers on the youngest daughter.

The youngest daughter was very flattered. She clapped her hands with excitement, and exclaimed: 'Everyone will think I'm a bird of paradise.'

And to tell the truth, it made her look very beautiful. The softest feathers were stuck around her navel, and the great proud ones along her thighs and her wiggling derrière. But the most magnificent of all was placed on her forehead, like the plume on a commander's helmet.

When the boy awoke, he was very happy to find his bird of paradise more enchanting than ever.

'I didn't know it was a girl,' he said. 'I can't have noticed in the dark.'

He left with his golden bird who was a girl, and had many adventures, too numerous to mention. For example, a prince fell in love with his darling, and came to romp with her when the boy had gone in search of the food they needed.

He was a very forward prince, and in an hour of unseemly frolicking a great many feathers flew.

Others followed and she began to look less and less like a bird of paradise and more and more a trollop like her mother. The downy feathers round her navel remained in place longest, but even there bare patches appeared as with someone with scabies.

And the boy? He became a disgruntled man, and gradually realised that that night in 'The Twelve Buttocks' he had been cheated. But he would never admit this. Again, as in his youth, he began whetting the knife with which he planned to sever the ties binding him to that feathered trollop.

As for the bird of paradise, the real one, was it still living under the skirts of the sisters, the other buttocks? No one knows. But the fact was that they kept anxiously guarding the hem of their skirts, as if some thing were hidden underneath that must not see the light of day.

This is something, moreover, that all women still do – even those who've never heard of such a thing as a bird of paradise.

Chameleon

Paul Claes

The Sister

La culotte ne sera pas le partage exclusif
du sexe male, mais chaque sexe
aura droit de la porter à son tour.

Breeches shall no longer be the prerogative
of the man, but may be worn
by both sexes in turn.

Requête des dames à l'Assemblée nationale (1789)

My parents had three children: a girl and two boys. Marguerite was
the eldest, little Théodore lived only briefly, and I was the youngest.
My sister (God rest her soul) was not basically a bad person, but
had an objectionable character. Despite all his contacts my father
couldn't find a husband for her. All her potential suitors were put off
by her three vices: capriciousness, a fiery temper and jealousy.

Years after my father's death I introduced her to a Scot with
a dubious aristocratic pedigree. I had got to know Thomas O'Gorman
in the Black Cabinet, the Royal Secret Service. As a matchmaker I
offered them both an honourable compromise: she was his chance of
a title, he her chance of offspring.

Marguerite bore her husband three sons, who brought him
even less pleasure than she did. The eldest went to the Orient (the
Indies and Cathay), while the second joined the royalist army when
the Revolution broke out. The youngest was an even greater disaster
than the others. As a lieutenant he was dismissed by his own men
when they were allowed to vote for their commander. Disappointed,

he returned to Tonnerre, just in time to catch his mother's last breath. He used even the letter informing me of her death to beg me for money, supposedly to buy himself a suitable mourning suit.

The husband and wife were so wrapped up in their own lives that they eventually completely lost sight of each other. They both became trapped in a gilded cage: he secured an ambassadorial post in Ireland, she was thrown into the royal prison because of a misunderstanding. When she finally died, he could sigh with the satirist:

> *Cy gît ma femme, ha! qu'elle est bien,*
> *Pour son repos et pour le mien.*

> Here lies my wife. Now all's just fine,
> For her comfort and for mine.

My sister and I didn't understand each other. Perhaps we were too alike. I've often wondered if I was not the cause of her misfortune. Perhaps my birth sowed the seed of her jealousy. She was my parents' first child, and all their feelings were focused on her, until the moment a baby son made his appearance. The child died shortly after birth. Then I arrived as the male heir, and as the son of the house I attracted all my mother's love. So my neglected sister became the impossible creature she remained all her life.

What pen can describe a gilded youth like mine? Three women surrounded my cradle like fairy godmothers, loading me with their gifts: my mother, my wet nurse and my nanny.

The first gave me her beauty: the slender body, fine wrists, delicate skin, the round head with fine blond hair, the red lips, and the fiery eyes.

The second gave me her strength: the tough constitution of a dragoon, able to cope with hunger and thirst, tireless in duels and endless nocturnal rides.

The third gave me her brains: quick wits, a ready tongue

and a diplomat's memory, the gift of adapting at lightning speed to each new situation.

Even before I was born my uncle in Champagne had found a wet nurse for me. Mère Benoît had become pregnant at the same time as my mother. She put me to her breast together with her baby daughter. I had heroic struggles with my fellow-suckler for the last drop of milk. I learned to walk together with Geneviève. On our crooked little legs we wobbled from the kitchen chair to the woman's skirt. Whenever we crossed, we held onto each other for support. Together we rolled across the floor half laughing, half crying.

Marie, the nanny, was my sister's governess. The fact that she was now also involved with my upbringing must have been a new source of jealousy for Marguerite. I remember the winter evenings when we listened to her stories side by side in our beds.

One fairy tale that has stayed with me is Puss in Boots, the only heirloom of a poor farmer's son. The clever creature sent the king hares and partridges, with the compliments of the marquis of Carabas. The king's curiosity was aroused and he and the princess travelled to the estate of this wealthy nobleman. The cat went ahead of the coach with seven-league strides. He told the farmers what to say to the king, and when asked who all this belonged to, they replied that everything was the property of the marquis of Carabas. The king was so impressed that he promised his daughter's hand to the marquis. And so the farmer's son married the princess. Why? Not because he was rich, but because he was shrewd. The world is there for the taking for those who know how to grab its riches.

My mother accused my father of being too strict with me. She dressed me as a girl until I was eight and called me Lotte. I wore my sister's childhood dresses until I was given my first pair of knickerbockers. They went with the blue silk suit that I first wore when my mother dedicated me to the Holy Virgin in Notre-Dame. I was proud of my lace frills and my high heels, but even prouder of my first wig, so much blonder and curlier than my sister's.

On Sundays we went together to High Mass. Marguerite and I led the way, side by side, like man and wife, and behind walked my father and mother, he with his cocked hat, she with her veil, the parental mirror image of their children. Passers-by slowed down to raise their hats to us, and to left and right of us the hissing of the working-class women was hushed, while a playmate of mine whistled in admiration when he saw my sword and had his ears boxed.

Who can describe my distress when one Sunday morning, just as we were about to go to church, I noticed that there was a hole at the back of my breeches? I tried to cover my backside in embarrassment, but only succeeded in attracting the attention of Marie, who came to fetch me from the nursery. 'Did you slide down the banisters again?' she cried. I sobbed and said I hadn't done anything wrong: the seam had come loose all by itself. Surely she didn't think I would ruin my best costume myself?

At that moment Marguerite came in. She began laughing like a madwoman when she saw me. I felt my cheeks glowing. My sister ran down the stairs to the hall, where my father was already waiting, walking stick in hand. 'Charles has torn his br...!' she screamed. 'Parbleu!' he exclaimed. He climbed the stairs and appeared in the nursery with his stick menacingly raised. His red face went purple. My weeping fetched my mother from her bedroom.

'What's wrong?' she asked.

'Just look,' he said, turning me round. I cringed. My mother, in an effort to calm things down, cried out: 'Do leave the child alone, Louis!'

'We're going to be late in a minute and it's his fault!'

'Can't you see how frightened he is?'

'Tell him to apologise, Françoise.'

'You're impossible, Louis.'

It turned into a drama. A musical drama, in which my father's bass and my mother's alto (which I still have) alternated in a tragic-comic duet, which was accompanied in the background by my obstinate sobbing.

The upshot was that my father and mother left me behind, since with my face red with tears I was no longer presentable. Marguerite was to keep me company, as the servants attended the service with my parents.

My sister smiled mysteriously when the door closed. 'I've got something to show you,' she said.

'What?' I said, wiping my nose.

'Beautiful clothes.'

'As beautiful as these?' I pointed to the blue suit lying abandoned on the bed now I had my other suit on.

'Much more beautiful.'

'Where?'

She pulled me after her to the corner room, as far as the wooden staircase, which led steeply upward in the darkness.

'We mustn't go up there,' I said.

'Don't you dare?'

'Daddy will be angry if he finds out.'

'You're still a baby. That's why you don't dare do anything.'

I pushed her aside and started climbing up. The open steps were so narrow and the staircase was so high that I didn't dare look down. At the very top, in the darkness of an alcove, I hit my head on a trapdoor. I pushed, but it did not budge. My sister, bigger and stronger than me, climbed up beside me and pushed with all her might. The trapdoor gave way and swung against the wall. We hoisted ourselves through the opening and found ourselves in an attic room.

'Have you been here before?' I asked.

'Yes,' she nodded, 'a few weeks ago. Marie showed me everything.'

The attic lay in semi-darkness. A purple curtain covered the round window. Gradually our eyes grew accustomed to the subdued light. There were chests, furniture covered in ghostly white, boxes, bales of fluffy wool, a dressing table with a speckled toilet mirror, and a commode, standing lop-sidedly on a broken foot, with drawers mysteriously pulled open.

But my sister paid no heed to any of this. She tripped over to the oak wardrobe, opened it and crawled on top of the piles of blankets and clothes inside.

'Come on,' she whispered. I climbed anxiously up to join her. What followed was rather like a puppet theatre. It was as if an invisible puppeteer were moving us, as we pulled on the sleeves of the dresses until they slipped off their hooks and enveloped us with their musty smell. Silk ribbons glided like shivers across our faces. We submerged our hands deep in the satin, we stroked velvet and finally each other.

Who began? I can't remember. All I know is that two caresses discovered each other like twins. Beneath her displaced wig I discovered her reddish blond hair, which finished in the fine down of her neck. Under my unbuttoned shirt she discovered my neck, my collar bones. I undid the countless buttons of her gown. It slid from her shoulders like a cocoon from which she emerged like a butterfly in her cambric petticoat. She took off my shirt and kissed my nipples, which grew hard. We sank to our knees in front of each other. Without daring to look I lifted her last item of clothing over her head. She found the gold button and pulled down my breeches.

'I tore your blue breeches,' she whispered.

'Why?' I gulped.

'Because I've been torn too,' she said.

She sank back and as she did opened her legs, so that I saw with a shudder the place where she had been mutilated for ever.

The Twins

Melius est ergo duos esse simul quam unum.

Two are better than one.

Ecclesiastes 4:9

One day in May 1743 Father Marcenay admitted that he had no more to teach me. My uncle Tissey, who far away in Paris was closely following my intellectual progress, wrote to my father to say that from now on he would take personal charge of my upbringing.

My mother gave me a long hug. I promised my sister that I would check with the Parisian couturiers what upper-class ladies were wearing at present. She rewarded me with a lukewarm kiss. My father and I boarded the stagecoach that was to take us to Paris. 'All we have to do is follow the water,' he said pedantically, as the coach climbed slowly out of the valley. 'First we skirt the Armançon, which flows into the Yonne and then follow the Seine, which will take us where we're going.'

I could scarcely restrain my curiosity. Was I finally to behold the glittering city of which I had read so many descriptions and admired so many engravings in the past few weeks? We followed the meanderings of the Seine, passed the toll gate and drove into the metropolis. I craned my neck in the hope of seeing imposing mansions and wide boulevards, but saw only wretched hovels and narrow alleys. Nearly naked children tapped on the window and begged with outstretched hands. I asked my father if this was supposed to be Paris. He replied gruffly that the Faubourg Saint Marcel wasn't the most pleasant quarter. Tomorrow we would visit the fashionable districts.

We lodged in the residence in the rue Neuve-des-Petits-Champs where I was to spend the next few years. My uncle received us jovially in the front parlour that served as the dining room. The servant poured tea. Trying to get used to the sickly sugary taste, I was dumbstruck by the luxury of the room.

The chairs, covered in moquette, were arrayed around the walnut table like sentries. Against the wall I saw a low sideboard in carved oak. A bulbous commode on four hind legs, in the style of the reigning monarch, filled another wall. Next to the clock was a porcelain water container for rinsing glasses. Between the windows the three mirrors of a pier-table flickered in the candlelight. The same light shone in the gilded frames of the four oil paintings and in the glass covering the thirty-seven engravings (how often I counted them as I sat waiting for my schoolmate, Turquet de Mayerne, who was never on time!).

My uncle pushed open a door and gave me a glimpse of his library. In the middle of the drawing room there was an ebony chest-of-drawers, on the walls two cases with copper fittings and oak bookshelves with a folding ladder. There I later read gallant love stories, tales of knights in battle, chronicles of campaigns and exploits. In my imagination the walls gave way to the horizons of steppes, savannahs and deserts. One day I wanted to have as many books as this, and even more.

The following morning we were to visit the capital. My uncle donned the chestnut-coloured worsted coat with gold buttons which he wore to the Port Royal every day. A carriage took us to the Place Louis XV, in the heart of the city. We alighted. A little further on the Seine divided in two to embrace the Ile de la Cité. Towering chateaux lined both banks. We walked to the Palais Royal, the residence of the duke of Orléans, down a majestic avenue of limes and chestnut-trees. With its hundreds of gleaming windows it seemed to me the most magnificent building I had ever seen.

I was amazed at the spectacle of aristocratic ladies who passed us in sedan chairs engaged in gallant conversation, while Moorish servants in sequined costumes followed them with parasols and folding chairs. My uncle noticed with amusement the astonishment with which I observed the extravagance of their hairstyles and make-up.

'What do you think, Charles?' he asked.

'It's so beautiful,' I stammered.

You'll find it quite normal soon enough.'

His indifference shocked me. But when I spoke to other Parisians in the weeks that followed, I found that they too treated the luxury that surrounded them with disdain.

'This is so beautiful,' I repeated. 'Why is it that yesterday in the suburbs I saw nothing but poverty?'

'That's very simple. Since the great wars of the last century this country has been bankrupt.'

'So where does all this splendour come from? Why doesn't the court share its wealth with the poor?'

Uncle Tissey shook his head 'What you see here is best compared to a backdrop. Behind the façade of the palace there are nothing but empty rooms. The beautiful semblance hides poverty. Our luxury serves only to hide our penury from foreigners. It is cheaper to keep up a court than to give everyone in the country a hunk of bread every day.'

'Why do the people endure that? Why don't they rise up?

'They console themselves with our wealth. Everyone cheers when the king's coach passes. His worldly palace is a prefiguration of their heavenly paradise.'

When my father said goodbye to me, I thought I saw a tear in his eye. Did this stern man love me after all in his way? My sleep was troubled that night. In my dream I swam across a river to an island where a mansion was on fire. At the window an old woman was screaming for help. But however high the water splashed I made no headway at all.

Before my father left he enrolled me at the Collège Mazarin. The school had been founded in the last century under the terms of the will of Louis XIV's cardinal. Sixty pupils from prominent families were to complete their education here under the country's most competent teachers. I did not know at the time that I owed this privilege solely to my uncle, the old regent's secretary.

We received instruction in grammar, rhetoric and dialectics: the art of conversing, stirring the emotions and convincing, the art of hiding thoughts and feelings in words. We dissected French, Latin and Greek authors, we read the lives of kings, statesmen and military commanders and we learned about the morals and customs of foreign peoples. In the library that Mazarin had bequeathed us, I immersed myself in economics, politics, diplomacy, strategy, history, geography and natural philosophy. But the body was not neglected for the mind. Quick and supple as I was, I soon excelled at dancing, fencing and horse riding.

Turquet de Mayerne was an even better dancer than I was. Though we were very different, he became my best friend. At his young age he was already a *Chevalier*, a Knight, while I was a provincial scion of dubious origin. He was tall and dashing, I was short and mobile. He had an angular, masculine head and I a round head with soft features. He had a wonderful moustache, while I to my despair remained beardless. He had a booming voice, I the falsetto of a soubrette. He was expansive, I was witty. But probably it was precisely those differences that made us so inseparable. Our comrades quickly dubbed us Castor and Pollux, the divine half-brothers from the ovum of the king's daughter.

Our initial comradeship was as playful as that of two young puppies. Sometimes we ran together along the Seine as far as the Champ de Mars, where we watched the king's soldiers. The marching, drilling and manoeuvring stimulated our belligerence. We broke off branches and made then into foils to attack each other with. I knocked his weapon out of his hand, he punched me in the back, I struck him in the side, he tried to twist my arm, but I slipped from his grasp. Then we chased each other through the fields, jumped over ditches, tumbled over each other and lay panting in the grass. Finally, worn out with fighting, we returned home arm in arm.

As we grew, so did our friendship. Turquet began to deck himself out like a *merveilleux*, a dandy. I begged my uncle for an outfit as fashionable as his. He shook his head at such frivolity, but he remembered his own youth and gave in. I tried on the flowered silk suit in my bedroom.

I stood in front of the full-length mirror and surveyed myself like Narcissus. Beneath the silver wig a rose of lips burgeoned forth between the powdered cheeks. My admiring glance moved down the delicate figure. My jacket hung half open as if it might slip off my shoulders at any moment. Beneath the vieux-rose of the waistcoat the blue breeches were as taut as a second skin around the thighs. An emerald gave lustre to the garter. The gleaming buckles of the red-heeled shoes were like gold butterflies.

I went to the antechamber to wait for my friend. My uncle had left a morocco-bound book on the table, and I opened it. It was *Le Prince travesti* by Marivaux. But my hands trembled so violently that I could not read a word (or was it my mind?) I heard the clock

45

striking the half-hour: that was late even by Turquet's standards.

Another quarter of an hour crept past. I was on the point of asking the butler to take a message, but I realised that such a course of action would needlessly prolong my suffering and decided to go to see him. I threw my red cape over my new suit and picked up my gold-headed cane. As far as my high heels would allow me, I ran along the quayside. It was spring, the lime-trees were in blossom, and the air was tingling in the light, but I felt sad. Where was my friend?

Suddenly, as if chance itself were giving me an answer, I saw a couple in a side lane standing together in an amorous tête-à-tête. The young man was bringing the girl's hand to his lips, as if he were saying goodbye. I was rooted to the spot, as I had recognised my friend.

So that was why Turquet had made me wait so often and so long: he was misusing our appointments for his own rendezvous. It was a betrayal of our friendship. I withdrew cautiously, so that he did not notice me. My heart was all a-tremble. His secret was now mine too. Perhaps one day I would be able use it against him. I hurried back home. There I gave orders to the servant to tell my friend that that young monsieur D'Éon had gone out.

With temples pounding I went to my bedroom, stood in front of the mirror and threw myself a bitter girlish kiss. While my eyes filled with tears, I removed one by one the precious garments that had been intended to seduce my friend. Then I removed my vest. Finally naked, I surveyed my nakedness. What was still coming between us? I hid what was superfluous between my thighs and then closed them as chastely as a virgin.

The Mask

- *Tu n'as pas l'art de deviner, beau masque;*
  tu te trompes de nom et de sexe.
- *C'est que l'un et l'autre sont fort incertains.*
  - *Tu deviens fou, beau masque.*

- You have not the art of divining, fair mask;
  You mistake both the name and the sex.
  - For both of them are very unsure.
  - You're losing your mind, fair mask.

Louvet de Couvray, *Amours du Chevalier de Faublas* (1787)

The following evening Turquet asked me why he had not found me at home the day before. I did not want to offend him and replied that I had gone in search of him but had not found him. I avoided his company for a week. One evening he grabbed me by the shoulder and said: 'What is it, Charles? Have I done something to upset you?'

'Why don't you love me anymore?' I said petulantly.

'Of course I love you, Charles. You know I'd sacrifice my last drop of blood for you.'

'So why didn't you tell me a word about her?'

'Who are you taking about?'

'The young lady you make assignations with by the Seine.'

Turquet blushed. 'Surely you're not jealous?'

'No, I'm angry that you should hide something from me, your best friend.'

'I was afraid of hurting your feelings.'

'There must be no secrets between friends.'

He kept his word. He told me what a revelation his first love had been. I shared the kisses, the promises, the tears. Later there were other loves and other courtships. I followed their entanglements more breathlessly than Marivaux's plots. One day he whispered to me that he had had a woman for the first time.

At my insistence he described what had happened. His father had taken him along to his mistress's apartment, and then had suddenly said that he had to go out for a moment. Turquet was to keep the woman company while he was away. She lay down on her ottoman in her negligée and asked him to sit beside her. He asked him to read something aloud to her: a passage from *The Sofa,* a risqué novel by Crébillon fils.

When his voice faltered after a few sentences, she asked him: 'Why are you blushing, young man? She had opened her mouth so entreatingly that he could not help planting a kiss on it. After that everything had taken its natural course. He had caressed her, she had kissed him, he had embraced her, she had undressed him, he had stripped her, she had deflowered him.

I had listened open-mouthed, but wanted to know what had happened next. How had he thanked the woman for her favours? What present had he given her? 'Myself,' replied my friend with a smile. 'My father had already paid her for her services.' I was struck by the heartlessness of the words.

It was the first of many love stories that awakened my curiosity more than my desire: gallant stories of conquests and disappointments, racy stories of affairs and liaisons, distressing stories of lust and corruption. I began to see that the world that until then I had regarded with a child's eyes concealed a secret that I had yet to discover. People were like coins: the front displayed a resplendent, noble profile, the reverse proclaimed their price.

Meanwhile my friend was astonished by my amorous reserve. 'You're as chaste as Lucretia,' he joked. 'No, actually you're even more chaste, since Lucretia was at least raped.' If anyone else had said this I would immediately have challenged him to a duel. Now all I did was blush: like a Vestal virgin.

I was and remained girlish. However assiduously I shaved, nothing appeared on my cheeks but down. My friend's moustache provoked my jealousy. My arms, legs and chest remained hairless. True, my voice had deepened in adolescence, but it still oscillated from alto to tenor. However, my feminine appearance was amply compensated for by my masculine character. No one was more passionate, hot-tempered or more choleric than I. When a classmate once ventured to question my origin, I grabbed him by the throat, and if the teacher's assistant had not pulled me away, I would have strangled him.

Hermaphodite, Turquet sometimes called me in jest. I liked the name. Wasn't the Athenian hero the son of Hermes and Aphrodite, the god of rhetoric and the goddess of beauty? Was I not the most fluent talker and public speaker in the college? Despite my short stature did I not have the elegance of an ephebe? Did my ambivalent magnetism attract both men and women?

In 1748 I graduated from the college. Then I studied civil and ecclesiastical law for a year. Since I was too young actually to be awarded a degree, I was given a special dispensation to become a lawyer. Turquet remained my bosom friend, and scarcely a week went by without the two of us appearing at a ball, where like the half moon I was able to glow in the light of his sun. One evening in March we spoke about the forthcoming carnival ball at the home of the marquise of C***, whom I did not know. We discussed what disguise we should wear.

'These masked balls are always dreadful,' said my friend. 'The people who do not recognise us annoy us and the people who do bore us.'

'Perhaps we can disguise ourselves in such a way that we don't appear to be in disguise.'

'That's it, Charles! You've given me an idea. Do you know what, we'll go as husband and wife.'

'You're pulling my leg,' I protested. But he explained his plan with great gusto. He would stick on the moustache of an older man and I would disguise myself as his young wife. With my falsetto there was no risk of my being recognised. Apart from that we would both be wearing a mask and a domino cape. His proposal tickled my imagination and I gave in.

Lisette, the chambermaid of my uncle (who must know nothing of our plans), helped me with my disguise. In the afternoon

Turquet had sent over the evening dress of his mistress at that time. In the mirror I gradually metamorphosed from a man to a girl. Lisette filled my underwear with rags and cotton wool. Over the bustle she draped the petticoat supported by whalebone. She pulled my corset so tight that I was gasping for breath. A cambric veil camouflaged my lack of bosom.

At the dressing table I had my face powdered, my eyes ringed with blue, my mouth painted with vermillion. On this canvas Lisette stuck a fly as a refined trompe-l'oeil, I was given earrings for my ears and a pearl necklace around my neck. She carefully lowered the pinkish satin dress over me. White as swans' necks, long gloves slid over my arms. A tall woman's wig was the crowning glory. I put on my Venetian mask, opened my mother-of-pearl fan and admired myself in the mirror. Was that me? The beauty making eyes and pouting immediately won my heart.

I walked through the room more nervous than a debutante. At eight o'clock the doorbell rang. I rushed into the hall and opened the door before the butler appeared. In front of me a man with grey side whiskers bowed stiffly.

'You look divine, Charlotte,' whispered an awed voice. Only then did I recognise Turquet. He led me to the phaeton. I had difficulty coming down the steps in my ball shoes. We crossed the city as if in a dream. Lanterns flickered everywhere. People paraded through the streets in carnival costume. There were countless Pierrots and Columbines.

When we arrived at the marquise's hotel, we looked at each other. 'Don't laugh,' warned Turquet, 'comedy is the one thing you must take seriously.' Arm in arm we climbed the stairs to the ballroom on the first floor. A sea of masks surrounded us. Unknown eyes surveyed us with curiosity. As if by magic the excitement gave me the air that suited my disguise. I turned alertly when I was addressed, answered with precise gestures, when paid a compliment raised a gloved hand to my lips, and flounced away coquettishly in shoes that were too tight. Eventually I became so intoxicated that I forgot my part and only then really did I play it properly.

I sat out the first few dances, drank two glasses of clairette and felt just tipsy enough to undergo the acid test. In the country dance my cavalier led me firmly to the dance floor. A Sultan's courtesan and a Moor joined us, and other couples followed.

We bowed, entwined arms, twirled, stepped and turned, changed partners and repeated the bows, steps and turns. Out of the corner of my eye I saw the square formations repeating our movements in ever new costumes. It was an unreal whirl of ravishing and weird disguises, a masquerade of stiff grotesque countenances and painted faces, a drama that was constantly freezing into a tableau vivant and constantly jerking back into motion like the mechanism of an automaton.

Ghosts of couples: I was a female dancer, I was one of the ladies turning and circling round him, the eternal dancer, until he took their place and circled and turned round her, the eternal centre of all the dances.

Becoming a little flushed, I made for the side of the room. Again I followed the spectacle, now splendid, now frightening. I was thinking of the skeletons that danced on the wall of our family chapel, when I became vaguely aware of a lackey with silver epaulettes bowing before me. The marquise wished to speak to me. My heart leapt up: I was to see my hostess. As I cooled myself with my fan, I picked my way through the labyrinth of gyrating bodies. Accompanied by the lackey I reached the end of the room. There was a knock and a cough of affirmation. He opened the padded door for me.

The boudoir was lit by a single elaborate candleholder. In an old-fashioned armchair sat the marquise of C***. She beckoned to me. I went towards her with legs weak at the knees. I curtseyed deeply. The woman in a blue mask motioned me to sit next to her, and surveyed me with a smile.

'Well,' she said. 'I must admit that I don't recognise you. Who are you, Mademoiselle?

I gulped, but regained my sang-froid. In my softest falsetto I said: 'You may call me Charlotte, or Lotte for short. I am Monsieur de Tissey's niece.'

'I didn't know that Monsieur de Tissey had such beautiful nieces. But I can understand that he prefers to keep such a lovely pearl to himself. Won't you take your mask off? Then we'll be able to speak more easily.'

The marquise removed her own mask. I bit my bottom lip: it struck me as too risky to expose my face to her dark gaze.

'But my mouth is not masked, is it, Madame?'

'You are as witty as you are beautiful. My husband will like that. I trust you will not deny him your beauty?'

At that moment there was a thunderous report from outside. I was startled, but the marquise immediately reassured me: 'The spectacle has begun, Mademoiselle.' She led me to the window by the elbow and opened the curtains as if on a stage. A rocket rose into the sky like a nocturnal lark.

Medieval

Hugo Claus

1.

The old man, who had been sent to bed after his bowl of gruel, crept out from under the horse blanket, stood almost upright in the moonlight, reached for the table and found the chalky serrated fragment, slipped it carefully into his mouth, to the back, where there had once been a molar, and rolled his tongue with its horny lumps against it, made the sign of the cross, and, almost laughing, hummed more than said: 'Now I mustn't swallow even once tonight.'

2.

The child found three teeth with a lump of gum and scabs clinging to them. The child prised the teeth loose from the hard tissue with its finger and a sliver of stone. It used them as knucklebones all afternoon. Then three boys from the fishermen's quarter came along and surrounded the child, which immediately hid one of the sacred knucklebones under its tunic.

3.

The people, once they had got hold of the king's head, chucked it around. His sepia brown hair clung to his skull and wound round his face, so that after a while this handball was indistinguishable from a coarse kind of red cabbage. Every time the king's head was thrown in the air, a raucous cry rang out, an exultation that had something of the ecclesiastical tones of the Roman-Gregorian liturgy about it. A little later a priest stole the internasal septum from the head, and the rest was dispersed in the swampy drains that ran alongside the houses.

4.

The weaver unleashed a scream that drowned out the din from the stage area. Because he was agile and furious and was standing near the front, he got to the king first, who was gasping for breath and resting on the shoulder of the actor who had played Mary Magdalene. This actor pushed the king towards the weaver, who caught him like a bale, hugged him, cracked his ribs, and pushed him away. The king wobbled and then the weaver grabbed him by his abundant curly hair, pulled the king's head back and showed the white neck to the audience, who descended on them both like bees.

5.

The king, who leaning backward and chewing on an elderberry pip stroked the neck hairs of a young fisherman, jumped up, climbed over the railing covered in bearskins and rugs that separated his seat from the stage and landed so violently on the floorboards that several candles on the stage fell over and were stamped out by the already rabid audience. The king raised his two-edged, blunt-tipped sword with two hands, swung it once from left to right and hit the centurion, whose face was cut in half.

6.

The actor playing the centurion made his way laboriously downstage, holding his lance close to his belly, and then pushed it in the direction of the cross. The actor playing Jesus Christ, steaming with sweat, asked his father why he had forsaken him. He was about to ask a second time, louder and more plaintively, when the actor playing the centurion, who had three children one of whom had died of swamp fever that week, felt the lance spring out of his powerless hands and run through the man on the cross. He just managed to hear the shouts, the amazement of the audience, and the groans of the king close by.

7.

The girl whose mother had promised her that she would be allowed to go and watch the Passion of Our Lord in three days' time, in which her father was appearing as the man who pretended to release Jesus Christ from his earthly suffering by pretending to pierce him close to his heart, was sitting by the dead body of her little brother. The girl thought: he isn't as white as snow but he is almost as transparent as ice. When the vesper bell rang, she went out into the street, where she woke a sleeping beggar by poking his nostrils with a straw, he blinked and immediately afterwards threw up.

8.

The monk brushed the dust off his habit, especially between the thighs, it took a long time, the dust particles swirled about in the light of the overheated cell where he had taken the gypsy girl who wanted to marry an actor. He barked and then cleared his throat. 'Girl,' he said, 'you know I haven't long to live?' She did not dare reply. 'Are you expecting a child?' he asked. 'No, father,' she said. Because he was aroused, but not sufficiently, he read to her (before siring a baby girl on her) a text by Le Père Vallandier, which he translated off the cuff from the French with a stutter:

'For see, see the two crystal fountains of milk before which the husband pales
for they are beautiful and better than wine on the tongue
and see, see the wonders and the sugar that the Creator has hidden in them,
and see, the blood softens there, like honey
and the arteries discharge there
with secret rivers of subterranean sweat
and their so salutary nutrition str-strokes-streams
there with providence and wise and powerful
such that if the mother had no ordinary food
she would corrode metals, yes, nickel and tin,
and that would let the last drop of her blood drip, trickle out
before she would leave empty these miraculous springs
and see, see how the whole being of the wet nurse
flows away in these two channels,

these two storehouses of manna,

two springs of ambrosia, that is, drink of the gods, you know, two fountains of nectar, two stalks of sugar cane, two jugs full of honey, two balsam plants, two dials of the inner clockwork mechanism of the mother, two parapets, two cake covers, two waterfalls of childlike nature, God in heaven, the husband discovers this before impregnation and is silent

just as St Jerome and other scholars say:

absque eo quod intrinsecus, and the secret and

the incomprehensible nature of this divine factory

is its seclusion and its silence

because the tits, you understand? are

an enclosed garden, so chaste is the bride,

a sealed fountain, so attached to her husband is she,

a well of living water, so much so that we draw life from it a sheaf of corn with a, with a, uh, uh, valatus lilüs,

(*The gypsy girl leaps back, she weeps, she crosses herself.*)

with a wall, a screening partition of lilies, so morally fruitful is she, so fruitfully moral, oh, storehouse of wonders of animal nature, which fathers, restrains, shapes, organises and leads that divine animal towards life, here before your eyes, dear girl, that must overpower that whole, full, complete, total nature,

(*He pulls his scapulary to pieces.*)

oh, part, oh, part, oh part that is removed from sight, don't go away, I shall soon die, but that, don't cry, child, but that is so linked to the two rivers of milk, part that was made by the Creator in such a way that you, don't go away, yes you!, precisely through that will display your affection, your possibilities, your symptoms, do you hear, child? and the foetus you will carry, whether you will carry or not, if it will be healthy or deformed, whether it will be male or female…

(*The book falls, the spine tears, and the tapping of his teeth against hers is heard.*)

Death On A Motorbike

Johan Daisne

In the course of my life I've tried my hand at a variety of jobs. I really was what's called a restless soul. But the most short-lived episode of them all was definitely the time I spent as a detective. I'd joined the police – well, how had I actually joined? By coincidence, you might say, but these days I no longer believe in coincidences. It just seems so.

The cinema and literature had given me a romantic picture of that 'quiet' profession. I say 'romantic': what attracted me was the adventure, which seems all the more exciting because the anonymity of detective work makes it appear both unperturbed and mysterious. So it was the disorder that appealed to me, and not the task of keeping order, which is the actual raison d'être of the police as a social entity. That moral point is, I think, of importance for what will follow, or at least my share in it.

That share was even less than minimal. In fact, I did not play the slightest part in what happened, but providence moves in mysterious, multifarious ways, and I saw in what happened a threatening finger pointing at me, although as a hapless minor character I didn't really count. But I was in the wrong place at the wrong time, and I think I've taken that additional lesson to heart.

I'd heard, then, that a fairly prestigious trainee detective's post had become vacant; virtually at the same time I met an influential acquaintance of my late father's under favourable circumstances, and I was eased into the job. I served for precisely one week. Until the penultimate day I had dealt with nothing but paperwork designed to help me familiarise myself with my new post.

A pattern was beginning to emerge, when the final day brought me the only case I ever dealt with. At first sight it seemed a trifling, everyday matter that we could wrap up with just a few formalities.

But seeing that it was my first assignment, I had spent some hours on it and investigated everything diligently and at length, with excessive thoroughness in fact, it seemed to me.

Yet there remained one strange, implausible point in the whole story that I couldn't make head or tail of. So my efficiency was designed in part if not to cover up that mysterious point, then at least to push it somewhat into the background and excuse my own deficiency. So I sat waiting in the corridor at once satisfied and ill at ease, waiting to be admitted to my boss's office in order to report to him.

It was summer, the end of August, but felt like a month later. There was mild sunshine between two drizzly showers. It was quite a while before I was ushered in to see the boss. I could hear his powerful, even voice in his office. I could not distinguish the sound made by his visitor, who must have been whispering. All sorts of people came down the corridor, ones I did not yet know very well. I had a final glance at my notes, so as to be able to present everything as smoothly as possible.

Then a bell rang, and a messenger led me inside. My boss was sitting all by himself. There was only one exit from his office, through which I had entered; so that he had not had a visitor. The only explanation for the noise I had heard was that my boss had been on the telephone the whole time.

There was no sun in his office, or rather it must have suddenly hidden behind the clouds, because no sooner had I entered than there was soft pattering on the large window behind my boss, a regular continuous patter of slow raindrops. At the same time, one by one, thick dollops of water spread on the pane like colourless, transparent blossoms, rapidly distorting the peaceful sight of the canal lined with young plane-trees.

My boss switched on his desk lamp and invited me to sit opposite him. He was a big, strong man, middle-aged, with grey hair and a friendly, though somewhat unfathomable expression. During the week that I had been on his staff, I had taken a liking to him, but still felt uncomfortable in his presence.

I plucked up courage and began my report, after assuring him in advance that I had omitted nothing that seemed in any way necessary or useful: I had gone to the scene of the crime, spoken to all the witnesses, besides carrying out some other investigations and making various calls. And here some minor possessions belonging to the victim had been found – I laid them out on the desk in front of him: a wallet, and pocket watch, a notebook, a clean handkerchief, etc.

My boss immediately seized the wallet and from it produced, with the sure touch of the owner himself, a letter, as if he knew all about it. He calmly opened the envelope and started reading. It was an unposted letter from the victim to his wife, at a seaside holiday address. I had not dared open it on my own authority; anyway, after my investigation I attached no further importance to it. My boss put it down again, still looking at me in his friendly and unfathomable way, and I started giving him an account of what had happened, as I had reconstructed it, rather neatly, if I say may so.

At about two-thirty in the afternoon, Mr Cornelis Willemse, aged 39, married, no children, had left his home on Bloksberg Boulevard. A neighbour had seen him calmly crossing the avenue, towards the tram stop diagonally opposite his house. Most probably Mr Willemse was going, as he did every morning and afternoon to the D… Bank, where he was deputy-manager.

In the neighbourhood the Willemses were considered quiet, pleasant people. Husband and wife seemed to be on the best of terms. When the weather was nice, they often went for a stroll around the block after dinner, in the winter they had season tickets to the theatre. They didn't have many guests. The cleaning lady, who had made lunch for her employer that afternoon, confirmed their good relations.

Mrs Willemse had been at the seaside with her elderly mother for eight days or so, half the time she planned to be away. Mrs Willemse had been reluctant to abandon her husband, who had to stay in town for business, but he had insisted that she should take a little break without further delay, as September did not look very promising.

In the front room of their house I had found a recent photo of Mrs Willemse: she looked like a nice woman, not exactly beautiful, and certainly not the type for amorous entanglements. At the bank too they spoke of Mr Willemse with muted praise, and sincerely regretted his death.

His salary was pretty average; he had not inherited anything to speak of from his parents or elsewhere; all his assets, which were on the modest side, were invested with the bank. The house he lived in was rented. So again nothing could be deduced from this that would put any other slant on the accident than a regrettable but everyday road incident.

So this was what had happened. The tram had been quite a long time coming. Mr Willemse, despite his calm disposition, may easily have got into a rather nervous state as a result. There were also quite a lot of people at the tram stop, mostly working-class people returning from the municipal hospital on Bloksberg Boulevard. Twice a week patients there were allowed visitors, and that had been the case this afternoon; but visiting ended at two-thirty on the dot.

A motorbike came roaring along, from the same direction as the tram, which still did not appear. The motorcyclist wasn't going fast and slowed down as he approached the stop. A few metres further, a little way from the kerb, he stopped; the engine was not switched off. I had gained this information from various people who had actually seen and heard everything, whom I had questioned separately.

The motorcyclist obviously wanted to ask something. He was a handsome young man, in his early thirties. He was wearing a crash helmet, with the earflaps blowing about, and had pushed his goggles up onto his forehead. Apart from that he was wrapped in a bulky one-piece motorcycle suit. He seemed to have come a long way, so dusty and even a little mud-spattered were the man and his machine.

Mr Willemse had not been closest to him; the nearest people were two working-class types, but since the motorcyclist obviously looked like a foreigner, whose language they might not understand, they hadn't budged and had simply let Mr Willemse approach him. I had reconstructed that moment with the utmost care, so that it was established that the motorcyclist had not called on the help of Mr Willemse in particular and that Mr Willemse had immediately rushed towards the motorcyclist.

He had simply stepped forward, with the obliging smile that went with his helpful nature, at the same moment that the motorcyclist, whom the awkwardness of the working-class crowd in the presence of the stranger had probably not escaped, had finally looked at the deputy-manager.

He did indeed then ask in a broken, foreign accent, as several bystanders heard, for Our-Lady-of Sleep Street, rue Notre-Dame du Sommeil. Mr Willemse immediately told him the way.

'Oh, that's very easy to find,' were his actual words, 'it's the first on the right, you just follow the tram lines.'

But immediately afterwards – without being asked – he offered to show him the way by riding pillion, since 'I'm in a hurry, and I'm going that way anyway,' he said. The motorcyclist simply nodded, and the deputy-manager immediately hopped onto the pillion with an agile leap. The last thing people heard him say with a smile, it seems, was:

'But you won't go too fast, will you?'

Then they left. Mr Willemse was dressed in a rather English style, in a light-grey suit, with a soft felt hat and a rolled umbrella. He held the umbrella wedged under his left arm, and with his right hand he had pushed his hat a little more firmly onto his head, after which he held on tight with both hands to the handlebars behind the driver's saddle.

The journey turned out to be comfortable; the bike did not lurch at all, despite Mr Willemse's tall build. The motorcyclist drove gently, more gently than when he arrived in the Boulevard, and everyone saw him slow down carefully as he turned right, into Our-Lady-of-Sleep Street.

Mr Willemse's pronouncement, 'I'm in a hurry,' seemed very plausible and yet was incongruous. He was certainly in a rush, because the tram was so long in coming, but Our-Lady-of-Sleep Street was scarcely three hundred metres further than the tram stop and still a long way from the D... Bank. No other tram except the one Mr Willemse had been waiting for went along it. So that Mr Willemse should have caught the same tram right there at the end of the street, without the lift having helped him very much. In fact, by waiting for the tram a few stops further the deputy-manager was in danger of not being able to get on at all: with all the people waiting at the stop on the Boulevard, it would already be jam-packed.

The only explanation seemed to be that Mr Willemse had suddenly given in to a boyish impulse. He had suddenly felt like a ride on a motorbike, and his mentioning that he was in a hurry had been merely a convenient pretext, since, with his quiet nature and respectable appearance, he was a little ashamed of his whim.

I was able to question an eyewitness, a second-hand bookseller in Our-Lady-of Sleep Street, on the subsequent course of events. This gentleman was just rearranging books in his display, when he heard the bike, with both the motorcyclist and Mr Willemse on it come clattering down the street. This tallies exactly with the evidence of the people at the tram stop on the Boulevard. The motorcyclist was not going fast, and had slid his goggles onto his forehead, Mr Willemse was obviously comfortable, as he was smiling. His umbrella was tucked under his left arm and he was holding on to the handle between the two seats. Then, a few metres past the bookshop the bike suddenly skidded. There had been some drizzle a little while before, and the tram rails were probably still slippery.

The bookseller immediately ran outside. The bike's engine was still running. Mr Willem lay half under the heavy machine and was no longer breathing. The doctor diagnosed a fractured skull and declared that the deputy-manager had died instantaneously. Apart from that there were no signs of injury on the body. His suit was untorn and not even dirty. The expression on the dead man's face was calm and seemed to be almost smiling...

I paused for a moment. My boss gave another friendly, unfathomable nod, as if he already knew all the details. I couldn't help thinking about the telephone.

'And... what about the motorcyclist?' he asked.

I sighed in annoyance – here came the weird, improbable point.

'He... was nowhere to be seen. Though only a few seconds can have elapsed, since the bookseller ran straight out of his shop. But by the time he got outside, the motorcyclist had already gone. It's just appalling. He couldn't have got to the end of the street or dodged into a house in that time. And the assumption that the bookseller gave implausible evidence, when he struck me as a most respectable and trustworthy man, doesn't make sense either. In fact, though no one else but him *saw* the accident happen, lots of people came running at the *sound* of the fall, that is, *at once*, and they saw no sign of a motorcyclist. They all thought Mr Willemse was the rider of the bike. And the motorcyclist must have had even less time to make his escape because he first took off all his equipment. Helmet, goggles, shoes, and his complete motorbike suit, including his shirt lay in a smouldering heap under the motorbike. The bystanders immediately pulled the bike clear and the bookseller even stamped out the fire. The various items were already half-charred but were clearly recognisable. The corresponded exactly with the various testimonies. But the craziest thing of all is yet to come. Just imagine, Commissioner: the shoelaces were *not* untied, the shirt was buttoned up to the neck, the tie still knotted round the collar... I... must humbly admit to you that this is quite beyond my powers as a beginner in detective work!'

My boss nodded, which pleased me for the moment, as I had expected a less smooth response. Then he handed me the letter from the wallet. I quickly read it to the end. It was a friendly letter, from husband to wife, the typical sort of letter a man left at home writes to his wife while she is on holiday. However, the last few lines were less ordinary.

Mr Willemse wrote that he was a little tired, his annual summer tiredness, nothing serious, and he would shake off that silly melancholy, *because hopefully*, he joked, *the Lord would not yet be sending his Angel to relieve Himself of me.* I re-read the line, suddenly bathed in sweat. I didn't understand, I could feel the boss's eyes resting on me, inquiringly, probably to see how I, as a would-be detective, would respond. Then I heard his voice, repeating:

'That motorcyclist was Death.'

I looked up. Was it a joke? And then I revealed my true nature, and how stupid reading had been the starting point of my interest. Stuttering like a child, I asked:

'Death with a small d...?'

My boss slowly shook his head in response, but said only, still in an even voice:

'*We* aren't writers.'

I had given myself away, and having got this far, I wanted to quickly ask him a few more questions:

'Have you ... Encountered that before in your job?!...'

I thought his head nodded, or at least he closed his eyelids for a moment as a sign of assent.

'We don't talk about it here.'

I can't remember how I took my leave. I downed one gin after another in the *Iron Cross* pub. That's where I met the landlord's daughter, the lovely Laura, who subsequently became my wife and bore me five strapping children.

After the death of my father-in-law I carried on running the pub. Business is good and the pub is now called *The Pedestrian*. I write the occasional story for the paper and every year I repaint our iron cross. I never went back to being a detective. The Willemse case has never been solved.

The press simply reported that the motorcyclist was on the run. A few years later the commissioner, who was my boss for a week, himself died in a motor accident. My children know that it is strictly forbidden to show motorcyclists or other messengers of death the way.

Queen

Saskia de Coster

The poppy offered herself like a scarlet mouth and the light kissed her petals. She stayed upright day and night while her roots filled with water. She never tired.

The older Charlotte got, the more often she wondered how little flowers managed to outshine people, who had to go to bed every night. Was it because the grown-ups didn't sow the plants themselves that the plants grew so luxuriantly? The grown-ups pulled up the weeds with contempt. The flowers stubbornly scrambled back on their feet, even on a dung heap. When the flowers are fully grown, we shall live in the shade of their leaves. The flowers wait with great dignity until the time comes. They have been sown all over the world in a long trail to point the way to the flower king, who is waiting for company. Every flower is a beckoning gesture. But no one wants to set out on a journey.

Whenever Charlotte came home with a rare plant, mother would ask if she was trying to turn the house into a pigsty with all the mud she brought in. Only one of the little tots in the playground was happy with the garland of flowers that Charlotte put round his neck. Charlotte knew every plant individually, but couldn't call one of them by name. That made her ashamed, since you can't just call every plant a plant and address every tree as tree. She herself had her own name: woman. Half her family had the same name. That was why they were family of course.

One day, when Charlotte was squatting by her poppy, whose stalk was softer than a toddler's neck, a sigh of wind brushed her cheek and she suddenly heard: 'Do I know you from somewhere?'

Her heart jumped up and down like a bouncing ball. This must be a joke. Many girls were in the habit of creeping up on a girlfriend from behind and saying hello invisibly like that. Yet this voice didn't sound at all playful and excited, but in deadly earnest. For that matter, Charlotte didn't have any girlfriends. Had a voice crept into her head that read out her thoughts like a radio news bulletin? No, that was nonsense.

Don't move. Give the voice a chance to return,

When Charlotte woke she turned out to have sleepwalked a long way. On all fours Charlotte groped her way back down the garden path. Only the moon was awake and gave a faint light. As usual mother was sitting by the fire. Every day after dinner she weighed buckets of horn, meanwhile greedily drinking a bitter drink. Then she slid her chair closer and closer to the open fire, until she almost merged with the flames and her eyes began to spew fire. Now her eyes had faded like the lamps of a lighthouse. Too late in the evening for unintelligible stories, usually something about three sisters and a bean. Grunts rose from her smelly gaping mouth.

When Charlotte entered her room the dog Midas cocked an ear, sniffed once deeply and went on sleeping contentedly in her bed. Being content with small things, said her mother, that's the trick. Charlotte was happy with the voice that spoke to her. Why should it want to get to know her? Because it liked her poppy?

Looking for the deeper meaning was not something Charlotte was good at. At school she could stand at the blackboard for hours with a piece of chalk in her hand, but the sum still wasn't right and the teacher was still giving her sour looks. The voice would come and get her, carry her away on the wind.

The door of her room opened with a creak and let a bright strip of light into the room. Mother was standing wobbling against the doorpost. Her face was as translucent as the bottle she was swigging from. She came towards Charlotte, who had just put her nightie on, and took a big gulp. She puffed up her cheeks like a baby who still doesn't know very well how to swallow. So that was what the night did to mothers, they turned into little children again. Mother muttered under her breath, stumbled over her own words and just managed to grab Charlotte's arm. Her eyes were glowing like coals. There was a droplet trembling on her lower lip. Furiously she spat in Charlotte's face. Those who come home late are punished.

*

Charlotte wanted to stuff her sandwiches into her satchel as soon as possible and run to school. Why wasn't the whistling kettle on the stove yet? She found her mother still asleep by the open hearth in which stalks and leaves were smouldering.

The whole morning Charlotte shifted to and fro on her school bench, until Myriam snapped at her that it was stopping her from writing. Charlotte stopped at once. I'm freezing up, I'm turning into a frost flower, this is my place for ever. She heard her teacher talking about the future. That was another world, inhabited by people whizzing around like lightning and not doing anything themselves.

During the art lesson the pupils had to draw a flower. As accurately as possible, stressed the teacher. The chalk marks on the board didn't look a bit like a flower, a real flower has a head like a flesh-wreath, not a circle surrounded by sloppy loops. And why fish bones instead of finely branching veins in the leaves?

Out of the corner of her eye she saw the teacher walking between the rows of benches. I'm not budging, she thought, a flower doesn't budge either. The teacher's head went from left to right. Now and then she pointed to a blot, a crooked line in an exercise book. Charlotte's body became rooted to the bench.

Charlotte felt the warm, inevitable hand descend on her shoulder. In a rasping voice the teacher asked what Charlotte was doing. The click of pencils falling into their boxes. Don't move. She was a flower. Everyone looked, no one breathed. The rats in the underground school corridors came flocking to see the change, the bars in front of the windows started to curl like snakes. Then the teacher's sour breath penetrated her nostrils. Flowers don't smell things, they give out a smell. Charlotte bent her head and looked at the blank sheet in front of her, which had one scribble on it. Two big tears fell onto the exercise book and extended the pencil line into a dirty rainy smudge.

'Is there a problem?' asked the teacher, surprisingly cheerfully.

Charlotte couldn't explain.

'Well?' Her eyes sparkled. Her fingers curled round the back of Charlotte's neck and sent faint jolts down her spine. Did this have a deeper meaning? The teacher went back to her desk.

'I love you all,' Charlotte heard herself say. That probably didn't mean anything.

Charlotte was sent home early with a note in her diary. 'We'll talk about this,' said the teacher before she let her go and she squeezed Charlotte's arm. The teacher's hair was full of specks of chalk.

*

There was a white van parked on the pavement. Its side was almost scraping the front wall. From behind the old oak tree Charlotte saw a burly man open the rear doors of the van and go into the house. A little later, together with another man, he lugged the sky blue sofa out of the living room. They had a lot of trouble loading it into the van. The small man grinned, revealing his decaying teeth, and rubbed his hands as if he were cold. They disappeared into the house again and came out again with the wall clock. Was the house emptied every day while she was at school? Charlotte went up to the men, who were hoisting the sink unit into the van with the aid of a pulley.

'What are you doing?' she whispered. The men were working hard and didn't hear her. She took a deep breath and repeated her question loudly.

The man, whose bull neck bulged out of his collar, looked at her from the side. The other man threw away a cigarette end, scanned the street and said: 'We're moving house.' And then, frantically, with a gesture to his friend: 'Come on, Staf, let's get out of here.'

They slammed the van doors shut and climbed into the cab. The engine spluttered and started, and the van drove off.

Moving house? She was never told about anything.

In the empty living room, which suddenly looked much

bigger, every step she took sounded like that of an intruder. Her mother was dozing by the open hearth. Her forehead felt as cold as stone.

The next day Charlotte got up much earlier than usual. He mother was still sound asleep in front of the fire. Only her gossamer fine eyelashes were ruffled by a slight draught.

The day was endless. They had to read, do sums and learn about countries for hours. During afternoon playtime the teacher called Charlotte into the classroom. With a trembling finger she leafed through a class diary, and laid it solemnly on the corner of the desk.

'Charlotte, why didn't you say anything to me?'

'I don't know,' said Charlotte.

'You really don't have to come to school when your mother has just died. You're a very brave girl, but it's all right to cry.' Was she supposed to start crying now?

Charlotte cried and was allowed to leave school. She walked home down the village street. She thought of the voice that wandered around on the wind and was blown about like a plastic bag. I'm walking lost among old houses and people I don't know, she thought. I even get lost in the playground. It's almost too late. I must disappear, I'll follow the trail. I'll become a flower queen, or a flower…

The flowers by the side of the road moved in the wind, and encouraged her to go faster. When she looked back from the path to the high mountain, in the distance she could see the sails of the windmill turning helplessly in the air. The mossy roofs of the village houses sank almost completely below the horizon. By late afternoon those shapes had also been flattened out. Charlotte decided never to look back again.

Thick clouds hung in a wreath round the top of the mountain. Narrow paths wound their way along its slopes. In the crevices between the stones, from where the wind could not even scoop out the dust, strange red and purple flowers bloomed.

By sunset, Charlotte had reached the mountaintop. The wind

swept all the clouds from sky, the sun winked at Charlotte and dived head first into the ocean. A little later the moon emerged. Charlotte lay on her back and looked upwards all night long. When she spread her fingers, they were stars made of flesh. If she stood up now she could almost touch the moon.

Soon she was living like the flowers themselves: alert and mobile in the light, quiet and tired when evening came. She followed the trail of flowers along a path that seemed to continue for ever, like an unravelling ball of string. One day a goat would walk with her, at other times a cloud would give her shade in the vast bare heath. No more walls, no more oppressive streets. She would walk until the path fell into the sea.

*

Always follow the path, she kept telling herself, I'm going on walking. There's only one problem, I've got to eat or I'll keel over. A real flower woman feeds on flowers. In a quiet mountain meadow Charlotte picked daisies and removed their mustard-yellow crowns. But her hunger wasn't satisfied by the handful of petals that were left. Couldn't the green leaves and roots of the plants be eaten too? Charlotte thought they could.

From the distance an old man came walking along. He was a little bent with age and waved his stubby arms.

'You're not allowed here!' cried the little grey chap, and he hurried closer,

'Tell me, lad, where are your parents?' he asked when he reached Charlotte. Charlotte could now see that his lower jaw stuck out quite a way. It was an effort for him to get the words out of his mouth. His glowing eyes were fixed on her for a long time.

'Are you perhaps looking for a place to sleep?' How was the man able to guess that?

His house consisted of only one room. Against a screen there was a huge pile of eggshells, and in another corner a stained mattress had been thrown on the floor. The man offered to give

70

Charlotte a wash, because, look, he said and his hard forefinger slid slowly across Charlotte's face, your little cheeks are all dusty. Charlotte preferred to have something to eat. The man looked in the virtually empty kitchen cupboard. Threw a handful of rice in a pan. Then he went outside and came back with a pail of dried walnuts. He hurried cracked the shells in his fist and dug out the dried nuts. He hadn't said much yet but looked eagerly around him. Nothing escaped his attention.

Charlotte shoved so much food into her mouth at once that she could scarcely swallow. The lumps of rice stuck in her gullet like corks. She looked up. The man was standing in front of her with no clothes on. His thighs were thick, mossy tree trunks. Was he going to wash too? He took hold of her wrist.

'You can take your clothes off too,' he said reassuringly, 'we'll wash each other.'

He knelt down in front of her. On the back of his head there was a big scab where the hair had worn away. The man was covered in fur. He was like an animal. The man pressed his face against her trousers, his nose pushed between her legs. He was snuffling as if he were looking for something, and put his hand on her crotch.

'You're not a boy,' he said slowly, suddenly tired. Red veins appeared on his cheeks, and a deep line divided his eyebrows. He looked her up and down from head to toe.

'Take your clothes off,' he ordered Charlotte.

The hand that went towards the thing between his legs trembled like a leaf in the wind.

Charlotte took off her vest and asked: 'My panties too?'

The man didn't answer, but pinched her chin hard between his fat fingers and stuck his tongue, like a wet chamois leather, deep in her mouth. A strong arm lifted Charlotte up by her panties, which tore, and swung her onto the kitchen table. A plate clattered to the floor. A bubble of spit ran down the man's big bottom jaw which was probably difficult for him to swallow. He took the frayed panties, stuffed them in Charlotte's mouth and plunged a branch between her legs. Deeper.

The stick bores into my guts, pricks my gall bladder, drills into my lungs, splinters my ribs. I'm a barrel of blood that's having holes poked in it. I can't breathe. I'm waiting, she said to herself, until the stick comes out of my mouth and pushes out the wad. Before that happened the man stopped abruptly and sank onto the mattress in the corner.

She walked for half a day, a whole day. Days. Flowers don't shed tears, they suck up water. She walked through a rain of light, under a rainbow, through fields where mice were shaking grass stalks, along paths where sails were congregating. In violent storms the wind tugged at her hair, she walked and sweated and shivered and forgot where she was walking. In the evenings the setting sun coloured the fields orange. She fell asleep as frogs croaked to each other from the mud.

Charlotte went on walking. Months passed. She could tell that from the flowers. Dandelions grouped into fluffy seed heads and sailed away on the wind, poppies and clover shot up in the fields, crocuses rested underground.

Once she was standing in a field and the earth suddenly piled up so that she could dig the mole out of its molehill. She ate only meat now. She saw pheasants in the woods and grabbed them by the tail, she plucked sleeping chickens off their perches. She felt a large juicy body growing over the old bony one. As if she were a sofa. Stones were no longer hard: she always sat on a cushion of flesh.

She could only live outdoors from now on. The one time she asked for shelter, she went into the tiny guest room, looked out of the window, and fled down the drainpipe back to the fields.

She had only one aim, one direction: straight ahead, right across meadows and hedges, over wet concrete, through sewers, over drying washing, past rabid dogs, to the one who scattered flowers on her path and was expecting her.

*

She came to a region where the heat paralysed your muscles,

squeezed you dry like a lemon. The people wore sandals but didn't walk around, just wrapped themselves in sheets and slept at midday. Lizards hissed in the dry bushes, bull necks carried baskets of grapes. The sun had a thousand arms. Instead of flowers there were hard thistles growing here, but the trees and bushes were full of oranges, shining tomatoes and purple figs ready to burst.

Charlotte was afraid that one day she would burst out of her dress like a fig. It was tight around her body like a crust. When a few months ago she was hunting for sugar beet along a railway, a soldier in a hurry pushed a parcel into her hands. He sprinted off like a flash, and his feet almost floated above the ground. Other soldiers tried to catch him. The parcel turned out to contain a coarsely woven dress that Charlotte put on immediately and since then had not taken off.

Now that second skin was getting a little tight. Soaking it off was the only solution. She went for a dip in a transparent, shallow river that was too lethargic even to flow. A few fish hung in the water as limp as teabags. The sun numbed her, her dress lay spread out over the water. Suddenly a boy surfaced next to her. He spluttered, and shook his wet hair back and forth. Like a trained athlete he swum to the shore with powerful strokes. Charlotte felt a lump in her throat. When the boy climbed onto the bank, Charlotte saw that he was as small as a dwarf. His body was dark-brown, burnished. Perfect. Water was steaming in clouds off his arms and legs. A straight nose, his eyes dark holes.

I need only stretch out my hand to feel the warm, dense flesh moving beneath my fingertips. I don't move. Heart of glass. Invisible in the water.

*

'Are just going to go on lying there?' asked the dark boy in a sun-drenched voice.

'If you go on standing there,' said Charlotte. After that she didn't really know what to say. He fetched a bag from near a dry bush and sat down. The cool water glided off her like countless fingers. Quickly she wriggled into her tight dress and the boy put out bread, cheese, jet-black olives and swollen tomatoes on a cloth. He introduced himself as Rasmus. He offered her the food and his slender fingers touched her forearm. His eyes spoke when his mouth was silent. He was the most beautiful boy in the world.

They walked together through the town, where the heat hung in the sweltering streets. They saw wrinkled dwarves climbing on each other's shoulders as elegantly as dancers. A chap with glasses picked up a ball of horse manure from the cobbles and brought it to his mouth, while another sucked approvingly on his smoking pipe.

For all I care, the dolphins here could have their snouts full of mustard, she thought, and be handing out parsley. I'm walking along and he's walking beside me.

No one seemed to notice them. Charlotte thought of ghosts that you can walk right through, and deliberately bumped into a dwarf. He waved his arms in the air furiously, as if shooing away an insect. At the crossroads Rasmus went into a house. She followed.

In the large stuffy space, which was sparsely lit, men sat at tables and stared straight ahead. Their job was to turn the glass and occasionally take a sip, smoking all the while. In a factory the smoke coming out of the chimney is a sign of busy activity. Rasmus led her over to a table and joined the queue for the counter. One by one the men were handed a glass of wine. The queue moved steadily forward. Among the heads Charlotte looked for the handsomest man, Rasmus. I'm becoming soft as wax, she though, he can knead me, do what he wants with me.

The more strangers she saw the more his image faded. He became as elusive as a horseman in a troop galloping past. It was dreadful. Charlotte felt cold; her body was enclosed in a cocoon of ice that the air could not penetrate. She fled into the street. Ahead of her a man came stumbling out of a side street. After a few metres he fell to his knees. He stayed kneeling for a few seconds. Then he turned on his axis and finally lay still on the hot paving stones. Water trickled from his trouser legs. The fingers that at first clawed the air went limp. The water dripped onto the street and evaporated.

74

She stood at the town gates alone.

A man who had bathed in a river. A man with a body of bronze and eyes that spoke.

I lean over the river and look. I see his image. I drown my thoughts in him.

Words to tell people something about him, to prevent him from dissolving entirely. No sheet of paper is big enough, I can't describe him, how can I set him down in ink? I don't know anything about him.

*

She walked for half a day, a whole day. Days. The villages were further and further apart, bathing in mirages; trembling oil stains on the horizon became houses, sheep, timid people. Black olives were charring on the trees. The sheep were almost suffocating in their fleeces. The villagers limited their actions to sleeping and brushing off flies. Each evening when the heat became more bearable, Charlotte roasted a sheep. The meat was beautifully tender and what's more made your lips supple and shiny.

Charlotte felt herself changing. Just as the bubbling water in a saucepan pressed against the lid, so her sweating belly stretched more and more against her dress. A shield of fat. Above it two protrusions that kept on growing, like the humps of a camel.

At night Charlotte thought of the brown body. The mouth with the milk-white teeth. The strong arms. In her dreams she bent over to feel his lips. She drew his nose in the sand where she was sleeping. She thought he was standing next to her and shifted to make room for him. She roasted two sheep.

The dirt path that she had followed for months became a paved highway. Roadside signs announced sacred games. Long jump, shot putting, javelin, triple jump, walk. Everyone was invited to take part or support. The only condition was that you had to be a man.

Rasmus.

Small, proudly muscular body.

Charlotte wasted no time on the way, she walked on without a break. For whole nights. Her feet could take her further than her dreams. They would be together again, she would place a wreath on his head.

On the opening day people flocked to the stadium in the holy city. A cloud of sweet honeysuckle floated above the freshly bathed priests with their fresh haircuts, legislators and military commanders. The ordinary people waddled after them, sprinkled themselves with water from leather pouches, pulled out bottles of drink. Friends drank together, ate the raw onions that were sold on the stalls, laughed and gossiped.

The day before Charlotte had gone to the market. Traders fluttered around her and brought scarves and beads. She held up different materials next to each other in the light, compared the price of carpets. Pretexts. She was looking for men's clothing.

At noon the traders withdrew to the cafés, the food was covered with cloths and flies. A languor descended on the square. Charlotte crept over to a pushcart laden with cotton, pushed at a thick bale and ran off after it as it whizzed down the steep paved road.

In the woods she draped the material around her body. She cut a deep notch in a tree and smeared the sticky resin on her cheeks and top lip. Over it she strewed coarse grains of sand. A touch of masculinity. She put a pine cone on her tongue and tried to speak. Deep throaty sounds welled up.

Panting with excitement Charlotte went to the celebration along with the masses. She shivered in the blistering sun, tension crept round in her belly like a worm. Twice she stopped and sat on a flat stone in the middle of the road in order to calm down. Her feet pounded the sand flat. Stories buzzed around the throng. About the biggest pumpkin in those parts, the filthiest whore in town, the pigeon that flew so fast it burst into flame.

Fiddling nervously with her dress Charlotte faced the guards. One of them walked slowly around her, then pointed to the red stain that was growing bigger and bigger. In order to hide her breasts she had tied a dead sheep to her belly.

'You OK?' The guard raised his eyebrows. A flock of insects was gorging on the sweet resin on her cheeks and under her nose.

'Boozer, stinking beggar!' The men behind her were waiting, impatient to go in.

Charlotte was let in.

After a whole series of speeches and prayers and a dance with a torch the first athletes entered the stadium. Oiled brown bodies shone in the sun. Thousands of hands waved, clapped, fluttered in the even blue sky. The men on the track shook their muscles loose and their naked genitals shook along with them. A boy struck the gong. Where was he? Heels were place against a white chalked line, eyes turned heavenward. Charlotte stiffened. The sacrificial sheep, with the knife at their throats, held their last breath.

'Go!' she cried suddenly, and accidentally swallowed the pine cone. The silence broke, thousands of eyes became bullets. Hands grabbed her, tore the dress roughly from her body. She jumped off the stand. A spear whizzed over her head and impaled a guard. Would he still come? He was as fast and unpredictable as the wind, after all.

'Sacrilege!' they yelled. The marble statues of divinities looked on motionless. Down the colonnade, past the temple, the river, the senate, the men followed each other in pursuit, got in each other's way, and screamed that the monster must die. Flayed, a skewer up her arse, roasted like a chicken, bottles, bricks up her cunt.

In front of a large stone building Charlotte saw a sign which read in bold letters: ENTER MY HOUSE.

With the palm of her hand she thrust against the heavy oak door, which swung slowly open. Calling on their gods, fists raised the troop of pursuers, which had thinned out, stopped at the foot of the steps and then shrank back as if poison gases were drifting towards them.

An unimaginable cold descended from the grey walls and spread over the granite floor tiles. The windows glistened like ice crystals, the chairs fought off the cold. From behind one of the towering columns rose a constant growl, as if a dull-witted beggar were talking to himself. Every step she took was an intrusion. And yet: in this world there was room for her; she did not have to squeeze through the doorway, the floor did not protest creaking under her weight.

A voice sounded behind Charlotte.

'Do I know you?'

Charlotte fell to her knees. Whoever or whatever was calling her, she had to surrender.

A bearded man with red cheeks and a strawberry nose appeared and bent forward. His friendly eyes were as round as hazelnuts. She was welcome, God had no opening times, said the voice that travelled from arch to arch.

The man showed her the cross arches with tableaux of half-naked men and women. An elder was afflicted by boils. A piglet licked clean a festering wound on his shin. A grimacing boy pulled an arrow from his ribcage while next to him on the burning grass a skeleton stared disgustingly at Charlotte. Charlotte looked quickly away.

The whole space was full of sculptures all of them serious or deeply melancholy. In a plea for attention they stretched out their hands. That attention, explained the bearded man, who said his name was Achille, was what God was giving her. Had she never heard the silence of nature? A silence that is more cruel and more silent than anything? And in that core of silence a singing reaching so widely that the whole world made sense and all things were lost for a moment?

He spoke in a whisper. She replied even more quietly. Two children peeping through heaven's keyhole. He told her about God and she saw it all in front of her: where He dwelt, what He did, what He wrote in his palm and His diary.

'But!' snorted Achille suddenly and was silent for a moment. 'It doesn't look good. The ship of the world is adrift. 'Look!' Charlotte followed his finger as it drew the ship in the air. 'The rowers have nodded off, the ship is tossed as the wind changes'

– his body rolled from side to side – 'it will be swallowed up by mountainous seas. The day when God calls the world to order is not far off. He will listen. Judge. Then there will be no more words. The very last screams will be blown away by the angels. Your swollen flesh will scorch, your heart will be charred.'

Terror cut off her breath.

*

My God who speaks to me and tells me what to do and sees everything. And yet, silent as the grave, is contained in this image. With toes round as marbles, ribs bent like hoops, with a body so thin my eyes miss it. There must be room for five of those Gods in me. They're in there talking to each other, I think, they're trying to tell me something and are pounding on the walls. It makes my belly rumble. I have to listen. Not understand. However many images he is, God is one.

Achille says I must look after myself and learn a lot. Every morning we walk through the wet grass singing. After breakfast we play chess for an hour. We spend the rest of the day in the church. We read the great book. The words boom against the walls, find each other, and meet like drops of mercury. The space, at first grey and dark as a cave, fills with colour when I give my canary-yellow dandelions to the statue. These are dissonants, says Achille and he pulls out all the stops on his organ. Above the thundering notes he bellows, like the skipper of a boat taking the full force of the storm. His white side-whiskers curl with pleasure.

*

'Do flowers suck the light out of the sky in the evening so that it goes dark?' I once asked Achille. He had to think about it for a very long time. Then he said that it was possible, though it wasn't certain. The next day he took me to the stables behind the church where a group of old monks lived. Elias, a jolly man who smelt like my mother, showed me round. Under wooden roof beams men and sculptures lived together, among clouds of dust and mangers full of tools. Hammers bit great chunks out of blocks of marble, files glided like human palms over the rough surface and calmed the mutilated stone. The very oldest monks shuffled about and sprinkled water over the white sand. Elias stopped at a block of bluestone. Achille had told him about my beautiful thoughts, said the fragrant, rich voice. With those thoughts I must be able to make a sculpture. 'Artists are the gardeners of beauty. And can do anything,' he said, laughing so that he showed his tonsils.

For a whole day and night I hammered, chiselled, and sanded until the Mother of God stood before me ghostly white and still. I moved her to the courtyard and dipped my hands in a puddle. When my palms were imprinted all over her body the sun appeared hesitantly. It was as if scores of people had touched her, brought her to life with their veneration. It was good.

In the early morning I went for a walk. I saw ants waking up, I saw beads of dew glistening and bursting like soap bubbles. I saw young shrubs being gently shaken to and fro. The hand of God. When I returned the sculpture had gone. To heaven.

It's now looking down to earth from heaven. At the people who want to forget the Lord because they know that he counts all sins like gold coins. He dispenses punishments: a child gets bubonic plague, a hunter loses his sight, and the handsomest boy in the world goes up in smoke.

He has his reasons that we know nothing of.

Sometimes I was afraid my belly would burst. I must convert faster and more intensely. My belly rumbled so badly that I started awake at night and thought there was a thunderstorm getting up. I ate pebbles to combat the roaring inside me. Something was pounding, pushed its arms through mine during such a spell, its bell against the wall of my belly so that my muscles almost tore. A kernel growing, a fat worm eating me that will open me up. I regularly spoke to God's immovable statue in the church. He always hears me, even at night when I'm asleep and can't hear myself. He lifts up my skull like a

lid and follows the thoughts snaking their way round. I never swear
because He sees me.

Where shall I begin?

I was born.

I was fed.

I spat my porridge out. For no reason. So it seemed.

I broke a commandment. Sin, filthy worm, crept in through
my open mouth, settled in my body and spat me out. It's stamping
around in that body. And I, I want to find myself again. Following
behind God like a chick behind a mother hen.

I said goodbye to Achille and swore not to return until I had
persuaded a hundred people to praise the Lord day and night, and to
stroke his statue until the skin came off their fingers. Achille laughed
into his beard. It made me furious.

*

*A farmer at first thought he had left a bale of hay in the field. The bale
slid closer. Came up the high street. As she entered the village the
market square emptied in a trice. Doors were locked, heads jostled
at the windows. From close to the creature looked the same. Massive
forms do not change with distance. A head balanced on top of the
mountain of flesh. The creature barked a few short sentences like a
dog and sat down beneath the clock tower. A few people protested
aloud when she put her mouth to the water-spewing lion's head.*

*The professor had observed the scene from his study. After
all those years of observation he scarcely turned a hair at a case
like this. An object of study was waddling across the square. In this
remote, backward village the scholar was working in the utmost
secrecy on the shaping of the body by the mind. A stubborn mind is
housed in a firm, well-proportioned body; a miser can be recognised
by his hunched shoulders. Perfectly functioning bodies are not the
accidental result of centuries of reproduction, a successful cooperation*

between sperm and womb. Minds are moulded by laws and speeches by the president. Enlightened minds ensure strengthened bodies. The president was counting on the professor.

He approached the giantess resolutely. Looked her right in the eye. Invited her to come and have a drink at his house. Gaining the confidence of lumbering people is easy since they always go for the easy option. With extremely docile cases: always be on your guard (but never show that you are).

In his study he offered the gigantic woman a seat, which she politely refused. He jumped up to get a cup of coffee and looked at his wristwatch. Like sailors did before jumping in the water he thought with a chuckle.

According to the law strangers should be removed from the village square. That had been done.

Admittedly inviting a stranger into your home was an infringement of the law. But who would come and lay down the law to him? He discussed, improved, and revised the law. He was the law.

He would look after the creature, he explained to the villagers. And she would look after his house and garden. After all he was often away observing. She was mentally defective and she could work like a horse. Not an unusual combination.

When Ralf the old sexton died she took on his job too. She polished the church floor daily and on Sundays she handed out hymnals in the church porch. At first the church-goers felt uncomfortable. Some of them had seen her kick the statues of the saints with devilish glee, others reported that the giantess spat at them when they didn't take the hymnals at once. All of them had to get used to the change. However, they were reassured when he explained that, although she was a bit bigger than average, she showed many similarities with the plodding, faithful farm horse.

So she was accepted into the rural community. In the evenings she exchanged a few words with the stunted old neighbour who was not as tall as her hand. After the service she distributed freshly picked flowers which the housewives gladly accepted. Like

82

everyone else she waited her turn at the butcher's. Like everyone else she was the subject of stories and gossip.

Very occasionally she stepped into the limelight. On Christmas Day she attracted attention by singing along at the top of her voice. The pews at the back slid forward over the carpet, those sitting on them were drenched with sound. During the annual polar bear contest she astonished the villagers by remaining under water for a day and a night.

Her stupidity inspired confidence in man and beast. During the elevation of the host Mrs Cijfer's dog, which had been thought lost, poked out from under the giantess's collection of junk. From then on she kept pets with her during the service. Soon toddlers too, who usually started bawling, were clinging to her skirts. They climbed the mountain of her belly, rode piggyback on her shoulders, played hide-and-seek round her body. During the hymns she put the tots under her armpits and rocked the squashed little heads.

*

'The sun went as pale as a ghost. Crocodiles wailed, women raved and men roared; the squeals of rabbits, which had never yet produced a sound, went right through you. The moon spewed fire...'

The children listened in fascination to my dream. They came and help me weed in the scrawny man's garden. I cleaned all the rooms, washed all the sheets daily and looked after the garden so he could shut himself up in his study. Sometimes he stood and watched through a chink in the door. He looked like a crust of bread with glasses. His eyes followed my movements, but when I looked at him he quickly disappeared.

The children ploughed up the lawn with their bikes, they hung on my dress or asked me for stories. Meanwhile their mothers were standing wasting their time chattering at markets, at tills and outside the gates of closed schools. They poisoned their children with their sloth. They spat in God's face. I should have killed the children. To save them from a worse fate.

Because their mothers ate idols, in their patisseries and works canteens, and then complained, counting calories and calendar dates.

Because they practised immorality in their children's homes and in public toilets.

Because they were old and ugly.

Because mothers should set a good example to their children.

*

We watched the lively tripping of pigeons in the garden; the little ones threw grains of cereal onto the grass. That is where it would happen. More pigeons landed.

'Here God's Kingdom will come to earth. A new house will descend from heaven and squash the old world flat. The sinners will be excluded. Desperately they will knock on the windows, red-hot candle wax will drip on their heads like rain.'

The children's heads turned to the watery-white ceiling of the sky.

'The stars fall from heaven like rotten figs. The earth's crust shrinks, beetles eat people. If you avert your gaze, your eyeballs roll out of their sockets like peas.

Perhaps you are thinking: we're children, we're good. If we eat up our sandwiches, don't speak with our mouths full and obey our parents. No!

Babies come into the world as lukewarm creatures, they're neither hot nor cold. Not a single baby scorches its mother's breast, there is not a single baby freezes fast in its cradle.

And yet. In the belly of every baby there is a seed.

It may dry up. That produces dry, heartless children. God hurls them into hell like firewood.

The seed may germinate. Those children radiate heat like stoves and need no fire to warm themselves by. God cherishes them day and night.

Can you hear the water when you turn the tap on? It is the voice of God rushing through the pipes. Put your shoes on, and you're stepping on God. He looks up through your soles. God comes to meet you in the smell of the fish stall round the corner. He leads the way, He follows every step you take. Follow Him, you have no choice. Avoid those people who sometimes help you across the street, put you in clothes that are far too big, and pursue you with lunchboxes.

Where are they now? What are they doing? Are they ever coming back?

You don't know.

Your life is a problem and God is the solution. They are strangers. Sinners. He will cut off the heads of sinners with a scythe. Don't be afraid. Your parents are bigger, they stick out. It'll be their turn first.'

They looked at me with big doe eyes. My heart overflowed. I enfolded the pale little creatures in my arms. And heaven enfolded me in its arms. God is everywhere.

*

I asked them if it sometimes hurt.

Of course they sometimes hurt. One girl showed the thorn on her finger, a boy pointed to the scab on his knee. Every day he scratched it off, and the next day it was back again.

Of course they wanted to be freed of their pain forever. Even if they had to suffer very bad pain for a moment and sacrifice a piece of themselves. God was laying a heavy task on my shoulders.

I got them to sit down in a row next to each other among the leeks. Then I told them to close their eyes and to stretch out their fingers in front of them. I took hold of the secateurs. Cramps in my belly. Better the short pain than eternal torment. Ten questions for ten followers. Ten fingers to uncover the truth.

Do you want to be dragged off to hell by devils that clamber up the legs of your chairs with their sticky bellies?

Do you want to eat their carbuncles there, drink their pus, knead their droppings?

Do you want to spoon the pulp of rotting brains out of a skull?

Do you want to watch with one eye as the other is peeled like an onion?

Do you want to have all the marrow sucked out of your spine, your legs, your toe joints?

Do you know what coffee is made of, the drink your mothers drink such vast amounts of? Do you know that rotting meat goes black?

Do you want to have a wart hog with its snout full of herpes poking about in all your orifices until you are the biggest sore in the world?

Do you want to have a pack of starving mice and rats gnaw your belly open and nestle in your guts?

Can you already taste the liquid from the corpse of the dead rat boy at the back of your throat?

Do you want to eat, digest, excrete, eat, digest, excrete, eat, digest your own tongue?

For each negative answer a finger fell on the ground. It was raining fingers among the leeks. The devil left them. The pain that they felt also passed through my body. They lost consciousness. I took their clothes off and threw them on a dunghill to make a bonfire. In the shed I found potato sacks.

Thinking of new garments for his young followers, thinking of sayings like 'put on the new man'. Sometimes I think too much and that's the cause of my suffering. The Lord thinks even more. So His suffering is beyond our understanding.

Now I had found followers for Him, He spoke to me again. No longer in words but in deeds. An iron needle pierced my neck vertebra, threading my vertebrae together. Lower down a cramp between my legs. Lower still, convulsions in my knees. Lower. I toppled. A fist toppled in me and dislocated my hips. The fist scratched me open from inside, and I was torn like a scrap of material.

It came out of me screeching. The monster. The lump of wild flesh. The devil that had lain low all this while in the cave at the bottom of my body, where I myself had never been. How could I discover anything where my hands could not reach? I got up out of the growing pool of blood, tore the tough intestine with which the thing wanted to suck from me and raised it to the sky. The children trembled and squeaked. It was the devil himself: a tumour, a boil full of pus that had not quite burst in me. I hurled the devil at the brick wall. A hundred times. Until something lay splattered at my feet, a tree of flesh in which shitty little eyes were still moving.

Now the devil had been driven out his retinue also came crawling out. A fat worm slipped out of me to the ground. Lather slid down my thighs. God had cleared everything out of me to be able to live there all alone. The devil had been driven out, I was whole again.

I asked the children if they wanted to go and see the fight between the elephant and the rhinoceros in town, but they shook their heads. A child's body takes a while to get used to changes. I promised to bring candy floss along. I felt light, liberated. Some people are annoyed at me because I take up more space than they do, but wasn't I feather-light, hollowed out now? A membrane like a pig's bladder.

The elephant and the rhinoceros also collided, thrusting into each other's sides as if into soft cushions. God freed them from the wilderness and took them to a circus so that they could perform daily in the arena. God led me away from a village and gave me words to ward off evil.

How the fight between the elephant and the rhinoceros ended, I don't know. I stood and watched and suddenly the scrawny man was standing next to me and looking at a policeman. Nodded.

When I was taken away, the animals looked at me earnestly. Perhaps they laughed invisibly.

Even without me the same thing would have happened. The children were only obeying a law of God.

Indian Summer

Jef Geeraerts

For Betty and Jef Barthels

And instead of lying half-stupefied in the orange glow of the overheated tent to escape the mosquitoes I now really must make a new daily schedule to impose the necessary discipline on myself, for example drinking less water or becoming absorbed in all kinds of complex tasks, then it may be possible that the water sloshing around in my gut won't immediately start dripping down my back in rivulets when the temperature soars in the afternoon and the mosquito netting is black with mosquitoes, or I must try to imagine as I chew on the leaves of the dwarf willows that the sap tastes of spinach and so is rich in vitamins and in particular I mustn't slowly start to panic by thinking hysterically of the most exquisite dishes, more and more the slightest movement is making me breathless, even just shifting position, pumping up the mattress is almost impossible now, I'm a trembling old man with acute pain in my joints and my gums are bleeding and if I sit up to look outside (to see if they're coming yet, if the plane is coming), I feel so nauseous that my mouth fills with spittle and my forehead breaks out in cold sweat and I start shivering and panting, in Herrbergsdalen I'd asked that woodcutter, in laboured German, to indicate the approximate direction of the journey in case help were needed, the only inhabited spot apart from Herrbergsdalen is Vargaren, that's where a Lapp lives with his wife, he said, a fisherman who receives supplies every three months in a seaplane belonging to the Forestry Commission, and to my question whether there were bears in the area, he replied yes, and on the map pointed out an area called Norra-Borgafjällen, there's nothing there, nothing, only reindeer, elk and snow, he said, have you got a good compass? That was sixteen days ago, perhaps he's forgotten us, I have to say the names on the 1:200,000 scale map carefully out loud once more 'Trykt av Generalstabens Litografisksa Anstalt Stockholm', in a slightly sing-song tone like the characters in a Bergman film, Swedish ordnance survey maps are freely available here, here they don't fear an enemy attack as they do in the Baroque south, reeling off the names hurriedly is the exciting memory game that will supposedly keep my mind resilient so that I don't have cosmic panics as always at about eleven at night, when the sun disappears behind the flat, snow-covered top of the Barkantjakk in a white, pale Saturn-like glow and the shadows slowly lengthen till I can no longer see the end of them and the lake-called-Sjougden clots in the line of mountains and the mosquitoes will sleep for four hours, three days ago I still leapt into action at that point, I'd boiled the last packet of soup, crispbread had run out long ago and so had the raisins and... yesterday I squeezed the last four pills that were left out of their plastic holder one by one and sucked up the sweet capsules, Sunday, Monday, Tuesday, Wednesday (Scorpio, Scorpio!) I have no more energy to lay a new supply of birch bark on you and the hard lump in my throat is creeping upwards because kissing is no longer possible, last night, or rather twenty hours ago, at the moment the sun hung in the sky like a yellow disc *and came closer* and the moon rose visibly and as always I suddenly became aware of an ethereal infinity, in which the earth floats like a discus, while the landscape lies frozen beneath a sun without warmth and at about two-thirty it rises again in a prehistoric silence above an unreal landscape from the Cambrian period with motionless crusty firs, ponds, lakes, mountains, no birds, no life, in which you suddenly have to jerk round, because someone is looking at you, the grinning slit-eyed Lapp from Värgaren, who when you see him slowly dissolves into the bog, twenty-four hours ago her features were still beautiful, peaceful, the skin firm, brown, hair shining, the hands... I carefully brushed away the mosquitoes and the flies, she was the only woman with whom I could embark on such a crazy journey through the wilderness, *Jämtland, that must be Lapland,* she had said, *it's the nicest name for Lapland,* with her small, intent face, happy, enthusiastic, she followed my finger on the map and spelt out the names that I now keep reciting in the correct order: Dajmasjön, Blierekij, Afvasjön, Gubbsjöhöjdon, Klöfverjället, Genjegetjem, Steurjenjuota, Köfåsen, Hjerpegalten... yesterday the patch of gangrene on the leg had not yet gone black and... either look in the notebook, impressions noted during the journey, *the colour of the copper church roofs in Helsingør is as poisonous as a green mamba*, and then, as they approached the Swedish coast, on the railing of the boat *the flat gleaming nuclear power station whose thin metal chimneys do not smoke, a hydrogen bomb has devastated Sweden,* we would travel through a charred, fissured land but afterwards they turned out to be petrol storage sites, smoke-free and hygienic as everything in that country, it drizzled beneath a light-grey sky, the further north we drove (sometimes six hundred kilometres a day) through uninhabited wooded regions, past lakes, over narrow wooden bridges, past rust-coloured wooden farmhouses with no people around, the air pure, ethereal, cool, *polar air*, finally along desolate, smooth earth roads between fir woods it got warmer and warmer, oppressive, not a breath of wind, the mosquitoes became unbearable, the sky was uniformly overcast, the sun glowed copper behind a thin layer of clouds, at the last petrol station a half-naked Swede said he had never seen anything like it, the thermometer stood at thirty-one degrees in the shade, that was the period when we drove practically naked through the monotonous landscape of frozen, thinly strewn pine woods, following the example of the few Swedes with reindeer antlers tied to their roof racks, who were zooming southwards at great speed and with full headlights on, the end of midsummer night when everything is permitted, after two days your breasts were as brown as your shoulders and that hair of yours was tied up in two buns, young, playful, Marianne, and at about eight in the evening we'd get hungry and invariably find a wonderful secluded spot with firs and short grass and a plunging stream full of icy, soft water that makes the soap lather and polishes your teeth as you drink it, and then I put the tent up while you cooked the evening meal, with swift, precise movements, babbling non-stop, full of plans for the big trip in Jämtland, the bear trip, the reindeer trip, the bottle of wine was

91

cooling in the stream, as we were eating French dishes, smoked salmon on toast and Chablis, imagining it was champagne and lobster, the bottle tinkling in the silver cooler, and then baked potatoes with steak and salad and a bottle of Bordeaux, and then I made a fire of birch bark and pinewood, *aromatic fire*, and we smoked and breathed and drank water, it was as if we were dehydrated; if at night we got up a lot to drink, we crept through the twilight like naked ghosts and drank from the stream flat on our stomachs, not a leaf stirred and it was sultry, not even the mosquitoes were buzzing, in the north we could see the vague glow that mesmerised us, we felt very relaxed and happy, we lay dreaming naked on our sleeping bags, dozed off, woke, asked each other if we were asleep and sat cross-legged smoking a cigarette we gave each other, we scarcely talked, we listened to the silence and when it got light at about two-thirty and the sun glittered above the woods, we got up and stretched and yawned noisily and went naked into the wood, the floor of tiny needles and moss was damp, we washed each other on a rock while the water foamed, where did all that water keep coming from? We felt like Germanic forest gods and I boomed out *'Duu saagest's!*, from the Matthew Passion and imitated an approaching bear with lumbering movements and appropriate growling until we rolled over the ground sobbing with laughter and kissed and… and then I boiled water on the wood fire with slow, ritualised, loving gestures, for coffee, strong coffee and you fried smoked bacon with fried eggs and we drank that unbelievable milk from pyramid-shaped cartons, everything slowly, relaxed, free from original sin, there was no god, only we existed and the earth was there too, fire, water, air, cosmos, we weren't bewitched by the landscape, that only happened on the fifth day of the journey, the day we decided to climb the mountain of the spirits, the Barkantjakk, to propitiate the gods I had first to beat the imaginary troll's drum and sing the sacred songs, recite texts from the *Edda*, drum first softly beseeching *dooboodooboodoob…* faster and faster, higher, more incisively and I had to ask our star signs, Scorpio, Pisces, love, death, violence, longing for Evil, the universe, Nothingness, whether the time was favourable for the trolls of the Barantjakk and whether the fatal day of Ragnarök had yet come, and let loose death cries and drum feverishly *dooboodooboodoob!* And scream hoarsely, and finally roll over the ground in a trance and wait breathlessly to see whether the spirits would answer... then we took a day's food with us in a rucksack, the summit seemed very close but when we emerged from the birch wood, a lush green plateau stretched ahead full of dwarf willows and a tangle of lakelets, ponds and streams, it took us four hours to reach the foot of the mountain, there we put on dry socks and different boots, we ate hastily, you were already tired, particularly nervous about the clouds of mosquitoes buzzing round us and when we started to climb, you asked if you could rest every quarter of an hour and you were panting, there were black rings under your eyes and you stubbornly refused dextrose, you drank too much water, my shirt was wet with sweat, even the rucksack was soaked on one side and at about two o'clock it got even hotter as there was no more vegetation and no water and the sun was reflected by the blocks of granite and made your eyes hurt, at the summit there were no mosquitoes and we sat silently on a boulder with our feet in the snow for an hour and then we suddenly heard the thudding of hooves, we looked up and about fifty metres away a small herd of reindeer came trotting in our direction, you jumped up and tugged the camera out of your rucksack, *reindeer, reindeer, the trolls' answer* you whispered and your whole face shone and your eyes, those eyes of yours, black with long straight lashes, and you ran off and took photos, the reindeer smelled our scent and made a timid swerve down the slope and you ran screaming after them and then I saw you fall, you lay there and you started to call anxiously for me and when I reached you, you were still lying hunched forward among the stones, your right leg had cracked and was caught in a fissure and when I picked you up you screamed with pain and then I saw it, the bone splinter was sticking through your trousers, which were red with blood and you clung to me and said quickly *don't leave me, I don't want to be alone, stay with me, don't leave me alone*, and then I took her on my shoulders, the leg dangled down loosely, we had no disinfectant, we had no string, no wood to make a splint, I tied a tourniquet above the knee with a shoelace, luckily she only weighed fifty-two kilos, I laid her face down on my rucksack, put my right arm under her left leg and took hold of her left wrist, she moaned incessantly and begged me to do or not to do all kinds of things, irrevocable things, promises for life, during the descent, then through the bog, searching for the tent, six hundred metres below, far, far away, near the lake called Sjougden which I could see in a white haze and when we got to the marshy plateau with the lakelets had already succumbed to exhaustion three times and recovered three times thanks to the last of the dextrose and at the first stream I drank till my stomach was bursting and gave her water to drink from my hand and there were bent birch bushes and I bound them round her leg with fresh birch bark and she bit into my arm with the pain and I had to help her to pee and when I saw it made me cry but it took another eight hours for us to reach the tent, in the dense birch woods her leg in a splint kept catching on everything and I simply didn't look and she lost consciousness and I felt faint and was covered in hanging moss and must have fallen over at least ten times and at the lake day filled the sky with swarms of mosquitoes and pale ponds and already hot and I had got the direction wrong, I said wait here, I'll go on looking alone and then I'll come and get you, because I was hungry and felt weak *no don't leave me stay here we'll die together here*, you said, your face was pale, twisted into lines I'd never seen, Marianne, in a few hours you'd aged ten years, I was over two kilometres out, in the tent I feverishly made instant mousse with raisins and drank two tins of grapefruit juice one after the other, gulped down the mousse and drank water till I couldn't drink any more, hung the bloody shirt on the tent pole, made mousse for her and stumbled, spitting and cough over to the spot where you were lying, you were swinging furiously at the mosquitoes attracted by the blood and I fed you mousse with a spoon, but you couldn't keep it down, it kept spurting out of your mouth and you cried, during the journey to the tent I felt stronger and I was able to carry you in my arms like a bridegroom carries his bride, in the tent at first you lay staring at the roof and the next day the pain started and you wouldn't let me fetch help from Herrbergsdalen, when it got too bad, I poured water over the wound and you lost a lot of weight because the fever became more intense, sweating, teeth chattering under two sleeping bags, throwing them off and sweating again, I held your head, your hair was wet and matted and you smelled and looked at me hollow-eyed, your lips were cracked and you swallowed water like an animal and the wound started to go green, but I didn't tell you that, nor did I tell you that amputation was the only solution, the knife was razor sharp and afterwards I would cauterise the wound, I couldn't bring myself to do it, after four days we were out of food, on the sixth day I came back into the tent with water and a sickly smell hit me in the face and I had to go out again, you lay breathing peacefully, the leg looked mouldy, the ankle and the knee were swollen and I had to hold your hand the whole time and talk to you and now and then you cried, on the seventh day you had a very high fever and you asked for food but there was nothing and your hands were narrow and bony like those of a ninety-year-old woman, at about eleven in the evening you became delirious and started shouting incomprehensibly and throwing your head about, deep red, eyes bulging, at a certain moment I was so tired that I fell asleep and when I woke it was strangely quiet in the tent, I sat up and took your hands in mine and laid them on your breast, closed your eyes and went outside, the sun was setting behind the Barkantjakk, the lake, the mountains were infinitely familiar, I walked into the wood and returned immediately, knelt by your rucksack and took out your towels and buried my nose in the material, then your toilet bags with its smells, your underwear, Marianne, my best companion, and when daylight returned I opened the zip of the tent and didn't dare touch you, I pulled the air bed out of the tent right down to the lake and sat for hours looking at you and brushing the insects away with a branch, I kept thinking: you won't be able to swim in the North Sea any more, where is your spirit now? is it on its way to the pole or are you floating in the cosmos like an atom waiting for second consciousness?... the next day I went into the forest to collect birch bark, which I cut carefully into strips, bone-dry and tough, from dead fallen trunks,

95

and began piling it in her, covering just her face with willow branches, to be able to see when I was there, and then I started chewing willow leaves... and when the mosquitoes became too bad, I carefully covered her face and had to go back into the tent, into the orange heat and had to try to sleep or not to think and recite the names once again and sometimes swallow the painful lump in my throat, but yesterday when brown liquid came out of her mouth and her belly started swelling over her belt, I summoned up all my strength and went to the forest and collected as much bark as possible and now it's nearly midnight and I can go back outside first drink from the lake and then crawl towards you on my hands and knees, the match strikes and I hold it under the bark at the four corners, the flames shoot up intensely and it starts creaking and cracking and spitting and sucking, a vertical column of black smoke rises up and in great astonishment I say: Dajmasjön, Blierekij, Afvasjön, Gubbsjöhöjdon, Klöfverjället, Genjegetjem, Steurjenjuolta...

Römnäsmyran, 12 July 1967
Knokke, 12 July 1968

Fairy Tale

Kristien Hemmerechts

Once upon a time a husband and wife had a child that lived. Then they had another child and it died and then another child and that child died too. The first child was a girl, the second and the third were boys. The children were called Katherine, Benjamin and Robert, but their names were mostly shortened to Kathy, Ben and Rob. After the death of the third child the man and the woman didn't have any more children, but did get a dog, which was christened Lady by their daughter. The husband took photos of his wife, his daughter and the dog, and then asked his wife to take a picture of him. The photos were developed and stuck in the photo album. 'The four of us together at last!' the woman wrote underneath, but less than three years later she left the husband, and hence also, without wanting to, the daughter and the dog.

Once upon a time a husband and wife had a child that lived. Then they had another child and it died and then another child and that child died too. The first child, who lived, was a girl, who grew and grew, until one day she stopped growing: she was fully grown, ready to have children of her own who would live or not live.

Once you've bled you can have babies, the girl knew, but she bled many times before it came to that: look Mummy, look Daddy, a tummy for you, there's a baby in it. The man, the woman and the daughter sat by the fire and stroked the tummy that grew fuller and rounder and brought the new baby closer. Months passed, but still the child wasn't born. They felt it moving in the full, round tummy and saw it turning over. Finally they realised that the child would never be born and would never die. The girl would stay pregnant for ever and ever, the pregnant tummy would be forever in their midst.

If I'd dared, I would have shorn off my hair and gouged my breasts with a sharp knife. I would have starved myself and gone around in loose black clothes. I would have become penance and mourning.

The night before you died your father drank some of your milk. Afterwards I could no longer bear my breasts to be touched. I didn't breast-feed your brother, who was born a year later. I wanted to be unsexed, disembodied. There were men, quite a few men, who found grief sexy. Who wanted to enter that body that was trying to disembody itself. The image I had of myself wasn't very sexy. A woman whose skin has been peeled off and who is put on display naked and rubbed with salt. There's a gale blowing. But no one sees that I'm naked and unsexed, no one sees my exposed veins and muscles and nerves, the salt biting into them. I must talk. I must open my mouth and let sound out. I'm surrounded by creatures that laugh and move and eat and roar. They frighten me.

I lie in bed and next to me lies a man. My husband. It's dark, pitch-black; we can't see a thing, only feel. I don't know what he feels, but what I feel is this: I'm in a deep hole and he's in a deep hole. When we've both clambered out of our hole, we'll be able to hold hands. It's not possible to dig a tunnel from my hole to his hole. There are no ladders on the walls of the holes.

The laws of despair are these: a despairing body tries to destroy itself. There can be no contact between despairing and non-despairing bodies. A despairing body that seeks or has contact with another body is no longer despairing.

Pure despair leads to suicide, the destruction of the body, that is, of the link with life, with experience. For the despairing person the decision to commit suicide is the end of despair. There turns out to be an escape, living is not a necessity. This is a reassuring thought. The problem remains: how?

My son has been cremated and all the people who have come to the party, because that's what the funeral meal is to some extent, have finally gone, I had to ask them – go away, please go away. I went and lay in my bed, always that need to go to bed, as if you're lying in your grave or crawling into the womb. I lie in bed, there are brown sheets on the bed – a wedding present. Not pretty, brown, but it doesn't show the dirt. I don't think much, I think: phew, now I can die. I think I'll do it in two weeks or so, I'll be abroad for a conference. Also tempting is the car in the garage, hose attached to the exhaust and into the car through a window, where I'll be calmly reading a book. The garage doors and windows will have been hermetically sealed with newspapers. I'm thinking of my parents' garage – that's probably connected with the longing to return to the womb. I don't think of who will find my body, I don't think of their despair. Not for an instant. I think only of how I'll do it.

'Mummy.'

My daughter is two and a half, and can't reach the door handle. She's standing on the other side of the bedroom door and wants to come in, into my bedroom, my bed.

'Mummy, mummy.'

How often does she say: 'mummy'?

Something topples in my head. I get out of bed, my grave, go to the door, open it, let her in. 'Darling.'

Later I will put my arms round her hundreds of times, feeling that she's alive, thinking: sorry, sorry that I forgot you for a moment then. Her father will hold it against me for ages. How could you? he says.

The despairing person forgets a lot. Much must be forgiven a despairing person, but she is not forgiven much. The despairing person wrecks a lot of things.

The despairing person feels dead, but she is expected to perform the actions of the living. The despairing person thinks: can't they see I'm dead? No, they can't because the despairing person isn't dead.

When does despair stop? The despairing body heals. It acquires a new skin that covers the raw flesh. Despair also stops when the despairing body meets another despairing body. Even if the two of them are together down a deep hole, that hole is no longer called despair. In the hole of despair there is no room for two.

8 September 1983
 I think he's cold. I can feel him shivering.

After Ben   AB
Before Ben   BB

9 September 1983
 Words.
 Black.
 And: the days are too long.

15 September 1983
 I wish there were an underworld I could descend into in search of you.

28 September 1983
 First people come because he's been born. Then they come because he's died.

1 October 1983
 Now I don't have to worry about you anymore. Now I don't have to be frightened anymore because you won't die anymore.

February 1984
 While it was happening: this isn't real, we're just pretending and once we've all cried hard enough, you'll come back.

Ben is a photo on the sideboard.

At home nowhere, because you aren't anywhere.

In the paper: 'Benjamin Karel Smith spent the lovely summer of 1983 with us.'

Sunday, 28 August 1983

My husband was going cycling with my brother, but I say to him: please, let me go, I need to get out for a bit. It's the second time I've left my son, who was born on 6 July. I did so yesterday to dash out and buy some clothes. I bought a long grey flannel skirt. Why did I do that? I don't know, it's summer and lovely weather. But I shall wear the skirt at my baby son's funeral. It's a second-hand skirt, perhaps that's why I bought it. I'm in a period where I don't find clothes that important and so don't want to spend too much. In a second-hand shop you have to be content with what's on offer. Yesterday I left my son with his father with a bottle from which he's refused to drink a drop. My Oedipal son did, though, scream loudly from the moment I left the house. I feel very proud, think: good for you, son, at least you know what loyalty is. Yet today I shall again leave him with his father with a bottle. I've started to cut the umbilical cord. He'll really blame me for this. When I came back from shopping yesterday, all kinds of people were sitting on the carpet in the living room, the window was open, that was unusual, normally only the window on the garden side is opened, but then it's an unusually warm summer. Your father was holding you in his arms and trying to shush you. I immediately took you from him.

But now it's Sunday morning. I go cycling with my brother, tell him how well I'm doing, how strong and happy I feel. When I get home my husband is standing with the baby in his arms. He's standing by the fence and showing him to the neighbours: what a bonny baby! What a little fatty! My boy, you don't need that bottle, you can drink from your Mummy. Mummy's got delicious milk for you. Look, says his father, and he shows me a plastic bag of what look like peppercorns. The sweet peas have finished flowering and he has collected the seed to sow next spring. I go inside to feed the baby.

I didn't know it was possible, a baby dying just like that. I didn't know and no one had told me. 'Babies don't die just like that,' I often said to my pathologically anxious mother. 'Certainly not a healthy baby.' She didn't contradict me, just looked askance. Her mother had lost two boys. I knew that, of course, but that was in the past, long ago. And there was something wrong with those babies. One baby was stillborn after a ten-month pregnancy (is that possible? I think now. Is it possible they left the baby in her womb so long?) and the second baby was infected with flu by a nurse who wasn't herself sick but came from a family where there was flu. Medical negligence. A thing of the past.

And that isn't true either. Friends of friends had experienced it. Their first child, a boy. He was five months. People talked a lot about it. The words 'cot death' were uttered. But they were different people.

How I loved my body in the summer of 1983. It could make love and get pregnant and give birth and suckle. I had been heavily pregnant, had sat naked in front of the mirror, hadn't been able to believe that that was all me, and it wasn't all me, it was you and me. After your death someone said: actually it's a kind of infertility. I suspect that was after your brother had died. And I, who had always been so proud of my fertility. Of my breasts, my hips, my womb. I thought: I'm giving birth to death. I wanted to destroy my body. Another girlfriend said: we were little gods. Little? I rode in a sun chariot, I was a universal mother, a fertility goddess. For me giving birth was the ultimate orgasm, pain and pleasure, life and death – well, death followed a few weeks later. I thought there must have been a great sadist at work. Someone who said: let's have a good laugh, that one there with the black hair, we're going to make her very happy, we're going to lift her up really high and then make sure she comes down to earth with a bang. Hubris. I have a mother who says she's a Christian, but actually believes in the Greek gods. Their indifference. Cruelty. Fickleness. You there, with the black hair. You.

I called you my talisman.

102

Did it matter that it was a boy? I think so. Lying on the bed with him – da da da, lovely, lovely Benjyboo – tickling his tummy – come on, laugh at your mummy, da da da, big boy laugh at his mummy – and then with a supreme effort: kga, kga, kga, deep in his throat. Mummy was hopelessly in love. Stupid people who are happy. Blind.

Nosy, nosy, nosy. There's a nipple on Ben's nose and a nipple on Mummy's nose.

When we knew I was pregnant, my husband planted a tree that never grew. It was planted in autumn, lost its leaves and never got any new ones. After Ben died, we sawed it off at the roots. We couldn't bear that dead tree. Whenever I passed the stump, I'd think: this is Ben's grave.

We adopted two stray kittens. One evening we heard squeaking at the front door. It was raining and it was cold. Two fluffy creatures were shivering on the threshold. They would be jealous when the baby was there, but we made a warm nest for them in the kitchen. First one was run over, then the other. Each time it was my husband who found the body on his way home from evening school. Stupid kittens, we said, but the house was on that kind of road. Not a street but a road that traffic roars along to or from the motorway junction. And the tree? Of course it didn't grow. It stood unprotected in the draughty gap between two houses. Whoever plants a tree in a spot like that?

4 July 1983

A boiling hot day. I'm heavy and round, tired of waiting. Go cycling, a friend had said, that will bring on labour. A doctor, he should know. So I put Kathy in the seat on the back of my bike, and go cycling. The area isn't flat, I pedal hard, hoping to bring on labour, and before I know it, I'm in Bertem in the cemetery behind the beautiful Romanesque church. How did I get there? I don't know. My bike is propped against the church and I walk among the graves with Kathy. It's a wonderful, sunny day. I look at the blue sky and the green crowns of the trees, and now I also look down. I'm among the children's graves, the graves of the little angels, two, seven, eight months, six weeks, called to be with the Lord, small, white graves. It's as if a cold hand is laid on my heart. I take Kathy in my arms and flee.

Sunday afternoon, 28 August 1983, about ten to three

Today is your father's and my fifth wedding anniversary and yesterday I was twenty-eight. We're sitting at the bottom of the garden at my brother's having a barbecue. My brother starts telling us about friends of his who've lost a child. Cot death. Or perhaps the baby was found in time and its breathing is now being monitored by a machine, I don't remember. In any case, the words death and cot death are uttered. My sister-in-law says to my brother: why are you talking about that? You'll worry them. No, no, I say, you're not worrying me, but I put my hand on my husband's forearm and ask: just go and have a look. And then the sentence: *Kristien, get an ambulance, quick*. My husband's British, everything takes place in English. And me getting up and running to the house and seeing my reflection in the window, seeing myself running and knowing: *it is finished*.

I'm grateful for the postponement I was granted. My husband found him. He never said anything to me about the shock. I'm telling the story purely from my point of view.

You had bawled a lot that afternoon and if we hadn't been visiting, I would definitely have taken you out of your cot. But you'd been fed and had your nappy changed, and you'd burped, so what else could I do.

You had crawled right to the front of your cot. Your sheet was wet with your tears and vomit.

Of course I felt guilty. Of course I was convinced I'd killed you. I'd left you alone in your cot. I was sitting in the sun having a great time at the barbecue, laughing, talking, while you were dying all alone.

Later lying on the bed in the room where his empty cot is. Whispering his name. Ben, Ben, where are you, your Mummy's here.

A cold little body. Purplish brown blotches on his eyelids and neck. It happens very fast.

The sweater he was wearing when he died was the one my mother had kept back until after his birth. She had knitted it but also wanted to embroider his name on it. Kathy delivered it at the hospital. 'For little brother Ben', she said. She could scarcely speak at that time, and those few words took a huge effort. She was wearing a white dress. There were beads of sweat on her forehead.

We're shocked when we go to look at him at the undertaker's. Now he is dead he looks disconcertingly like his sister. As if she is lying there.

Sunday, 28 August, 5 pm.
        We come back home without a baby. There is a cake outside the door. Friends have put it there and on the box they have written: much happiness on your fifth wedding anniversary! We take the cake inside. We put the box on the table. We think: we're never going to eat cake again. We're never going to eat anything again. But then we get hungry. And visitors arrive. We cut the cake.

Each of us had our story.
        My mother spoke of hubris, fate, and the gods and said that we were no more than flies that they toyed with.
        My father saw the will of a wise God, whose plans we could not and must not fathom.
        My husband talked of guilt and retribution, the sacrifice that had to be made to restore our karma.
        Kathy said Ben was in a plane and the plane had flown into a long tunnel.

I spoke about the tree that had not grown, about kittens that had died, about children's graves.

Each of us had our story, but there was no story.

Kathy says: I've done that. I dieded once too.

There is war in the heart of the woman who walks in the night with the child at her breast. No longer her child, but the child of the night.

There is war in the heart of the woman whose child is in the plastic bucket, blue, wrinkled, stinking slime. Soon she'll be sewn up. Soon the bucket will be taken away.

I am the woman in the black clothes.

I am the woman with the torn-out hair.

I am the woman with the gouged breasts.

I am the woman in black.

February 1984

Pretending for a moment that Ben is still alive and I'm not the stricken mother.

The attendants wear a grey uniform and a matching cap. Because it's so warm most of them have taken off their jackets and rolled up their sleeves. Some have beads of sweat on their foreheads. Whenever they address us, they first click their heels and salute us with a powerful sweep of the arm and touch the peak of their caps. Not one of them speaks Dutch. They keep intoning the same sentences. 'La cérémonie va commencer. La cérémonie est terminée.' But there isn't much ceremony. We're doing this without a mass. We don't want God or a priest, no soothing words. We enter a small building, stand in a semi-circle around the coffin, which has flowers on it. We watch intently, curiously, since none of us has ever been through this. Two minutes of music, not Handel as promised but something else, what difference does it make. The two small doors slide slowly open, and the little coffin starts to move. Completely under its own power, it seems, it glides without a sound into a dark hole. Disneyland, I think. Things like this happen in Disneyland too. I wave goodbye. The doors close, the next family is waiting. 'La cérémonie est terminée.' We have to leave. There's a bar, La Silence, where we can have a drink while you are incinerated. Black smoke issues from the chimney. We drink coffee, talk about the weather and about what a hoot the attendants are. With an adult it takes an hour and a half, but a baby is quicker. But after three cups of coffee, it's still not over. We go outside to wait in the sun. Look at the graves in the cemetery.

It's very hot, tears mingle with sweat. Because we have paid a thousand francs extra we're allowed to watch them scattering the ashes on the grass. 'La cérémonie va commencer.' We are allowed to go in front as we are the parents. The attendant is carrying a tin. It's a little like a collection box for missionary work.

He salutes again, steps resolutely onto the lawn, heads for a small monument – 'A nos morts bien aimés'. He salutes, stands still. We hold our breath. A flap in the bottom of the tin opens and the ash slides out. The man does not move his arm. Later he will apologise to my brother for the fact that there is so little ash. One of the most important topics of conversation at the funeral lunch will be: how can they know that they were Ben's ashes and what difference does it make? The tin is empty and the flap is closed. The man salutes. 'La cérémonie est terminée.' But it hasn't finished yet. 'Voulez-vous la plaque d'identification?' he asks, rummaging in the tin. We all think the same; he'll bring Ben out now, a second birth, a rabbit out of the conjuror's hat. But we are given a white stone with a number on it. The proof that it was you they cremated and scattered. Later everyone who missed the cremation will say: I wish I'd been there.

We resolve to scatter the seeds of the sweet peas on the lawn one night next spring. We won't do it.

We had the following cremated with you: your bedspread that my mother had knitted for you, your bear, your nicest baby-gro.

You were already laughing.

You laughed selectively.
You laughed only at me.

La cérémonie va commencer. La cérémonie est terminée.

The day after Ben was cremated, we took his sister to the zoo. Life had to go on. A coach full of Downs syndrome children were dropped off. They laughed a lot.

While they were trying to resuscitate Ben: the fear that he would pull through and would have to go through life with severe brain damage. Like a cabbage.

Now I see you as a wise old baby. Wrinkled little chap, an oversized head on a body that never fully grew. You're a little astronaut spinning through space.

Do you know the one about the people who lost a child. They lost another one too.

Rob was a time bomb. No one dared to have him to stay for fear he would suddenly die like his brother. I was firmly convinced he would live, but first we had to get through a difficult year, the high-risk year for cot deaths. He ticked like a time bomb, too, or rather the machine that monitored his breathing ticked. It was a small device attached to his little body with a blue wire and electrodes. The device ticked with each breath and if he didn't breathe for ten seconds, an alarm went off. The tick was irregular, since like everyone his breathing was irregular. Consciously or unconsciously I was always waiting for the tick, I didn't sleep, I dozed. After his death I thought: now I can sleep at last. The next day I went to the cinema.

In my notebook it says: 'That I didn't say goodbye to you. That you lay there, cold, pale, grey on the hospital bed that was too big for you, and that I didn't have the courage to say goodbye to you. To take you in my arms, to warm you against my heart, to hug you.'

I didn't even have the courage left to cry. I had stopped that because it was so terribly painful. Tear glands get exhausted at a certain moment. If you have to cry anyway, you get a splitting headache. But I became afraid that Rob would not be at peace because he had not been accompanied lovingly to the 'other side'. That he would be doomed to wander, to circle the earth like a stray space capsule. With his brother we had sat for a long time, alternately in my arms and in my husband's. We had wrapped him in a baby blanket so that he wouldn't catch cold.

After Ben's death I saw omens everywhere, was convinced that what had happened that Sunday afternoon had been preordained much earlier. We – my husband, Ben, my brother and I – had done what had to be done. We were actors in a necessary drama. I even had a déjà-vu experience: what happened that afternoon was a film I had once seen. After Rob the world was empty and meaningless. A joke. I wrote in my notebook: there is no way, no truth and no light. The key is lost and all the maps were burned long ago.

It was terrible having to go and tell my parents again: the baby's dead. I stayed in the car, let my husband tell them. I didn't want to see my mother crying. I couldn't bear having failed again.

I thought: I must be a really bad person to have been afflicted twice. I was amazed that people still wanted to talk to me. Hadn't it been proven how bad I was?

I thought: broken on the wheel and branded.

I thought: soon I'll be forced to pin a big letter B on my jacket. B for bad.

I had my hair cut even shorter.

Rob died on Wednesday 17 October 1984 at about seven in the evening. That afternoon I'd gone with my mother to buy clothes for Kathy for the party to celebrate Rob's birth on Saturday. After shopping Kathy stayed over at my mother's and the next day my father took her directly to school. There were prayers for Rob there, but Kathy still didn't know that her brother was dead. I heard from the girl next door that the village priest had come to give a talk to

109

the older schoolchildren. Rob would go to heaven, he assured them, even though he hadn't been baptised. I can't remember how Kathy reacted when we told her. All I remember was that her father forbade me to cry and wail. That would traumatise her, he said. On Saturday morning my mother-in-law came over from Wales as planned for the party.

A misunderstanding: there was nothing wrong with his breathing. But there was with his heart. Actually he went on craftily breathing after his heart had given out, so that when the alarm finally went off he could no longer be resuscitated.

His father did not want to come with me to the mortuary, so I went alone.

They had made him a cap of cotton wool and pulled it over his skull. They had to do that because they had taken some cells from his brain to examine them.

Rob was cremated like his brother, but it was bleak autumn weather. There were more people than for Ben. For most it was their first cremation. Two of them said that in our place they would eat the ash. They would go onto the lawn, fall to their knees, scoop up ash in their palms and lick it up.

I wore the same black blouse, but a different skirt, black with a white stripe. Apart from that I wore a black jacket, black stockings and black shoes. A woman who'd been in my class at school said I looked like a nun and how the hell did I manage that.

We laughed.

30 July 1987

It's my husband's birthday. He's thirty-one. I pick him up from work. I tell him I've rented a flat in town. He'll tell Kathy: mummy has lots of work to do. So she's staying in town.

This happened, and that happened.
>It happened that you died and I died,
>it happened that you died and I didn't die.
>Didn't die yet.

Lock-Up No. 14

Stefan Hertmans

'Where the wanderer ventures alone and pensive, no machines can penetrate.' Gian Pietro Lucini.

Jossif Romanenko was about to rent a lock-up garage. For years his red Panda had stood in the Botersteeg, rusting away in the early morning dew and acid rain. The clocks ticked and the stars set, and the half-light before dawn was full of voices returning home from the night before, hoarse with smoke, while the first starlings whistled in front gardens.

Jossif loved the very early morning and strong coffee. He sat in the big back room that opened onto a huge veranda, where tropical plants bloomed and parrots flew. There was a small blue enamelled bird on the mantelpiece. He sat there, waiting for the sound of his mother, who appeared just after six-thirty in her pink peignoir and took her place silently in the big armchair by the window, just under the banana tree. They sat together silently and blew on their hot coffee. In the street, a woman's voice shrieked, high and incomprehensible.

'Will you try and get hold of that key again this afternoon, Jossif?' his mother asked. Her coffee cup slid towards the edge of the saucer. Her grey hair stood out sharply against the tangle of leaves behind her. Jossif nodded, slightly irritated – but not with her. The irritation was directed at something in his thoughts, a whole heap of annoying thoughts jumbled together.

It must be about seven weeks now since Jossif had tried to get his hands on the key in question, the one for the lock-up garage he had been allocated. In the meantime, the previous tenant, whom he used to see quite often in the Botersteeg, had moved house. That was why Jossif was eligible for the lock-up that had become vacant.

112

Renting the lock-ups was a privilege accorded to those who had lived longest in the Botersteeg, and anyone wishing to claim one was put on a waiting list that changed less quickly than the hairs on your mother's head turned grey. When he heard that lock-up no. 14 was becoming available Jossif hurried off to the MORE, the Municipal Office for Real Estate as it was called, and stood in front of the huge grey gate at a quarter to eight, an hour and a half early that is. At about eight-thirty a motorbike and sidecar came screeching through the narrow street. Two men sat side by side laughing. The vehicle seemed to drag a blue thread of smoke behind it which, oddly enough, created an impression of stasis. Jossif was allowed in at nine o'clock. Half an hour later he was assured that he had a good chance of renting the lock-up, after all, he had lived in the area his whole life and his Panda had been parked outside the house for a good ten years. Every Saturday Jossif polished the bodywork with a soft cloth. He swept grains of sand and small stones out from under the pedals, wiped the glass over the speedometers clean and polished the old-fashioned chrome work till it shone. Afterwards he opened up the bonnet and checked the oil and the ignition. He let the engine turn over while he tuned it with his screwdriver and heard, ever lighter and more finely regulated, the rustling of wings and elytra and, far away in the depths of the engine block, something like hundreds of children's voices shrieking with laughter. Sometimes he was so enthralled by the sound that he became confused and careless and hurt a finger. The taste of the drop of blood that he sucked from his fingertip was mixed with the tang of oil – warm old dark oil from the deepest depths of his red Panda.

That day Jossif had strode home from the MORE and sat in the conservatory whistling like a starling. You could do all sorts of things with a lock-up like that! You could turn it into a real garage, with your spanners, pliers and screwdrivers hanging on a rack. You could get to grips with the maintenance in peace and quiet, store all kinds of useful clutter at the back, take the bike out of the narrow hallway at last and hang it neatly on a rack against the back wall. On rainy days he could sit and watch moss growing on the corrugated iron of the roof, and see who got into which car in which lock-up before driving off across the gravel. Yes, it was as if, on days when you were at a bit of a loose end, you could take off and live wherever you wanted for a while.

In the months that followed, Jossif's excitement subsided into a disappointing wait. More than six months passed before he got a letter confirming his right to the lock-up. The letter was friendly, but nonetheless officially worded. He was requested to collect the key from the previous tenant and, as of the following month, to pay the rent regularly at the local MORE office.

Jossif floated triumphantly just above the wooden floor under the date palm, the mango and the banana tree and suddenly it occurred to him that he had not got the key to lock-up no. 14. His short-lived euphoria disappeared immediately. Jossif had found out, meanwhile, that the previous tenant had vanished. Only his mother still lived in the big, dark house round the corner. But though he had rung the bell there repeatedly, the door remained shut. He had no alternative but to pay the rent for the as yet inaccessible lock-up and to try once more to get hold of the previous tenant's address. So Jossif went along to the MORE again, where he was received with a certain condescension. An official promised him, after hearing his convoluted story, that he would check whether there was still a duplicate of the key at the office.

At night Jossif dreamt of lock-up garages like gaping mouths. To his horror he swallowed his own red Panda and then flew above the city with what seemed like gauzy wings protruding from his ears, he saw the previous tenant sneaking furtively through a lane, darted down and bit him in the neck. The taste was so bitter, like used oil, that he woke frightened and out of breath.

The next day it rained. Jossif went and stood in front of the closed up-and-over door and sighed deeply. The wind crept through a narrow slit and rattled the door a bit. In the middle, the lock shone like a bullet. Around it the metal seemed to quiver slightly, and move. Jossif put his hand on it for a moment. The lock was lukewarm and he felt it shiver. Then he laid his hand on the metal, a zooming like thousands of insects quivered on the other side. He pressed his eye to the small slit at one end. He could picture clouds sailing in the sky, bits of fluff and petals blowing round, and a warm, damp wind slapped his face. Oh God, thought Jossif, if only that were my mother there. He thought of rivers and swing bridges, reeds waving in the wind. He went home quickly and fell asleep under the banana tree. The clocks ticked and the birds were silent. Only two blue butterflies still fluttered around. His mother dropped two stitches from her knitting and fell asleep too, her mouth open.

One evening just before twilight, Jossif bumped into the previous tenant. He was around the corner, ringing his mother's bell. He looked at Jossif, who immediately broached the subject of the key, with a sort of greenish contempt in his eyes. The man made as if to speak, but the old woman opened the heavy door and her son disappeared inside. The door closed flawlessly and lightly, with a click like a bubble of saliva in a moist young mouth, for which one waits behind the hawthorn hedge but which eludes kissing. Jossif pushed the bell with his hot fingertip and waited. At almost the same moment the door opened again noiselessly. Jossif saw a long, empty corridor, hushed and white as in a convent, far removed from the hustle and bustle of the street. He entered hesitantly and the door closed behind him with the same overwhelmingly intimate click. Ah – latches and hasps, knobs and handles, joints and lips of silence, hinges and grooves, flaps and spy-holes, keyholes and fingers in the wound. Jossif stood inside and felt suffocated. The man stood behind him, his hand still on the doorknob. Before Jossif could say anything the man took him by the arm and steered him lightly but firmly to a large room at the back of the house. Jossif blinked at the light. In the blinding white workshop countless contraptions zoomed and quivered, little machines and strange mechanisms, as touching as blind, floundering insects on their last flight before death sets in and they dry out and are blown away like feathers on the wind.

They streaked past each other flawlessly, so that nothing touched anything else: glass bees, mechanical moths, propellers and hovering rings, squeaking dragonflies, a zeppelin and flying shrimps, a sort of bicycle with wax wings and above it all, just under the transparent corrugated roof, was a mechanical condor, screeching and squawking like bagpipes. Jossif had to duck fast as a madrigal-singing priest just missed his head. In a distant corner on the other side he could see a life-size copy of the old mother, sitting fixedly, muttering continually, though what she said was lost amidst the flapping and zooming.

'The only thing that's missing,' said the man reflectively, with a finger on his chin, 'is an angel. But I really need some live organs for that, I can't manage it with electronics alone.' 'I just want my key.' Jossif's insides hiccupped and clicked as if they were made of aluminium. 'My mother will take care of that,' said the man sternly. He seemed insulted by Jossif's egocentric anxiety. A weirdly animated eagle owl started squeaking like a guinea pig. 'You just don't seem worth this initiation.' It sounded as if someone were tightening a belt round a groaning body.

'I've got a little experiment on the go in lock-up no. 14,' he went on, rather brusquely, 'ah, but the creature's too miserable to behold and it won't stay in the air for two minutes. As soon as it can it creeps back into the box where I keep my pliers and spanners, and sleeps for days amid the smell of grease and iron. On top of that, my dear friend, I am afraid the creature's lost the key somehow or other. Unfortunately, I noticed it just too late. I'd already let the door drop into the lock.'

Thirty seconds later Jossif was back on the street. Plumes of smoke formed bushes on the roofs, and in the streets the paving stones shone with spring and space. Near porches and doors Jossif could hear a whispering as in conches and shells. Something that comes from inside you, that flows in your blood and gets you high and hooked on the world before you really know what's what – a feeling you can't explain later, but by then it's too late.

Jossif strolled over to the large gravel-strewn plot and stood in front of the lock-up garage. He laid his hand on the metal again and felt how his body heat flowed straight back into the palm it came from, like an oyster that keeps its shell shut and seeks the seed, the place where it smarts and hurts as the pearl grows. The door quivered and shivered again, like a wing of light breakable metal. The lock and handle glowed so hot and bright, he noticed now, that he almost burnt his fingers.

He could see only darkness now through the slit and somewhere, lost in the depths, a bluish light that seemed to rise and fall like breath. As he pressed his ear to the slit, he heard the frantic wheezing of a weary mosquito, but louder, as if that spot of blue light moving in the air was enough to create non-existent words.

In sudden panic Jossif fled back home, sat under the date palm and shivered for the rest of the day, while his mother slept on the sofa, smiling and muttering incomprehensibly like that other image of a person, somewhere amongst the flying contraptions round the corner.

Jossif could not sleep. No sooner had he closed his eyes than sails and doors tipped open and closed with kissing and sucking noises, and abandoned him suspended in an abyss of wings and antennae. In the early morning, Jossif drank his coffee hotter than usual. Then he walked through the hallway, chose a hammer and chisel from his workroom, stuck them in a red bag and went out, slamming the door behind him. There was not a breath of wind. The air hung motionless between the houses, as if it were still asleep. The lock-ups, too, were as quiet as his mother, asleep at home. Jossif put the point of the chisel against the lock and sighed. He aimed the hammer and struck. But instead of the ear-splitting, unholy thud that he had expected to ring out in the early morning air, the lock gave only a fleshy plop. Blood suddenly spurted over the point of the chisel onto his hand and he pulled it away in alarm.

Behind the thin metal skin, a wrenching, groaning and sighing started, as if someone was trying in vain to free themselves from the other side. Jossif threw down his tools, tried to staunch the

117

flow of blood with his hand and whispered despairingly: 'Have I hurt you? What should I do? Can I help?' And then, almost suffocated by a surge of incomprehensibly sad and foolish emotion: 'Will you please let me in'. For a moment the wrenching, groaning and sighing fell silent. Then it started again.

Well, the Holy Fathers, with their stories about the Evil One and his Work, have given us enough warnings about the eye of the needle through which the camel must pass, or about entering any sinful paradise, the smallest gate of the city, or the most intimate part of a much loved body that we cherish and caress; beloved skin that transforms the lover into a grovelling idiot, fallen angels who plunged dizzily backwards into the dark chasm of time; examples of strange transubstantiations, bleeding bread and flesh full of leaven, blasphemy, the sudden lasciviousness of a God who tires of the forms of his own spirit and plays illicitly with life. But how could that pleading voice be staunched? How could the shivering of that flightless wing be stilled? And what must Jossif do with his red, rusting Panda in a world that bleeds if you beg for access? Would it not be better to remain banished forever, part of a race of wandering exiles who at least have no unintentional blood on their hands? Perhaps every diaspora once started like that, in desperate sympathy for something unknown, waiting eternally beside a closed door with a bleeding lock – something like birth that can never reach completion.

Jossif received no answers to his despairing questions – unless the wailing of the sirens in the harbour might be so construed – there was only that hiccupping, choking, wrenching near the lock. Jossif rushed home for ointment and dressings, and bandaged the bleeding door. The shivering did not stop. Through the slit he saw white light flying to and fro, a dazzling ball in a small, enclosed darkness that otherwise only smelt of motor oil and rusting metal, a plaintive panicky noise flashing and jerking to and fro. No matter how he begged and pleaded, there was no sign of understanding from the other side. Blood seeped through the newly applied bandage and there was a first jagged streak across the door. Jossif squeezed his eyes closed, shook his head hard and desperately. He felt that if he stayed another second he would start to cry - howl and never stop.

He grabbed the gauze, the ointment, the hammer and chisel and ran from the site. Meanwhile, time had gone on and the morning was alive with humdrum activity. He ran through a sea of office workers till he heard his front door bang shut behind him with a hollow thud. In the letterbox he found a large envelope with the letters MORE on it.

With a feeling of relief he tore open the envelope and clutched at the key. In his palm, lukewarm and shivering, lay a miniature but otherwise perfect copy of his other hand.

The City That Never Was

Hubert Lampo

There is much that is strange but little that is coherent in my account of the city that never was, my friend. So I'll begin with the story of the train, although this was all going on long before that, you understand, in my childhood. Yes, this adventure probably began in my childhood accompanied by the shriek of the locomotives which at night rumbled across the flat area behind our house on the edge of town, and apart from that in the nocturnal ships' sirens on the river, in the hum of the telegraph wires along the railway, in the smell of the rubbish dumps, which were sometimes set alight on autumn evenings with bunches of branches and in the whistling sound in the convolutions of the sea snail shell with 'Souvenir d'Ostende' on it, when you pressed it to your ear. There was also an old coffee tin, which as far as I can remember was always on the mantelpiece, with coloured scenes of children in the snow and little figures got up in wigs like aristocrats and involved in gallant exchanges, on skates or in horse-sleighs. It is all connected and much more, but I'll begin with the adventure on the train. It really is best for me to start with that.

So I was on the train. I say *so*, but for you, unknown friend, that is not axiomatic, you realise that of course. I was on the train because I went to Brussels and back by train every day, where I worked at the ministry – oh, a very modest position. I'm a schoolteacher, you should know. Ten years before I had graduated from training college as an excellent student – however strange that may seem to you – a serious sacrifice that my parents, working people, had made. But I must have been a feeble schoolmaster, since on the very first day I was hooted at and pelted with paper chewed into wads by thirty unwashed snotty-nosed kids. What had this got to do with all those wonderful, idealistic stories that had been held up to me at training college, almost like a fairy tale? I fled the class head over heels, never to return... The inspector, a good man, took pity on me. He arranged for me to be found a place at the ministry. You can tell from my glasses that I'm short-sighted. But intellectually I was short-sighted too, which made the world appear to me in frightening shapes and with constantly threatening perspectives... Forgive me; I'm digressing. I sometimes find it difficult to hold on to the thread of the story.

I was sitting on the train, then and was probably reading the paper. Or no, reading is not the right word. I generally held the paper open in front of me. Otherwise I didn't know what to do with myself. Sometimes it was enough for a fellow passenger to look at me for no reason, for me to feel completely annihilated. Apart from that, I was still a shy boy, who had never dared to look into a woman's eyes. Now I think about it more deeply, that paper must have been meant as a protection from women's looks. Forgive my digression. I simply wanted to make it clear to you that from behind the newspaper I probably hadn't noticed that a woman had sat down diagonally opposite me. In the novels that I eagerly devoured at training college, my ears burning, it would have been a young, attractive woman, whose helpless look when we left the train at the terminus would prompt me to carry her case. But this woman was neither young, nor attractive. The best thing would be to call her a matron. At any rate I said to myself at the time that she was a matron. I remember very well using that unpleasant word: a matron. Nevertheless, my gaucheness in life had always prevented me from lacking respect for my elders. Had she not found a seat, I would probably have offered her mine. Although even that would have demanded an enormous effort of will. Every necessity for contact with my fellow human beings paralyses me, makes me nervous and clumsy, and makes the blood rise straight to my head. Consequently I've often allowed myself to be messed around with like an old rag... I should, though, add that this woman did not intimidate me. On the one hand I seemed simply not to exist for her, on the other her appearance was so extremely vulgar that it made me forget my embarrassment for a second. Although she was

121

probably about sixty-five she had platinum-blonde hair, which made her complexion, despite the thick layer of rice powder, seem even paler and threw into relief the rings round her eyes, whose natural blue harmonised with the artificial blue with which she had painted her eyelids, in order to give her eyes God knows what sort of charm, which she intended to enhance further with her ridiculously false, upwardly curled eyelashes, which were caked with mascara as far as the red, obviously inflamed rims of her eyes. You see that I remember everything precisely. It costs me not the slightest effort to see her clearly standing in front of me. She was wearing a pink suit, for which she was forty years too old, and as was the fashion at the time, a very short skirt. She sat with her legs crossed and through her fine stockings I could see the knobbly varicose veins, which continued up her pale waxy thighs, a strip of which I could see beneath the skirt, which was far too short for someone of her corpulence. Never in my life have I seen such a pathetic and at the same time ghastly assemblage of human, or rather human mental decay. The fact that I kept staring at her was due entirely to a feeling of deep revulsion, to the point of nausea, which rose in me, thought not entirely without an embarrassing, almost fascinating compassion. You should know that since my earliest youth I have had a strange and mostly completely unmotivated compassion for some of my fellow-creatures, a compassion that sometimes moved me to tears, but for which I did not know the reason, as if it was in my subconscious that the pathos of this world evoked a poignant echo.

All this did not take very long. Almost immediately I immersed myself again in my newspaper, though nothing in it grabbed my attention. It was a long time ago. Now I hear myself retelling it, I feel some remorse. I was young and foolish. Looking back it all sounds terribly hard-hearted. I didn't occur to me for a moment that the elderly woman, despite everything, remained a woman. She was still doing everything possible and maybe the impossible in order to remain attractive. You could tell from the efforts she made. Perhaps her husband was dead and she was hoping to find at least a lover, why not? Stupidly I imagined that an ageing woman is without feelings, yes, I really thought that, physically without feelings, you know, that she had no more need of a man to satisfy her. In my day such subjects were never discussed at school. My parents simply never thought of them. The fact that there might be something more between them as healthy middle-aged people than sharing the same bed from habit, was quite beyond my powers of imagination...

When I again involuntarily peered over the paper, I was ashamed of my own stupidity. Why had the woman made such a deep impression on me, inspiring in me a revulsion bordering on the physical? On closer inspection she turned out after all to be nothing but an elderly woman, making fruitless efforts to look like forty or fifty, like scores one passes every day, without staring at them in annoyance. Afterwards I had to admit that the varicose veins, like the blue rings under her eyes, were a figment of my imagination. I immersed myself once more in the broken arms and legs, the lost handbags and the shameful treatment of the police, which still attracted coverage in those days, when the certainty shot through my mind like an electric charge. I can't have been wrong, the image of the varicose veins and the bags under the eyes had been simply too vivid. Wasn't it after all precisely that, which had filled me with revulsion at first sight? It annoyed me, when I felt myself get worked up about it – the feeling I had back then in front of the class, as the wads of chewed paper shot past my head and spattered messily on the board. Wit feigned nonchalance I laid the newspaper on my knees. At this moment it was as if my nerves were inadequate for me to follow my original excitement. The woman in the corner by the window had *neither* varicose veins on her thighs, *nor* bags under her eyes and couldn't have been more than forty. Through her powder and rouge shone a healthy, wrinkle-free skin, while there was no question of undue corpulence. In fact, the best description would have been the blonde plumpness of a mature woman, who still possessed all the attractiveness of youth. Under her opened jacket she wore a blouse of white silk, through which the embroidered hem of her petticoat was dimly visible, with above it as low as possible the beginning of her breasts. I sat staring at her as if transfixed. She seemed to be aware of

123

this. Obviously she enjoyed the attention, since she turned her gaze on me. Rather ambiguously, I thought at first – with boundless purity, I judged afterwards. Suddenly I was afraid she wanted to strike up a conversation with me and with my face burning I again slid the paper in front of my eyes. I breathed more easily once I had done this, since it seemed to me that her gaze was threatening inexorably to clamp onto mine, and thus to plunge me into a confusion of which I dare not foresee the limits. Then I realised that there was no question of confusion. I felt completely calm, despite the fact that apart from us the compartment was completely empty. I felt almost happy – I use the word *happy* very advisedly – with the awareness of her attractive proximity. The inexplicable feeling of happiness, which had never before suffused me, by now went hand in hand with the vague awareness that something totally out of the ordinary was happening. What's more, now I was able to think a little more calmly it became completely clear to me that I had not been wrong the first time, any more than I was wrong now. The matron of a moment ago really had existed, just as the young, desirable woman of now was sitting in front of me in the flesh. Despite the calm that had been so unexpectedly awakened in me, I did not dare look up at once, but nevertheless folded the paper into eight, while my eyes slid furtively along her crossed legs. They were slim and strong as those of a thirty-year-old, with aristocratic ankles, in close-fitting gossamer-thin nylons. Then I looked up, as if wanting to surprise her unexpectedly in the process of that incomprehensible metamorphosis. But it was as if I was drugged; that is why I was aware of nothing for the next few seconds, except for the fact that she adjusted her clothes since we had almost reached our destination, although the misted-up windows made it impossible for me to do anything but surmise. A kind of bluish, naturally imaginary mist had drifted across my eyes, which initially blurred all details. But when the fog lifted a moment later, I observed that the stranger was not forty, but could be no more than thirty at the most, in the full flush of her now unmistakably slim, full womanhood.

The train had meanwhile entered the station. Only now did

it become clear to me that the clanking of the wheels had stopped a long while ago; even the screech of the brakes when we arrived had escaped me. The windows wet with trickling teardrops blocked the view outside. Heavy clouds must have closed in, as the light was now an even grey, almost blue. Everything might have provoked my astonishment, indeed even helpless fear. However, all that filled me with astonishment as she got up with a look that seemed to command me to follow her unconditionally, was the pristine calm in myself, which seemed to me completely strange and yet familiar as if despite my years of faint-heartedness I had always had a premonition that one day the supernatural moment was bound to dawn when I would at last feel like a man. 'Come with me,' said the stranger. She led the way in silence and I followed the scent of her dizzying perfume, which wafted towards me as if from distant times. I don't know myself what I am to attribute that impression to, yet it was a ravishing perception.

When I stepped onto the platform I had the feeling that time had stood still or, more exactly, that there was no time, that it was not it, but we who were passing. The woman laid her cool hand on my forearm, and as if she wanted to force me to look around. Suddenly I noticed that we were the only living souls on the platform. Meanwhile I automatically raised my wristwatch to my ear. It had stopped. The completely unknown world around us penetrated only slowly – or was it very quickly in this timeless space – to my senses, to my consciousness.

It was a huge station with endless platforms, between which the rails lay rusting as if no train, apart from ours, had arrived for years and as if the slightest touch would be enough to make them crumble into reddish dust. The sleepers were coated in moss and in some places covered in small, poisonous purple toadstools.

Slowly we made our way towards the baroque-style buildings fashionable last century. Here too everything was completely deserted and horrific vines climbed up the iron pillars, telegraph stations, water pumps, telegraph poles, information boards and railings. Yet I can't speak of neglect, since the word neglect conjures up an image

125

of an absent human hand. There was nothing human about these weathered complexes, some parts of which seemed to have collapsed and reminded me very strongly of the basalt fortresses of a legendary lost world. The whole scene was commanded by a massive tower, the top of which had disappeared. Immediately I saw that the sky was clear, without a single cloud, pure purple, like glass above frozen time. The sun was at its absolute zenith, huge, and giving scarcely any light and I thought I could observe it in three dimensions, hence spherically. This strange light seemed to me to be due to the glowing sky, rather than to the burnt-out, blue sun, on which I could make out the spots.

Although apart from the two of us there was not a living soul to be seen anywhere, I did not feel lonely. At most I could speak of a vague melancholy. It was precisely this melancholy that so fascinated me for a while. Never before had I felt myself so supremely capable of focused analytical thought and I reflected that only familiar things can inspire melancholy, a melancholy that issues from unspoken nostalgia. I had waited all my life for this moment, not as the moment when all the drawbridges to the secrets of our souls and hence to the hieroglyphics of our strangest dreams are lowered, but on the contrary as the return to a country that seemed very familiar and the cabbalistic signs which I had sometimes intercepted when I was young in the light of the gas lamps of my childhood, the landscape of advertising posters on rain soaked fences, the inky smell of a fresh newspaper, the frost flowers on wintry panes, the restless howling of dogs at the moon as I lay in bed waiting for sleep, or the singing of girls, invisible in the evening, playing on the waste ground behind our house. Then I noticed the silence too. I had never known what silence was, I thought to myself. Sometimes I believed I had experienced it when I walked at dusk in my father's garden among the climbing roses, the raspberry bushes, the hydrangeas and the geraniums, smoking my pipe, far from the outside world with its buffets, which often blocked my path like barbed wire. Although not a sound penetrated to me from the falling dusk, I suddenly realised that it had not been complete silence. At every moment, even the choicest, life gnaws away at our souls and the awkward cogs of our rusty thoughts grind through the spirals of time. I had never known that total silence, which expressed itself not so much through a complete absence of sound, as through a two or at most three-tone Aeolian harp sound, which seemed to waft through everything – including myself like a constant wind moving to and fro, coming from everywhere or nowhere and which reminded me of music as yet uncomposed...

We arrived in the tumbledown station building where stalactites hung from the tall ceilings, disintegrating posters covered the walls, alternating with large patches of mould, and blue signs announced the platform numbers of trains that would never leave. I walked around alone smiling. I remembered the nights in the past when as a child in bed I listened to the familiar roar of a train under the nearby viaduct. The railway line that divided the suburban landscape into two equally bleak halves was not an important one and I couldn't possibly imagine what the destination of such night trains was. Gradually my imagination took control of this perception on the border of waking and sleeping and I imagined the locomotive, by the fierce glow of the furnace, charging unmanned through the night, followed by a long string of carriages, towards morning, to disappear at daybreak in unknown distances and to reappear the following night like a comet in the sky of my fearful childish imagination.

As we left the deserted station my companion took me by the hand and for a moment I had the impression that a great sorrow had been waiting all this time to descend on me. I did not dare look at her, ashamed of the inexplicable tears that began to obscure my vision. I closed my eyes and allowed myself to be led by her until I was once again to some extent in control of myself.

We found ourselves in a strange city – if that is the right word. The fact is that all the words I use to tell my story are only vague shadows of what I should like to evoke in tangible form. For example, I was talking about a station. Is every building where railway lines come to an end between long platforms and blue signs

127

announce distant destinations, necessarily a station? And what was the meaning of the dead sun in the firmament of time that had congealed into immaterial crystal?

We walked, then, through a strange city. Did this city actually exist? But no – walk is not the right word. We strode through it, making only slow progress. When I looked at my companion, I was struck by the dignity and purposefulness of each of her gestures, while I was almost embarrassingly aware of every muscle movement that the almost ritual striding demanded of me. Never before had I been so intensely aware that I was alive, never had I felt so mentally lucid, so free of fear, suspicion and humiliating doubt.

But I wanted to talk to you about the strange city, undulating over the slopes of the surrounding hills in the dusky light, of which I cannot possibly say whether it was now purple or green. First I thought of Pompeii, although I had never travelled further than the caves of Han. I don't mean the real Pompeii, or the city as we know it from photos and postcards, but the way I imagined it as a boy when I first heard people talking about it. I can't remember exactly where I heard tell of it – perhaps at school – but in my childish thoughts it was a dead, non-existent city, built in the elaborate style of a hundred years ago, which had been artificially awakened from its sleep.

So we wandered through a kind of nineteenth-century Pompeii, where grand house-fronts rose on both sides of wide streets, mostly adorned with protruding loggias and balconies supported by earthen or even glazed pottery mermaids, fauns or bacchantes with vines and grapes in their hair, surrounded by climbing plants, sometimes carrying bell-shaped flowers that glowed in the indefinable light.

As we advanced some squares, crossroads and parks, all equally deserted, without the slightest trace of human presence in the present or past, awakened a shapeless memory in me and I felt a vague familiarity rippling through my whole being. Despite my unusual mental lucidity I could find no explanation for this fleeting feeling and it remained the kind of slightly irritating sensation of spying a familiar face without being able to put a name to it.

Meanwhile, I had absolutely no anxious thoughts. Still, I felt an inexplicable aversion when I realised that the light behind the countless windows was nothing other than the same purple light, that there were usually no interiors behind the façades and that we were therefore wandering through a gigantic, pointless theatrical set. At the same time I had the sudden urge to laugh out loud at the deceptive presence of the tram rails, at the five-branched lamp posts, urinals, fire alarms and imposing letter boxes in French Empire style. I observed my silent companion, who was walking beside me like a sleepwalker and whose gaze now reminded me of the expressionless eyes of the Caryatids, with which many buildings in this deathly metropolis had been lavishly decorated. Even the presence of the stranger proved incapable of troubling my resignation at the incomprehensible nature of this adventure. Under normal circumstances the proximity of a woman tended to throw me completely. Don't misunderstand me. What up to now had deterred me and at the same time attracted me to her, had unfortunately never proved sufficient to draw me out of my shell or prompt foolish behaviour. I mean that I had always behaved in a feeble and cowardly way, whenever a woman happened to address me. I would have given ten years of my life for a woman's glance, I sometimes thought, a single woman's look, in which I read no contempt, even if it turned out to be replaced by nothing but pity. There was no longer a question of any of this now. I felt calm. None of us knows, I think, what complete calm is. Even in our happiest moments secret fears and desires, suspicion and hate, passions and prejudices lurk within us, like lichen and mould. But *once* in my life I did feel calm and hence happy. It was while I wandered the godforsaken streets of my own unconscious side by side with this ghostly woman.

This whole story sounds rather obscure. I know it wasn't a dream. At the same time I am aware that my adventure conflicts with physical possibility, and does not accord with the imponderables of matter that rule our world. I am not looking for an explanation. I know I will never find one. I spent many sleepless nights, experienced many restless hours before I found an answer to the question what actually happened to me. I am anticipating my story, but that doesn't matter. Somewhere, my friend, there must exist another landscape, not *outside* us, as in the books of Plato, who is called the divine, but deep *within* us. We are almost never allowed to enter this landscape, but it was *once* given to me to experience this miracle.

Still without exchanging a word we walked up steeply rising streets. Between the uneven cobbles thistles, foxgloves, nettles and horsetail ran riot. Finally we reached a hilltop from where I could look out over the city. I saw an uninterrupted basalt landscape, but there were nevertheless occasional huge greenish patches where all kinds of plants had overgrown the buildings and crumbling walls. We followed a wall leaning obliquely backwards and so reached a house. The façade showed fewer signs of decay than the rest. Nevertheless it was built in the same style, richly adorned with carved wreaths of flowers, baroque shell-motifs, complex wrought-iron railings in front of the windows, in turn surrounded by columns with Corinthian capitals. Above this the roof was supported by Caryatids and crowned by a balustrade of bulbous columns.

My companion slowed down. I wondered what awaited me, ready to accept anything unconditionally, even the world of death. From her handbag she produced a key. I wondered whether in this case too the impressive house front would prove to be nothing but a theatrical set.

My suspicion did not prove true. We immediately entered an imposing entrance hall, built entirely of white marble. On the floors were Oriental rugs that creaked underfoot, as if crumbling to dust at each step. The wide spiral staircase was illuminated by high windows. Each time we passed on I moved aside, realising that here too the curtains would disintegrate at the slightest touch with an oppressive smell of ancient fabric.

On the first floor the woman opened the door of a room looking out onto the street, furnished in a style that a hundred years ago might have been a model of good taste. The gaslight hissed intimately – these actually were gas mantles - wrapping everything in a yellowish glow, warm in colour after the aquarium coloured atmosphere beneath the purple light. A tiny carillon in a musical box tinkled and, inexplicably, annoyed me, but fortunately immediately stopped. The room was halfway between a drawing room and a bedroom. That at least was my first impression, due mainly to the blue plush armchairs, the jewels everywhere and the wide low bed with the satin canopy.

But don't let me waste time on such descriptions. As regards the rest I shall be brief. Anyway words are inadequate to convey the impressions that were shortly to overwhelm me. Many details have nevertheless remained with me with unusual clarity. If I half-close my eyes, I can again see the line of her matt-white back, just outside the cone of lamplight, with below the shaved armpits the curve of her perfect breasts, as she raised her arms to let down her blonde hair, which fell silkily over her shoulders. The fragrance of that naked female body has also stayed vividly with me, like that of lilies on a rainy summer evening, when the heart is heavy with memories of things never experienced. I also see before me how she casually let her underwear fall around her tiny feet and how her breasts became sharper and more mobile when she bent forward to take off her nylons, as if wanting to drive me out of my mind.

What had to happen happened. I possessed her. So, after years, I finally became a man. And not only did I possess her, not only did I greedily quench the passion that had lain deep within me for years. But I also loved her, however incredible that may seem. As I looked at her almost incredulously, all my youthful dreams seemed to awake in me. I clearly remembered how strangely alarming the first desire for a woman can be, how nameless the longing is when one listens to the rain gusting on the roof tiles, to the singing of the water in the drainpipes, or how overpowering the poison was that once seemed to flow through me on sultry summer evenings when a thunderstorm threatens and one longs for the smell of the rain in the dust or on the hot cobbles. I loved her. Now I know that my life has not been in vain. I learned that woman is a miracle. But it was my privilege to experience a double miracle: the explosion of my own manhood and the discovery of the infinite land of female desire, of

131

which, naïve bungler that I was, I had scarcely any inkling. Suddenly a woman had come into my grey life and I seemed to exist for that woman as she lay under me, asking for more, her head against my shoulder, her lips half open. Outside the window lay the city that never was.

Then, for the first time during this adventure, I felt anxious – for a short while at least. I had turned down the lamp. The feel of her body beneath my hands, at first uncomprehending, now gradually knowing, had already seemed too much for me and I felt deeply uncertain about doing it. Suddenly I shuddered. I was still stroking her body, but suddenly the image of the old woman from the train loomed up like a gruesome memory, a nightmare.

I shuddered. My heart was in my mouth as I listened to her breath, rather laboured and rough-sounding, like that of an asthma sufferer. Hesitantly I felt her body again. My muscles froze out of pure fear. I became freezing cold and my skin seemed to be slowly contracting. Under my touch I felt this desirable body turning to a substance without inner consistency or resilience, while a sickly, unhealthy smell of old age and organic decomposition came towards me. With a supreme effort I got up, left the bed and tore open the closed curtains. The material turned to powder in my trembling grasp. A chilly dusk filled the room. With revulsion I recognised the matron from the train, with her jellyfish-like folds of flesh, revolting in her shameless, blue-veined nakedness. I could scarcely suppress a cry of bewilderment and disgust and wanted to flee, although I had no idea where to. I was sure, though, that this was not the same woman.

At this point my memory fails me. I do not know what else happened to me. Or rather: I cannot come to terms with what I know. And anyway, why should I immerse myself in speculative reflections? Why seek an explanation for what happened to me? I have a quiet life here, people are kind to me. I know once and for all that there is a world that extends beyond the cool exterior of things, further than the boundary of our senses, my unknown friend. You could ask me how things went after that, how I found the way back to what we unthinkingly call reality. I can only answer that I don't know and never will know. Where time stands still and we submerge ourselves in the sunken continent within ourselves, reason based on our paltry premises like one and one makes two is no longer any good to us. Go on, you can have a jolly good laugh! Sometimes I suddenly find it pleasant, no a relief rather, to talk like the books I read – reading is my favourite activity. And now I beg you, don't ask me any more questions. But let me say that I'm grateful for your patience…

Why are you shaking your head…? Do you really not think I dragged the story out too much…? Of course I should have thought about that, as I now understand. You're the new doctor, the new psychiatrist, as they say here… So I can go ahead and tell you everything – even what I keep secret from the others. For example from the man I thought you were, a friend from the past, from college, I imagined… I'll tell you my secret, doctor. So as not to be laughed at, I talked about the city that never was… People sometimes make up stories that are only half true. Not in order to lie, you know, no, just because of that other half you're never really sure about. Does it mean something, doctor, that I've started doubting the made-up half? I mean that I've probably imagined some things. Sometimes, sick with longing, I wanted to return to that city. Each time I thought to myself: it's impossible, isn't it? Stop that nonsense! Nonsense or not, I once spoke about it to some predecessor of yours. He called it a good sign… Secretly I laughed at him. I lied about it, although I don't think it was really lying. I simply knew something he didn't. The station I always took the train from, you must have heard of it, that strange South Station, which I sometimes thought wasn't real, was demolished over thirty years ago. So I can't go there anymore. I'm not sad about it. The fact that the station has been demolished, I mean, is of no importance. The main thing for me is that the city *does* exist. Is the Queen of the Night still waiting for me there…?

Who knows, sooner or later…?

1947-1992

Ammetis The Sleeper

Rachida Lamrabet

Hyles euphorbiae; the pupae of the spurge hawk-moth may remain in diapause for up to 5 years.

Going off the rails. That was my mother's greatest fear. She was terrified of people who with staggering impudence left the beaten track as they zigzagged on their way leaving a trail of havoc without giving two hoots about the mayhem they caused. It kept her awake at night, that fear.

Sometimes she thought she was very close to an explanation. She would get up and fetch her notebook, in which she jotted down a few ideas, scribbles on which she could later base explanatory theories. But the next morning she always had trouble reading what she had written, and much to her annoyance she couldn't remember much about her nocturnal ideas and brainwaves, so close to breakfast.

Yet she never forgot the task in hand, her greatest obsession: to reduce the risk of going off the rails to zero.

When she had finally worked out how she could minimise the risk, how she could protect herself from undesirable contingencies and turns of event, she decided after all to become pregnant.

It was one chance in two. One chance in two that it would be a girl, and then she would be running less than half the risk of something going wrong. Statistically speaking girls had more chance of reaching the age of twenty-one. Girls were well-behaved and fearful. She was convinced of this since she herself was a model of good behaviour. She was caring and thoughtful, and she loved her parents, whom she would never hurt. And if she were to have a boy, her responsibility would weigh on her like lead, but she was prepared to carry it just as an intensely pious woman was prepared to

134

bear her fate, bravely and silently. Apart from that, nothing at all was certain.

And as I budded like a young tree in her body, her plan ripened.

Perhaps going off the rails was not inevitable.

Every joint and every piece of bone that began to take shape hurt. It was as if I were becoming an old man.

At first I hadn't realised that other things were growing besides my head. Tiny legs and arms and a spine that linked the upper and lower sections of my body like a curved sea horse.

I felt it in every tender fibre, in each opening palm, in the minute organs, which at first let the blood circulate slowly and tentatively and then impelled it forward with conviction as if they had never done anything else.

Life was terribly painful, tugging at me like a spiteful bully who wanted to give me a taste of what lay in store for me.

And in the tenth week, on top of everything else, there were genitals. They had taken a long time to manifest themselves. In comparison with my heart or brain they were pretty primitive, and yet this organ was to be decisive for my identity. My mother had taken a deep breath when she heard that she was expecting a boy, and that fear would never leave her.

'Rayel, rayel!'

'Great, isn't it? First child and rightaway a real rayel!'

The gynaecologist slid the scanner across my mother's abdomen once more. I did not care at all for these shameless intrusions into my privacy. At first I didn't realise what this unseemly peeping tom was looking for.

'Fine, fine, fine,' he muttered contentedly as he moved the instrument to and fro. In an unguarded moment I opened my legs. The gynaecologist held the instrument still and crowed triumphantly: 'Khouf, Khouf, rayel, do you see? No doubt about it. Well, Mr and Mrs Aboulakal, that's the icing on the cake!' He spoke very colourful

Dutch, which made his enthusiasm sound a little like mockery.

It was odd. Genitals. It looked as if the fully-grown had built their world around genitalia. That their norms and values were shot through with a genital view of the world. And the thing just hung there characterless and ostensibly useless. The fact that I was a boy raised my parents in the gynaecologist's eyes to the level of super-parents, and almost entitled them to look down on parents of girls.

And it made my mother nervous: the risk of going off the rails again reared its head.

I thought it was improper behaviour and kicked out at the machine. Surely mothers look into their baby's eyes for the first time when it's born?

It wouldn't surprise me if immediately after my birth the gynaecologist grabbed me by the legs and hung me shamelessly upside down to display the characterless organ to all and sundry.

How could an organ that just seemed to hang there for no good reason be so important?

'I don't care for that Doctor Volkers with his pidgin Arabic,' I heard my father say when we had left the surgery. 'Don't you think he was going a bit over the top with that rayel stuff.'

My mother laughed it off and looked tenderly at the ultrasound printout. 'He's just perfect!' I was flattered.

It's nonsense of course, but when my sex became known, I had the feeling that the temperature of the amniotic fluid fell a little. After the gynaecological examination my mother took the copper-inlaid mahogany box permanently out of the cupboard and set it prominently in the middle of the kitchen table. There were already lots of receipts in it. It took me a few weeks to work out what she was up to.

My mother has the need for certainty, for the knowledge that everything will be as she wants it to be. There mustn't be too many unknown quantities.

She was quite anxious, my beautiful, young mother, pregnant for the first time.

Let me introduce her to you all. Twenty-five years old, intelligent and pretty. A mother whom as a toddler I should have liked to marry. Of whom I would be proud when she stood waiting for me at the school gates at the end of the day. Later she was to spark secret fantasies in my spotty adolescent friends.

But we haven't got that far yet, nowhere near.

My mother had decided that I would be successful and good. I wouldn't grow up to be like all the others, she would see to that.

No pampering, but straight talking and accountability.

She would keep track of everything. The nine months that I had lived in her body, her strength that I had sapped, the morning sickness, the pallor. The ugly stretch marks on her belly and breasts, and the sleepless nights. And my dad wasn't allowed to come near her. She thought he smelled of chicken. She kept an account of the money she had spent on me, down to the last cent. The doctor's bills, the countless receipts for vitamins, ointments, baby socks, romper suits, the buggy and the cot, the cuddly toys and pillows. The whole works. Not that she didn't enjoy choosing everything, checking carefully to see that everything matched. She had an eye for detail. My future bedroom could have come straight out of Ideal Home.

After all, I was her child, her first child. She wanted me more than anything in the world. She loved me already. But she was on her toes and would leave nothing to chance. And that was all about risk analysis. Because my mother was convinced that I ran an increased risk of going off the rails, of becoming terribly bad.

She knew of enough examples, and the most painful of those was her brother, my uncle. She wanted nothing more to do with him. She left the letters he wrote her from prison unopened. As if she were afraid of admitting anything from his world into her house. She had banished him from her life and so ensured that he could no longer be an example to anyone. And the accounts that she began to keep, were for use in the event that, despite all her efforts, I still went to the bad. She didn't doubt for a moment that she would be just as capable of rejecting her own son as her brother if I should stray from the strait and narrow. But before she allowed things to get to that point, she kept accounts. So that I would be able to see, later, that she had made a great financial and emotional effort on my account. That she had sacrificed a lot in order to have me. So that I would think twice before getting into bad company, dabbling in drugs, haranguing my teachers and leaving school far too early. Would think twice before breaking into cars. If I went off the rails she would take out a civil action against me, and her accounts would enable her to work out exactly how much loss I had inflicted on her, down to two decimal points. I would pay back everything she had invested in me to the last cent. And once her loss had been reimbursed, once her books were balanced, she would behave as if she had no son. That was her avowed intention.

My own mother! I mean you've got to give a guest a chance, haven't you?

Time out, guys. Hold on a moment. You don't expect me to go on in these circumstances, do you?

So in my twentieth week I took a difficult but necessary decision.

My mother began feeling nauseous again and was worried because she could no longer feel me.

'Come on, Zinedine, kick my hand. Do it for mummy.'

I refused to move a muscle. Not just yet, mother.

Yesterday, during her routine monthly check-up, the gynaecologist had reassured her that everything was going perfectly. I met all the indicators, fell nicely within the growth and weight curves. Statistically there was absolutely no cause for concern. Once she had dressed, I went calmly into sleep mode, and curled into a small motionless ball. With my thumb in my mouth I closed my eyes. On the way home I was rocked to sleep. The rhythm of my heart slowed down and everything was bathed in an off-white haze.

'Don't worry, darling, he's probably just tired from all that kicking over the last few days. Babies can take a day off too, you know. And you're moving around a lot, so it may be that you can't feel him when you're so much on the go yourself.'

My father tried to put her mind at rest for the first few days after that, but she knew something had changed. On the third day she was back at the gynaecologist's. She had rung him in a panic. And he had said she might as well come in. 'Better an examination too many,' were his words. She was put on the monitor. From the moment she heard my heart beating she breathed a sigh of relief. Doctor Volkers went on listening.

I know that what she would have like to do most would have been to spend the remaining twenty weeks hooked up to the machine, to be able to check my temperature every second, count the heart rate and follow my movements.

'Why isn't he moving?' she asked.

'He's asleep. Babies need lots of sleep, lots and lots of sleep.' The doctor answered as he made notes.

'His heartbeat is slow, though,' he said finally.

My mother shot upright.

'There's no need to worry,' he hastened to reassure her. 'For the moment everything else is normal, but we'd prefer to keep you here tonight for observation.'

I felt guilty because she tossed and turned in her bed that night, She couldn't sleep. But my mind was made up, she had gone too far with her receipts. Every bill, irrespective of the amount, had been carefully recorded, from the day after her first gynaecological examination. And when she knew my sex, she took the mahogany box out of the cupboard as if she were now in earnest. Every Sunday evening, when she couldn't spend anymore, she did the previous week's accounts in a large soft-blue 'scrapbook' with the cheerful title *My First Baby!* Under each receipt she stuck into the book, in the place where normally the first ultrasound picture would go, she wrote the date, the product purchased and added a short personal comment.

Alongside the Body Shop bill of 23 March she had written 'According to Freya this is THE wonder treatment for pregnancy

139

stretch marks. What they tell you is to start rubbing in early. I'm curious to know if it will work, but at any rate it smells nice.'

Under the bill next to it for the same day for baby socks: I couldn't resist them!!! So tiny! Unbelievable, so sweet!'

After the first two months she reached a total of 421 euros including doctor's fees. In pink marker pen she underlined her provisional final amount and commented. 'Amazing what a little zygote like this costs!'

By the end of the week the doctors had discovered that my vital functions were operating at a very low level. My metabolism had slowed down and after three weeks they were unanimous about the grim diagnosis. Stalled physiological development.

They had finally realised that I was no longer growing. Doctors from renowned university teaching hospitals were tearing their hair out because they could not find a similar case anywhere in medical history.

And my future grandmother raised her hands to heaven, because there was no shortage of myths and fantastic stories, far from it. Her daughter-in-law had an Ammetis in her womb – a sleeping foetus, and that was very serious. She knew women who went round all their lives with a foetus that refused to wake up, never wanted to be born. It had kept countless women childless and unhappy.

My grandmother herself knew a widow who gave birth to a child years after her husband's death. A theologian certified that it was an Ammetis. In that way the child acquired the same lineage as its brothers and sister, and the widow was above all suspicion.

My poor mother was pricked and weighed. She was hooked up to drips and catheters that pumped saline solutions and vitamins through her body via the swollen blue veins in her arms. And careful nurses with kind voices attached electrodes to her abdomen, where a few minutes before my father's warm hand had rested.

All to induce a reaction from me.

Foreign gynaecologists were called in and squabbled animatedly about the test results. Finally it was proposed that a daring experiment be conducted and an attempt made to stimulate me. The four-strong squad of doctors was unanimous: this was the final attempt to reverse the situation. There was no time to lose – I already had a four-week growth deficit.

One gynaecologist acted as spokesman. 'Mrs Aboulakal, you should know that this is a most exceptional situation. Diapause does not normally occur in humans. It is a phenomenon found mainly in certain insects, and only in response to particular unfavourable environmental factors. We are of the unanimous opinion that the organism, I mean of course your baby, can only be released from diapause if we use very specific, but not risk-free stimuli.'

My mother sat up in her bed, looked the four-headed white dragon straight in the eye, thanked it for its help and asked it to tell the nurses to disconnect her from the dripping machines and croaking catheters.

By the time my mother had got dressed, my father was in the room and carried her case out of the building with the white dragon in their wake, nervous but speechless. Deeply indignant that its most unusual patient could leave just like that.

My father, despite the circumstances, had tried to make it a pleasant homecoming. The flat had been nicely tidied up and to judge by mother's brief reaction he had even provided a nice bouquet of flowers for the kitchen table. The mahogany box had been banished from its central position.

She didn't touch the tea he had made for her.

He tried to take her in his arms, but with a gesture of her hand she kept him gently but firmly at a distance.

'I'm going to lie down for a bit.'

'You'll call me if you need anything?' was how he tried to convince her he was there for her.

Without taking off her clothes or shoes my mother crawled into bed. Later in the evening my father put his head round the door.

She didn't reply when he asked if she needed anything.

When he closed the door behind him, my mother turned onto her back. She held her belly with both hands. Her right palm grasped the crown of my head.

'Why don't you want to grow?'

I listened intently.

She softly stroked my head and I felt like nuzzling her hand with my head, like a kitten.

'Aren't you curious about what it's like out here? Don't you want to learn to walk, and play football and cycle?

Football, now that appealed to me. I knew that my father hoped that one day I might achieve what he had never been able to because of his damaged knee.

'The other day I saw a really nice bike. It was terribly hard not to buy it on the spot, but you wouldn't be able to ride it until you were about three. Daddy will love teaching you to ride. He's very good at it, you know. Last summer he helped one of your cousins get over her fear. She'd already fallen off a few times. Her father was very impatient and thought she was a wimp. And then your father got involved and before she knew it she could cycle with the best of them. He's very good with children.'

She was silent for a while.

'It's really devastated him.'

She said it so softly that I almost didn't hear. As if she were thinking it. Perhaps she didn't want me to hear. Perhaps she didn't want to make me feel guilty.

I tried to swallow my discomfort.

She held her breath for a moment and tightened her grip on her belly.

She had felt something.

It Will End In Tears

Ivo Michiels

Baby Blue And Candy Pink

In Memoriam Lucio Fontana

Was it a palm, a weeping willow and a plane-tree? Was it two palms? A palm and a weeping willow? Two weeping willows? A weeping willow and a plane-tree? A plane-tree and a palm? Two plane-trees? Were there a number of trees, a number of weeping willows, a number of plane-trees? I'm standing at the window, I can still see it clearly. I see myself standing at the window looking out across the lawn, green, undulating towards the green of the trees, of the weeping willows, the palms, the plane-trees perhaps. I can see Fontana clearly too: he is standing close behind me, scarcely three paces away, and behind him I see the studio, the dark establishing itself more firmly in the corners, the storage space up there that has already almost dissolved in the midday darkness that has suddenly fallen, and beyond the studio the gallery, the inner courtyard enclosed by high walls, and in a neat row along one wall – the wall on your right when you stand with your back to the studio – the egg canvases, great ovals of gold or green, a green that doesn't even exist except on this one unique two-dimensional egg, and black, candy pink, white, red too, and baby blue, a blue that doesn't even exist and in it, in the gold, the green, the black, the pink, the white, the red, the blue, in them the tiny craters, minute gateways you might say, quirkily round with crusted rims of baby blue and candy pink, in a row along the wall so that the camera can glide past and feel its way along the eggs, the chocolate box lids, the gateways with the crusts, and way beyond these craters – the largest of then no bigger than a fist and yet with the whole of Vesuvius in it, to name just one volcano – beyond it the

143

depths of the earth, arranged against the wall of the inner courtyard, and on the other side of the courtyard the caretaker's flat and just beyond the caretaker's flat the gate, then the street, and as I look out over the garden where at midday it is gradually turning to evening and night, I see clearly behind me the Corso Monforte, busy, oppressive, without a sound being audible. I see this clearly and sharply: Milan as it were wiped off the map, behind me and around me, and so I in the heart of the city that as it were no longer even exists, it is so unbelievably still, I, the lawn outside, the palms, the weeping willows, the plane-trees, the studio at my back, and Fontana, as was said. The woman too. She stands slightly to the left of him and a step or so closer to me. Her belly almost touches the small desk at which he writes his letters, laboriously and with abandon and in a language you can't read anywhere, a mishmash of something resembling French and Italian, with possibly a Spanish suffix added, a language of baby blue and candy pink and minute craters with crusted rims. *Cher ami Michils, je suit très très content d'avoir reçu votre lettre.* I don't look at the woman. If I turn my head just a fraction I'm bound to see her. I've never met her before, I'm sure of that. She came into the studio a moment ago the way so many people enter this space, the young and the very young and the no longer so young: laughing and with abandon already in their hips. He must have kissed her hand and introduced her to me, he must have, but I've forgotten her name. She is, I seem to remember, a countess. Or perhaps her name is Contessa, signora Contessa, it's possible. At this moment she bends slightly closer to me, as if he is pushing her towards me because I can now smell her perfume very strongly. I suspect him of pushing her in my direction with gentle pressure, placing his hand on her shoulder and without saying a word saying that she must move closer to me. I tremble slightly. And at once I see that I want to go, I know myself, my attitudes, my staring out across the lawn, the green beyond it that is becoming increasingly mixed with black. Soon, I hope, he will begin to talk, calmly and agreeably, like a man. But he says nothing. Until I hear only the cries resounding in the studio behind my back, raw gutturals that suddenly descend on me, accompanying the thudding sounds, the rhythm of the screams that keeps time with the rhythm of the thrusts, loud and piercing. No, I'm wrong. There *was* no cameraman there that day, there was no sound man, there was no director and the canvases were not arranged along the wall of the courtyard, not that day. That day not a leaf stirred, it was so calm it was almost as if the city had been wiped off the map. I've already mixed up too much, I see, confused too much. Confused what I know with what I see, knowing with knowing, hearing with hearing. That's how it goes. I must begin again. Was it a palm, a weeping willow, a plane-tree? Was it two palms? A palm and a weeping willow? Two weeping willows? A weeping willow and a plane-tree? A plane-tree and a palm? Two plane-trees? Was it a number of trees, a number of weeping willows, a number of plane-trees? I'm standing at the window, I can still see it clearly. I see myself standing at the window and looking out over the lawn, green, undulating towards the green of the trees, of the weeping willows, the palms, plane-trees perhaps. The rain pours down vertically and from very deep within the studio, from the storage space up there that has almost dissolved in the midday darkness that has suddenly fallen, the storm trundles over us. At regular intervals flashes of light flood the surroundings with intense brightness and I see the garden outside turn ear-splittingly white, the trees white, the studio behind my back a white space and in it white in white, myself standing at the window looking out, not moving a muscle, and close behind me Fontana, he is scarcely three steps away and slightly to his left stands the woman, she has now edged closer to me and her belly is pressing gently against the small desk at which he writes his letters, for a second or less that white triangle frozen in the white space and so as it were submerged in each other, the triangle submerges in the space, in the studio with the canvases arranged against the walls back and front, the eggs, the gateways, the minute craters in them, or the cuts, sharp gashes and the lips of the canvas curled, inward, outward, merged with the lips, this one instant drenched too intensely with light so that there is too much to be seen to truly see, that's how I see it. How at regular intervals we are obliterated in the light and return in the dark, for hours and hours on end. *Beaucoup de foi je mai souvent de vous y dé les beau jour que nous avons passé avec Jef y notre discussion sur l'art y l'amitié que vous m'avez donné, y la stime sure mon travaille, cette'éte un gran incouragement pour travaillé.* From Genoa to Ventimiglia the whole coast is a strip under bombardment. It's already quite a way past midnight and the three of us are still standing on the balcony, high on the hillside, so that we can follow for kilometres how the sea is constantly under fire. We've put on our sunglasses, so dazzling is the light that descends on us from left and right and from all directions, now and then the cameraman makes a joke, we laugh with united terror at the violent crashes and sometimes we do after all dodge back into the room. Tomorrow, or rather shortly, at dawn, we shall hear that within living memory the area has never experienced such an uragano, only the very old will remember such a storm, vaguely. When much later the storm subsides a little and the power station has obviously been repaired so that below in the village the lights over the motorway come back on and the echoes also gradually retreat behind the hills, when it's over the director says that we have to be up again in three hours' time and the cameraman says that there won't be much point, getting up he means, because we surely don't expect him after a night like this, and I say: he'll be there, you can bank on it, although I'm not absolutely sure, after all he's not that young anymore, he's famous, he's modest, he really doesn't need it. He's just promised and this is one thing I know about him: that he's a man of great gifts. It makes me start when I see him a few hours later amid the havoc, slightly chilled and with his jacket collar turned up. Something resembling the skeleton of a deckchair lies at his feet and from the flooded tunnel under the motorway a broken palm comes drifting in his direction. Then I see still more torn-off palm leaves strewn around him and there he stands: calm amid the torn-off leaves and the piles of mud and here and there in the mud a picture postcard and a little further an orange pennant, crumpled and covered in mud but orange and he stares and stares at the patch of colour that has withstood the storm and he raises his hand when we approach. In the bar where they've not been to bed all night we drink a cup of coffee. Afterwards when we get into the car we scarcely speak, only the occasional word comes out: *uragano, cornuto, macchina, Picasso*. Sometimes there are at least twenty kilometres between one word and the next and all that time I consider how we are going to arrange the canvases along the wall, the eggs, the chocolate box lids, the minute craters in them, unless we place a single canvas against a pillar in the courtyard and get the camera to make a plopping movement down the column onto the canvas below, plop onto the colour, onto a gateway, a few square centimetres of gaping black with crusted rims of baby blue and candy pink, it must be very quick, and then another canvas and so another colour, perhaps penetrating the gateway, just for a moment, and later on the soundtrack the ringing of bells, plop-bang, plop-bang. But I know immediately that it's not true, that I wasn't thinking of that at all, the whole endless route from Genoa to Milan and actually it's obvious that I can't remember anything of what went through my head then, those hours when we zoomed along in silence, pushing through some late shreds of the storm and succumbed imperceptibly to sleep yet did not sleep. The ringing of bells too was added only months later, in Berlin, and all that is clear in my mind is the storm, that midday, that night, low over Milan, the whole coast a bombarded strip so that we have to put on our sunglasses against the harsh light that descends on us from all directions. Until finally somewhere in the darkness behind my back Fontana says that we must undress, the contessa and I. And because of that I squeeze my eyes shut in panic and press thumb and index finger against my temples: because again I have mistaken one darkness for another and one light with the other, have mistaken silence for silence, and talking for talking and hence cannot possibly distinguish what does not belong together remotely or closely so that it will soon seem as if it does nevertheless all belong together, then and then and then and now and night and midday and beach and interior and south and so on and so on. That's how it is. I must begin again.

Was it a palm, a weeping willow, a plane-tree? Was it two palms? A palm and a weeping willow? Two weeping willows? A weeping willow and a plane-tree? A plane-tree and a palm? Two plane-trees? Was it a number of trees, a number of weeping willows, a number of plane-trees? I stand at the window, I can still see it clearly. I see myself standing at the window looking out over the lawn, green undulating towards the green of the trees, of the weeping willows, the palms, the plane-trees perhaps. The rain pours down vertically and in the blackness of the studio, occasionally lit up by flickering I notice (in the white? In the black?) how I make a hesitant movement, or not even, a movement that scarcely reaches the status of a movement, at most an effort to make it, as if I make a timid attempt to turn to him and don't make it, from the look of it try to resist, to contradict him, or possibly haven't understood his language and of course I understood him, every word, every colour, even the baby blue, even the candy pink, their meaning, the rhythm, the sound, understood what was said and not expressed, said at least a hundred times and never ever expressed, not even in his letters. *Vous avez 45 année, il sont rien, vous avez encore beaucoup de chose a faire, y Jef ma dit que vous fait de chose très important, tout ça je pense c'est naturelle.* He keeps repeating it: you're young. He says it first in French and then in Italian, for the contessa. Her elbow is now touching my arm, so close has she come to me. Only for a second, because I already see how she detaches herself and actually begins, raises her arms above her head with a graceful gesture and shakes her hair. She throws her dress onto the small desk at which he writes his letters, and on top of it, over the dress and under the lace underwear she takes off, my own clothes fall and I can't even explain this, watch breathlessly as we gradually appear in our nakedness and before we run into the rain a moment later I catch a last glimpse of him. It seems as if he has retreated further back into the studio, among his canvases, the eggs, the gateways, or the cuts, sharp gashes and the lips of the canvas curled, inward, outward, hands stuffed in his pockets like a boy and he's so young that he calls after us that it's fine like that, calls it very softly, and from then on I avoid looking at the window, feel the rain streaming warm and dense over my skin and I know that close by in the garden the rain is now streaming warm and dense over her skin and I avoid her skin for a little longer, I hold my arms stretched out stiffly in front of me, palms turned skyward like a chalice, they fill up and overflow and like a little dancer she rises up and places a nipple in each chalice to drink and while the rain leaks from her breasts then fills my hands, it is as if at the same time she drinks and offers me drink and the next moment we are running madly after each other, whirling around the trunk of a tree. Brown and gleaming she dashes ahead of me and when I stop unexpectedly and turn round she bumps into me hard and I think: now she's laughing, but it's not laughing, her lips just stay slightly parted, not stiffly, or merrily, she wipes a strand of her long drenched hair from her forehead and slowly retreats from me, although she has not moved her feet at all, so I think, she slides further and further from me until she is right in front of me and wonder which of us has moved, which of us sank to their knees, whether she had lain full length on her back or I laid her in the grass, pressed her eyes closed, slid my hands over the wet marble of her torso, over her belly and then lower, towards her vagina, sharp gashes and lips curled, inward, outward, finally sink in the lips and cry, to the sky above, the rain, the dark midday light over the garden, over the courtyard, and beyond the courtyard the street, the city, I scream till I see everything again and see clearly that he has unlocked this door for me too, simply because I am his friend and because of that, because I am a friend of his, put out a virgin canvas for us and nods in assent when I say that the tape is running and the camera is running, for that reason clenches the pricker in his fist and charges at the canvas with a scream so that I am able to hear what up to now no one has known about him, this strength, this violence, the screams resounding in the studio, raw gutturals that reel right over me, drill right through the canvas, as it were drag space in through the window, brought up from what depth? What darkness?, what light?

They say you're an aesthete.
They can't hear me.
They say you're only thirty.

149

They can't see me.
They say you're almost seventy.
They don't believe me.
They say: candy pink!
With gateways and craters in it.
They say: baby blue!
Pierced through gashed through.
They walk past your door.
They're not looking for me.
They're coming to greet you.
They won't find me.
They say: chocolate box lid!
They can't taste me.
They say that you're famous.
Now that I'm dying.
They say you've died.
Now I'm alive.
They say you're alive.
As long as I'm looking?
Look for what?
For example.
The whole time?
The whole time, constantly, non-stop, without interruption, in the Piazza, in the plane, eating dessert, in bed, in the bath, on the beach, at the bar, in the clay, with the paint, alone, not alone, with a woman, with another woman, with a friend, with another friend, with a fool, with another fool, with a thief, with another thief, with a parasite, with another parasite, with a king, with another king, at a grave, at another grave, with a god, with another god, friendly, merry, embracing, unmoved, stiff, excited, trouble-making, playing, asking, denying, affirming, believing, doubting, helpless, hoping, failing, mutilating, mauling, gluing, washing, disinfecting, forgetting, finding, relieved, grateful, exuberant, saying yes, saying no, saying no more, saying everything, only then.

J'espère de vous rencontrer très tôt ici a la campagne, douve je pense passé les dernier anné de ma vi. Je été très malade, pour beaucoup de mois, maintenant ça marche meilleur, mai je doit fair beaucoup de atantion, y travaillé très tranquilment. La vi c'est joli ici le meme, il vient beaucoup des ami a moi visiter. Pardon pour mon francé, cher ami Michils, j'espère vous rencontrer le plus tôt possible, y continuer notre discussion sur l'art. Mon salutation les plus afectuose y amicalle de ton ami Fontana – Comabbio 17.5.68.

Fontana. Lucio. Lucio Fontana. Fontana Lucio.

Lucio
lustro
lupo
luogo
lunario
luna
lume
ludo
luce
lucente
lordura
lonzo
lontano
logoro
logico
lodo
lode
locanda
livido
lite
litania
litigio
lirico
liquido
lingua

linea
limpido
limosina
limone
limo
limite
lima
lieto
libro
libra
libito
libidinoso
libertino
libero
liberale
libello
lesto
Lesbo
leone
lento
lenti
lene
lena
legnata
legione
leggero
leggiandro
leggenda
legge
legato
legale
lecco
lazzo
lazza
lavoro

lavina
lavato
lavanda
laura
laude
latte
lattante
latebra
larva
largo
lapide
lanzo
lanterna
lanfa
landa
lancio
lancia
lancetta
lana
lampo
lampana
lampada
lamia
lamento
lago
la.
Let.
Let's.
Let little children come unto me.

The Straggler

Yves Petry

We haven't done at all badly, ladies and gentlemen, as a human race. We've every right to be proud of that. And since there's no one else to congratulate us, we'll just have to do it ourselves. We can't expect any praise from the other animal species. They don't have the capacity to assess our achievements at their true value. They are imprisoned in their natures and whatever lengths we go to in order to penetrate their experience of themselves as animals, it would be unrealistic to expect a reciprocal effort on their part. We set them down in our labyrinths and measure their brain power by the degree to which they are able to adapt to their new situation. But they will not measure *our* brain power by the complexity of the labyrinths we have built around them. They have no interest in the scope of our intelligence, let alone understanding of, or even respect for it. The only respect our species can gain is self-respect. So let us at the start of this lecture allow ourselves a few seconds of self-respect and commemorate our species with a modest but well-deserved round of applause...

It struck me as rather improbable that people would actually respond to this humorous prompt by applauding. Consequently I did not consider it advisable to insert a pause that could easily turn into an embarrassing silence, leaving me red-faced. But on the other hand, boldly extending the silence that has fallen without lowering one's eyes, looking out into the auditorium until a few obliging souls are finally induced to a burst of hesitant, watery applause, obviously not quite sure what for – that would immediately create the right atmosphere for the turn my lecture was about to take. Because it's true there wasn't that much reason for applause.

But, ladies and gentlemen, I was thinking of continuing, with or without a pause, there's not that much reason for applause anyway and we should certainly not take that self-respect too far. After all, we're only animals, with all the limitations that implies. I'm certainly not telling you anything new. The evolutionary biological paradigm, the naturalisation of human beings as a conceptual novelty has by now found wide acceptance among the public at large. Nowadays energetically popularised versions can now be found on a daily basis in even the most mindless printed matter. One does not need to be a genius to join in the discussion. Every Tom, Dick or Harry can explain it to you in broad outline. Some people have quite a problem and find it extremely hard to agree with this way of thinking. But for many people it is quite a relief, a true liberation from a painful state of lack of identity. I believe I can assert that for women it all generally makes little difference. The fact that they are animals, may be an intuitive insight that always issued quite naturally from their intimate bodily self-awareness – they didn't need any science for that. Apart from that over the past few millennia they have heard little else. In the ontological spectrum they have often enough been placed between man and animal, often closer to the latter than the former...

　　　No, perhaps this wasn't such an appropriate digression. It would take us too far back into the past, whereas my lecture must be totally oriented towards the future. It had become totally irrelevant, that future, so why go on talking about it? Besides, there would also be women in my audience and what did I actually know about women. My relationship with the other sex was, to put it mildly, very reserved and in fact I had few concrete indications to justify the general assertion that women derived the direct insight from their intimate bodily self-awareness. Such statements might even encounter vigorous protests from the audience before my argument had even got off the ground. Suppose I were to be accused of sexism from the word go, over there in America, in Carnitec headquarters! I had never had any problems with the women who worked for Carnitec, and it would be better not to run the risk of suddenly provoking a backlash. The reason why relations between myself and the women at Carnitec went so smoothly was mainly due to the fact that I had very little contact with them professionally, for the simple reason that there were no women working in my department. And if I ever did have anything to discuss with members of the opposite sex from another department, I never succumbed to the temptation to pronounce on the specifically female aspects of their presence. For that matter, they gave me no reason to do so, since they did not project the image of woman, or not the kind of modern woman you might encounter in the street, on TV or in pubs. They dressed and behaved in a very distinctive way. They did not have the weary, half-hearted aura of women who were mothers, lovers, career women, housewives and citizens all in one. In the cool, professional surroundings of Carnitec they did not display that arbitrary combination of weakness and strength, neediness and self-sufficiency, subservience and assertiveness, which make contemporary woman such an easy catch but such a drag to live with. The women at Carnitec seemed, to judge by their appearance and behaviour, to have opted not for half-heartedness but for extreme clarity. They never tried to find out what you actually thought of them. They themselves made it perfectly clear how they wanted to come across and left no room for ambiguity that needed comment. Consequently none was required of you. If you kept to this rule, misunderstandings never arose. They were almost as predictable and unambiguous as caricatures. You wouldn't even be doing that much violence to reality by dividing them, by way of a caricature, into two groups. The first type, the dolly, often had a great mop of hair, held in check by one or more giant braids, sometimes hanging loose, sometimes draped around her crown in some way or other. Beneath this high-maintenance hairdo, this keratin octopus, there was usually a small, delicate youthful-looking face without make-up, sometimes adorned with an elegant pair of glasses. Apart from her hands and a thin, pale neck, you didn't usually get to see much of her body. Because even on hot days she showed a stubborn preference for loose-fitting, sack-shaped dresses with long sleeves and pleated collars. Underneath she usually wore tights, which made her look like a life-sized, old-fashioned doll. You might wonder who, apart from herself, would ever dare to dress or undress this doll or comb her hair. You'd almost have to be a girl for that, or else a paedophile. Did she menstruate? Did she have a womb? Or at least pubic hair? You were inclined to think not. Of course she had a shrewd, industrious and meticulous brain; otherwise she wouldn't be working for Carnitec. And besides being such a good worker she was also highly appreciated for being a silent worker. You didn't often hear her and whenever she did say something it was invariably sensible. She was a perfect team player. She adjusted modestly to her subordinate role. She was never a project manager. She was content with an anonymous share in the success of the project she was working on. She didn't seem to have the ambition of seeing her name in lights linked to some success or other. She had no problem about ceding that honour to someone else. She was really no trouble at all. She was the nun of science, the chaste bride of the universal intelligence. The other type in contrast, the butch, had developed into the complete opposite. From beneath her short haircut, probably do-it-yourself, often on the greasy side, she looked out at the world with surly belligerence. Seen in profile, the silver nails that she sometimes wore in her ears looked less like female jewellery than the hinges in a suit of armour. Sometimes she had children, funnily enough, since it was difficult to imagine the man who would dare approach her with his penis sticking out. Don't let's pay any more attention to her clothes than she does herself. Carelessly applied make-up was intended to give her a semblance of femininity, but the average painted horse had more charm. She behaved as if she were wearing a suit of chain mail made of Y chromosomes. She wasn't stupid, of course not, and whenever she got the chance she made that abundantly clear. You had constantly to brace yourself against her bossiness and competitiveness. The older she was, the more domineering she became. And you mustn't think that you could impress her with your male attributes, your lower voice, the taller stature, your more developed sense of humour. Forget it! She wanted to hear arguments, useful arguments, and apart from that you could hang your prick down your back for all she cared. She seemed to be moulded from testosterone-reinforced concrete. Like a real bloke she sometimes came up with complete nonsense and for days after stubbornly defended her mistakes. What was wrong with this woman? Did she have hair on her nipples or what? One thing you must put right out of your head, was making a remark like that aloud. Because in her eyes jokes were only funny when she could laugh at them. And she had little patience with unfunny jokes. She could cut up really rough, for example, if you made over-explicit allusions to organic or gender differences. She didn't find that funny at all, as I once saw a careless male colleague learn when he was given a thorough tongue-lashing. I hadn't followed the scene right from the start, but the woman's view seemed to boil down to the fact that she had a kind of penis as well, and obviously a much bigger one than he had, though an internal one. And there was actually no difference between internal and external. Try denying that! Because in the light of the profound intelligence that was the norm at Carnitec, and the even more profound one that was being aimed for, the difference between inner and outer had indeed lost all relevance, as had that between men and women. Everything is contained in everything else. There is no interior that cannot be exteriorised, there is no exterior that is not itself contained, every inside is also an outside and vice-versa, every front a back and vice-versa. Anyone who felt obliged to introduce naïve dividing lines, between inside and outside, hadn't got a clue, and never would have a clue and should simply never even have applied for a scientific post. She was not going to deny that she was a woman in her daily life. She was actually proud of the fact. But in her position as team leader she did not want that alluded to, unless there was a good reason. Had she heard that reason perhaps? No, all she had heard was a dirty, shitty sexist, joke! It was an embarrassingly stupid argument, in which she got increasingly heated. Why did the bloody woman keep banging on about something that all of us had long taken for granted. He tried to pour oil on troubled waters, the poor guy, to apologise, he really hadn't meant it that way, it was just a joke, but she wouldn't let up, the humourless bitch, purple as an erection of inextinguishable rage she kept pounding him, as he shrank into a pale, limp thing that looked around timidly for a corner to crawl into. What exactly had he said that could justify such an outburst? No one had heard and no one defended him. Three months later he had left Carnitec and no one seemed to miss him. Oh la la, you'd better be careful with Carnitec women, I told myself. But what about the men then? Yes, you can say things about the men, the men can take it on the chin – for now. And even if my relationships weren't much less distant than with my female ones, there was at least one man I knew quite well, with whom I slept and got up, with whom I showered and whom I jerked off, namely myself, so no one could deny me the right to talk about men, tell tales out of school about them, and if necessary tell lies about them to slander them if it suited me.

For men on the other hand, ladies and gentlemen, for men things are usually different. Darwin and evolutionary biology have offered them a welcome way out of what over the centuries has become an increasingly acute lack of metaphysical potential.

Over the centuries? Why am I starting on about that again? The only century that mattered had only just begun. And besides they were all very easy, those guided tours of the past. It was over, it was as harmless as the dead in their graves, it couldn't contradict you and as a result you could flesh it out according to your needs. As a living product of the present you were always superior to your theme, you were constantly in control, but it was a very lazy form of superiority that had cost you very little. It was the superiority of a public that watched the craziness of the past from a safe distance and did not seem to realise that, seen from the future, it also consisted of lunatics. No, really, you don't really show your most brilliant side by going on about corpses. Let the dead commemorate the dead. Actual it's downright annoying, the facile behaviour of an intelligence that uses its night lamp to illuminate dreary history instead of planning a future with its morning light. But all right, on we go, for the sake of the argument. Once more, briefly, and then never again: the past.

God had left man abruptly in the lurch and at a certain moment history too turned out to be nothing but a bloody mess, to which he could scarcely appeal in order to award himself exceptional privileges or a special position. What was he to do? Where was his place? What was left that could give him the right to sound off? And then, right on cue, along came biology, and finally gave man a place in the scheme of things. Of course he has to share that place in the scheme of things with woman, it's no longer an exclusive niche, of the kind he used to have. But OK, better a niche than none at all. And that's why men still have a lot to say for themselves, since they still have a self-image. For obvious reasons the naked mole rat is a less popular role model but in the power-crazed chimpanzee or the libidinous bonobo men recognise with profound empathy their true hirsute nature. They too are hominids, only with their coats turned inside out. The fact that these are threatened species that are no longer viable in the jungle and whose future, if they still have one, lies in zoos, is an irony lost on most men. What matters to them is the ninety-eight percent genetic match they share with their wild fellow-males. They are as proud of that figure as if it were an exam mark. A man likes the ape in himself. The fact that there is so much that is human in apes, in turn gives prestige to what is ape-like in man. It points to a mythically long blood line, giving him a hint of animal nobility. So, a little respect for the gentleman, please. He may be a bungler, but this is bungling with a respectable prehistory. It comes from afar. From prehistory to the bedroom is a long way. Of course he can't always know what he feels; his feeling is older and more powerful than his knowledge. Eons of struggle are stored in his genes. He is the victor of an endless number of fights. He would like to express this sense of triumph, but often find the present is too small for that. That is why he often makes such a frustrated impression. But even his subjection still carries the stamp of his pre-human ancestry. Primordial instincts are at work in even the most domestic mediocrity. Inside the couch-bound channel-hopper lurks the eternal hunter. And the cyber-surfer surfs the wide plains of porn with the doggedness of the wolf that has smelled blood, even though it will yield him not much more than a momentary release of tension, a solo spasm of dancing on the spot. He likes to imagine that around all he does there hangs a whiff of the steppes. That is not only his pride but also his consolation when things go limp.

Oddly enough, the ninety-nine point nine-nine percent genetic match between a man and an arbitrary woman does not lead to a correspondingly strong identification. You won't easily find a man flaunting his inner woman, and that probably wouldn't be helpful for mating behaviour. In this it is precisely that hundredth of one percent difference on which everything turns.

However inconsistent that may be, such inconsistencies are quite simply unavoidable with an intelligence that for reasons that have nothing to do with intelligence, exists in two variants, XX and XY, which are constantly confusing each other and will never coincide. A universal intelligence would not tolerate such inconsistencies. A universal and total intelligence, ladies and gentlemen, may tolerate copies of itself, but no variants. Total intelligence coincides totally with itself. Only one total intelligence can exist. That is why history, here it comes again, has countless examples of men who in their longing for total intelligence refused to recognise the sexual variation, who suppressed it, eliminated it or simply ignored it, which was all well meant but completely in vain, of course, since even their own intelligence was only a murky variation of a pure intelligence that was beyond their reach. But in daily life most men fortunately abandon a longing for total intelligence. Half an intelligence is more than enough. After all, the planet runs simply on brute force.

In the field of relationships this view has created new possibilities. A no longer tenable romanticism of stereotypes in which love was a key concept, has given way to a more rugged, science-inspired bio-romanticism in which power is the new buzzword. Of course this does not solve all problems. The old conflict continues, perhaps even more acutely than before. Because if man is an ape, then woman is a female ape. If both of them want to occupy the same niche in the scheme of things, then one day there will have to be a formal discussion of the division of the pleasures and responsibilities attaching to that niche. The struggle may be intense, as is the way with apes, and it will continue for as long as there are apes. But it has at least become a sporting contest, a trial of strength between equals, which can no longer be decided with false arguments based on prejudice. So good news on the sexual front.

But the conceptual comfort provided by this new image of humanity, ladies and gentlemen, is again threatened with disruption. Because we may be animals, but animals are ultimately only machines. There are better machines than us on the way. I mean powerful, imperturbable and tireless machines that work in a way none of us will be able to explain. It's really as though humanity is allowed no rest. No sooner have the sexes accepted an equal image of each other, than hypermachines are now being developed which in their efficiency won't give a damn about our sexual and ultimately also human determination. Total and sexless intelligence, until recently only an impure dream, will become crystal-clear reality. It would be enough to make you cry or shiver, ladies and gentlemen, had not a happy coincidence selected us of all people to be present at the start of this development, enabling us to call it, to a small degree, ours.

At this point I could, I think, without risking loss of face, insert a short pause to allow sniggers of amusement from the audience. I saw the bearded face of Dr Miami in front of me, undoubtedly somewhere in the front row, a bespectacled, grey, grinning bush, swaying gently in assent. But, as I foresaw, there would be other faces too, with non-committal frowns on their foreheads and glumly pursed lips. Because not everyone at Carnitec wanted to hear that machines were on their way that would no longer take account of the human factor, that tender fragment of verbosity and prophecy. They preferred to imagine that they were involved in a project serving human interests. Yes, even at Carnitec there were quite a few humanistic types walking around who believed that they were developing machines whose exponentially increasing capacity would benefit the welfare of mankind. For example, they hoped to make human beings cleverer. Hence their experiments with microchip implants and their research into nano-bones for strengthening natural brain capacity.

'Look at it this way,' Dr Miami had once said, 'those people produce top-class work, you can't fault them at all. And what they do often has useful applications. Increasing people's speed of thought, for example, patching them up when they've deteriorated through Parkinson's disease or providing them with prostheses that function almost as well as the limbs they've lost...'

Then he had had to smirk a little behind his beard again and it looked a little apologetic. Often when the subject of man, people, human beings or human interests came up, Dr Miami produced a rather uncomfortable grin, as if he had made an indecent joke. That was probably because of the enthusiasm attaching to such concepts, their idealistic tenor, the concern and involvement they expressed and seen from a distance, viewed from Dr Miami's perspective, made such a sadly confused, hopelessly naïve, irretrievably outmoded impression. I grinned along with him. His perspective was mine too.

'But the whole idea,' he had continued, 'the whole idea that the relationship between man and machine will be one between a master and his obedient, helpful servant, well, that is largely a marketing ploy, I fear. It serves mainly to give Carnitec a good image with the public at large and soothe it with the illusion that we are guided by what is in their interests. That our efforts are geared exclusively towards their welfare.'

But in our department, of which Dr Miami was chief and I a highly valued member, we were working on a different project: Baby.

Let me introduce you: 3XSS-111.ULIMACHINE is its official name. Baby is the nickname we have given it. It has the memory and computing capacity of the most advanced supercomputer. It is endowed with the capacity for self-development. Yes, Baby can learn. And without our intervention, completely independently, it is capable of drawing more precise conclusions from what it has learned. He's a smart cookie, if I may be so bold as to give him a gender. He not only learns, he's alive too. Because we ventured to supply him with a crucial characteristic of life: no, not consciousness of course, no sense of self, the eternal beginner's mistake, that fairy

163

tale with which we bring up our children (we have to, or else they will wilt or grow crooked and who has the heart to do that?) and in which of necessity we go on believing in ourselves. Baby is untroubled by consciousness, he doesn't waste his precious brainpower on that. He has no need to project fine images of himself, to adorn himself with names, or to imagine a loft destiny or noble mission for himself. Baby has no need to believe in anything in order to act. His activity is not based on an identity. He acts purely on the basis of his power to analyse and manipulate. The increase of power is his pre-programmed instinct; reduction in power is no option for him. That is his way of life. He never has to struggle with motivation problems. He lives and grows like a real baby. Except that he will never grow up, not by our standards. That is, he will never stop growing. Nor will he ever shrink, no as long as the universe doesn't shrink. And perhaps this ultimachine will one day even devise a way of surviving a shrinking universe. Some people sometimes call him The Monster, for quite defensible reasons. For without going into detail I can tell you that Baby isn't as nice as his pet name would lead you to believe. He also has some fairly aggressive features. The fate of our genes, for instance, is a problem of trivial importance. Baby's silicon brain constructs an intelligence that is definitely focused on self-preservation, but not on ours. At his present stage of development Baby still needs us, but we've been virtually written off. Baby's machine grammar reflects fairly absolute and immutable views of self-preservation and he has not been designed to see in the material of which we are made something whose preservation is worth striving after, or in the long term even possible. He doesn't believe in us. Our collaboration with him will be of relatively short duration. One day his intelligence will have surpassed the limits of our own and he will resolutely opt for the preservation of his own, irrespective of the results. That is simply the most intelligent choice. Would you have made a different one if you had had a choice? Yes, just you wait until Baby is big and strong. He won't look after us, he won't worry about us, that would amount to a reduction in strength. True to his design he will abandon us with our genetic stigmata, our intellectual limitations, and the needy cry of our blood. Perhaps, if we ask him, he will be able to predict with inexorable exactness the date when humanity will be finished. Yes, provided that he has the correct data, he'll also be kind enough to calculate to the exact second when our Last Day will begin. We'll have to grin and bear it: our good old Christian chronology, our earthly, seasonal calendar, our solar years, our beloved human time, abruptly and finally demolished by catastrophes of eschatological proportions. The end of history, but this time for good. 26 July 2067, to take a hypothetical example: the critical point has been reached at which the atmosphere will have changed its composition to such an extent that it is unsuited to harbour aerobic life. Or 8 January 2298 at 9: 35 42 GMT: an asteroid, for the moment still designated by a neutral letter code, unavoidably attracted by the iron heart of our planet, will reach its destination and burn away the biosphere with its high-energy kiss. After having shown us the prospect of this ultimate sunset Baby will have done with us. We'll hope he's wrong. We'll know if he's right. The chance of Baby being wrong is many times smaller than the chance of whatever improbable catastrophe he predicts.

What will be left of human beings when Baby is finished with them? They'll become stragglers, all of them, belittled by Baby's intelligence, in the sad realisation of their redundancy, waiting calmly for the inexorable, their bodies full of sedatives, unemployed, robbed of all the pride their intelligence once engendered in them, their gaze wandering with sickly slowness across the bleak walls of their room in rest home-cum-madhouse Earth...

The Smell Of Fresh Linen

Hugo Raes

It's the boss of the laundry himself who delivers the washing to your house, there's no need to give him anything. And the fact that he gives you sour looks isn't because you don't tip him, but because he's a sourpuss.

Granny had wanted to test the truth of these words of her son's after yet another sour laundry delivery and had asked the chap in his white coat straight out. She had asked him: Are you the actual manager of the laundry? Before answering he first puffed a stinking cloud from his half-extinguished cigar and mumbled, seemingly with great reluctance: madam, if I were the manager, I'd be playing billiards in The Fat Ox now, instead of working. Thereupon Granny had started to tip him as before, as if it were an inescapable duty.

The washing was delivered promptly, every two weeks. She smiled when she couldn't help thinking of a joke she had heard on the radio, the one about the lady who wrote a letter to the laundry saying: you should use more soap. And who got a reply saying: And you, madam, should use more paper.

Granny examined the laundry list and the accompanying bill. The standing charge had gone up again; she lifted up the handkerchiefs on top and looked underneath.

Then she heard a car pull up outside the house. And the child's voice. She pushed the laundry basket aside and opened the door. Hello, darling, what did you say? she asked, her heart melting. Granny, granny, said the child, supporting itself on the wall with its hands as it raised one leg high to reach the next step. It paused by the laundry basket for a moment and asked: What Granny doing?

She laughed: Granny's washing has just come from the laundry.

Granny doing? the toddler repeated mechanically.

And what's Loesje doing? she asked, picking the child up and hugging it to her. Playing, said the child.

So, mother, we'll come and collect her at about seven o'clock. Aren't you staying for dinner then? she asked, rather disappointed. No, because this evening the architect's coming round with the plans, and so we've got to be home, otherwise it'll get complicated.

But yesterday you said you were staying for dinner, didn't you?

Yes, mother, I did, but this morning the architect rang and he can either come tonight or not for another five days. But we'll come tomorrow afternoon instead.

Good idea, said the grandmother.

And then we'll take a drive to the sea in the afternoon; the beach and the dunes are covered in snow and that must be a wonderful sight.

Will these freezing temperatures never stop? she thought after her son had given her and his little daughter a kiss and left. Winter is lasting so long this year. Slowly, holding the hand of the little one who took small, sometimes faltering steps, he went into the living room, and shut the door to the hall. Come to Granny, my darling, she said with her lips pursed and teeth clenched. She could eat the little angel. She lifted her slowly up and crowed oooh! What a nice coat Loesje's got.

And the child said: Nice coat!

She had to fumble quite a bit with Loesje's sleeves before she could get the red coat off. Loesje was already fiddling about with the gleaming empty ashtray with the revolving circular top which when you pressed the button hurled the extinguished cigarette-ends with centrifugal force into the interior of the container. The ashtray was there for her son's benefit, since she herself did not smoke, and there had been no other visitors since her husband's death except for a lady, also a non-smoker, who lived nearby or one of her nieces. The child was a handful, and no object was safe from her. She picked the little girl up again, to distract her from the glamorous ashtray, and asked: How old is Loesje? Two, she said, but meanwhile she was thrashing about like an eel, trying to wriggle loose from grandmother's arms. Laughing, she put the toddler down again and she grabbed immediately for a bowl in which she put her pearl necklace. Heavens, those little fingers, those little mitts! crowed Granny, and moved the bowl from the side table to the cabinet.

Then she pointed to the big basket full of second-hand toys that she kept for the days when she had to babysit. But the little one wasn't interested. Loesje drink, she said. And Granny gave her some milk in the white mug that she brought carefully to her mouth.

Here, she said, giving the child a pack of playing cards. That would give her time to carry the laundry basket from the hall to the kitchen, and sort the linen.

Then there was a ring at the door.

She went over to the window obliquely to the side, in the hope of seeing who was there. But she couldn't make out the person. She opened the door and from close up saw an unsavoury man's face, and instinctively she drew back a little, while the man asked if she would like to buy any tea towels, and started praising his wares. She said, no, sir, I don't need anything, but the man pushed further forward, jammed his foot in the door and sang the praises of his goods, looking past her into the hall. She pushed against the door, but the pedlar prevented her from slamming it in his face. Rather nervously she repeated that she didn't need anything, and had almost no money. She said that out of fear, because you hear so often of old people who are attacked, and she was frightened of pushy, impertinent pedlars. The way that this one, after having insisted even more, withdrew his foot tantalisingly slowly. As she pushed the door into the lock she wondered whether this man hadn't rung the bell last week or the week before. Something clattered in the kitchen, and she rushed in that direction, in time to see the plastic salad bowl bobbling across the floor. The salad, which she had already tossed with oil and vinegar, was sticking to one of the two kitchen chairs and the floor tiles.

Is Loesje allowed to do that? she scolded.

What Loesje doing? said the child in bewilderment.

Yes, what is Loesje doing! Loesje mustn't do that! she said accusingly, and with a towel she wiped the child's fingers clean.

After she had cleared everything up, and had given the child a sweetie to keep it quiet for a minute, she looked at the kitchen clock. Almost three o'clock. She thought of how busy it would be now, in the centre, on Saturday afternoon. She thought the light was becoming whiter. And when she looked at the window, she noticed the powdery clouds or smudges of fine snow. That's the kind that settles. She poked the cast-iron cannon stove vigorously, opened the door at the bottom a little further, and when she emptied in half a scuttle of coal she heard the flame suddenly start loudly droning and purring and a sharp smell prickled her nose and eyes.

With the natural movements of someone who had done this regularly all through her long life, she sorted the linen. Then she picked up the pile of handkerchiefs and took it over to the tall cupboard. In the middle of the room she suddenly felt a terrible piercing pain in her head which made her pause and groan and go aaah. She breathed deeply and held her breath. The lightning-like pain of a brain haemorrhage immediately became so intense that she closed her eyes violently and tottered. She collapsed and fell with her head against the leg of the table and her chin on the pile of towels. The newly-washed smell of fresh linen was the last thing her senses registered.

The little girl, stepping awkwardly in the high-heeled white box calf shoes, approached Granny, who was lying on the floor. Granny doing? said the delicate little voice.

She turned round and then turned back to the old woman near the table and watched her steadily. Granny sleeping, Granny bye-byes. Granny doing, Granny sleeping.

Loesje squatted down next to Granny, pressed an index finger against the closed eyelids of Granny, who was lying with her mouth half open against the towels. Then she took the old rubber animals out of the toy basket one by one. And then pulling the duck that made a clattering sound when she pushed it across the floor a little. She laid the teddy bear next to Granny, and then went back to the toy basket.

Loesje did not hear the four rings of the kitchen clock. She went on playing happily, absorbed and in her own world. It gradually became dark. Outside there was a blizzard. The only sound in the room was Loesje's foot, which she slid rhythmically to and fro as she played with a stick with wooden rings. She scrambled to her feet, and went over to the side table with the revolving ashtray.

There was a crease in the rug and the child tripped over it and fell sideways against the purring, red-hot stove. She screamed loudly, and then stopped, as she was stuck by her cheek and one of her bare arms. The child seemed to be suffocating, and only then did air returned to her lungs and did the screaming follow. The smell of burnt flesh spread through the living room. Still the child was lying against the stove. The whole side of her face and arm were burnt away. The child struggled to raise itself up and fell onto the linoleum in front of the stove. She tried to say something to the figure on the floor nearby.

She wept heartrendingly.

At seven o'clock there was a ring at the door. When no one opened the door after the second time, the man tapped on the rather tall window and tried to see through the curtain. It disturbed him when he noticed that there was no light on. He now knocked loudly on the window pane together with his wife and looking in shielding their eyes with their hands they heard the crying. And when after long peering their eyes became accustomed to the darkness, they saw in the red glow that fell onto the carpet from the open door at the bottom of the stove, a large shape on the floor.

Covering his fist with his hat the man smashed the window pane.

The Slugs

Ward Ruyslinck

'There's another one!' cried the bailiff in horror. He hurriedly pulled his legs up under the sheets and, resting on his left elbow, pointed his extended arm at the foot of the bed. Then he sat up a little further, dipped his fingertips in the bowl on the bedside table and sprinkled the place where his feet had just lain.

The deacon, sitting on a chair by the bed and playing with the cord of his cassock, followed all these movements with an impassive stare.

'I can't see anything,' he said in a voice that seemed to emanate from his stomach, 'why don't you just lie down again.'

The bailiff remained sitting in the same position, half sitting, and his parched lips, which resembled old flaking leather, parted as if he were gasping for breath.

'You're not seeing things through your own eyes, father, you're seeing them through the eyes of your faith. You keep saying it's my sins that are hounding me and that the curse will be lifted the moment I convert. But I can see it with my own eyes, which have never deceived me in forty-four years; I can *see*, just as I can see you sitting here: they're there, really and truly, they exist. When I think of them, I see them, and even when I don't think of them I see them: black, the colour of your cassock, but shiny, with oiled backs and two antennae. Fat, slimy garden slugs. It's not a hallucination, as you say it is, and certainly not a ruse of the devil's, since I don't recognise the devil. If you can't see them, it's because you don't want to see them. In 1940 I attended a spiritualist séance and sat next to someone who turned out to be a priest (he was wearing ordinary street clothes like me, but I was assured he was an investigator for the Roman Catholic church, an assistant to a bishop, no less). He was in the same room as me and the other three witnesses, when the table rose in the air and stayed hovering about half a metre from the floor, but he maintained he couldn't see it. It was quite simple: he didn't want to see it, because the Church had instructed him to close his eyes. He couldn't see it, the Church had removed his eyes and given him the eyes of a blind man instead. He was bound to the Church not only hand and foot but also by his eyes. And you, excuse my saying so, are tarred with the same brush. What I see is reality. They're there, I'm not crazy. They are leeches, living black leeches. What have my sins got to do with it? It's the third one that's come to taunt me today. This morning there was one on the wall, just opposite, above the watercolour, and less than an hour later there was one on the commode. Perhaps it was the same one, I don't know. There's only one sure way to get rid of them: a few drops of ammonia and they're gone. I don't think you can banish your sins with ammonia. Ammonia isn't holy water.'

He fell back exhausted and closed his eyes, but didn't dare stretch out his legs. The deacon, who had listened to him calmly, now looked pityingly at the face of the bed-ridden man, which had the shape and colour of a turnip. Then he glanced around the room: here and there the linoleum, the walnut wood of the wardrobe, the commode and the bed had small pale patches, where the ammonia had eaten into it. He sighed.

'If you were to use holy water, they would never return. They would be destroyed. Ammonia just frightens them. And it wouldn't damage your furniture.'

'Oh yes, I could try holy water,' said the bailiff indifferently, as if trying to please the priest with this answer.

'Although I'm convinced the holy water won't have the slightest effect, if you don't first confess your sins,' announced the deacon calmly.

The bailiff did not answer. Beneath his still closed eyes his nose hooked into his face like the blade in a plane.

'I'm tired,' he said.

The deacon thought: he really does look tired, but above all frightened. He's frightened to death, his sins are weighing heavily on him.

As if the bailiff was embroidering on the unspoken thought of his visitor, shortly afterwards he asked, with a breaking voice:

'Do you think I'm going to die, father?'

'I know for certain that you will die, Mr Bailiff.' He paused for a moment to allow the merciless reality evoked by his words to penetrate, and added in the same measured, but faintly compassionate tone: 'But when, God alone knows: tomorrow, in a year, in twenty years...'

'Yes, I'm not immortal,' said the bailiff. 'The doctor has admitted that I'll never live beyond sixty, but that on the other hand there's no serious reason to suppose that it will happen before next month or next year. That's another of those ambiguous statements that you must like or lump.'

'Those who believe in eternal life are always prepared for death.'

'Yes, so they say,' said the bailiff with gentle irony. He opened his eyes into narrow chinks and peered suspiciously at the steel-blue curtains that were tied up in a loop with gold tassels. Beyond them shone the daylight, mother-of-pearl and autumnal, converging around a coffee-coloured stain that was the sun. 'Mr Bailiff, this world is like a feudal domain. We should prepare ourselves every day of our lives for our release, which is death. Even if we have reason to assume that we have many more years to live, it is desirable that we should expect the end of feudal service, so that we still have an opportunity to discharge our debts and make up for obligations we have neglected. In other words: this life is burdened with a mortgage and it would be irresponsible to accept the afterlife without paying off that mortgage. I'm speaking your language, Mr Bailiff, so you'll be sure to understand me. You're a sensible person and I hope you'll reflect on my words. In any case I'm giving you this advice to consider. And now I must be going. If you need me, you can always send for me.'

The deacon got up from his chair to take his leave. With a rapid movement he recovered the broad-brimmed hat hanging over the back of the chair. This was his hat. He brushed the dark satin with his sleeve, as if to remove a piece of fluff, but did not put it on.

'I enjoyed your visit,' said the bailiff and it really did look as if he were grateful to the priest. He cautiously stretched out his feet towards the end of the bed. It was if a snake were slithering slowly beneath the covers. Then he added with gloomy spitefulness: 'Please bring a horticulturalist along at the first opportunity, someone who knows about garden slugs and how to eradicate them. And course some holy water too.'

The deacon paused by the door. He was going to say: 'My dear sir, it is not your room that is overrun with vermin, but your soul,' but then he remembered that he had said something similar previously. He was silent and stared at the white, emaciated turnip face on the pillow. He's frightened because he's being left alone, because I'm going and leaving him at the mercy of the slimy incursion of the slugs, and that why he's made that spiteful remark. He's frightened to death.

As he was going downstairs, still holding his hat, he heard someone call out: 'Padre!' The kitchen door, which opened onto the hall, was open. He put his head inside. The housekeeper was standing at a low table scraping salsify roots. She was wearing red rubber gloves and a blue apron. She always called him Padre, he had no idea why.

'Has he seen them again?' she asked. Her voice, moist and harsh, always reminded him of a hot mist that rose quickly, sank down again and immediately froze.

He stood in the doorway and said:

'Yes, while I was sitting with him: at the foot of the bed.'

She shook her head in pity and rinsed a long milky-white root under the tap.

'It's dreadful. What do you think, will he ever recover, Padre? It's gnawing away at his eyes, his belly, his heart. If it continues much longer, he'll go mad. Yesterday he saw one floating in his soup. You can't imagine how discouraging that is for me. I can't dream of serving green salad vegetables like lettuce and cabbage and celery, but what am I to do if he finds them even in the soup?'

It was cold in the hall and the deacon put on his hat. 'It's a serious, although not a hopeless case,' he said. 'His conscience is burdened with a sinful past. Each slug is one of his sins, slimy and black. He will go on seeing them to the end of his life, unless he sees the error of his ways and turns his face towards Christ again. They will multiply, they will constantly grow in number, they will crawl over his body in massed ranks like ants. Yes, you said it: it will be an ordeal that drives him to madness.'

The woman looked at him in dismay. 'Padre, you are invoking the terrors of hell!' Her face lengthened and broadened, flat as a skimming stone at her temples, She had a vivid imagination.

He smiled sadly: 'God is merciful to sinners.' And then: 'Why does he shun the Church? It is regrettable.'

She shrugged her shoulders. Her face sank back and she took the end of a long, curved salsify root between her thumb and index finger. She resumed scraping, slowly and distantly.

'I don't know,' she said. 'He's quite withdrawn, at least with me. It's hard to fathom him. But he does think a lot, I can see that.'

'I see.'

'Yes,' she said, 'he thinks *too much*. Perhaps that's the reason.'

She pared a long strip of skin from the root. The deacon made a vague, ambiguous gesture with his head: her reasoning did not strike him as sufficiently convincing, but he did not wish to pursue it now.

'Perhaps I'll drop by tomorrow,' he concluded. 'I hope he has a quiet night. Should anything happen in the meantime, you can always call in my help. In fact, I insist you do.'

She wanted to see him out, but he prevented her: 'Don't worry about me, I can see myself out.'

As he left the house and crossed to the other side of the street, he had the feeling that this was where the world began that was inhabited by living people, people who had pored over Homer at school and from then on had had a horror of any epic poem, people who had never read Homer and would never hear about him, people who lived consciously, happily or unhappily, but consciously. He thought of the bailiff, of his deep-rooted godless attitude, his emaciated waxy face, his stubbly chin, his fear. He also thought of the slugs, with a feeling of discomfort. He believed only in God – not in the chilling second existence of the bailiff, not in the grotesque monsters of the imagination, not in the slugs. At this moment – and always, it was true – God was a white layer of foam that floated on the black river of his own fear.

The night the bailiff now spent was the most restless he had known. The housekeeper, who was sleeping in the room next to his on a straw mattress on the floor and had left the door ajar, heard him, like Jacob in Pniel, wrestling with the angel all night long. As day was breaking he fell into a comatose state that lasted for two days and nights. His face had taken on a yellowish, translucent colour: a hollowed-out turnip with a candle burning inside. His dry, curled top lip revealed a few incisor teeth; he seemed to be smiling. A terrifying death's head. His doctor was summoned. He brought his bag with him, but did not open it. For about two minutes he stood motionless at the foot of the bed looking at the patient, blinked indecisively and went away. Two hours later he returned, accompanied by a colleague from the local medical institute. He too had brought a bag, but left it downstairs in the hall. He felt the bailiff's pulse, raised his eyelids, tapped the bared teeth with the nail of his index finger and held a pocket mirror under the patient's nose, all this without taking his left hand out of his trouser pocket. Then the two of them, the general practitioner and himself, went downstairs without exchanging a single word.

When the bailiff awakened from the coma – it was a Friday around vespers – the deacon was sitting calmly beside the bed, legs crossed as if he had been sitting there all the while, two days and two nights, like the page of a tear-off calendar still indicating the day on which the fatal disruptive event had begun. Over the back of the chair hung the black skull cap and on the linoleum there was a faint square of light. The bailiff opened his eyes and let out a deep sigh.

His blind gaze was directed steadily at the low ceiling, and seemed to be trying to lift it up. There was a dark, damp stain and perhaps that was what he couldn't take his eyes off. But the deacon knew that he couldn't see anything, that his heart was beating in a vacuum and he had only regained consciousness, not life.

Patiently the deacon folded his hands. He did not pray. He was waiting for something and that waiting demanded all his attention. From outside came a monotonous screeching sound, as if an automatic garden sprinkler had been turned on somewhere.

The death's head on the pillow moved slightly and the bloodless lips parted. A word rose up like a bubble. The deacon leant forward and listened intently. He recognised the word. It overwhelmed him. He frowned, and squeezed the beads of the rosary in his pocket. He took the word into his own mouth and swallowed it down. It sank towards his stomach and swelled like a sponge. It made his stomach swell.

The bailiff repeated it, groaning: 'The slugs...' He's delirious, thought the deacon, it's the malignant fevers that are starting – could this be the end? Instinctively he folded his hands again and under his breath intoned the beginning of the forty-second psalm: 'As the hart panteth after the water brooks, so panteth my soul after thee, O God. My soul thirsteth for God, for the living God; when shall I come and appear before God? My tears have been my meat day and night, while they continually say unto me, Where is thy God?' The patient lay still, as if following the words of the prayer with heart and soul. For a moment his eyes seemed to float towards the closed window, where the cold air pressed against the glass. And then, as the priest's voice faded and in the sudden advent of silence the screeching of the garden sprinkler again became audible, he moved his lips once more.

'God is a slug,' the deacon heard.

He looked at the unfortunate man with pity. Poor soul, the slugs had eaten his brains. God is a slug. Yes, *God* had eaten his brains. It wasn't blasphemy, it was not the challenge of a mindless person – what he said was the truth. It was an answer to the complaint in the psalm: where is your God? When Christ hung on the cross at Golgotha and in a moment of weakness raised up His voice to His almighty Father, a gleaming black slug crawled up the back of the upright of the cross. God had never forsaken Him, not even in the hour of death. But *He* did not know that. He clasped the yellow, sinewy hand with the tapering fingertips bleached by the ammonia, which was resting on the sheet. 'Mr Bailiff, can you hear me?' The skin of the hand he was holding felt lukewarm and moist. Like a freshly tanned hide, he thought. The sick man's nostrils were flared. His breathing was irregular and he did not answer.

Probably he heard only the silence that was growing in him: like a sound. Or like a colour, against a dark background? Death would come, as a servant of the supernatural law, to seal the doors. To take possession of the soul and make an inventory of undischarged debts.

There was a faint knock at the door. It wasn't death yet. The housekeeper entered the room. She stationed herself silently behind the deacon's chair. Obviously she was looking over his head at the sickbed, at the translucent, hollowed-out turnip face on the pillow.

'Do you think he'll make it?' she whispered in the priest's ear. He did not look round. She was still panting for breath, like a pair of bellows with its spout pointing at his neck. She was no longer young and could only tackle the twenty-six steps of the tall staircase with great effort. He did not answer her question directly: 'He's obsessed with the slugs. They're poisoning not only his imagination, but also his blood. If only he would confess his sins; the confession would free him of that monstrous obsession.' He tapped the bowl on the bedside table with his index finger: 'Tomorrow I'll bring some holy water with me to replace this stuff.'

'He'll notice.'

'He *won't* notice: he's not fully conscious yet. Anyway, it doesn't matter if he notices.'

'He won't want it.'

'It's for his own sake. At present he's in no state to judge what's good for him.'

178

She hesitated and moved closer to his side.

And… what about the bill?'

'It's free, don't worry.'

She nodded. For some reason his magnanimity seemed to move her.

'In any case it's a lot cheaper than ammonia,' she said. 'He's already used half a litre. She cast a despairing look around her: 'And the furniture. It drives me mad when I think about it. I shall have to toil away for six months to get a bit of a shine on it. Is holy water corrosive too?'

He smiled reassuringly: 'No. It costs nothing and it doesn't corrode. And besides that it does a lot of good' 'Yes,' she said with a contented nod of the head, 'the doctors…'

She didn't finish her sentence. The sick man had moved for a second. The deacon's hand motioned for her to be quiet. The bailiff had turned his face towards them, but he could not see them. His eyes were dead and the colour of his iris seemed much paler. His breath must be scorching hot, since his nostrils were not only wide open, but seemed deep and charred.

The housekeeper took a hesitant step closer:

'Sir, can I do anything for you?'

'He can't hear you,' the deacon assured her.

She looked at him quizzically.

'No, he can't see or hear you.'

Her eyes grew wide with fear.

'Is he … dead?' she whispered, grabbing the back of the chair.

'No, he's alive inside. We are dead – for him at least. It's like a dream, an intoxication, a sleep during which his senses are sensitive only to internal reality.'

'Do you mean he will stay like that? I mean: will he never be able to see or hear us? Or…?'

He knew what she meant. She had used the word just now, but it mustn't be repeated. That would give it a dangerous, inexorable power and provoke the threat of what had been enunciated.

He shrugged his shoulders and slowly got up. 'I can't express an opinion, I'm not a doctor. I can only penetrate his soul and make a prognosis about the disease raging there. But since diseases of the body sometimes originate from a disease of the soul, as it probably is in this case, we cannot ignore the connection.' He took the rosary from his pocket: 'Come, let us pray together for the salvation of his soul, which is in desperate straits, to obtain forgiveness for his sins.'

The housekeeper suddenly started and raised her arms in a despairing gesture:

'The milk! Excuse me, Padre, I have to go downstairs: the milk is on the gas.' She made straight for the door, with long strides. The deacon heard her clumping down the stairs. He knelt on the rug in front of the bed and remained alone in the room, together with the bailiff's soul and the invisible slugs.

The spireas under the window had finished flowering and the dull daylight was starting to fade over the hanging bunches. In the sky, low over the hedge and kitchen garden, floated a fragile, gossamer silver fabric, the autumn dew.

The deacon was sitting at the open window. He put his prayer book on the windowsill and looked out for a long time, at the shadows in the presbytery garden. This is one of those evenings when most people die, he thought, but he couldn't say why. One of those evenings that make the heart of person living quietly and introspectively restless and full of premonition, that make him reflect on the beginning and the end, on everything in between that he cannot understand. And on himself, the sinful man, the eternal beginning and the eternal end, the clay jug in which the potter had left a stone.

Soon his thoughts turned to the bailiff, whose fear of death was obviously so great that it kept him alive. Simply through his fear; for those who are small when their last hour has come are also small enough to pass through the eye of a needle. This may be a paralogism - but what other explanation was there? The whole past of the bailiff had obviously been dominated by paralogisms. He

180

had roamed around in the night of unbelief, full of haughty self-deception, and his sinful behaviour had hatched the slugs that were now making his dying such torture. Once, at the beginning of his illness, during one of their long conversations he had maintained that a sinful person was never wholly sinful, and that was true, but he had not found those words in himself. He had read them in the work of the novelist Arthur van Schendel, at the beginning of the moving story 'Angiolino and Spring'. All through his life he had stolen words from others and appropriated them without the slightest sense of shame; all through his life he had chased after other people's ideas, like a dabbler after the banner of a corporation. In so doing he had not only deceived himself, but also God and other people.

The sun, beyond the garden, was shrouded cold and red in evening mist. It grew cold in the room and the deacon got up to close the window. A few seconds later the bell rang. It was like a human voice uttering a cry of pain. The maid showed in the bailiff's housekeeper. The deacon was still standing by the window, with one hand on the back of the chair that he had pushed up to the window and was at that moment just about to pull back. He looked at the woman with curious bewilderment. Her face, he saw, was chalky white and her greying hair seemed to be damp with the fog.

Her scarf, which he had draped loosely over her, fell to the ground. She was about to bend down and pick it up, but she changed her mind halfway and only then did she say what she had to say, quickly and breathlessly, not as quick as the bell, but in the same dominant key:

'Padre, I believe the hour has come. He's nearing the end. Will you please come with me? I…'

'Have you called the doctor?' he asked.

'No, I came straight here. I'll…' She picked up the scarf with a groan. 'I'll come with you right away,' he said.

'I'll go and get the doctor first. Here is the key, then you won't have to wait for me.'

She gave him the key. Suddenly he was reminded of the pretext she had used a few hours before to get out of an urgent duty:

the milk's on the gas, I have to go downstairs. But now the danger was imminent; death took no account of a litre of unboiled milk.

As he prepared everything he might need – the stole, a palm frond, the capsule with the holy oil, the cotton wool – he heard the housekeeper talking to the maid in the hall. The heart and the mouth are communicating vessels, but why isn't the same true of the heart and the soul?

He left the presbytery just after the housekeeper. He walked on hurriedly and in less than two minutes reached the bailiff's house. It was a gloomy old mansion, whose dark-green louvred shutters on the ground floor were almost never opened. It was a house in which a murder might have been or might yet be committed. A house that in fifty or perhaps a hundred years' time, tumbledown and uninhabited, with an ominously creaking floor and a ghostly, monotonous drip-drip of rain in the stairwell, would be given over to the timid and peaceful rule of spiders, millipedes and slugs.

As he turned the key in the lock, he tried to remember the rest of the opening of 'Angiolino and Spring' (Van Schendel had been one of his first loves – how he had rhapsodised over heroes like Tamalone!): 'A sinful person is never wholly sinful, just as a poor person, however abject, is never utterly poor...' It was a beautiful opening, but the end was beautiful too – it was what you could call a meaningful story. Angiolino was resurrection, rebirth, spring itself – but the bailiff was error, self-damnation, the way of destruction and unbelief. So was there no hope for him, who passed Truth by, haughty and with head averted, like the many wealthy people who passed Angiolino by as he put out his hand toward them on the bridge? In the hall he stopped to listen. The cold stone silence came to life. Far away, probably in the neighbours' house, a vacuum cleaner hummed. Was this the sound he had heard before which at the time he had taken for the screech of an automatic garden sprinkler? He went upstairs; the steps creaked louder and louder. Outside the door of the room, where he found himself for the second time today, he stopped again. He turned round, looked down the stairs and saw the depths from where he had climbed up. It made him feel uncertain, since no one knew how far he could climb before falling back into the depths. He stood there and visually calculated the distance to the bottom and it was as if he had time, as if he had come to examine a recovering patient's collection of impaled butterfly specimens. Finally he removed his hat and opened the door gently. A strange silence, totally different from the silence in the rest of the house, forced him backwards. The evening twilight had poured into the room like grey water and the sick man's bed, the mirror-faced wardrobe, the commode and the bedside table floated forlornly between the walls.

On his previous visits he had noticed a lamp between the wardrobe and the door, on a small table, part of a nest. He groped for the switch and turned on the light. The bailiff was lying with his face towards him and was looking him straight in the eye. His mouth had fallen open: a black hole in which the teeth gleamed like knives – the sharp, uneven teeth of a beast of prey. The sharp nose cut the grey face into two halves, one in the light the other in shadow. It was as if he had fallen asleep in an uncomfortable position and had tried to support his head with his hand. His hand, bony and clenched, was indeed underneath his chin. He was sleeping with his eyes open and seemed to be staring straight ahead in terror.

The deacon saw all this without moving. The despondency that came over him was like the onset of a severe attack of guilt. He's not that old, he thought, forty-four. That thought resounded audibly through the room. It was an actual sound, as if he had uttered it; and heard in this way there was something disrespectful about it. But he pulled himself together: good gracious, I'm becoming more involved with this one man who has gone astray than with all my pious parishioners; I know that this is not wrong, since he above all others needs my help and intercession, but it is unfair.

He went to the window and closed the steel-blue curtains. Hurried steps approached in the street, but then receded again. It wasn't the housekeeper, I must do my work, before the doctor comes, he decided. He went back to the bed, with something gnawing at his insides. He closed the dead man's eyes, straightened the head and knelt down, hands together, to do his work.

Then he caught sight of the bedside table and the white glazed bowl. Without knowing why he got up again. The bowl exercised the same attraction on him as a fortune-teller's crystal ball: mysterious and enchanting, one could read a future event in it, which could inspire hope or fear, happiness or sadness.

He stretched out his hand, but immediately withdrew it. He stared in horror at the bowl and his blood froze. 'This is the Devil's work… this is the Devil's work…' he groaned. The bowl was empty, but at the bottom, fat and swollen, lay a slimy black slug.

Apostle Of Artillery

Paul Snoek

I

Since I'm not a Jesuit and so don't pester people at work with the intention of converting them to the Catholic faith, I decided, after a period of idleness and all that entails, to learn the technique of casting a cannon, fanatical as I was about everything that smacked even remotely of the military, Christian spirit of Jesuitism. Whether the manufacture of these utilitarian objects was compatible with an apostolic mission, I leave to the critical discernment of the reader. But in no way could the world accuse me of mendacity, when I pointed out to society at large, using numerous obscure writings, that the Society of Jesus, during the great religious clean-up in Japan, besides performing mass baptisms and pursuing dialect studies, also occupied itself with the forging of cannons, which were indispensable during their conversion work; cannons patented by the Holy See in Rome. It should incidentally be emphasised that at this period the Society of Jesus, in its free time, occasionally helped a French absolute monarch rid himself of his queen, despite the fact that there had been some question of biological contact between the monarch and the spouse in question.

So I wanted to embark on an apostolic mission and chose the manufacture of cannons in preference to the engineering of divorces in royal circles, since the latter are less common in our society than was the case in those days. After all, the cannon had the advantage that its manufacture was edifying, while the arrangement of divorces in royal circles presupposed more destructive and lucrative tendencies on my part. So I decided to learn the art of casting cannons, *ad maiorem dei gloriam adque salutem ecclesiam catholicam, magnam, universam et perpetuam.*

II

The building of my first cannon, my very first, did not, as the reader will be able to establish from what follows, go smoothly. I was scarcely nineteen, young and inexperienced. I began work on 1 April in the year of Our Lord 1955. The day before I had pinched a biro from my youngest sister's pen case and on the back of a mourning card I carefully noted down everything I needed for a successful outcome. My father, a do-it-yourself enthusiast and water-polo player, approved my plan and let me have various tools that he kept in the loft and that dated from the first years of his marriage, when he had knocked together a few cupboards and beds, which although nice, subsequently turned out to be less useful than they should have been. Of course children arrived and the furniture lasted only four months, although the solid hulks were intended for years of use. Despite all my respect for my father I felt I could not hide these facts from the reader, since my father's partial failure was a razor-sharp precedent for me, a lesson for the future. I made an inventory of what I had been given and found myself in the possession of a hammer, a spirit level, a blunt chisel, a hacksaw and half a kilo of gleaming copper rafter nails. In the garden I marked out a space in which I would give vent to my enthusiasm and in a ramshackle chicken run – during the war we had kept chickens and rabbits – I stowed the gear I had inherited from father.

That evening I was a happy man. An uncle, who had heard about my plans, lent me a book by Jules Verne, *The Monster Cannon of Steeltown*, the reading of which did not dampen my energy, since I devoured it at one sitting in the night of 1 April. On the morning of 2 April I rode to Brussels and with my savings and the small amount I had earned by giving a number of talks (on the poet Rodenbach) for a regional broadcasting station, bought the necessary machines and raw materials. I combined three factors in production: nature, capital and labour, in the most advantageous way and when I inspected my workshop that evening, reader, it brought a tear to my eye.

Because I found that I could start work the following morning and was aware of my responsibility, as I admired the materials and machines I had purchased and knew I was the lawful owner of a hydraulic press, a lathe, a furnace, an alternator with automatic voltage control and a company registered in my father's name, since I was still a minor at the time this took place and hence still not legally responsible. I kept to the rules and regulations, even the unjust ones, since in this regard I always follow the example of the great Socrates, who when given the chance to escape nevertheless drained the cup of hemlock to the dregs, saying to those who came to besmirch his good name: 'If the good citizen does not obey the bad laws, the bad citizen will not observe even the good laws.' The following day (it was the third of April) I purchased the booklet *How to Cast a Cannon,* in the series *Making Things at Home*, do-it-yourself guide no. 4, and crossed my Rubicon.

First I dug a trench about thirty metres long, as a mould for the barrel of the cannon. Later I was to regret not having begun with the base, but as I said I was young and inexperienced. I melted bronze and cast the barrel, which I allowed to cool for three days. Then I cast the base according to the same procedure, and when this component had also cooled down, started working on the thing with my father's equipment.

I drilled it through and polished its pitted bronze surface with abrasive paper. Finally I mounted the barrel on the base, but since I did not have a hoist, this manoeuvre was slightly complicated, as you can imagine. Even my patient work was a form of prayer and without joyful resignation my suffering was no missionary work. But even without a hoist everything worked out.

As far as the internal structure was concerned, namely the mechanism that loads and unloads, fires and automatically aims the barrel at the target, I will be brief about this apparatus, since giving too detailed a description would tire the reader unnecessarily and since these purely technical and scientific details fall outside the scope of our story, as the main thing for us is to establish that the cannon was ready for action. For details on the built-in cogwheels, the clinometers, manometers and shell sorting systems, I refer the reader to the writings of the Jesuits active in Japan around 1650. The fact is that the inner mechanism is of little value, compared the apostolic mission, which was my true goal. In short, things were fine and I was a proud man, as proud as Hippodamus of Miletus, when he surveyed the finished harbour of Piraeus.

III

But that's where my troubles began. My original intention had been to donate the cannon to the missionaries in Africa; I was even prepared to pay the shipping costs out of my own pocket, but the local branch of the Society of Jesus informed me by registered post that they had already got wind of my excesses, that they did not appreciate my jokes and that as far as they were concerned I could go ahead and melt down the cannon and sell off the bronze, since financial contributions were always welcome in their missionary fund. They had enough cannons; it was ammunition they were short of. Somewhat confused by this missive, I decided to go on working on my own account, to look for a market and to transfer annually half my income to the account number of the local branch of the Society of Jesus, missionary fund division for the conversion of kaffirs and Zulus, since in their registered letter the order had been kind enough to divulge the account number of their missionary fund.

For a few days I hesitated whether or not to continue with my apostolic mission, since manufacturing ammunition, if I were to change tack, would entail new difficulties. On the one hand there was the experience I had acquired concerning the casting of cannons and accompanying love of the craft; however, on the other hand because of my lack of qualifications in ballistics and the theory of ammunition and also the fact that there was no do-it-yourself manual available on the subject, I decided to suspend production for a while and to look for a customer who would buy my cannon and might be interested in a number of them. I met the man, an Iranian businessman, who had erected medieval monuments all over the world and had use for my merchandise as a decorative element in his field. We entered into a contractual agreement, under which I undertook to supply each month ten miniature cannons in medieval bronze, cannons with a religious aura. He undertook to distribute these items worldwide and payment would be quarterly in the currency of his country and would be transferred via an international exchange bank to my father's account, since as a minor I was still not legally responsible.

I received a fairly large sum as an advance. The manufacturing process went well and I delivered my goods on a monthly basis. The cannons took up two square metres and at the beginning were very much in demand in film and other sophisticated circles, since the Iranian's daughters, who moved in these circles, helped publicise our goods, partly through their attractive appearance, partly through the brochures in impeccable English, which they distributed among the distinguished guests at numerous cocktail and garden parties. So for two years, in my spare time, since I was studying Thomist philosophy, I manufactured cannons, always in bronze – the adjective medieval was intended as an advertising gimmick during our sales campaign in America – cannons, whose religious character, however, varied with the price. The most expensive were those whose barrels were decorated with relics set in gold of mainly European saints: let me make it clear, genuine relics. Most in demand were the sacred relics of Saint Thérèse of Lisieux, Saint Rita, St. John Berchmans, and the Holy Innocents. I once succeeded in picking up a relic of St Ignatius Loyola, but as my suppliers made clear, this was something unique in the history of their business, since such a relic only became available every 269 years. The cannon in which I had inserted built-in music boxes, which when the cannon was fired played Gregorian chants and hymns. The song 'In Lourdes in the mountains, there appeared in a cave…' was my bestseller.

Cheaper still was the cannon with a Perspex barrel, which was transparent as an aquarium and in which tiny fish swam around in healing water from the fountain in Lourdes, symbolising the figure of Jesus as Ichthus, without there being any question of transubstantiation in this case. Cheapest of all were the cannons

whose barrels were decorated with palm fronds, which framed
sayings of the Church Fathers applied to them in Gothic lettering.
I later produced the last type in a smaller size, to allow the less
well-off to have one of our by now world-famous artefacts in their
drawing rooms. It goes without say that my associate also supplied
his goods on credit without a deposit. In brief our products sold like
hot cakes, so that I earned a tidy sum from them, half of which I
paid as promised into the account of the local branch of the Society
of Jesus, missionary fund division for the conversion of kaffirs and
Zulus. After two years' work I became rich and seeing that there was
a future in my business, after having obtained the B.A. degree in
Thomist philosophy, I gave up all further study. At this time I owned
a luxury apartment in the capital and a thatched house at the seaside.
Apart from a Firebird with a seven-speed gearbox I also financed a
hospital in Goa, which every year invited me to spend a few weeks in
the Portuguese enclave, an invitation that I was never able to accept
because of lack of time. In conclusion it should be mentioned that I
received many honours, including the title of Papal Cannon-Founder,
a title that had not been awarded since the end of the seventeenth
century.

IV

One day, arriving in Knokke-Het Zoute, I gave a lift to a hitch-
hiking soldier, who after expressing his humble admiration of my
blue car, discussed artillery with me, a subject for which I had a great
appreciation in view of my manufacturing business and because of
any tips I might be able to pick up for producing new models. The
short conversation with him made me reflect deeply when I got
home. A few days afterwards I decided again to think over my talk
with the soldier, since I had the feeling that the ghost of this rainbow-
coloured young man was still pursuing me. 'Did I get the right end of
the stick?' All my activity had nothing more to do with an apostolic
mission and I had offended the spirit of artillery. Not against religion,
since the ignorant cannot sin, but against artillery.

I wondered whether, having dishonoured bronze, I was still worthy of touching a real cannon; a steel cannon, of flesh and blood. Could I with my sacrilegious hands still operate a cannon? I already saw myself on the battlefield in a blood-soaked uniform, deep in a trench and far from my beloved cannons. An officer acting on orders from above, forbade me to lift so much as a finger in the direction of a cannon, on pain of court martial, execution and an all that entailed. Would I ever be able to clutch the heated barrel of an ant-aircraft gun to my bosom?

I would be granted no glimpse of these wonders.

The next day I surrendered my whole thriving business, warehouses, machines and raw materials, patent and liquid assets included, to the Society of Jesus, which they eagerly accepted, and I withdrew for a long period to my humble abode. I knew my behaviour was reprehensible, and despite the fact that my mother was prone to wishy-washy, insignificant ant-militaristic prejudices, I decided to join the artillery, on the one hand because I wished to impose a penance on myself for my sinful past, on the other hand out of idealism and perhaps also because I was about to be conscripted into the military as part of next year's intake.

For, supposing I had continued with my profane practices, would I still have been able with equal softness to stroke the neck of a horse, the flank of a howitzer? Would I, reader, have been able with equal love to warm the belly of the mortar, and the breast of my beloved?

Clean-Up
Or
The Adventures Of Abdullah And Me

Peter Terrin

One day I received a short note, saying I was being sent for a job. I examined the envelope for the date of the postmark. How long had the letter taken to reach me? I didn't know when I was to start. It may have been yesterday. I couldn't tell anything from the note or the envelope.

In the afternoon I thought it appropriate to take a walk along the municipal canal, to renew my acquaintance with it. But the weather was changeable, with wind and rain; there was no sign of a boat, not even a motor launch. Whenever I got the chance, I looked into the water for a long time. The more intense the light, the greener and less transparent the surface: I noticed that even then.

By five o'clock I'd got pretty hungry, fresh air is good for you. It's nice here, I thought, as I hung my jacket on the empty hat rack. There was a lady sitting by the window, at which she was blowing the smoke of her cigarette in thick clouds. In front of her on the check tablecloth stood a tall, jolly-looking glass. I chose a seat where she couldn't help noticing me. I had something to celebrate, and so ordered soup and a main course. The waiter brought me a spoon and a basket of bread. He asked me what I wanted to drink. I thought about it, but wasn't thirsty. When I told him, he stood at my table for a moment as if he couldn't believe it. Yet I was only telling the truth, because I really wasn't thirsty.

In the middle of the night I was wide awake. I just lay there till the alarm went off. I shaved at the washbasin in the corner of my room and carefully combed my hair. No one in the building seemed to be awake yet when I closed the downstairs door.

I had the letter with me, neatly tucked into its slit envelope, although in the event of a complaint the document could prove nothing to my advantage. I followed the route I had sketched out yesterday evening on a scrap of paper. The city was preparing for a busy day with lots of tourists. Outside every shop there was water on the pavement and it smelled nice and clean.

Where the canal widened, tucked away behind a shallow curve, I saw a jetty with some motor launches moored at it. They were all the same orange colour. Some steps had been built in the earth bank, leading to a shed on the quay. The shed, a converted container, was orange too.

I couldn't find a door, only a doorway.

A man at a small desk looked at me unhappily.

'We'll have to do something about your hair,' he said.

A coffee-maker was bubbling away on the desk. Against another wall of the shed, on a bench, sat a foreigner. He was an Arab. He was wearing orange trousers and jacket.

'You're now working for the Sanitation Department,' said the man at the small desk accusingly. 'Don't forget it.'

There was silence for a while. I'd carefully combed my hair this morning. Perhaps the man meant that my hair had grown rather long. In that case he was right. I bided my time and said nothing – I had nothing to say. Both men surveyed me in exactly the same way. They showed no interest in the coffee. The man at the desk, the boss, had shaved carelessly, and I could see black hairs on his cheeks that he had overlooked for a day or two, judging by their length. The Arab smelled of onion or some such thing.

Finally the boss told me the Arab was called Abdullah, and that we would be working together from now on. I replied by giving my name, and also said, as we were shaking hands, that I thought Abdullah was a funny name. I said it sounded to me like a swearword. He exchanged a glance with the boss, got up off the bench and left the shed. I resolved solemnly never to address my new workmate by his name.

193

Our launch was no great shakes. It was an old rubber dinghy, with a motor scarcely bigger than a biscuit tin. There was a pool of water at my feet, which was obviously a permanent fixture. Abdullah went forward and sat on the inflated side and I was to operate the rudder, a stick with a slippery handle. The boss had decided this, because Abdullah was younger and broader-shouldered than I was. It would be easier for him to scoop up the rubbish, the wet rubbish, sometimes heavy as lead, than for me. That was quite possibly true, but still I said that I'd never steered a boat in my life. At that the boss laughed for the first time, and poured himself a cup of coffee. He said we wouldn't be putting to sea. Then he said it was easier than riding a bike.

It was a very long time since I'd been on a bike, but I couldn't remember any problems. When we got onto the municipal canal, it turned out not to be as simple as expected. But all in all, I quickly got the hang of steering, and I also soon got to know the idiosyncrasies of the launch and the motor. I noticed immediately that the motor occasionally spluttered if I went flat out for a while. Because of the blunt prow we lost a lot of speed. As if someone were hitting the brake. I impressed on Abdullah that he must never stand up when I was going full speed ahead, since he might fall in the water. He nodded, keeping his eyes focused straight ahead, at the surface of the water. Again I trained my gaze on Abdullah for possible clues.

Most litter was found under the long jetties and landing stages that the city had built for tourists. Once upon a time the canals were kept out of sight, as they were open sewers. That had changed meanwhile, and the water even appeared to flow. The waterfront now offered relaxation and recreation; on a refurbished quay, a jetty or a landing stage. Nevertheless the water was muddy green.

There were two long poles lying in the boat: one had a formidable hook on the end, the other a nylon catch net. On that first day we retrieved mainly broken branches from the canal as well as small dead animals or birds, which stank terribly. Abdullah wasn't so much bothered by the stink as he was sitting at the front, with his head in the wind. I stuffed the bag of carcasses as far as possible under the other rubbish. When we arrived back at the shed in the late afternoon, the boss said the worst was over; the last clean-up had been three months ago, which explained the large number of carcasses. As from today Abdullah and I would clean the municipal canals every day during the summer, starting at six in the morning. We wouldn't have much trouble with carcasses in future, he said.

On my way home I bought some potatoes, which I would boil later. My mood was pleasantly light and I walked slower than usual, though not as slowly as the tourists. The season had started quite early: you really saw them in every part of town. The fact that people walked the streets half-undressed never ceased to surprise me.

The sun had made my room very hot. I undressed and washed, and then washed my clothes and hung them to dry over the back of the chair. I loved the smell of household soap. I got the clippers out of the drawer and cut my hair, especially my neck hairs. Then I peeled the potatoes. After I'd cooked them I let them cool off a little, as they had no flavour when hot. I used very little salt, and with the plate of potatoes in my hand I sat at the open window and looked at the street below. There was a lot of activity. I saw people on their way to restaurants or shows, most of them elegantly dressed in light, loose-fitting clothes, women in clicking heels. After nine the street quietened down; loving couples strolled along the pavement hand in hand, silent and content. When the unpleasant streetlights came on, I went over to my bed, lay down and started reading. It was a gripping book about an epidemic with lots of innocent victims. As a result at about eleven I washed my hands and face again thoroughly, and brushed my teeth. Shortly afterwards I fell asleep.

The next morning the boss, to my surprise, was sitting in the shed drinking coffee. It was five to six. Although he seemed to me to be fully awake and I was sitting directly opposite him waiting for Abdullah to arrive, he said nothing about my haircut. Perhaps I now met the standards in force in the Sanitation Department, and this required no further comment. Whenever I shot a sideways glance at the puffing coffee-maker, he always looked up, but didn't offer me coffee and said nothing about my short hair.

I shook Abdullah's hand politely again, as we'd only known each other since yesterday. The boss remained silent, although the Arab had shown up at least four minutes late. It occurred to me that he might have been working there longer than me. Perhaps he and the boss had come to an understanding.

I felt a lot better, the moment I had taken my place in the motorboat, the motor roared and we left the jetty behind us. At first the canal was wide and windy, and we seemed insignificant and useless; but after about a hundred metres we made our way into the narrow sections between the old inner-city buildings as if we were on a special mission. I learned that the canals we were cleaning had a total length of 18 kilometres. Abdullah and I were not in any great hurry, we were expected to work until four in the afternoon; at least, we were paid up to that time.

'Have you got any family?' asked Abdullah, after a while.

I thought that was a funny question, since everyone has family. I replied that I didn't have any family that I met regularly, and apart from that I didn't feel like having a conversation. I liked gliding undisturbed across the glittering water, close to the chunting of the motor; I also liked the view. In some parts of town we were completely invisible, whereas we had a free view of silent medieval cellars and other storerooms, where hardly anyone ever ventured these days. People on bridges generally took no notice of us, although Abdullah liked being admired as he was handling the hook, and stood up as if he were a primitive hunter.

Abdullah said that he had a lot of relatives.

The silence that followed this statement made it appear ambiguous, as if what he actually meant was that, in his view, he had too many. I knew that Arabs as a rule had large families, and I could well imagine his discomfort.

We had taken off our jackets, as the sun was boiling and the water didn't offer much relief. I put Abdullah in his early twenties;

196

he was wearing a vest, snow white, which contrasted strikingly with his dark skin.

'I live at my cousin's place,' he said. 'My uncle has a house, and he lets me share a room with my cousin. My cousin is two years older than me. He thinks I should refuse to work for the Sanitation Department, because it's dishonourable.'

Abdullah had a moustache, no more than a slight shadow on his upper lip, which was a constant reminder of the boy in the man. What's more, he spat compulsively in all directions with pursed lips. Blobs of bubbly spittle that floated on the green water.

I didn't go into his cousin's comment, but I did find it an odd remark. Did his cousin mean that all work in the Sanitation Department was dishonourable? Or only dishonourable for his family? Or for Arabs in general? I decided not to express an opinion on the matter, which after all was none of my business. Besides, Abdullah hadn't asked me a question.

We worked on in silence.

Half an hour or so later Abdullah said he was a sinner, and cast a brief glance over his shoulder to measure my reaction. He said that he received letters from his father in Algeria, forbidding him to smoke or drink alcohol and telling him to pray at the right times. Then he said above all he wanted to be a good Muslim, so that his family could be proud of him. But his cousin often took him along in his nice car with loud music with other guys, and things got out of hand, I thought it was pretty childish of a twenty-year-old to tag along like that, but then I didn't know any other young Arabs, and ultimately it didn't surprise me. On the other hand I couldn't care less. I repeated that I didn't feel like talking and told him to sit down, for his own safety.

The next day Abdullah didn't appear in the shed until ten past six. The boss made no comment, not even when I said that my workmate was ten minutes late. He looked me straight in the eye in annoyance and then said that he was in charge here. I asked him if I too could come in at ten past tomorrow morning. He said: 'No.' It seemed to me that he tolerated Abdullah's behaviour because he was a young Arab; I wasn't sure and so said nothing more about it.

The boss said that he had received a letter from the council. It seemed that the historic city centre was being plagued by the droppings of countless pigeons. The situation was untenable and in the long term might do serious damage to the tourist industry. We were instructed to destroy every nest that we could reach from the water. Meanwhile the pigeons had begun a second breeding period, the ideal moment to act.

It had struck me that every hole or opening in the quayside was occupied by a pigeon. By the waterside they were quiet and safe. They always looked at us unperturbed, cooing deeply, even when we came very close. According to the council they were a flying plague.

Abdullah and I had our hands full that day.

At the first nest we were awkward. The mother pigeon made a high-pitch cry of lament that oddly enough seemed to emanate not from her beak, but rather from the top of her head. All in all I thought it was an inoffensive creature, which had done nothing but follow the call of nature. At the same time I made the point that this was an emergency and that our intervention did not really constitute a threat to the survival of the urban pigeon as a species. As was his habit Abdullah wielded the hook. The pigeon got up from its nest but did not fly away; flapping wildly it tried to dodge the probe. It had two chicks, still featherless and blind, which screamed at their mother with their disproportionately huge beaks open wide. Abdullah was not very persistent. He withdrew the long pole and said that he couldn't help thinking about his father in Algeria: he wasn't sure if his religion permitted this. He took up his forward position, in his usual place. The pigeon nestled half across her chicks. It became silent, as the water lapped irregularly against the ancient brick. On the jetty opposite sat a piebald cat, attracted by the commotion.

I got up and asked Abdullah for the long pole with the hook on it. He peered at his hand as its existence had only just got through to him. Then he said that there was no need, and that he'd take care of it. While I drove off the mother pigeon and pulled the nest into the canal, he said he would pray for the birds. The chicks sank screeching under the water; I fished out the unsightly carcasses and put them in a plastic bag. The pigeon crawled back into the hole and hopped restlessly back and forth, head nodding.

Only in a few nests had the eggs hatched. Abdullah worked with the hook and I caught the whole lot in the net, so that we didn't pollute the water. Eventually the work went quite smoothly; Abdullah again spat in all directions and swore forcefully.

The next day his breath smelled of alcohol and he looked shattered. A little later he blamed everything on his cousin. He had it easy, Abdullah claimed, because his father, his own father's youngest brother, wasn't nearly as religious. He simply wore a suit, not a djellaba. Besides, his greengrocer's shop was doing very well, and over the years he had adopted a lifestyle in stark contrast to Algerian custom. His father wasn't aware of this, either no one dared tell him or he simply refused to believe it when any news did reach him. Everyone knew that the old man would never leave his country, so everyone left things as they were. But his uncle did keep his father informed about Abdullah, as had been promised years ago. Exactly what he said or wrote was unknown to Abdullah, but it was a fact that the letters from Algeria invariably upbraided him. While his cousin of all people was constantly leading him into temptation. In Algeria, said Abdullah, his poor father had no idea how difficult life was here for a young Muslim like him. His lament was beginning to get up my nose, and I said he was a hypocrite; I said I was certain that there were plenty of young people who had problems with the strict rules of their religion, but didn't for that reason always blame someone else, when they proved weak. Abdullah looked over his shoulder, with his offended look. Because I was speaking the truth, he said nothing in reply.

Nest-clearance became a routine job: I scarcely slowed down, and in one fluid movement we brought the booty aboard. If there was still life in the plastic bags, we hit them briefly with the poles. Sometimes at about midday, in parts of town where people had a good view of us, there were sounds of protest and we were booed, but we were doing it, after all, for their convenience.

It got hotter every day. The water reflected the dazzling heat, as if we were not on a municipal canal, but in the desert. The pigeons did not appear to have any problem with the heat: they showed astonishing persistence, since usually they had built a new nest two days after our clean-up, albeit without eggs. To begin with we let the pigeons brood on their empty nests, but after a while, when we checked for eggs a second time, we cleared away all the rubbish anyway.

The continuing heat made itself felt in the increased number of cans and bottles bobbing in the water. Abdullah and I worked in unpleasant conditions. I stopped the motor launch under every bridge, so that we could escape for a moment from the brutal sun, and I wiped the drops of sweat out of my eyebrows. I soon grew tired, simply because of the temperature, while Abdullah, as an Arab, coped with it much better than I did; he did not want to get behind and went on working, because his cousin was waiting for him at the shed in his open-topped car.

In those weeks I closed the curtains in my room at about eight, and went to bed. If I'd wanted to read a book, there was no need to turn on a lamp, the evening sky was so light, and the building was still full of sounds made by its occupants, but that made no difference to me: I fell asleep exhausted.

One evening I had undressed and had just slipped between the sheets, when I heard the doorbell. I lay there and listened carefully: again my exact code sounded: three long, one short. My upstairs neighbour didn't dare knock at my door, although that would be easier, and always went all the way downstairs to ring, whenever his cat had got lost. The animal, ancient and ailing, let no opportunity go by to hide, preferably in some out of the way corner; to die quietly, I assumed. Although the cat had never yet ensconced itself in my room, my neighbour always checked with me first. He would stand in the door and say that the situation was very unfortunate, with which I agreed. Then he wondered, as if he were asking me, what he was supposed to do with the poor creature – he was at his wit's end. If I replied that he should have the cat put to sleep, he shrank back as though I had done away with the cat and he was looking for a clue. I said that he was just too compassionate, and that it would be better to be brave, especially with a beloved pet, but that struck no chord with him. He turned away in dismay and then went on searching the stairwell; later I usually heard sobbing in his room, which could mean either that he had found the cat or he hadn't. I always hoped the agony was over once and for all; I disliked his visits.

I got out of bed, poked my head between the curtains and looked down out of the open window. I couldn't see anyone at the front door and assumed that my neighbour would shortly be knocking, which happened exactly at that moment. Too late to get dressed, I unbolted the door, pulled the sheets up to my chin and said aloud: 'Come in.'

It wasn't my neighbour but Abdullah who appeared in the doorway. I didn't say hello because I didn't understand what he was doing here and had expected my upstairs neighbour. He asked if he could please talk to me, because it was important. I said that in that case it would be best if he came in and shut the door. I hoped he wouldn't spit in my room, purely out of habit. He was wearing a purplish vest and a flashy chain, which I didn't think suited him and probably belonged to his cousin. We had never met outside working hours at the Sanitation Department. The boss must have given him my address. My room was small for two people, and Abdullah was standing uncertainly by the wardrobe. Clothes were hanging to dry over the chair by the washbasin, so that he finished up half sitting on my bed, by my feet. His presence was very annoying and I was sorry I had invited him in.

He said he'd received a letter from his father in Algeria, a letter containing bad news. It struck me that I was always careful not to trouble anyone, and consequently really appreciated not being bothered by anyone, not by my upstairs neighbour and not by

Abdullah, and I told him exactly that. But that didn't put the Arab off. On the contrary, with an affectionate smile he maintained that he had sought me out precisely for that reason, because with me he at least knew who he was dealing with. I found that a confusing answer to my request, especially when he said that I was the only person who really understood him; without pausing for breath he told me that his father had found a wife for him, in Algeria. He would have to return to his home village and marry a girl he didn't know, someone chosen by his father. Up till then I had heard only of girls being forced into marriage, whereas there were obviously also young men involved, who were not necessarily acting of their own free will. But that was never talked about, as though it was less traumatic for young men. Be that as it may, I wasn't familiar with their culture and wasn't very surprised by what I heard about it from Abdullah.

He told me about the girl, summarising the vague descriptions given by his father in his letter. The house that the married couple would move into was only a stone's throw from his parents' home. Abdullah leant on his thighs and stared intently at the worn carpet, as if the rest of his life were passing in front of his eyes. I had no idea what he expected of me after this confession, I was lying naked under my sheets and it was only out of polite sympathy with his lot that I said nothing about how annoyed I was that in a little while I would certainly have to read for an hour to calm down and get some sleep, when I was dead tired. However, not long afterwards Abdullah got up; visibly relieved he shook my hand and thanked me for listening. Perhaps over-eagerly I asked when he was returning to Algeria.

The next morning I was sitting in the shed with the boss, waiting for Abdullah to arrive, when I asked him straight out why he'd disclosed my address. He looked up listlessly and said: 'Because Abdullah asked for it.' I had the distinct impression that he had no idea what I was getting at. I doubted whether I could explain it to him.

During the days following the visit nothing seemed to have changed; Abdullah said nothing about his forced marriage, and babbled on all day about trips or incidents with his cousin. It seemed to me that he enjoyed thinking about the near future, to fill his life with trivialities and petty emotional problems. It made me impatient, especially as other members of the family gradually came up; I wasn't in the least interested in his aunt, who after years of trying still couldn't get a certain type of cake to turn out right. Fortunately there was the roar of the outboard motor, which wiped out many of his stories, and I helped him look for litter, so that we kept working.

There was no let-up in the summer, the days were hazy with heat. I felt dazed, because I found it hard to get to sleep at nights. One afternoon, near the marina, where the canal was wide, I looked up from the dreamy play of the light on the surface of the water, to the silence in our boat: Abdullah had gone, and the motor had cut out.

I wasn't sure if I was fully awake. I turned round in the direction we had come from. The situation struck me as so exceptional that I tried to reconstruct the morning to see whether I'd perhaps set off without the Arab. In my mind I saw myself sitting in the shed with the boss, but I couldn't distinguish this morning from all the others. I started on the usual route, and had gone a couple of hundred metres, when I thought of the tennis ball between my feet. Two angry coots had been pecking at the yellow ball against the bank, and for a laugh Abdullah had scooped everything up, while the coots went on pecking imperturbably. Now lots of other memories surfaced, more or less up to the time I fell into a daydream. Abdullah had definitely been in the boat. I looked into the green water around the rubber dinghy. Because of the strong light it was hard to see more than a few centimetres down. Obliquely in front of the boat the strong undercurrent of a discharge of sewage made the canal as smooth as a mirror. Abdullah must have slid into the water gently, head first, or else the splash would have attracted my attention. Perhaps he was standing upright when the motor spluttered and cut out. By now it was pointless to jump in after him; he was caught in the churning undertow, and had been for quite some time.

I restarted the motor. I knew from experience that bodies

did not float straight up to the surface, and that I would find the Arab in a few days' time. I saw no reason to take the short route back to the shed: the long way round wasn't that much longer and there was lots of work to do.

I soon began to enjoy the work, though it was hard. It was a relief to be skimming the surface of the canal by myself, finally rid of Abdullah. The work was fiddly, yet I had the feeling that I was only losing a limited amount of time compared with a two-man team. I imagined that the boss would be interested in that idea. I worked up a sweat, hoping for a future without a mate.

I moored the boat at ten to four. Pleased with my efforts, I went down the steps to the shed. The boss was immediately curious about Abdullah's absence. I stood at his desk and told him everything. I told him about the spluttering of the motor, about the spot in the canal where sewer discharges deep underwater. The boss was hot, and shifted about uncomfortably on his chair. I told him I hadn't seen anything, and that I was in a bit of a daze because of the shimmering water. Then I said that I had warned the Arab, but that five minutes later he had ignored them. I said his father was going to force him into a marriage and that his cousin thought the Sanitation Department was dishonourable. I told him about the times when he had called himself a sinner, and added that he was now free once and for all of such feelings.

The boss suddenly seemed to remember something. He hurriedly got up and went outside through the doorway. On the edge of the quay he looked out over the jetty and the municipal canal. Then he walked right round the orange container. Back in the shed he sat down in his chair and asked: 'Where's Abdullah?'

I said that he must be underwater, somewhere around the marina, in the deep section where the sewer discharges. I had just told him that, but I could well understand his confusion.

The boss grabbed for the phone, while he asked me excitedly for the exact spot, the street he could direct the emergency services to. I answered his question, but felt obliged to mention that the Arab had disappeared five hours ago.

'Five hours ago,' repeated the boss. He put the receiver on the hook and stared strangely at my face.

I assured him that despite this morning's incident the cleaning of the canal had been completed, and in exactly the same time. When he did not react and kept staring at me, I said I wasn't frightened of hard work, especially if in future I could work without a certain annoying colleague. 'Besides,' I concluded, 'this is a saving for the Sanitation Department.'

He picked up the telephone again. I heard him asking someone to come urgently to the shed. As we waited in silence I thought the boss would offer me coffee, but he seemed too distracted for that.

A little later two policemen arrived. They were wearing smart, dark-blue uniforms and caps with shiny badges. They asked me for my name. One of the policemen wrote it down it in a notebook with squared paper and a red margin. Then the other policemen said: 'What exactly happened?' I was hoping that the boss would say something, since I had only just told him everything. Nevertheless the boss also waited expectantly for my reply, as if he wanted to hear the whole story again.

I gave the policemen a dutiful account of my experiences with the Arab. I started with our first meeting in this place, overlooking no detail. I told them about his father, cousin and aunt, and said that he had also come unannounced and disturbed me in my room to tell me about his forced marriage. I said that, on his own admission, he was a sinner, and that I had warned him. I mentioned the powerful undercurrent of the sewer water, in which one could get hopelessly caught up. I said that bodies automatically came up to the surface after a few days. I said that it might have been deliberate, but I didn't really believe that. I said that it was most probably an accident, and that it any case it was a release for everyone, for his family, for me and not least for Abdullah. I told them everything as clearly as possible, and yet the two policemen looked at me as if they did not understand, as if I were speaking a foreign language.

The notebook, in which only my name had been written down, was snapped shut. Then the other policeman said I must come with them.

The White Vase

Felix Timmermans

The world lay on my heart like a heavy weight, and I was forced to abandon human company in order to give expression to the workings of my soul in some silent place. The time had come when it was languishing, exhausted and stifled amid all the rottenness of society, and yearned to enjoy a wholesome life of its own. I left for an extended stay in a Trappist monastery, which I knew was located in the wide, flat, arid heathlands, with open horizons all around like the sea.

I had been there a few days; but how those had had actually rolled by in the well of time I could no longer say. The brightness of the third day too was fading into darkness without my having undertaken any action, when as the sun set I realised I was a completely changed man, and that a strange mood had arisen in me so simply, so imperceptibly, that it seemed as if I had always been like this.

Had these two days of prayer and silence freed my soul of its worldly burden, so that it only now made itself felt?

A strange, nameless feeling had arisen in me, a kind of unconscious terror of something far away, whose tangible presence I nevertheless felt in myself and all around me. I tried to push it away, but I was fooling myself, because the thing was lodged in my body like the blood in my heart, and it began to spread, like the mist that rises from the meadows at evening. I became afraid of what surrounded me. I suddenly felt the finiteness of the country in which I stood so utterly lost and alone. The bare sandy heath, dotted only sparsely with wild cypress trees, stretched endlessly into the distance, far, far away until it stood out dark and sharp as gorse against the pale sky. Neither woods nor towers awakened any hope of continuing human habitation; it was as if the world ended right there and I myself became the boundary of human life. And very low overhead were thick, heavy banks of dark-blue clouds. Only when the resonant bell of the monastery had stopped ringing did I notice its sound, and as it hung silently in its distant tower, a sudden arresting silence descended on the countryside. This caught my attention, and I strained to hear that silence, and I heard nothing, nothing, nothing at all, an unimaginable silence. Because I was feeling so anxious, I began searching for sound. At first in the distance, for the barking of a dog, the rumble of a train, but nothing came from afar, there too things were in the thrall of that strange motionlessness of sound, and the cypress trees were stuck there like iron skittles, the dry, prickly wands of gorse thrust from the ground as if petrified; if one had moved around me, I would have heard, so motionless was the silence and no wind, not a breath came, and I waited; but nothing came, everything was held down by that great power, hitherto unknown to me.

My own heart stood still. I wanted to break the silence with a cry, a scream, but it was choked in my throat, like a soap bubble bursting.

Was that eternal motionlessness preparing to explode at any moment in a thousand-fold boom of thunder?

Oh, it weighed on my soul like a stone, that unending plain. It made me close my eyes and I became so afraid that I started and hurried away to the monastery...

Only as I stood beneath the monastery gates did I dare look round, and there, right ahead of me, in the centre of the gloomy avenue of poplars, very low on the horizon, was a half moon, ungainly and blood-red.

When I arrived in the cold church, the monks, in their richly draped white habits were praying in silence, and one brother was just lighting a long candle, which dotted half the mysterious darkness with a fiery flower, and the eternal sanctuary lamp, floating in red glass, brushed a very thin stripe of pink on to the Gothic vaults. Three monks in brown habits each grasped a bell rope and began pulling; booming sounds rang out above my head from the tower and soared away across the mysterious evening countryside. The church boomed with them. And now the monks started praying aloud in Latin.

The prayers were chanted. Rapid words were mumbled, at times sustained for longer, at times abrupt, but always equally dry, without surges or swells, and it went on and on, and as it grew it became repugnant, and increased like something that would never stop and would continue for ever. It was as though a single person were praying; eventually one forgot the monks and it was nothing but an accumulation of hollow words in the useless dark. It was as if these eighty monks were one creature with one soul and one thought, with one heart and one will; like a machine with various cogs operated by a leaden hand. It troubled my heart, and I thought of the night before me. My room was down an endless white corridor of the deserted wing of the monastery, where I had to spend the night completely alone. I was terrified of something that I felt intensely, but could not define. I had the impulse to go home at once. But I was unsure of the way and the nearest station was over an hour from the monastery. I was about to smother my terror with prayer, when the praying suddenly stopped and an oppressive silence ensued, which fortunately did not last long.

The monks were now standing facing the altar with their arms opened wide and stretched out towards the image of the Virgin Mary, Greek in its loveliness, that stood above the altar in the feeble glow of the candles like an approaching vision of a holy twilight. Suddenly the stops of the organ opened and gave forth sweet, calm tones, which gently filled the church one by one, creating a limpid song that made me forget my fear. And with a clear, warm voice the cantor sang: *Salve*. It was heavy with inner tenderness and the other monks immediately responded in unison with *Regina*, and sang the sacrosanct words of the old hymn. The air trembled with sublime love and divine observance, with a deeply-hidden undertone of extreme suffering. The song swelled and bent, surging to and fro like the song of the sea. It was as though from time to time a wind caught the sounds, carried them up to heaven, and descended again when the time was ripe. And it mounted in ecstasy like the flames of a fire, and the organ mingled and wreathed and sprinkled its full-grown clear notes among them, extending the song higher and firmer in its beauty. It was like a host of white flowers, blossoming one by one around the mysterious silence where God himself dwelt.

I had forgotten my unpleasant mood; tears trickled down my cheeks and I expected, with the simplicity of a child, that the image of the Virgin, affected by all that profound devotion, would move as a sign that our prayers had been heard.

Suddenly a silence descended on the church, the monks were absorbed in inward prayer. The time was approaching when I would have to go to my room; my heart stood still at the prospect. And the monks shuffled mysteriously down the long corridors, the tiny candle was snuffed out, the doors closed and the church was left in cold silent darkness, in which the blood-red sanctuary lamp with its eternal glow flickered like an eye opening and shutting.

Without kneeling I left the dais and stood in the long white corridor. I stood there; in the far distance, lit by a reddish candle flame, was a large, ugly statue of the Virgin Mary. Then I crept down the corridor to my room, which I plunged wildly into. I bolted the door, lit the candle, and slumped into a chair, feeling half relieved of the great burden weighing on my heart. I was about to breathe a sigh of relief, but when I saw the white candlelight falling on my pale and bony hands, I became alarmed and again such a great silence descended, but now it was as though it were tangible, cloaking and enclosing everything. It was as if the whole room were brim-full of water that was forcing me into the chair and my arms down onto its arms. I tried to laugh at my fearfulness and stupidity, but I couldn't because I could feel that there was something too serious behind it. After all I was completely alone in that wide wing of the monastery where holy relics were stored, filled with bones, skeletons and skulls. Yet it was not those dead things that I was afraid of; my heart was seized by such a sense of doom, which may always be present, but which can only manifest itself in silence and solitude. I did not dare follow my thoughts to their logical conclusion, but they kept recurring, gaining in clarity: I would die here tonight... I would have liked to go outside, sleep on the bare, frightening heath, but I was sitting here as in a secure prison, the warders of which lay dead. I was so convinced of my powerlessness in the face of what was imminent, that I abandoned all hope and no longer believed I would live to see morning. I no longer dared move; I felt cold and bathed in sweat all over my body. I thought neither of home or of my parents or other things that I had left behind for ever, it was as if they had never existed and I had been sitting here like this forever; I had eyes only for the things around me. Next to me on the table, covered in a white cloth, was a porcelain vase with two lilies in it. It caught my attention because I suddenly noticed its beauty. I admired its gently swelling shape. It was so pure and elegant and was undecorated. It was nothing but a curving line upwards from base to the top, where it opened into a smooth straight neck.

The candlelight played beautifully around it, splashing luxuriantly down on it in the centre, fading almost into invisibility on either side. Right in the middle the light continued to penetrate, brushed the back of the vase, where it cast a luminous shadow, a white shadow on the table. I wanted to possess that vase. And that calm beauty, which kept to a single line, made me forget my horrid thoughts. Then I noticed that everything in my room was white: the wall, the closed curtains of my bed, the vase, the table. All that whiteness seemed to wrap my warm heart in snow and I looked for something dark. My eyes moved towards the window; there were white curtains over this too, but one had been drawn and revealed a coal-black window pane. I sprang to my feet in amazement: there at the window was an ugly man's head with a wild beard and huge eyes, which gave off a deathly yellow gleam. I was about to scream, when I saw that my anxious face was reflected in the pane. Now I could no longer control it, everything was conspiring to make me more afraid, even my own image. I blew out the light, and too cowardly to get undressed, jumped into bed with ruff collar, stockings and all, and hid under the sheets.

And now I felt satisfied and without fear, as if all that unpleasantness were entering me from outside and was being excluded by the cover, but again that did not last long; I was gasping for breath, and lifted the covers a fraction, I felt the cool air approaching, while I listened. There was a deep silence in my room, but in the corridor I could hear the deep ticking as if the large clock I knew was there; I was greatly startled when I heard that this noise was growing louder and louder until it was no longer ticking, but the steps of someone slowly coming closer. The person came to my door; then the sound stopped and began again, but returned the way it had come; it slowly retreated until in the distance it again assumed the sound of the ticking of the clock on whose face death was swinging a scythe.

I soon set out to discover what these steps actually were, since I was not dreaming; I pinched my cheeks very hard; no I wasn't dreaming; were the steps perhaps those of a monk, coming to listen to see if I were asleep? It couldn't be anyone else, as there was no one in that wing of the monastery. I was about to reassure myself with that thought, when again I heard the usual tick-tock changing into the same step, again, like before, coming slowly closer. Now I no longer knew what to think. It was definitely not a human being, since the sound of the steps, rising and then merging back into the ticking of the clock, was far too strange for that. So what was it...? The power of death that was to come for me in person tonight... The power of death that as it walked down the white corridor was waiting for the exact time to throttle me? My heart pounded like the banging of a child's frightened fist on a dark door. I listened, but only ticking reached my ears. I suddenly became convinced that the steps, returning a third time, would finish their work. I shuddered. I now felt the finality of what I had thought; I knew I was so helpless, so insignificant in the face of that great power. I would have to die here, very soon, so far from home in the night, in a monastery full of silent monks! The other facts about which my presentiment had always proved true, surged up and strengthened my own perceptions. I listened, things were the same in the corridor and suddenly a lucid thought went through my brain: I might just have time before the steps returned to creep into the adjacent room and so deceiving the *thing* that was about to return; *it*, not finding me here, might stop looking further. This resolution gave me very little hope, but made me laugh, since something that is bound to happen to you will happen in any case, with no regard for ocean depths or heavenly heights. On the other hand I knew that we can sometimes turn around a predetermined life with a simple gesture. I got up, picked up my slippers and went into the lonely corridor from my dark room and closed the door again extremely carefully. Then I looked down the corridor, which was as lugubrious and mysterious as it had been just now. The mysteriousness, which was identified with the corridor, seemed to have become tangible. And the candle in front of the statue of Our Lady lit it and the clock gave it a sound; yet there was no sign of that other *thing*; still that *something* could be heard, but not seen – perhaps it was standing peering at the end of my life with great gleaming cat's eyes. I felt unsteady on my feet in my dismay, but suddenly plucked up my courage and went to the other room, bolted the door and pushed the first chair I could find in front of it. I looked for the bed and again hid beneath the sheets, but now curled up, hands clasped over my ears and praying. But I did not illumine the words of the prayers either with my feelings or thoughts. I did nothing but think, think of the thing that was approaching and that I had tried to fool, and filled with intense fear I awaited the outcome. The thoughts stampeded through my head like maddened goats in the night; I shivered and the sweat ran from my head and arms, it trickled and sometimes tickled, but I did not wipe it off, I no longer dared move: only now and then, when it became stiflingly hot, did I raise my elbow a little for fresh air. It continued, on and on as if two days of light and dark were passing over me. I dared not take my hands from my ears; I did not want to hear a thing, anything. And so I lay there waiting in the dreadful uncertainty whether death would find me or not. And I lay there even longer cringing with terror, until I suddenly turned my head to the side and raised a corner of the bedclothes. I don't know how, but suddenly my blood, which seemed to have solidified in my veins, began to flow and boil like the sea. I had seen a patch of faint grey daylight. The scant light, scarcely visible, drove out my fear, and I jumped out of bed full of happiness like someone raised from the dead. Look! The first glow of day was appearing beyond the world. I laughed with joy, and began to think it was just the darkness that had provoked all those gruesome thoughts

The bell in the tower struck two-thirty. So everyone was still sleeping their monks' sleep. So I would have to wait before I could go outside. I was about to sit on a chair when I became curious and wanted to see the abandoned room. God knows what had happened there. My God, the door of the room was wide open!... I went closer, and a violent gust of air struck me in the face; look, the window was wide open too! I went in, God! – on the white sanded planks the beautiful vase lay smashed to smithereens, while the grey daylight crept over it. The stately lilies seemed to be buried under it, with their calyxes crumpled and bruised. Only the base of the beautiful vase remained in the centre of the table!

For all my deep astonishment I felt inundated with happiness; that open door, that open window and that broken vase! Oh, my God! I knew exactly what had happened! My presentiment had been correct! And suddenly the bells rang out in all their bronze richness! From far away shuffling and scuffing approached; the monks had got up, and I waited for the kitchen monk of the closed order to come and prepare my breakfast in the kitchen. When I heard him turn the key in the lock of the gate, I rushed downstairs to tell him what had happened. He was astonished to see me so early, but I explained everything, my premonition, my terror, the changing of rooms and the dreadful discovery of the beautiful white vase. The dear man was completely carried away by my story, and when I had finished he said, shaking his head and with his eyes closed, with great conviction: 'It was the devil.'

I knew differently and the very same day I returned home, for how would I dare spend the next night there? As I walked across the broad heath in the morning sunshine, I rejoiced at the top of my voice, for I had evaded death!... I had fooled death!

Successor To The Throne

Walter van den Broeck

While He works on His tower, I sit here under the pear tree – yet again
under the pear tree! – with clammy hands and back muscles that can
scarcely cope with the prickly bark of the sweating trunk. And I look
at the monument that he has planted in fronted of the house, the
monument with its hundreds of levers, its thousands of metal objects,
which He began in 1955, and which now will probably remain
unfinished forever, since He is already busy with the construction
of His tower. Initially it looked like an inoffensive, large metal table
on which we could play all kinds of games: king, giant, jumping (off
and on), mountain, Mass (as we had once seen in 1948 when He fled
with us into a church because it was raining so hard), general, martyr,
statue and lots more. But that didn't last very long, because one day
– He had come back from the fields earlier than usual – He leapt
off His bike at the open gate and gave us a long, penetrating look.
We could see that clearly from the peak of His cap that remained
horizontal and covered His eyes with a black strip of shadow. We
went quiet, Alex and I. The rusty top of the table was burning under
the soles of our feet, and I though we would have to stand still for
ever, if He didn't go away, if He didn't do something, put His bike
against the gate, for example. And I saw Alex sweating profusely,
and pushing His teeth forward through His open lips, as if he were
blinded by the sunlight that was behind Him and wreathed Him in a
halo carved from brightness. We were afraid He would never move
again, so that the glowing steel would consume our feet, our legs, our
trunk, our arms and finally our heads in a seething apocalypse. I can
still hear exactly how Duke tugged at His chain and barked, barked
like the dog from Pompeii just before the lava engulfed it, and I can
feel the heavy drops of sweat sliding down my temples. Now the red
hot sheet is boiling all the liquid from our bodies, I thought, now

we are slowly evaporating. Come on, let Him move, let Him give a sign with one of His ten fingers that He is now casually resting on the handlebars of His bike, let Him do *something*: jut His chin out a bit, whistle, shout, ring His bicycle bell, click His tongue, nod, just for a moment! And it was if He had read my thoughts: He coughed. (A cough without germs, as there was no sound of phlegm coming loose). He simply coughed across His vocal cords, yet it liberated us. We leapt off the table, hopped around a bit, since even the sand was hot, and then disappeared into the barn, where Alex kept His book of hieroglyphics hidden.

The next day, when we looked down from the flickering window of our attic room, we saw four tubes on the table top. And shortly after, when we stood at the table and felt the tubes, we noticed they were welded to the table, and realised that in future we would never be able to play on the table again.

I sit here under the pear tree and listen to the ring of His trowel on the bricks, to the plaintive scraping in the mortar hod and to Duke, who is now blind, and growls at every insect he imagines is close by. I also listen to Alex, who is wearing himself out in the barn, landing thudding punches on the leaden sandbag. He used to wear boxing gloves, now he pounds away at it with His bare hands, since for some time past he has been practising karate. Without much ceremony Alex smashes through the top of a kitchen table. With two fingers, squeezed together into a razor-sharp knife, he can dislocate a couple of your ribs.

And meanwhile, while the bark is hurting my back and I can still smell my sweaty feet, though I stick them as far forward as possible, His trowel is also ringing in my head. It chops up every thought before I have finished thinking it. Now and then I look at the kitchen window, behind which mother is quietly working. I'll wait until she sticks her head outside again, like in 1961, because I can't stay much longer sitting in the shade of the pear tree. He's taking me away from our place, he's making me invisible to the stupid workmen who live at the foot of the hill and look up at us every day and tell each other exactly what we (He, mother, Alex and

I) are getting up to here. Perhaps they also look at Duke, because they know he can't see anymore, and can't bark anymore, when they crane their dry, inquisitive necks in our direction. And although the pear tree is my friend, a silent soother, I can no longer tolerate its isolating me, because I love what is ours.

Mother *must* look today. At me. While He makes His trowel ring, and Alex lands dull blows on the sandbag, and Duke lies growling in His kennel at insects that land on His drooling snout, and slowly nibble away at him – a little more each day. Mother *must* look, because somehow I've got left behind. The prickly bark, my sweaty feet, the monument... I can't sit here any longer, I must stand up and take the lead like on that day in 1955, when He came back from the fields and saw that someone (me) had laid a large plank across the ends of the tubes, and on it the chamber pot from our bedroom. I lay staring at Him through the open barn door. Alex was lying next to me, but he wasn't looking. He just swore because he couldn't decipher the Egyptian letters, and out of rage stuffed handfuls of hay into His mouth, as if that was likely to do any good. I saw Him go up to the table holding His bike and saw His lips moved soundlessly for minutes on end. He let His bike fall sideways onto the ground, clambered onto the table, and had an arm that was just long enough to lift the plank a little, so that the chamber pot tipped and broke on the ground. Alex prodded me between the ribs – he didn't yet have those razor-sharp fingers – and he panted in my ear that the symbols, which were framed by an oval shape, formed the name of a royal personage. And I replied that I couldn't care less what they formed, that He had tipped over the chamber pot, and I crawled as far as possible over the hay, wondering all the while why I was doing that, until I finally knew for sure, that He would leave the fragments lying there, would not even ask us who had dared to put a plank on the tubes with a chamber pot on top. He would leave the fragments lying there as an example, as a warning. So the result of my act of violence was turned against me. Because who would come and get rid of the fragments? Mother certainly wouldn't. (She never comes outside. She only occasionally sticks a duster out of the window to scatter a cloud of grey mist over the yard. Sometimes she also sticks her head out, as she did in 1961, but that seldom happens, so seldom that at this moment I would really like her to do it again.) Nor would Alex; at that moment the study of the Egyptian symbols absorbed him too much. And we didn't have any pets that could run off with them. (Except for Duke, but he was already chained up. Even if he had wanted to, he wouldn't have achieved anything but some pain in the moist furrow in His neck.)

He lets His trowel ring on the bricks. Sometimes I hear Him coming down the ladder, and I don't know whether it is the rungs or His knees that creak so. Behind the house, where I can't see Him, He mixes fresh mortar with much slurping and sloshing. We've never been able to see Him. If He dies today, I will have difficulty remembering His face. I see only a green cap, a grey face and a tightly closed mouth. And also a shadow covering His eyes. I have never be able to establish empirically whether or not He has eyes. Of course He has eyes. Probably He simply doesn't want us to see that He sees us. That makes it impossible for us to count the times He looks at Alex or at me. That means that we always think He's looking at both of us, and that makes us good friends, although… the bark of the tree in my back, my sweaty feet, the steel monster and especially the punching Alex, get on my nerves. I loved my brother when he studied hieroglyphics in the barn. Unfortunately that came to an end, because one day mother found the book and showed it to Him-who-must-be-obeyed. Since there was no reaction on His part, it was obvious that He approved of Alex's study of Egyptian script. It immediately lost all its attraction for him. Later he collected the skulls of mammals. After skinning them with a pocket knife, and allowing the ants, which swarmed about the place in their millions in the summer, to pick them clean, he fixed them to the cross beam in the barn. He constantly got irritated with me, because I just stood and watched without doing anything myself. So he thought. Because before he started on the study of Egyptian hieroglyphics, I had already started burying things. Gaudy little marbles, a plaster banana from mother fruit bowl, the doll with the royal robes that

Uncle Casimir's little daughter left behind here one May day, and for everyone in the house searched high and low, an alarm clock, a crumbling, decaying truncheon, a scout knife, a trowel: I buried them all without anyone seeing. I had the biggest problem with a three-rung ladder that mother used to wash the windows or painted the shutters in the spring. I had to devise a ruse for enlarging the hole, which given the dimensions of the ladder had to be very wide and deep, at various times without arousing suspicion. I chose the spot carefully. Right in front of Duke's kennel, with him growling because he wasn't allowed out while I was working, I dug up the earth. In this way on the first day it looked as if Duke had dug a hole. The second day, at midday when every one was sitting down to lunch, just before He gave a warning whistle signal, I dug quite a big hole as fast as possible, which still could have been made by Duke. The third day no one noticed that the hole had become much bigger. In an empty moment I smuggled the ladder outside unnoticed, threw it in the hole and in a flash covered it with earth. That must be the greatest triumph I have ever experienced, because they hunted for the ladder for longer than for the doll with royal robes. Even now I sometimes see Him going restlessly from the barn to the locked cellar and from the locked cellar to the loft, and then I know He's looking for the ladder. Sometimes He evens stands in front of His monument peering, as if He's wondering whether He hasn't incorporated it by accident into His metal construction. I have often wondered why I actually bury all those things. Usually there is no answer. Sometimes there is, when the weather is very mild, so that my attention is not distracted by anything, when the wind is wind and the sun sun, and the sky sky. Perhaps I did it to start with because I liked digging holes, but today that explanation doesn't hold water. All I know is that it used to protect me from the progress Alex made with His Egyptian hieroglyphics, and later with His skulls, and still later with His boxing exercises on the dirty black sandbag that smelled musty when the rain lashed the jute through the open barn door, and made black water trickle down the bag's black belly. Even now it protects me from His karate practice. I also know that I sometimes have to go outside to find an object to bury, although it also happens that I keep a found object for later, for a moment when the burying demon drives me out into the yard. In 1963 I drew a map of all those burial places. I still carry it around with me, since I'm frightened that one day might dig up an old object. That would be terrible. What has been buried must stay buried, otherwise there is no progress.

Now He goes back up. His old legs look for support on the rungs of the ladder, which is growing longer and longer. At the foot of the hill the stupid workers' wives watch tight-lipped. They can't make out clearly what is going on here, because between their hovels and our house there are great meadows on which a few scrawny cattle eat their own gastric juices. The distance clouds the vision, and the sun that shines in their faces tears up the images on their retinas. The bucket scrapes along the ladder, and now Duke stops sniffing, I hear the plop of a load of mortar. Obviously He has filled the bucket to the brim so as not to have to go up and down the ladder too often. The prism-coloured stars and circles that the sun draws around me through the foliage of the pear tree, hold me prisoner, as I still can't get up, although the bark and my sweaty feet, the monument and punching Alex make me long for some movement. Yet here, with my backside on a buried pencil, I must wait until mother pops her head outside and smiles at me. If she smiles, I can get up and go and watch Alex and annoy him by doing nothing. He doesn't know I bury things, because I've never told anyone. Alex always gives away what he feels like doing, so that He-who-says nothing-and-works soon finds out, and wrecks the whole plan with His approval. We have that in common, Alex and I: we can't stand His approving our plans. Our resistance must drag on and on, drag on and on like His monument, that grows higher tantalisingly slowly. Because after the tubes, and so after the plank with the chamber pot on it was pushed off, it still wasn't finished. He welded a shiny metal top to it, so that from far off, from the foot of the hill it looked as if two giant tables were standing on each other. To prevent us from climbing, he painted the whole monument bright red. The smooth paint gave nothing to hold on to. (It was then that He attached the first extension to His ladder.)

So now mother must look to give me the edge over Him and Alex. I don't count Duke. He's blind and so can't compete with us any more. I know that if she laughs now, I will suddenly peel my back from the tree bark, I will immediately smother the smell of my sweaty feet in the sand, and I will walk across the yard as if I am finally lord and master here. I shan't have to bury any more things. It will be possible to call an indefinite halt to the work of undermining because mother's smile will arm me against the unexpected attacks of the stinging sun, the ringing of this trowel, and the pounding of Alex's fists. How I need it, this day, in this yard, under this pear tree! This day never was, and will never be again and yet it will become very important. The sun – I know for sure – is now ours alone. It shines only on our place. I forbid it to shine and warm anywhere else. I may not be able to see it, because I'm sitting under the tree, with a wreath of shadows and points of light around me, but my blood boils at the thought that at this moment it is shining and warming the hovels too. Perhaps that is why He is building the tower. Perhaps he is trying to catch hold of the sun, narrow its rays into a single narrow beam that is focused only on us. It's about time it finally became true that we: He, mother, Alex and I – I don't count Duke – rule this misty country of sunken cheeks and anaemia. And Duke? Why on earth did he go blind so early? With His sharp teeth and the uncontrollable fits of anger he used to have, he would have been able to keep the group of labourers down below in subjection without much trouble. If mother looks, I'll get up and walk over to the monument – as long as I can hear the trowel and the plopping of the mortar onto the bricks, there is no danger – and if I sabotage something; pull an object out of the tower, twist a lever out of true, although there isn't much point, since He Himself, since He has been working on the tower, pays no more attention to the thing. Now and then He dives into the locked cellar to rummage about a bit and sneeze, but mostly He sits in His tower, a little higher every day, making a little less noise every day, because He is growing away from us and the sound of His work is borne away on the wind.

No, Alex and I are no match for Him. Whatever we try, He is always able to neutralise our moves with magisterial counter-moves. From beneath the kepi, which He has taken to wearing, the day after we had thrown a few rotten pears onto the top platform of His monument, He surveys the situation, making sure that His eyes remain in the black strip of shadow below the peak. Arms crossed and feet astride He stands there defying our attacks. The doorway frames Him, as if He is a family portrait. Beneath His gaze our plans crumble to powder. Then when a little later He walks over the smouldering ruins of our revolt, all His movements are so minutely balanced, that I can seldom help nudging Alex and saying: Look how He walks, doesn't He walk beautifully? But Alex never listens. He just thinks about our next move.

No, since He has started on that tower, there is not much left for us to do, and we gradually lose mother more. Because look, she doesn't even look outside anymore. She doesn't even stick her hand with the duster attached out of the window. And however much we rack our brains: there's not we can mess up on the tower, since in the evening He collapses His telescopic ladder and stows it away in the locked cellar. (We often hear Him sneezing down there, as it's very dusty, since not even mother is allowed in to do any dusting.)

Duke is growling again, though there are no insects on His gummed-up eyes. He produces a shapeless growl from His rusty vocal cords. It irritates me. I don't like things that happen without an acceptable reason. Something has to make sense if it is to happen. Without sense it's better if it doesn't happen. It always upsets me, because I myself never do anything senseless. Because even the burying of objects makes sense in spite of everything, as I can tease Him with it. No, teasing isn't the word. Because I can thwart Him. We, Alex and I, have been thwarting Him for years. Everything He has made, we have damaged or destroyed. I don't tease Him, I thwart Him, slowly, respectfully, with an intensity that is worthy of Him. It is necessary, because from the strength with which I break a stick on His ribs, He realises how much He means to me. It is the only way to show Him love. His boat keeps floating downstream and with each attack we, Alex and I, drag it a little upstream again.

Now the siren of the stinking factory is wailing in the distance. Soon the trail of servile, stupid workers will emerge. They're just like Duke: if you shout 'up', they straighten up, if you say 'down', they fall flat on their bellies. Behind your back they growl, and firmly resolve to tear your throat one day. But they're as old and blind as Duke is. As they growl they try to keep off the insects.

They cycle in a great arc around the hill to their uniform hovels. They eat hurriedly, so that they can go and look at the tower as soon as possible, and argue with each other about the how and why of His construction. Later, when they slip between the sheets with their drooling wives, they still won't be able to make head or tail of it, and they will dream of palaces and thunderclouds, of working hours and bicycle bells, of TV sets and a way of getting rid of their wife. Under this pear tree, with the rough bark that cuts into my back, and with my sweaty feet lying in front of me wet and rancid, and in the barn Alex's punching, I look at the monument that He began in 1955 and has now left to rust unfinished, and I lack the strength to get up. I lack the strength to do anything at all, because the ringing of the trowel, the plopping of the mortar onto the flame-red bricks, the soft creaking of the rungs, the occasional growl of Duke's, weigh heavily in me, press all the strength out of my limbs, so that I cannot even excise the boil on my neck, just above the last prick from the tree bark. It doesn't often happen that He leaves me so far behind, for despite His success, I have always had a counter-attack in mind. This time it's as though I've been completely beaten. Nailed to the ground, slowly drying out, with a buried pencil under my backside, I sit waiting for mother. (Pull the window up and smile at me!) Because she is the biased referee, who follows the centuries-old duel between Him and us as an interested party, that's true, but she has to. A woman doesn't have the right to oppose her husband: she has to leave that to her children. After all, she had undertaken to grow old with Him. If she also opposed Him, by for instance cleaning out the locked cellar, she would make Him younger again, while she herself grows older. The distance that would be created between them, would mean an inadmissible distortion of time. She has to be biased, and now and then she has to encourage us in our attempts at destruction, since she is our ultimate target: we undermine Him in order to please her.

Why doesn't she stick her head out of the window to smile at me? What's wrong? Perhaps Alex hasn't played the game by the rules. You never know with Alex... Since he deciphered hieroglyphics he's had lots of crazy ideas.

If it doesn't happen right now, I'll call 'up Duke' and wish he were young and randy again.

The Saint Of Number

Karel van de Woestijne

I have not created for you the fabric of this spiritual life, complete
down to the steel needle, white and sharp in the bleakest but purest
of heavens, out of realities. I would shudder had I compiled the
life of this saint, for whom I shall not even invent a name, from
authentic facts and deeds, from historical actions accompanying real
events. Deriving purely from an imagined, albeit almost incredible
possibility, this story is only the expression of some people's most
fervent desires. I know those who, feeling themselves isolated, will be
surprised to recognise in the brocade robe in which the most cerebral
of dreams is enveloped, the precious tissue in which they themselves
had come to shroud their shivering and bashful nakedness.

Oh, my friends, the pride of your withdrawn solitude, the
arrogance of your most heroically abstract thought, the impenetrable
shape of your self-blinding and ultimately bitterest hope: you
imagined you knew their image only within yourself, their darkly-
veiled or brazenly shining likeness only in the hermetically sealed
chambers of your own heart and brain. But lift up your eyes: you
will see them realised, probably to your amazement, standing bright-
faced under the weight of their regalia. And perhaps you will then
understand that you have harboured within yourself too many lies,
only now acknowledged, which had taken on the appearance of
complete truth.

My hero – he is one – was able, even before his heart grew ripe
enough for a love other than that of young animals for their mother,
and when there was no other urgent drive in him than towards the
natural exercising of muscles and lungs, to experience his life as the
actions and reactions of Number. The fresh ethereal nature of his
understanding was not filled, even when he was a child, with fixed

or changing visual images. From play and rest, from happiness or sorrow he preferred to commit to memory the motion, regular or slow, more heated or more subdued, of his blood that surged or crept along, constricted his throat or stung his eyes, pounded his temples, or made him see gentle, rhythmical throbs on his wrist. When, tired from running, he sat down on a chair, he felt a twofold squirming motion, ascending and hurrying downwards, like two armies of ants. When the end of the day sounded in his more sultry head and he had gone to bed, he relived internally the hours that had passed, prompted not by the figures of his friends or the quiet pool of light shed by the family lamp, but by the happy roaring in his ear when rapidly tapped and the beating of his heart growing louder or calmer... In later years, those of his maturing and mature age, he was scarcely able to picture from that earliest childhood, even roughly, how his father must have looked. Of his mother's death he remembers only, albeit very clearly, the way they woke him at night in his cot and said very gently: 'Up you get, little lad, your mother is with the Lord' – he had the sensation, painful at first, of suddenly no longer being able to feel the inner pulsation. And he is quite sure that he has never looked in a mirror, but that he has never fallen asleep except from taking his pulse. So that one can say that at that time he lived much less by concrete than by purely rhythmical experience.

From the period when he was being prepared for his solemn First Communion he retained throughout his life the very first, sweet feeling of the meaning of a spiritual life. Learning to read had given him no joy in knowing, learning to write no joy of recognition. The words, expressed in sounds or written in script did not for him mean any deepening of his knowledge. – There are children who delight in knowing that a table exists both in its actual presence and also as its transposition in letters: the table acquires an enhanced, more intimate value as a result; its reality derives from its own distortion, a self-distinguishing form. For *him*, who never used many words – never spoke much – they were no more than useful sounds, which evoked no image in him that might be an inward and inalienable possession.

– However, when he learned to pray, which was useful and necessary for admission to Holy Mass, the prayers awakened something tender in him, which he preferred to simply listening to the alternating pattern of his rising and falling blood. Not that their strings of sound sequences achieved a heroic sense for him, though he suspected that he was being taught them because their power was greater than their immediate meaning for him. Yet it was as if their even swell, their rise and fall, as they sang out, loudly at school and softly in the silence of his own self, had created, alongside the natural motion of his own life, and independent of it, another, less simple motion, the joy of which was not as simple, and which demanded more restraint from his ear and more concentration from his understanding. The prayers, with their balanced order and form, had opened up for him the sultry chambers of an inner life, whose sense was still obscure, but no longer purely physical. As his first, uncomprehended poems, they taught him to understand the rhythm of the spirit. Beyond any actual meaning, their undulations were necessary for him to become aware, however furtively, of the churning and gyrating life of the emotions.

Though initially somewhat strange and accepted with some suspicion, that situation did not sour his humour until he started to suffer the torments of the flesh. He had always been a sturdy lad and, as you know, without much imagination. The maturing of his senses had not been preceded by the painful and anxious intimations and fears of the senses. Chastity had not been difficult for him, since his mind was pure and honest. Then, however, the blood started stubbornly coursing through his swollen neck and firmer calves with the constant pressure of a siphon; when for the first time, as if from outside himself, the terror of his awakened, already urgent, already loudly imperious male potency; when his head started spinning in panic at the violent conflicts with desire and resistance and all his joints ached from sudden urges to act and the weight of sweltering languor bordering on despair: then, together with the roaring through his whole body of the conflicting demands of the flesh, there flashed through his brain, wallowing in the churning chalices of his burning brain, the sudden revelation of the changes of value, tragic and bewildering, in and of spiritual Number. He, the reticent one, who had lost his mother at an early age, who was known not to be too quick-witted, but over whom punishment and threats had no hold; he, the passive one, who up to then had been content with first the throb of his active or calm pulse, then with the brilliant procession in his head of the words and sentences: no longer was he afraid of new events. He regarded the call of the flesh as a commandment. In obeying that command, he learned, he became aware of his male destiny, and of his duty to pursue it. – Yet though the storm in his blood had abated, still the turbulence that hammered in his brain as if because of a storm, the uncomprehended fear that gripped his throat, would not soon be explained in his eyes, or arranged in the order of a natural logic, the one that must satisfy the semi-consciousness in his understanding. In a word: disunity had been born in him.

Unity returned only when a woman, older than himself and full of wisdom, fell in love with him. She satisfied his passion; in doing so, she introduced him to a calmer love, which remained love. When his limbs were exhausted, the rhythm that governed his brain evened out. Recalling the act of love or anticipating it made his brain pulse more amply or hammer more hastily. Yet whenever he spoke of memory or desire to his lover or to himself, when she demanded that tenderer or fierier variety, again he found no images, but only a song. A song which for him had no precise, no pure, no easily comprehensible meaning. Just a song, which was all his love, and in which he confessed and recognised that only hesitantly and timidly. A *song*.

The poet that he had thus become, the kind of poet that he had become, was not very highly regarded. Most people found him largely incomprehensible. There were also those who said he was cynical – and those people had a slightly better understanding. When he showed his poems to his lover, he found that they did not satisfy her either. – She was a woman who had known many men.

Some of those men had loved and also expressed their love in verse. In the poetry of all those men the same beautiful expressions kept recurring, within the same facile, swaying metrical scheme. Not so in the poems of this her latest lover. She laughed as she told him this. He was disappointed, but remained attached to and in love with the woman, fearing that she was right, and that he really should compare his poems with those of other poets.

The accompanying sense that he was helpless, and also that the woman might return to the men who *did* know how to put things in the right way, made him deeply unhappy. However, where, as a result, his passion cooled and he began to recognise the need for discipline; where therefore spiritual Number began demanding greater obedience from his blood; where that blood, where Number demanded supremacy, demanded that he sing, sing as he must, inexorably – then he gradually became the poet of spiritual wretchedness, pathetic desperation, the poet of the inexpressible and unquenchable thirst for complete expression, the poet who, doomed to absolute honesty, knows that he will never reach the mountain lake amid the ice cliffs whose water is so clear and so deep, that by its absolute translucence he will see the sediment on the bed of his being. Lie – how could he have done so? Anyway, he was too poor in images and had only his sensuality, the roar of his turbulent or languorous blood, the disgust and flame of his desire – and then as its reverberation the rhythm in his soul, which he would never master and could never serve properly. He was tortured deep in his flesh by the necessity of expression. It dragged him in its wake like a pack of raging dogs. He tried to smother his passion in vice and over-indulgence; he chastised his body with the lashes of self-contempt; he also whipped up his sensual frenzy so that it might subside the sooner. But exhausted, chastised or seemingly defeated, what remained from the crude passion was shame-filled melancholy, which tortured him more than the black fire from which it emerged, and above which there rang out inexorably, louder and louder the Law of Song. And only when he had sung – in what words? Oh, the poverty of words! – only then did he feel, did he enjoy, did he drink sacred peace. – Until when? Alas, the all-powerful flesh constantly claimed the helpless song as its own, the song in which no one wanted to recognise only flesh, the sickly song in which the Number of his blood and the Number in his thoughts could never be brought into harmony.

His song – he had come to love it like a young, ailing son. He cherished it, with the care and melancholy of a mother pampering her child, knowing it will never recover. The conflict that raged within him, and in which his spirit, the immaculate brother of his flesh, was always the loser made him prefer increasingly the former's wounds, which he feared he would never be able to nurse as far as the clean scar of recovery. – His life was impure and uncertain. He would not, he had already divined, love that woman, older than he was, who had introduced him into the thorny gardens of love, until the season when the bright roses bloomed. Physically very healthy, he had the weakness that goes with health. His will did not keep pace with his sensuality. – Well then, he left that first lover, who disgusted him: he had experienced the same constriction and the paralysed relaxation in other arms, but never the deeply moved gratitude that he yearned for. Oh, to rest upon a tender breast, under the watchful gaze of peacefully loving eyes!...But no, lust drove him onward or snapped at his heels, and invariably he found himself between the same sour sheets, and invariably – worst of all – he could see no way out, knew no other resolution of the question of security than in his song, than in bruised and impotent Number...

'Since,' he said to himself, 'since the balance I seek between the onset of passion and its expression in what we are wont to call poetry, turns out to be impossible, and since it is at the same time quite clear that it is not passion that is found wanting, but its expression; that it is not the body but the spirit that falls short; since, in addition, it seems to me that the expression becomes more painful the more complicated the thrusting power of motion is, greater purity of life might perhaps...'

The truth is that he began to feel very tired. The violent exuberance of his life would have imposed excessive tension on the

231

strongest nerves. Added to which, certainly, there was a restlessness in his poetry. It had lost none of its sincerity; how could that have been possible given its strident motivation? But the knowledge that it was both imperfect and incomplete had automatically deprived it of its unforced, free tone – although the latter was only haltingly expressed, and this ordered structure, which had initially seemed so desirable to him, now struck him as *untruth*, as fancy dress, a hypocritical disguising of what was dearest to him: the spiritual Number.

Then he fled the town where he had glowed like jet: black, with sparkles, but without the sacred flames. He moved into a small country cottage, by a river. When he arrived it was the season when the fourfold wind with conflicting gusts is also able to turn the head like a barn empty of grain, and that even early sunshine can plant a living warmth in people's hearts. The day on which he left for his new home he sank, cursing, up to his knees in bogs. But those bogs were full of thousands of moving frog's heads, countless frogs with gold-ringed eyes, swimming, leaping and suddenly sitting motionless, staring into the sun, on their broad bottoms. Soft, rounded swathes of primroses descended towards those bogs from the carpeted verges of yellow velvety flowers, huddled together as if against the cold, so close together that a bitter balsamic scent, squeezed out of them wafted over the clay soil. From those bogs, towards the drier paths, rose the grasses, the smooth, azure coated grasses, and the beetles were already scuttling over them. And across the bogs lay the cobwebs, the weaving cobwebs, the singing cobwebs, the cobwebs with the first flies shimmering in the sunlight… For him, as a town-dweller, it was a surprise. His senses: were they really intended for something other than an unfortunate and searing passion?... For the moment it remained a question. And that first night he slept as if in a bath of lukewarm water perfumed with lavender…

He remembers how there in the country, by that curving water in which he no longer thought of going to look at his reflection, but where he saw the reflection of the sky, and the meadows, and the heifers and three-year-old cows in the fields, and the beat was that of rhythm of the winds, the rhythm of undercurrents, the rhythm of the sea and tides, the rhythm of the planets, the rhythm of the universe – he remembers how he experienced there a love for the most humble of realities, provided they could show him a beauty that did not come from himself; a love without profit, which, where he began to suspect great unifying interests, drove him towards what was so far beneath him according to his own great comprehension: from the insect to humble human beings. His long walks and the pure weight of the sky had banished almost all passion. He had become a man at peace, if not a completely happy one. For the fact was that he was a poet.

Already his first efforts to realise in simple words a paltry part, and the most precious part of his new experiences, had been rewarded. In the simple expression of his fresh receptivity, his verse had gained a purity of line, a measured lightness, a playful seriousness, which seemed to him a sign that he had be rescued from his sombre fears. It had the suppleness and sudden joy, the twinkling of stars and velvety nocturnal sweetness, the mystery and translucent clarity of Number, as it had resolved into spiritual and physical harmony and inhabited him. His calmer blood, no longer so brashly imperious in demanding that it should be expressed fully in song, also made the song more joyous and especially easier flowing. His experience of being part of the outside world, whose life seemed to derive from the same heartbeat, appeared to adjust the resistant rhythm of his heart to the beat of the Universal One. And he was actually happy, since he was in equilibrium.

Yet the fact that day after day, month after month, and after the accumulated translucence of years, at long last perceived transformations in the expressions of his spiritual number, transformations in value that were like the siren voice of previously unsuspected abysses, that were again to rob him of his peace of mind and inspire him with fear. Up to now he had had unexpected warnings that clove his spirit with anxiety like the onset of a disease.

233

Certainly, he considered himself to have been saved from the flesh. Not that he had banished his male sensuality: that would have seemed unnatural and hence unnecessary. But he no longer experienced it as a commandment, and if, in the hot season, it became too violent a master, then his heart, his overflowing, but now so conscious heart was able to channel it properly into song, albeit sometimes sombre, sultry song. In this way he really was no longer a slave to it, and it depended, he recognised, on his spiritual Number. That undertone, new and – he felt – less pure, obscurely contrary, sometimes false and surly, which, without his ever being able to identify its origin, sometimes rose to the clear surface of his even and smooth poetic utterance like the dark fragments of peat that leave bubbles like pure gold on still, silver-shining ponds where they rise suddenly and inexplicably to the surface – was that not a sign to him that some new feelings had been awakened in him that, independent of his senses and disciplined passion, nevertheless existed outside his purified contemplation of nature, which had helped saved him...? For a while he fought against it: he wanted to remain the simple man who has finally learned to express himself. But he soon realised the dissatisfaction of his spirit, which was no longer content with facile observation, where the words had anyway already rendered pious concentration unnecessary. And one night he had a vision, which clarified for him the deeper dimension of things, the premonition of which had disturbed him as another threatening disruption of his peace. He was in a limbo between waking and sleeping. It was as if, freed from all weight, all heaviness, he were suspended in a sphere far removed from the tangible world. He did, though, first and foremost and as clear as could be, see the earth as it appeared to him every day, with the magnificent water and the charm of the tiny creatures and humble plants. The silent, smirking farmers went past him. And it was true: it was perhaps the first time that he, surprised by a higher consciousness, by an awareness that afforded him an overview, understood the actual value of an image in itself. But beneath and above the level of the soil a mysterious life became equally clear to him. With different kinds of clarity, true, but equally clearly from above and below, he saw the work of quiet, peaceful beings. They were like young people; but their white robes and the gold of their hair, bright as if it were up in the sky, turned to blue and bronze by the shadows in the subterranean mystery, were too hazy to be attributed to creatures like us with a sex and a fixed form. Their activity also made then unearthly. By gestures alone they made ears of corn rise from the fields, while they brought food and nourishing sap for the same ears from the depths of the earth. He saw them taking children to school unseen. And one sat with a dying woman, on her pillow and told her stories, making her smile blissfully...

At that time he was subjected to several such dreams, to the point of irritation. Though it was not that he did not see them as a warning. Was the intention, if this was (as he soon reasoned) an incentive for him to get to know, scientifically, the immutable origin, fixed nature and precise use of the phenomena that previously provided him with too facile an expression of Number? He suspected it was so, and studied. It brought him, he was forced to learn, nothing but disillusionment, and made his love no longer disinterested. Then he devoted himself to what the laws of faith might offer. 'Woe is me,' was his first experience of these.

Of course, of course, these laws contained beneficent explanations, which were also clear. More than those of science, they offered comfort, and permitted one to love without ulterior motives. They were, in fact, so appropriate and so accommodating they were bound to contain truth. For is knowledge, knowledge heightened and unified, any different and does it require anymore than knowledge of the most suitable relationships, than the appropriateness of the various individual components...? Dogma, then, and fixed science, although they complemented each other so easily, what could they give him to explain what was again making his spirit restless and turbulent, and his spiritual rhythm so feeble and fearful?

For his uncertainty had been reborn; this time no longer from anything material, but from the very suspicions themselves, and from the longings of the spirit. Liberated, by what grace? From stubborn physical torment; loose in his limbs and unsuspicious in his thoughts; sensually unselfish and very relaxed in his sensuality, he was, as he felt, not without some bewilderment, definitely open to a new view of things. He was like a prepared and spotless house expecting uninvited but definitely arriving guests. He knew them, he thought, from long ago. They had undoubtedly visited him since he was very young, but only when darkness had fallen, and shrouded in dense veils. Now, however, in the early morning, they had scarcely fully entered before they stood there without draping garments. From the moment they started to approach from the furthest avenues, his eyes trembled at the sight of their brilliant necklaces. Their smiles shone like a white rose through the morning mist. Plucked from the distances like lilies they advanced like shafts of sunlight through white curtains in the eyes of a waking patient. And whenever they crossed his dark threshold, his happiness was infinite...

Alas, this transubstantiation – which is what it had become – in the least contestable of realities, in the most secure and inalienable of possessions, of powers and decisive causalities, in which he was all the more compelled to believe, that were all the more evident to him, to the extent that he did not know them through people or from books, but that they were revealed to him, repeatedly and indefatigably revealed; oh, his beautiful, infinitely beloved guests, whom he had come to know one by one, not as laws, as inexorable laws – only, consciously, as the companions of his day's journey: how he had suffered, not being able, though he rejoiced at their approach, to celebrate them in song while they were close to him...

Did he feel unworthy, perhaps? Was he silenced by the feeling of undeserved insignificance? No, because he was far from having submitted in simplicity and trust. In the beginning he had been enraged by explanations that seemed to him unnatural. He himself had not prepared the house for the sometimes undesired visits; only after their repeated knocking, after their stubbornly persistent and intrusively charming, had he entertained the guests each time.

This was what troubled him so, that he could not receive the beloved uninvited guests fittingly, and his words lacked the ability to do so. He was aware of the favour that was being bestowed on him: and was all the more aware of his gaucheness. And the more numerous and more forward the visits became; friendly and giving more generously of fruit and noble metals – the more ashamed he became that he was unable to say the simple words of welcome, the rich words of thanks on parting or the glorifying words of remembrance.

Because again he felt the same impotence as when driven to sing of his carnal passion; the same kind of despairing powerlessness in the face of this purity from on high as when the lower depths sucked him under; again the lack of balance between commandments from outside and the expression of the inner Number. More than ever he felt himself to be once more impoverished by his own images, his figurative craft, his aesthetic transformations. And never at the same time did he feel the fear, which gripped his chest, of necessary utterance.

He had, though, beyond significance, beyond actual meaning, gradually observed parallels between some sounds and some of the visiting figures. Each approach awakened a special shimmer in him, for which he found an equivalent in his human language, albeit in the most abstract metaphorical form. True, he experienced, at times, the joy of a sudden identification, the happy surprise of absolute harmony. True, he sometimes felt himself standing on the horizons where they, his guests, had their natural abode, and it seemed to him that whenever he started to speak it was they, with their voices of vibrating crystal, that forced his teeth to articulate. True, he was occasionally able to hear his own language very promptly as no longer distinct from theirs. But what agonies he endured, immediately after such grace had been received, finding himself back on the hard earth, with his coarse humanity, exhausted from otherworldly tension, shattered as it were by a fall from on high! And then, how little he cared whether his song of the most sublime moments still accorded with human language; how little he cared whether he would be understood (was the inner Number not blissfully content at such disinterested moments?): he was oppressed by the thought that that his successions of sounds and words would be unable to escape the doom of sensuality. Oh, the images of his inwardness, they stood up – he knew it, they formed a circle, they performed a splendid dance; they hung like garlands of otherworldly flowers, like the interplay of countless cherubs, like the circling motion of meteoric dust. They were not of this world. They did not belong where he himself, alas, knew he still was, irreconcilably. He felt that his spiritual Number had risen to a higher plane, that it had been purified into a higher, more certain, more steadfast, no longer fragile and transient essence. However, to follow it with his word – the way that, albeit only at rare moments, it was granted him by special dispensation to reach it in the ethereal realm, the purifying and subtle ethereal realm where it dwelt – to embody it approximately was a torture under which he suffered dreadfully. For could he express it any other way to a poor human being than with human signs, even though those signs had now lost their value, and attained the significance of symbols? Could he do it better than with means that were pleasing to his senses, when they originated in his senses? Had he gradually, after all, unwillingly – for he never lost his mistrust – outgrown a sense of community with his fellow-men: was it not still from their vernacular that he must derive the ingredients of his utterances, if he wanted to rediscover in his song the shapes of what was to be from now on his only true life? And was it not so – this became the worry of his least-visited, his most earthbound days – that he was unable to commemorate his most precious days than by bringing them in to contact with what remained of the doom from his previous existence full of demonic passion?

And so he found himself facing a dilemma: either, through the most stubborn denial, to strangle in himself the nobler, the revealed, the finally comprehending life; or to give up trying to continue to feed his need for numerical utterance from it. He tried, rebelliously, again to dedicate himself totally, to the purely visible, audible, tangible. He went further: using black and mysterious means he tried to awaken his drowsy flesh through a powerful new surge of blood. Yet in every flower he saw reflected the face of one of his heavenly visitors, and from the experiments with his body he retained nothing but the nagging certainty that that it had died for good – perhaps, he thought, murdered by himself... Still, however, he did not abandon his desire, to flee the succession of beautiful images, which no longer left him and accompanied him everywhere. In philosophies he sought the proof of their insubstantial nature: he found only the unambiguous confirmation of their existence. He hoped to find that the doctrine of the priests contradicted the truths they had held up to him: but what he came to realise was that what the priest stammered was nothing but the reflection of his most humble experiences. And when he gave himself over to ecclesiastical practices, with the intention of savouring their worthlessness, he saw them, his guests full of blessings, sitting next to his pew, praying like him, with a smile...

So there was nothing left for him, he felt, but to silence Number in himself. He would impose on himself the chastisement of spiritual destruction. He no longer wanted to react to the angelic visits. The determined paralysis of his tongue, rather than let it stutter impotently and bring shame on the inexorable spiritual rhythm: it would make him truly worthy of their heavenly grace.

And he began to devote himself to the inexpressible, on what is bound to be absent in all human utterance, since it can be expressed only in ideal correspondences, beyond all sensuality. He would no longer express himself in any way that might contain or provoke any earthly perceptions – certainly therefore that henceforth he would not often break his silence. Averse to anything direct, even the subtlest forms such as light and sound, he no longer wanted to know anything but relationships in the abstract. He wanted to know whether Number would be able to withstand this ordeal: transformation of the shape, the beautiful shape of his now daily Guests into the Aridity, the seldom-possible explicability, the eternal abstraction of a formula. He wanted no more than to dwell in reflections, albeit with the inconstancy of flowing water: it would be recognised, in the indelible, although changing relationships across time and space, which display no form save in the spiritual realm of generalisation, which have no value save in complete abnegation, which no beauty and no goodness save as a token of the energy of heroic induction. So it would become, his spiritual Number: so, now and ever after, it would witness and profess the reality of the joyful and innocent visitors – or it would cease to exist.

On the contrary, he derived ineffable delight from it. In practising such utterances, deprived as they were of all sensual benefit, naked as they were in the innocence of their bright truth, they offered an aesthetic joy in which Number could be absorbed into itself, in which it could annihilate itself to create a constant succession of lasting renewals, they dispensed practical satisfaction, in which Number could immediately recognise its essence in complete clarity and certainty, and see itself affirmed most precisely and independently in its relationships for all timelessness...

And so he felt, my hero, my indeed most ruthless hero, he gradually felt himself to be in unbroken communion with the visitors who honoured him, absorbed into a world, which was without any trace of earthliness and which he was able to express according to impersonal but all the more eternal, enduring principles, in their ethereal firmness, with their invisible, inaudible, but thereby less relative, more absolute truth.

Rising from the diseased, uncertain and impure sickness of the flesh to the incorruptible health of a purified spiritual life; within him the law of metre and number, of sounds and rhythms absorbed into the virtue of the blind yet by the same token less hesitant harmony that hold the worlds together...

And yet: he still sometimes suffered anxieties. – He no longer dared doubt his chosen status. Nothing could any longer undermine the certainty of his knowledge. But did that not leave the fear, that the mystery of the first cause, the creative beginning, the Being that had appointed everything for all eternity, for ever and ever, would remain hidden from him? Would he not be allowed to know the instigating and expanding Unity, the initial and eternal abstraction that was the reason and essence of everything comprehensible...?

He dare not conjecture; he was forbidden to know; and he could not blindly believe... Must he content himself with the great grace, which had, incomprehensibly, fallen to his lot? Would he, who had been granted a sojourn on the ultimate horizons, would he have to look straight ahead, and never into the abysses above and below him, on whose rim, on whose extreme edge he dwelt – would he never, without the danger of vertigo, be able to plumb and know the depths, he who knew everything, the comprehension of their being...?
He, who knew everything...

Oh then, my friends, the miracle happened. One day he lay in the cell he had built himself on the highest of the glaciers, he lay on the ice crust that was its floor, and the bed of his despair; he lay there, he of the god-given gifts, in his despair at the fact that something was still withheld from him, and that this Something must nevertheless be all he was given. He lay there, and thought to himself and powerfully within him sounded the demand of Number, for the sake of which he was denied the joy of that unique knowledge, that knowledge of absolute Unity, while all the rest was revealed to him. Would he then, the knower, have to resign himself to forgoing the latter? Would he have simply to accept this one thing, where he could only intuit it? Would he not be able to get to the bottom of it, he who was able to plumb the darkest mines with his gaze; would he have to acknowledge its evident truth solely through the fragile, precarious authority of a paltry faith? Would the all-powerful knower...

– But then his closed eyes were surrounded by darkness. Bewildered at first, and full of fearful timidity, he did not dare look. But when the inner demand that he should look grew more urgent, and the suspicion that it would be to his advantage grew stronger, he opened his eyes. He rose to his knees: before him there stood, in mourning garb, and with a face pale with deep sorrow, an Angel, who was very familiar to him. The Angel had visited him repeatedly, but before in a robe of matt white, with a presence full of rosy tenderness. It was, he knew, the Angel of Humility... Now it, the Angel, was shrouded in darkness, and its face full of sadness. And the resentful, despairing man, whose heart was black, though not with the blackness of mourning, was bewildered and suspicious that his former guest, who had always appeared to him in such white splendour, should be standing there clothed in such dark colours and with such sad features, and was about to ask it: 'What is it then that robs you so of your peace, and makes you sad?'

But he did not ask. Penetrating the very depths of his soul, the Angel, through a veil of tears, had fixed him with its stern but pitying gaze, its bitter and yet infinitely sympathetic gaze, so long, so constant, and so inexorable...

Again he was about to ask, in the fear that suddenly seized his heart:

'How is it that you, the Angel of Humility...'

But the Angel anticipated him, and:

'So you recognised in me the Angel of Humility?' it asked with its tear-choked voice, both tender and reproachful...

- Then the despairing man, who refused to believe, refused quite simply to believe, then he realised why the Angel was sad. It became clear why ultimate grace was still denied him. For a long time he looked deep into himself. And, sobbing, he let his head sink into his lap and, as the Angel had done, wept bitterly at his plight... When he raised his head again, the Angel was still there. He raised his eyes in entreaty to those of the Angel, and the Angel's eyes began shining peacefully. Then he prayed for forgiveness; and lo, there where he knelt with his eyes fixed on the Angel's black robe, the robe suddenly became translucent. First a sweet brightness; then, imperceptibly, a still more subdued brilliance; soon afterwards the mounting blaze of a piercing white glow; and then, and then...

'But I can see God!' he cried out suddenly.

And it was true, he had seen God.

May 1912 – May 1913

The Lost House Key
the reason why, or I told you so

Paul van Ostaijen

"The striving of the human spirit to perceive everything as interconnected is so powerful that in remembering a disconnected dream it involuntarily compensates for the lack of coherence."
JESSEN, *Versuch einer wissenschaftlichen Begründung der Psychologie.*
Berlin, 1856.

Mr Hasdrubal Paaltjes[1] was an Inspector of Bridges and Roads. Furthermore, he was a universally respected man. He lived in a city of half a million inhabitants. This gave him metropolitan stature, without his fame being swamped in the seething anthill of a metropolis. The male sex and women not inflamed by passion honoured Mr Hasdrubal Paaltjes because he was a serious civil servant with the prospect of a pension. Also because he was a lovable human being and because he participated without youthful passion in all discussions on politics, world wars, earthquakes, Turkish immorality and art. But women who *were* inflamed by passion saw in Hasdrubal a vigorous man of forty and did not doubt his capacities. Many young women had Hasdrubal's portrait immediately above their beds or on their bedside tables. Others, who had experienced bitter disappointments in their marriages, persuaded their husbands to invite Mr Paaltjes round. In this way they also obtained a signed photograph. In hours of direst need this photo became an acceptable surrogate. The husbands knew this. As long as it goes no further than the photo, they thought. Whether it went no further than the photo, they of course had no idea. It was simply a pleasant interpretation of something unpleasant. Only the wife knew the state of affairs

---

1 Some accounts speak of Asdrubal Paaltjes. This Asdrubal Paaltjes is identical with Hasdrubal Paaltjes. However, most chroniclers use Hasdrubal. We consider it advisable to use this form. It is probably the case that a French stenographer, unable to distinguish between A and H, gave currency to this incorrect spelling, in so far as it can be considered to have currency. (Author's note.)

between herself and Hasdrubal. Reality, an overheated fantasy or just an idyllic dream. The women were never wrong. They really are like X-rays penetrating male potency. Perhaps they are scientifically more accurate. A woman is never wrong. And if she happens to be wrong, she says: how on earth could I have been wrong? In this way she unites both her disappointments in one. And she says it so naturally that one thinks only of a fault in the psycho-physical X-ray system. Yet her heart harbours a deeper melancholy.

People in the city did not realise the extent to which Hasdrubal Paaltjes was becoming its pulse, the engine of the city. If only they had been able to realise that! How many ills would have been averted! But such things are realised only in their inexorable effects. So posterity will write: those misfortunes befell the city of X because Hasdrubal Paaltjes, that monster in human form, had become the engine, the pulse of the city. Pointing things out is a special delight, a kind of intellectual self-abuse. It will be seen from the continuation of this story that we are dealing here with no less a catastrophe than that of Babel or Sodom.

The story is as follows. Mr Hasdrubal Paaltjes had been out on the town with some friends. When the drunkard had found his house with the help of his cabman, he could no longer find his house key. Drunkenness is a sober state. It is the state of sober balance. Yes and no are constantly cancelling each other out. No one has yet been able to prove with mathematical logic whether he actually lost his key. Some maintain that he had not lost his key, and that he was actually probably holding the key in his hand, but that this minor detail had escaped him.[2] Most people, however, regard this as an unfounded hypothesis. Those who hold the first opinion belong to the movement they have called neo-psychologism. Those in the second camp deny the former the right to any scientific title and call them

---

2 People will object: if the case of Hasdrubal Paaltjes having or not having lost his house key has not been settled, why do I choose the title: the Lost House Key. My answer is: the view of the rational realists is the generally accepted one; it is sanctioned by religion, the state and society. The psychological interpreters are regarded as tasteless eccentrics, cerebral clowns and unscientific fanatics. Their arguments are called as idiotically speculative. We mention them for the sake of completeness. But the first view, that of the rational realists, is the one that has cultural-historical value. Culture and society have pronounced their unambiguous judgement.

sneeringly the hyperbolic hypothecists, claiming for themselves the title of rational realists. Some silly readers, eager for the Paaltjes story, may not be very interested in these digressions, which they may dismiss contemptuously as details. For their benefit we shall say right now that these two opinions have provided the raw materials for an all-embracing cultural conflict. If we quote with statistical accuracy the fact that 209 women murdered their husbands – the women were psychologicals and could no longer endure the slander of their rational realist husbands – one may judge to some extent the importance of the conflict.

With or without his house key, Paaltjes could not get to his bed that night. Outside his house he spoke to himself more or less as follows (not verbatim, but according to popular tradition): since firstly I've squandered my money, and secondly with great effort and the help of a cabman I have discovered my residence, but thirdly cannot find my house key, I must now, in order to preserve my equilibrium, introduce a positive element into my evolution. Since I am in addition obliged to spend the night in a hotel, I do not see why I should do this in an ascetic and egotistical way. I can unite these two conclusions by seeking out the last streetwalker, probably the only one who has not yet found a customer, and share my bed with her. I think it's idiotic to spend the night alone in a hotel. I don't see why I should spend the night alone. I think sleeping alone is stupid in any case and, apart from that, champagne has a highly erotic effect on my constitution. All praise to fate that caused me to lose my house key. Otherwise I might have forgotten that champagne is an erotic stimulant. Paaltjes found the last available sample of whoredom in a rather *Weltschmerz*-ish mood. Good old *Weltschmerz* (the reader is kindly requested to read this last sentence aloud – with full and resonant intonation). But when Hasdrubal addressed her, she brightened up, like a lamp filled with fresh spirit. Tomorrow, she thought, she would be able to lure new customers with: yesterday Hasdrubal, you know, Hasdrubal Paaltjes slept with me.

Still, she hesitated for a moment when he spoke to her. The space of a lighted match. Then it had gone. Paaltjes noticed, but didn't try to fathom it. *C'est la vie, que voulez-vous.* Later he often thought: that's why she hesitated.

They had a wonderful night. Hasdrubal was glad he had followed the champagne to its ultimate consequences. She was glad to be having Hasdrubal. She said repeatedly: Hasdrubal, my Hasdrubal. Her voice a vanquished Loreley.

For the next few days too Paaltjes was content. The escape brought no unpleasant consequences. So he thought.

There's no harm in waiting. And a solid dose of syphilis should not manifest itself immediately. The name guarantees quality.

That is why the tart had hesitated for the space of a lighted match. Remorse or a bad conscience? Certainly. And Hasdrubal. The pride of the city. The living poem. In a flash of realisation it became clear to her that this escapade was bound to have a profound effect on the future development of the city. And so it came to pass. As in the flash of lightning. Hasdrubal noticed the symptoms. Then a doctor. Then a professor. Finally the dean of the faculty. Hasdrubal was given a stern talking to. Very difficult treatment. And especially, sexual abstinence.

Hasdrubal echoed the words. Sexual abstinence? So, no sex in his diet. Or what? What did they mean by this paradox? Vaguely, lost in dreams. He felt like a trapped eagle. Torturers and red-hot needles in his eyes. Inquisition. Was that sexual abstinence?

Hasdrubal understood; abstain or commit suicide, one or the other, but it was all the same. His fame: he never thought of abstinence. He must cling to that fame. *Taureau ardent. Torrent ardent.* That's right. That's what women who had read books on Red Indians called him. Giving up fame wasn't the end of it. It also meant making a terrible fool of himself. He had obligations to himself. There was no getting away from it: he was Hasdrubal.

Abstinence proved impossible.

Come what may. This was Paaltjes' fatalistic conclusion. And he continued as normal. Which for him, Paaltjes, was quite normal.

Once on the wrong path it is difficult to turn back. Paaltjes was on the wrong path. And now he set many others on the wrong path. First, through Paaltjes' agency a number of women found their way onto the wrong path, which actually is no great feat.

One fact is beyond doubt: the women had limitless trust in Paaltjes. They did not check, which was their Achilles heel. Why not be objective? A quasi-governmental organisation like, for instance, the customs service, livestock control on foreign imports. Now, in Paaltjes' city, women were already bearing the brunt.

The specialists' doorbells never stopped ringing. These specialists believed they were acting wisely by doubling the consultation fee. Something like a practical warning. Be careful, because it's very expensive if you're not careful. Women should be more careful. But it was a futile gesture.

Slowly the men's caravan also began to swell. Because the women whom Hasdrubal had loved were in the know. Aflame with love. Not just the flame of a lighted match. And Hasdrubal was worth ten others. If Hasdrubal broke, they must keep quality in quantitative equilibrium. And so the procession of men became endless.

Finally the tenfold multiplication was sufficient to send those women who had not frequented Hasdrubal, the same way as his lovers. And so.

The waiting rooms of the specialists turned out to be useless. The distinguished male and female patients were put in the dining room, in the bedroom, in the kitchen. In the street the patients formed long queues. In the streets where these specialists lived, no trams or other vehicles could move. Soon it was necessary to build hangars where those waiting could spend the night without losing their place in the queue. There was a roaring trade in places. The unemployed queued up and reserved places for the rich. The city and the central government levied a tax as they did at fish and other markets. A good idea, which restored the shaky finances of local and central government. Folding chairs sold like prawns. Countesses and suchlike engaged menials to bear their lace-curtained litters. They brought some refinement to the new situation. A new fashion.

Casinos were opened in the vicinity. A new industry flourished: litters, casinos on wheels, libraries on wheels, rolling desks on wheels. Eccentric ladies even tried bedrooms on wheels. The streets smelled of perfume. And literature. What everyone should read in special cases. The secret of the casino on wheels.

Such a situation was bound to worry the heads of the state, the guardians of communal welfare. A motion was tabled in parliament. Too late, in the opinion of the right and the centre. This objection is an attack on human rights, was the opinion of the left. Everything is pigeonholed in advance. Perhaps this is an excellent thing; it is certainly pleasant in any case. The comfortable life.

The debate degenerated into a purely political conflict. The right considered the city of X a danger to the state. Measures to isolate the city were urgently needed. The left wing was in uproar, shouting: priests and moral blackmail. The leader of the social-democrats made a speech about human rights. An ethicist maintained that people must be cured by good deeds and good examples. But not by fighting one evil with another. No ethical homoeopathy, gentlemen. One must show these people who have gone astray the *a priori* superiority of the good. The right replied with a well-rehearsed *a capella* chant of: *libera nos, Domine.*

The right wing of course won the battle. The right always wins the battle. This is tradition. The necessity of this can be proved *ab absurdo*. Just imagine, for instance that the left-wing were to win. Yes, the left wing. You laugh. You see. It would look like a censored film.

So, the right wing was triumphant. The socialists finally accepted the right-wing bill, on the understanding that the right must promise to study the question whether an act of parliament on child and female labour might possibly be considered at the earliest opportunity in the narrower confines of its party executive.

The city of X became a free city. A perfectly clear term; it's a matter of using the right interpretative criteria. Everyone has a say on the future of the free city, apart from the inhabitants of the free city. That is precisely why the name free city was chosen. When a quality is totally non-existent, the word expressing that quality is repeated a hundred times in order to convince others and oneself. The creative word balances out what is non-existent. A polarity.

In a trice this free city gained unparalleled notoriety. It provided the material for the weightiest discussions in every city on both continents. Indeed, in every village and hamlet. No wonder the daily press believed there was huge business to be had in featuring as much news as possible from the free city. War, sport, politics and obituaries, everything is overshadowed by the new feature 'Life in the Free City of X'. Psychological studies appeared. And there were three-cent instalments. All about X. One could read adverts: Journalist wanted. Only those able to reduce life in the free city of X to brief telegrams need apply. Or: Publisher interested in all manuscripts concerning the free city of X. In all the arts a new movement emerged that was sometimes called the neo-fantastic-naturalistic trend, because it again tried to represent scenes from nature, but only such as were a more cerebral form of empirical experience than the simple noting of optical pseudo-truth. However, this artistic movement was generally called X-ianism and violently combated by conservatives of all nations. Its aspiration was simply to represent the city of X, unknown to most artists, naturalistically with the aid of fantasy. The conservatives could not understand how people who laid claim to good taste and appreciation of the concept of aesthetics could be guided, indeed misled by such a theme. It is an artistic debacle, they said. Every daily sent its correspondent, and the large dailies several to the city of X. Most states in Europe, Asia and America felt obliged to close their borders to returning journalists. Soon only bankrupts, exposed card-cheats and other freelance workers were taken on as correspondents. They undertook never to return to their homeland. For which they were paid exceptionally attractive bonuses.

Never had a city been the destination of so many exiles as X. Consider: so many unhappy people found a home in a place where they were no longer outcasts from society, but on the contrary were the healthy norm. The few people healthy by our standards who still lived in the free city, had of course long been labelled as black sheep by the vast majority.

    There were special voyages from America for emigrants.

    The Japanese requisitioned the Trans-Siberian railway.

    The city of X soon became known as Megalopolis.

The city of Megalopolis blossomed as if reborn. The great powers did succeed in isolating Megalopolis, but further interference in the internal politics of the city soon proved impossible. Anyway: after the great powers and neighbouring states had for some time behaved venomously towards Megalopolis, fired by a merciless urge to destroy, the idea launched by the United States suddenly gained general approval. The city should be considered rather as a dustbin for elements that in other cities and states would undoubtedly constitute a danger to national security. The American argument was as follows: instead of destroying Megalopolis, we should contribute much more to ensure that the city flourishes. The Supreme Council came to the decision that Megalopolis should be isolated and that the city's foreign policy should be monitored by the powers, but that in domestic policy the people of Megalopolis should be given a free hand, and that the economic support of the city, since it could be used as an external prophylactic, should be approved; the existence of this city kept away venereal diseases, by concentrating the carriers of such diseases.

    So it was that after a brief crisis Megalopolis flourished as never before. All opinions were the result of a completely changed view of life. One cannot say that these opinions were completely new. They simply emerged from juxtaposition and hence in absolute terms were as old as the other opinions, as there is no extreme without its opposite. But at least as manifestations they were an antipode to our generally accepted opinions. Especially from an ethical point of view. This ethical turnaround can be seen as having tipped the balance. It is crucial. All the other inverted views of the people of Megalopolis can be traced back to it.

    Creating a fetishistic cult in honour of the great names among one's fellow-countrymen or fellow-citizens is a glorious aim to which every city has aspired. And the same applied to the people of Megalopolis. It was just that they had a different criterion. Is it wrong to establish the tree of good and evil as the beginning of human value differentiation, or at least the tree of a particular good and a particular evil? Should one not see good and evil as abstract poles with a constantly changing concrete interpretation, according to the environment, the nation and the individual? That is, good and evil as just a symbolic representation of pole and antipode. Probably our concrete Judaeo-Christian interpretation of good and evil has put the abstract recognition of this suprapolarity in the shade.

Megalopolis' hero-worship was neither greater nor less than that of other cities. The heroes were simply different; not personally different, but different in principle, measured according to a different ethical scale. You can't imagine, for instance, that the archbishops of Paris, Cologne and Mechelen would dream of presenting Hasdrubal Paaltjes as a candidate for local beatification, let alone desire his canonisation. The attitude of the people of Megalopolis was quite different. Even during his lifetime Hasdrubal Paaltjes enjoyed the veneration that is the lot of great men. He, neither a bishop nor a king, but much more than that. When Paaltjes spoke, others were silent, and when he was silent they were silent too, so impressive was his very silence. When children were born they were brought to Paaltjes for his blessing. He cuddled them and said: keep the ways of Megalopolis purely and loyally in your hearts. A monumental statue, about the same size as the Battle of the Nations sculpture in Leipzig, was erected to mark his 60th birthday. It was a work from the school of the only true X-ians. They had abandoned the antique symbols, both Phidias and Archipenko, in order to raise the contemporary life of Megalopolis to the level of a new mythology. Four bas-reliefs had been applied to the base. One of these represented Hasdrubal Paaltjes losing his house key. Beneath it were the words: Birth of Megalopolis. Next there was 'The Development of Megalopolis'. This bas-relief was divided into various sections: the procession in the streets in front of the specialists' consulting rooms, the Trans-Siberian express, the overseas voyages and a panorama of the free city of Megalopolis. The framework of this division was formed by a key. The third and fourth bas-reliefs had mottos attached, reading: 'Know thyself' and 'To thine own self be true'. Which testifies to the ethical sense of the people of Megalopolis.

Street names in Megalopolis included: Key Street. Lost Key Street. Hasdrubal Paaltjes' Key Street. The square in front of the town hall was called Lost Key Square. Later people said simply: such-and-such key avenue or street. Eventually the word key completely ousted the tag Avenue. The people of Megalopolis had distilled their life into its mythical quintessence. The great path: raising ordinary life to the rank of eternal symbols. And Megalopolis followed this supreme path. Never had a myth been more logical and natural than this. Megalopolis was a single ethical whole. It is said that this wholeness is sadly lacking in us. A concentrated myth, an ethic instilled in every citizen, of social, political and artistic life were the consistent specific expressions.

Take marriage as an example. Here one can already see how strongly antithetical the society of Megalopolis and our society are. With us everyone recognises marriage as it now is as immoral, at least in a large percentage of concrete cases. And yet this institution remains. A basic principle is soon forgotten in the case of marriage, where other advantages emerge. Here and there one still sees an old evangelical monarch opposing his children's proposed marriage to Catholic princes. This conviction also vanishes where attractive opportunities present themselves. Everyone criticises such an attitude. With reservations: everyone has plausible reasons for doing the same when the opportunity presents itself. Hence a complete rift between ethics and social mores. Things were quite different in Megalopolis. If anyone approached his parents-in-law-to-be he had immediately to produce a medical certificate, proving that as a citizen of Megalopolis he was no exception. If he was unable to supply such a certificate, he was immediately shown the door. He was regarded as a black sheep; someone betraying the established customs and honoured mores of Megalopolis. Not only the parents, but the children too behaved in this way. So deep-seated was this view of life in Megalopolis. In our society we often see a girl defending her beloved against her parents, indeed having her way, if necessary using dramatic evidence. Nothing of the sort in Megalopolis. The first thing girls asked for when they were attracted to someone was his medical certificate. If he could not prove that he was in the usual state for Megalopolis, this was a barrier to the possible development of her feelings, what is generally called love. Most girls hated such a man. Women are of their very nature conservative. And young girls are romantic into the bargain. So girls were bound to hate such a rootless person with the fervour of romantic conservatism. More mature women were simply sorry for him: although an inhabitant of Megalopolis he was in reality without any moral anchor; a poor wretch, who lived in Megalopolis without understanding the ethos of the city.

Of course no doctor in Megalopolis thought of using preventive medicine against the disease. The few who had tried had been lynched by the women. All the doctors had done was quickly find a way of making the disease bearable. Necessity is the mother of invention.

An American philosopher had once said of Megalopolis: through consistent immorality this city has become moral again. On the one hand the people of Megalopolis rejoiced that people were obliged to recognise their ethics. But apart from that they could not understand why this was derived from consistent immorality. They laughed at the American's childish philosophy.

In Megalopolis it was taken as axiomatic that the population level must rise through immigration. So many people were wandering around the world without a homeland, and they were an inexhaustible source for Megalopolis. They also knew that whole black tribes belonged to them. To concentrate all these people in a happy homeland was a dream of the true patriots of Megalopolis. So procreation was not excluded. However, those too old for procreation were regarded in Megalopolis as a threat to society. The people of Megalopolis were a peace-loving people. Only a few, who had taken the philosophy to the level of fanaticism, dreamed of using the black

253

tribes to obliterate the old philosophy. They formed the extreme right wing in Megalopolis and even their opponents had to admit that they held an idealistic position. It was just, the others believed, that the world must be imbued with the new doctrine in a peaceful way. The right wing called them '*des apôtres de la manque*'. All this pacifism endangered Megalopolis, as long as the free city was dependent on its neighbours. Not for a crust of bread: it was a matter of higher merchandise. Of two philosophies. And it was not the time for going to extremes like the Christians in the days of the catacombs.

The origin of Megalopolis already lay far in the past. It was around the myth or reality of this origin in particular that the weightiest problems developed. Sceptics believed that one would never be able to penetrate further than a paraphrase of the hypothesis. Proofs. Heaven help us.

We have already spoken of the friction between the psychologicals and the rational realists. The view of the latter was shared by eighty per cent of the population. There was also a third group, the nominalists. They believed that Hasdrubal Paaltjes was a mythological figure. The lost house key meant more or less that a family (in the state which now was the healthy norm in Megalopolis) had emigrated to Megalopolis, as a result of banishment. The lost house key was nothing more than the mythical representation of the fact: the impossibility of returning to one's homeland. The head of this family, they argued, soon gained prestige and influence in Megalopolis. The adherents of this nominalist view were few in number. They were not only ridiculed, they were hated by true sons and daughters of Megalopolis. Decadents and drifters, they were called. Some heads of families denounced them as Belials, who were trying to undermine the ethical unity of the people. A defender of the nominalist philosophy, was once appointed by accident to a professorship. The students – the heart and future hope of the nation – stripped him and paraded him round the city dragged by a team of horses. Nominalists were never invited in polite society, an honour that did, however, once befall a psychological, even though it was only to make fun of him. The situation of the nominalists was vaguely like that of the Jews in our society.

However, the greatest rivalry was between the two well-known groups. The psychologicals acted as though they were the connoisseurs of the truth. The realists were undoubtedly in the overwhelming majority. University professors, the toffs and the nobility, the farmers and the agricultural workers from the countryside around the free city were realists. The artists, some Jewish bankers, ladies from the various worlds, called 'mondes', the wives of university professors and the shop-keeping classes were psychologicals. The last two categories had an erotic interest. The thing was that many realists were impotent: for instance, the university professors. And the shopkeepers allowed love only a very tiny part in life, from, say, from about 10.00 p.m to 10.05 p.m. So the wives of university professors made an erotic compromise with Jewish bankers. Of course there was also 'spiritual affinity'. They spent enjoyable hours while the professor sweated over a new work against the psychologicals.

The argument of the psychologicals can be easily summarised. Starting from Hasdrubal Paaltjes' individuality, it is easy to see that it is impossible to maintain that Hasdrubal lost his house *by accident* or perhaps failed to find it. There must be a very precise cause. Hasdrubal was too careful a person to behave in this way with house keys. Paaltjes must have been drunk, they take as a starting axiom. And it then clearly follows that: he had not lost his keys, but in the nervous excitement of the drunkard had failed to find them. And anyway, argued the psychologicals, debates about this local story of Paaltjes' house key are finally futile. It is not history, but psychology, or better still immediate consciousness that matters. One must determine the causal link between the outward manifestation, which becomes history and inner psychological necessity; reason and cause. Even if the story of the key is true, it in itself says nothing about the inner necessity. And this necessity *exists.* All that remains is to investigate the controlling psychological mechanism. One can, for example, hypothesise and then deduce that Paaltjes had a creative or imaginative relationship to the idea of a state. The loss of the key is the external trigger for creativity in Paaltjes' urge to create a state. Or something of the kind. The loss of the key is ultimately an act of fate, without psychological value. Value has subjective necessity as opposed to the one represented in this story which is like the relation between cause and effect.

The realists scoffed at this argument. Why should Paaltjes have been drunk? Clearly: chance plays no part in the loss of this key. That is also their view. But there is no proof of this development. It is childish to presuppose this drunkenness axiomatically as the result of the empirical experience of a detail. It is immature and incongruous. And then you have these psychological 'delicacies' with a new conclusion inspired by empirical experience: drunkards do not find their keys; Hasdrubal Paaltjes did not find his key either. That is total madness or dilettantish philosophy. One must hold on to the most elementary point: Paaltjes could not get to his bed because he had lost his house key. That was the naturalistic version in the charter and that was how it was. However, the charter was too close to the facts to worry about the causes of the loss of the key. This is regrettable. But beware: how easily one sinks into speculation in hunting for such causes. The realists freely admit this. But various simple causes are possible. The fact that so many people in Megalopolis are redheads, may perhaps be connected with the fact that Paaltjes, in closing a mahogany desk, forgot his keys. The realist carefully pursued this line of inquiry, before emerging with a cast-iron system. The psychologicals in turn ridiculed this – calling it speculative. But most realists were convinced to the point of mania of the truth of mahogany, which after all was in fact nothing but a cerebral game.

But the realists! A realist philosopher of art had written a very strange book. He showed that all the artists in Megalopolis had a preference for red, flame red, as in mahogany and for deep madder colour. The realists see mahogany everywhere, said their opponents, and in fact they could use this as an argument too. Such irony was of course well received by women and revolutionary students.

The realists were forced to admit history as found in the

charter did not penetrate to the ultimate cause. This was a very dangerous gap. Because after all Megalopolis lacked the foundation upon which specific development of the ethos of Megalopolis could be constructed in universally valid terms. The psychologicals said: Admit that he was sloshed and that's that. The psychologicals presupposed drunkenness as a genetic postulate.

In this way yet another new shade of opinion was introduced. Realists who admitted that Paaltjes had been drunk, but clung to the *loss* of the key.

In this context there still remains the argument between a realist and a psychological to be mentioned. This debate was concluded when the pyschological smashed a mahogany bedside table over the head of his fellow debater. The gesture of the infuriated debater was so violent that a few moments later nothing was left of his interlocutor than a pile of philosopher's brains amid splinters of wood and slivers of porcelain. This incident alone was grist to the mill of the realists who saw it as added proof. Why should this murder, committed by someone who had very consciously opposed the rational realists, once again point so clearly to mahogany? Did his whole subconscious life not now force the psychological to a confession? And with his psychological weapon?

The philosopher committed suicide in his cell. He felt the blow all too well. And with this blow at one fell swoop the view of the psychological realists took a huge leap forward in public opinion. And slowly the lost house key and the mahogany reached out to each other. In a manner of speaking, as one is wont to write.

Love, Hope And Dwarfs

Annelies Verbeke

Laetitia Blommaert turned off the engine and found she liked being stationary here. The wind turbines by the hard shoulder turned to the rhythm of the music surrounding her. She hadn't compiled the MP3 herself and didn't know what the track was called, but it sounded fabulous. She wanted to be the double bass player, embrace the instrument full of echoing resonances like a long-lost friend, nestle the side of her head against its neck. She'd learn to play the double bass. Why not? Everything was possible again.

Wind turbines. When a newsreader spoke the word, sometime last year on a supermarket radio, she had understood 'winter blinds'. Government grants for winter blinds. Ben laughed as much as she did. They pinched each other's bottoms and took turns pushing the shopping trolley, piling it high with everything they liked or had never eaten before. In the following weeks he said regularly that he wanted to draw the winter blinds, and she led him to bed. For months afterwards they pointed at winter blinds by the side of the road, until they no longer needed to repeat the phrases.

He was bound to have forgotten that. He forgot a lot and Laetitia didn't think it was a physiological defect. His mind possessed the disconcerting quality of purging itself of all events and pronouncements that were of great significance to her. Of everything that in daydreams she continued to trace in exquisite lettering on the walls of important buildings. His sentence 'No one has ever meant so much to me' occupied the whole right-hand wing of Santa Maria Maggiore. 'Why didn't we meet before?' covered the ocean façade of the Sydney Opera House. At nights the words 'What a sexy body' appeared in lights on the Eiffel Tower. To 'Will you marry me?' subtly incorporated under the main dome of the Taj Mahal – she had added a reservation of her own in brackets: (somewhat flippantly, yet in earnest).

She compared his memory to that of a fruit fly, a frog or a mother-in-law's tongue. She repeatedly tried to explain that what had not been retained, might just as well never have happened, and that she didn't trust people with no memories. She was quite happy to seize the day but not if even the near future whisked it away so casually. Not if she were doomed to lose herself in his past-free life.

He felt that she'd gone on a bit about things recently.

'So that means I must have remembered after all, babe,' he added.

That same weekend he had laughed heartily when she had crushed her fingers in an attempt to use the door as a nutcracker. Then she was sure.

But it had taken the drip-drip of hundreds more reservations before Laetitia Blommaert had opted for hara-kiri. She couldn't bear the thought that only losers did the right thing. She was glad she had left Ben and not the other way round.

Fortunately she was hardened and wouldn't necessarily have to die. She could opt for a less dramatic form of freedom. Although she'd rather forgotten how she used to define the concept, she seemed to remember that it suited her down to the ground. Probably it had something to do with tambourines and endless dune landscapes.

Sitting in her car on the hard shoulder Laetitia realised that her toes were free again too. She removed the sock from her right foot and studied it intently. The remnants of nail varnish were crying out for varnish remover. Almost at once she noticed a piece of loose skin. At the spot where it had left her middle toe, it had gone thin and white. She picked at it at length and with great concentration made sure she did not hurt herself. Ben thought this was a dirty, even disgusting habit. According to him the cheese on his spaghetti resembled the dead tissue that Laetitia carefully collected in the ashtray. After that comparison they stopped eating spaghetti.

Even when there wasn't a single piece of dead skin left to remove, she kept the bare foot on her left thigh. She scarcely noticed that sitting half cross-legged was causing her muscles to stiffen.

When a large 4x4 passed in the inside lane, her car rocked to and fro for a moment. Children waved from the back seats. She wanted to change places with them, play with their toys and wear their Bob-the-Builder jackets. She wanted to be them, all four of them, and waved back. One of them showed her his little middle finger, after which the others, screaming with laughter, turned their little bodies in the direction they were driving. Laetitia decided to close her eyes for a moment.

It took a while before the knocking on the window got through to her. At first she thought the sound was part of the drum solo that the rain was playing on the windows and the bodywork. She turned the music off since it was scarcely audible anymore. Outside the weather and the night had thinned out the trail of red tail lights. Her bare foot felt numb and she had got very cold. As she started putting on her sock, she saw the gnome. Unlike other gnomes, he was wearing rain gear. Instinctively Laetitia crawled as close as possible to the driver's side door. Without taking her eyes off the gnome, she checked with trembling fingers whether the door was locked. The rain streamed off his purple K-Way. The little man again knocked insistently with his small broad fist on the window by the passenger seat. He looked worried.

Very slowly Laetitia's brain formed the thought that the person tapping more and more excitedly on the window was not a gnome, let alone any other imaginary creature.

'Sorrysorrysorry!' she screamed, throwing herself half on the passenger seat in order to open the door for the dwarf.

'Are you unwell?' he asked.

'No,' she said, surprised at the question. She scrambled upright and straightened her hair, which because of the dive for the door had fallen over her eyes.

'Has your car broken down?' He had an affected voice, like an erudite elderly man, which he possibly was.

She shook her head and could clearly see that his concern was increasing. The rain was trying to disintegrate his rain top. Thick drops slid from his hood to his eyebrows and cheeks.

'Get in and sit down,' said Laetitia.

'Right,' he said. 'The weather is exceptionally harsh.' He supported himself on the seat and jumped in with a reasonably athletic motion.

Only then did Laetitia see that a red Volvo was parked a few metres ahead. That must be his car. She wondered how it had been adapted to his size.

'Well,' said the dwarf. 'We're sitting.' He pulled his hood off, revealing his white hair. Laetitia understood why he had no beard. She nodded and tried to smile.

'So, your car's working?'

'Yes.'

To prove the point, she started up. After the diesel engine had growled for a bit, she took the key out of the ignition.

'Were you involved in an accident?'

'No.'

'And you don't feel unwell?'

'No, not really.'

'Not really?'

'No.'

He waited for a moment and said: 'Forgive me. George Clooney.'

Confused, she shook his proffered hand.

'Your name is George Clooney?'

'That's right.'

Since he didn't move a muscle, Laetitia suspected he wasn't lying. She didn't make any remarks about his name, as he probably heard quite enough of them. She introduced herself in turn.

'Laetitia means joy,' said George Clooney.

'Yes,' Laetitia sighed. She had heard that many times before – from Ben, among others, when they first met. She tried to absorb an escaping tear with her eyeball, and failed.

'Oh,' said George Clooney. He looked away and stared tensely at the road lighting. Although he was holding the door handle, he obviously felt that he couldn't leave her alone. Laetitia

261

went from restrained sobs to quite hysterical weeping. Twice she actually screamed: 'Why?' George Clooney bit his lower lip. For a moment she tried to touch his arm. He drew back in alarm when she screamed 'Bastard!' He correctly assumed that the despairing cry was not intended for him. In his jacket pocket he found a paper napkin, and after checking that it was completely clean he offered it to her.

'Thank you,' squeaked Laetitia after blowing her nose. 'I'm so sorry.'

'No problem,' said George Clooney soothingly.

'I've left my boyfriend. I don't even know where I'm going to sleep tonight.'

'Oh.'

Laetitia realised she had to put an end to the charged atmosphere. First she must thank George Clooney most kindly for his kindness and then say in passing that she was sure she could find somewhere to stay. She had planned to spend the night with Opa and Oma Ganzendries, her grandparents, who had been named after the street they lived in. For a moment it had also seemed attractive to wallow in a victim's role and find shelter in an inhospitable place. She had imagined an empty, run-down playground that she had not visited since her childhood. She could sleep under a rusty climbing frame and get a tetanus infection. But she kept these misgivings to herself: she wanted George to stay with her for a little longer.

The rain and wind made it clear as loudly as possible that they were not nearly done yet.

'You can spend the night with us,' said George Clooney.

Laetitia had not expected that. Still, she hesitated for a moment. She didn't like the idea of calling on people she knew and getting ill by sleeping in a playground seemed on second thoughts to be going a little far. The aloof hospitality of a strange house was exactly what she needed.

'Are you sure?'

'We have a guest room.'

Not until she was driving behind the red Volvo did she

wonder who 'us' and 'we' were. For a second she pictured six other dwarfs, but immediately condemned herself for this thought. A slight panic seized her when she realised that 'we' and 'us' might not exist. She didn't know George Clooney anymore than she knew his famous namesake. Would she be able to handle the dwarf if he tried to assault her? Images loomed up in which she was running up a staircase pursued by him. Although her legs were much longer, he trundled along and managed to catch up with her. As he did so, he laughed constantly and bared a row of pointed teeth, which he then tried to sink in her calves. She kicked out and bent down to push him away. What if he was a martial arts practitioner? What if he was armed? Ben would call her naïve, irresponsible and weird. He would also drop everything and rush to her aid, should that prove necessary. But she had resolved not to allow him any further rescue missions. She mustn't get herself into a mess now. As they approached the next exit, she considered turning off and driving away at high speed. The fact that she did not may have had something to do with instinctive trust. Or resignation. Or simply naïvety.

He lived on a new estate. A garden gnome stood by his drive.

The other half of 'we' and 'us' turned out to be his wife. They kissed each other lightly on the mouth. Her name was Nancy. She was slightly bigger and younger than her husband and greeted Laetitia with a firm handshake. She obviously found it perfectly normal to take in confused young women that George Clooney had found on the hard shoulder.

The couple left Laetitia on a low sofa. She suspected that George was telling his wife in the kitchen that she had left her boyfriend. Nancy's reactions sounded sympathetic and curious. When a little later she set down a tray of tea and chocolate on the coffee table, she met Laetitia's eyes with an extremely neutral gaze.

'Out of the way, puss,' she said.

A fat grey tom nestled on the lap of its master, who immediately began stroking it.

The low furniture made the ceiling look much higher.

Laetitia immediately took to the sober house with its distorted dimensions and white-painted walls. The garden gnome by the drive was obviously intended as a joke. They had taste, and a sense of humour.

'I don't want to be a burden. It was a weird day and your husband was so kind,' she said, hoping that Nancy would interrupt her with a reassurance. Her hostess, waved briefly, as if brushing away a piece of fluff. That was all she needed to do. She had a pleasant face. There was no sign of children in the house. Did she want them? Laetitia could imagine her working with toddlers. Would it seem very pushy to inquire about it?

'What do you do?' asked Laetitia. 'What job, I mean?'

'I paint bodies,' said Nancy.

'Oh yes? At trade fairs and so on?'

'Yes.'

At Laetitia's insistence George Clooney showed a few photos, and Nancy acted very embarrassed, but couldn't hide how proud she was. In one of the photos she was standing on a stepladder next to a naked man whose shoulders she was decorating with a zebra motif. Laetitia didn't immediately relate to painted bodies. She said she found the finished models in the photos impressive.

'And what about you? What do you do, Mr Clooney?' she asked George Clooney.

'Just call me George. I'm an insurance broker, and an actor. Not as great an actor as my namesake, but it's a nice sideline,' he said. He explained that he worked mainly in children's theatre. His name was a nice entree in both professions.

'And you?' asked George and Nancy at once.

'I'm an arts administrator,' said Laetitia, who had just sat a compulsory examination for this job. She left various questions unanswered and to pass the time had counted the other entrants. There were a hundred and four. Laetitia had read Classics at university, but had completely lost interest in her studies. Even the philosophers she had once raved about scarcely interested her any longer.

'Where?' asked George.

As smoothly as she could Laetitia mentioned a remote municipality. When the couple observed that they had never yet visited a cultural centre there, she felt relieved and ridiculous. To avoid having to answer further questions on her imaginary job, she pretended to yawn. It worked.

'You're tired,' said Nancy. 'I'll show you your room.'

'Good night.' George waved briefly as she followed his wife upstairs.

'See you in the morning!' she called back quite loudly.

In the bathroom Nancy took a new, vanilla-scented bar of soap from its wrapper, pretended not to hear Laetitia's protests and showed her the guest room. The big bed seemed to be awaiting a princess. Over the silk sheets lay a white tulle bedspread and little mirrors edged with pink yarn.

'How lovely,' said Laetitia. She thought of Snow White and blushed.

'What time do you have to be up tomorrow?' asked Nancy.

'Doesn't matter,' said Laetitia, immediately regretting it.

'Don't you have to go to work?'

'No, I've got the day off.' Laetitia quickly added that she had another week's holiday. Nancy nodded. Before closing the door she glanced round at the glowing cheeks of her guest, who had sat down on the bed.

Left alone by the light of the bed lamp, Laetitia, despite the bedding, felt more than ever deprived of all princes and fairy tales. Although it was two in the morning, Ben didn't seem to be wondering if she had really left him. Perhaps he had completely forgotten her, like the rice dish she had left for him. As she undressed, she slipped down to the part of hell that she had passed by many times in the last few months. It was an assembly area for all those who at that moment were waiting for a call from their loved one, a text message if need be. Anyone giving in to the temptation to make a call themselves was reprimanded. Laetitia was able to control herself just in time. Anyway, what would she say to him? 'Don't think I'm coming back. I've met a dwarf and his wife who are looking after me.'

Their unintelligible voices sounded monotonously through the floor. Laetitia found it incredible that her spending the night here caused not the slightest excitement. Did they have people to stay that often? She liked to call herself hospitable, but in fact she had never offered a bed to a stranger. Once to the friend of a friend, that was all.

To her surprise she was poised over the yawning pit of sleep when she heard George and Nancy making bathroom noises. She had expected the break with Ben to keep her awake all night. Obviously it had mainly exhausted her. She did not even start when the door was pushed ajar with a creak. George and Nancy were welcome to come in and watch over her sleep. With pointed hats and gas lamps if they wanted. It was the fat tomcat that nestled at the foot of the princess's bed. The moment she moved a finger in his direction, he started purring. Laetitia was good at stroking: Ben thought so too. She could picture him exactly lying in their bed alone, with his head protruding only a tiny way from the lilac duvet. And then she imagined precisely that he kept his eyes shut but was not asleep. That he gave a slight groan and laid his hands above the blanket on his head below the blanket. 'Why didn't we meet before' he said to that head, whereupon a young woman crawled out and lay smiling on top of Ben. Laetitia knew the bitch. She had a good memory.

The night turned into vague nightmares about playgrounds where she got her hair caught in climbing frames and tried to escape by pulling on that hair. If she yanked hard enough, she might be able to remove her brain together with the roots. But she stopped because the pain could not surpass the pain of loss. She slept for an hour, perhaps two. When she at last woke up her consciousness played tricks with her. For a moment it was able to convince her that the warmth pressing against her lap was caused by Ben's buttocks. Then she suddenly remembered everything. She pushed the cat off the bed and saw it disappear through the chink between door and frame without looking round. The light coming in through the window indicated that the morning had not yet completely detached itself from night. Bad days often begin early.

Reluctantly Laetitia went with her full bladder to the low toilet in the bathroom. Grief emphasises the compulsory banality of everyday actions. She brushed her teeth with a brush that had been put out for her, and bent down to be able to survey herself in the mirror. Her appearance and feelings were in harmony. She hated everyone.

George and Nancy's bedroom door was also ajar. When she went and stood in front of it, her body cast a long, almost invisible shadow over the medium-size wooden bed. They were holding each other. Laetitia wanted to be the tomcat lying at their feet.

It was six-thirty when she walked past the garden gnome. Her car was parked fraternally next to George Clooney's Volvo. It was impossible to start it silently. As she drove down the drive she hoped she had not woken her host and his wife. She had not wanted to run into them in the intimate clarity of morning. Perhaps they had caught snatches of her nightmares. She sometimes dreamt aloud. After making up the princess bed, she had left a note on their kitchen table: 'Thanks for everything. I'm feeling a lot better already. I slept well. The soap had a really lovely smell, thank you. Laetitia.'

It had to get better, with her and Ben. She put her foot on the floor and started overtaking lorries. She was going home and it had to get better there. If it was still possible.

Laetitia noted with delight that his car was still parked outside the door. She went quickly up the stairs. She heard the radio alarm clock and suspected that Ben was slowly waking up. When she was almost upstairs she had the idea of lying next to him, with her face turned towards his. She would copy the dwarfs, and the rest would take care of itself.

The empty bed crushed Laetitia and filled her with languid fury. The floor was like a powerful magnet sucking her metal heart and knees downwards. Still, her hands reacted promptly. She forced her way to the mattress through the stack of blankets and pillows. The mattress was not particularly cold, but not warm either. Perhaps he had slept in the flat. So why wasn't he here? She wished she had been the radio alarm clock last night. Then she would have seen him, or not. Alone, or not.

She sat on a chair in the living room. She would wait for him here, stiff but calm, dignified. She was dying for coffee, but did not want to eat or drink anything before he arrived. She didn't want it to look as if she were not waiting, but just having breakfast. Because if he came in, in a minute, tomorrow, some time, she wouldn't raise her voice. She would look him in the eye and wait to see what he had to say. Cautiously, as if she'd come back to weigh him up and find him wanting. After which she would give him a last chance.

She heard the key in the front door lock. Her muscles tensed, as she braced herself to see it through. To ward off fate, she had to tap her left knee five times with each finger, which she quickly did.

He looked at her, curled his lip in annoyance and walked past her. He was holding a small loaf wedged under his arm. She got up and followed him to the kitchen.

'Where have you been?

'The butcher's.'

'The butcher's?'

'I bought a sausage in the shape of a loaf.'

She tried to make her laugh sound spontaneous and carefree. He remained tight-lipped. He put coffee on and didn't ask if she wanted anything. On the stove stood an untouched rice dish. It had taken her two hours to make. In the last few weeks they'd argued quite often about the food they ate.

He drank his coffee behind a newspaper.

'Have you got someone else?' she asked. However many times had she asked that by now? Less often than she had thought it. The question would probably not go away until it provoked a devastating answer.

'You never go out for bread this early, do you?' She was an idiot with a heavy head of clay. Her mouth was modelled in the shape of a holy water font and the bags under her eyes had been exaggerated to the point of caricature. Mushy, scarcely liquid secretions accumulated in her. Any minute she would start dribbling or crying. At this moment he was without doubt the least amiable being on earth. His look did nothing to contradict that.

'What exactly are you insinuating? Do you think I'm having a secret affair with a baker's wife or something?' His annoyance was total.

She didn't think it was the baker's wife, but Laetitia's rival might live next door to a bakery. Suppose it wasn't the first time that Ben had been to see her, that on his last visit they'd eaten cakes together, that the cow had pretended to like butter cream, because that was his favourite. The worst thing that Laetitia could imagine was not their making love, but their laughing at something together afterwards.

'I thought you'd decided to leave yesterday? For good? Farewell? Where did you sleep, anyway?'

He knew she hadn't been there. It might even have upset him. He'd missed her. His anger gave her hope.

'I stayed with some dwarfs,' she said. Her face turned back to flesh.

'What?' asked Ben, on his guard.

'I stayed with some dwarfs,' she repeated and then she told him how they'd taken care of her. She got lost in details: the purple K-Way, the body painting photos, the tomcat. Her story faltered, the words disappeared. The content babbled along between them like an insignificant brook. She could see that he had abandoned all hope for her mental stability, and didn't believe her.

It didn't matter what she said, what she experienced. She didn't matter. His mind was made up. On the corner of the kitchen table lay the glass she had broken the night before. Suddenly a snatch of a nightmare from a few hours ago came into her mind. In it she had put the glass in her mouth and crunched it up. Not until she started spewing slivers and glass did she realise she had harmed herself.

She was seized by a momentary urge to glue the glass back together and announce solemnly that she had come back to start over again.

'There's no one else,' he said slowly.

Oddly enough she hadn't expected a 'but'. More like a hug.

'But I don't love you anymore.'

Being left is not the complete reverse of walking out. Nevertheless between the two things there gapes the most important distinction imaginable. Laetitia Blommaert had never understood that some people seek comfort in the thought that it can always be worse. She herself thought there was nothing worse than that. The supportive squeeze of her shoulder, just before he left for work, was so unbearable that it stunned her.

She was left behind with the broken glass. She turned it round and round, felt the edges, which in her dream had been much thinner. She lacked the courage to stick the glass in her veins, or the art of meditation. Still she wanted to try the latter, as a kind of first aid. Her weak heart pumped heavy blood.

She walked through the playground. Her pace quickened as she passed faded climbing frames and worn windmills that turned squeakily with the wind. Under the autumn leaves lay wet, trampled grass. This was the only spot she could recall. She seemed to be deliberately heading somewhere. At the same time she suspected that the recurring places in other people's meditations looked less ominous.

The minutes ticked by. It occurred to her to call Ben at work, but she didn't know what else she could say. Now there was no hope left, no angry thought could yet be formulated. She thought it was quite an achievement to get up off the chair. There must be people who would be stuck in these circumstances forever, who would go on feeling sorry for themselves until they choked on their tears and slid onto the cold kitchen tiles. Laetitia looked for a long time at the dirty floor beneath her feet. Fending for herself was not alien to her, and nor was a social safety net. When she tried to remember what visits she had put off for ages, she thought first and foremost of the dentist and the gynaecologist. Naturally, there were others waiting for her too.

She rang two girl friends, both of whom expressed their

sympathy. Then one said things would turn out all right after all, but that she would ring back later as it was hectic at work. The other, who had been without a relationship for a number of years, announced somewhat triumphantly that you were better off alone. Then she rang another, male friend. When he tried to find a solution, she interrupted him by saying that his arguments didn't apply to straight men.

Her parents didn't qualify as rescue workers. Years ago, for the last time, she had told them a highly personal and hugely sad love story. Alternately, from two different homes, they talked about self-pity, victim behaviour, divorces, genes, history repeating itself, fits of rage, denial, an urge to destroy, fate, wanting to be right and the wisdom that age brings. The final judgement was: 'You asked for it.'

Laetitia decided to visit Opa and Oma Ganzendries. They wouldn't ask embarrassing questions and would definitely be home. What's more, she always felt purged after a visit to her grandparents. It was their simplicity and the naturalness with which they seemed to love each other – and with the certainty that you could always get in by the back door. Laetitia could imagine that in their old age, George and Nancy Clooney would be a miniature version of her grandparents.

For years she had seen Opa and Oma Ganzendries making Yule logs together. They took notice of the seasons. Winter and summer they spread whipped cream, strawberry jam or chocolate sauce over a round section of rolled dough and rolled it up slowly in synch into an oblong cake. Whenever she tried to picture happiness, Laetitia thought of Yule logs.

It took almost an hour to reach their house. She tried to bridge the distance with loud music, which worked pretty well. She saw Ben's back only once or twice, as it was turned on her for the last time.

Oma Ganzendries was sitting next to the central heating radiator, with one leg lying carelessly on a sofa. On the other leg sat an old man frozen in a tense attitude.

'What's wrong with her?' cried Laetitia.

She had seen at once that it wasn't Opa Ganzendries bent over her grandmother. The permed, dyed blond hair could only belong to Uncle Désiré, her grandfather's brother and the only person who wanted that kind of hairdo. Uncle Désiré and Laetitia looked at each other in confusion. Laetitia rushed to Oma Ganzendries.

'It's nothing,' she squeaked to Laetitia's great delight. She really didn't look at death's door, though her blouse was unbuttoned and her wrinkly neck was disfigured by a red blotch. Laetitia pointed to it and asked what it was.

'She had a nasty turn!' The panic in Uncle Désiré's voice made the hairs on the back of Laetitia's neck stand on end. There really was something wrong with her grandmother, something irreversible. It was not unusual for a day to contain more than one disaster. Briskly she placed her fingers on her grandmother's temples and lifted her eyelids with her thumbs. She didn't know herself what she wanted to see in the whites of her eyes, but was convinced that if there was something wrong, she would be able to tell from them.

'Ow!' cried her grandmother. Her nostrils flared angrily. Yet it was as if she didn't dare contradict her granddaughter. Her eyes kept nervously avoiding Laetitia's.

Then Laetitia saw the women's thermal underwear and the flesh-coloured tights lying next to her grandmother on the sofa like faithful snakes. She looked at Oma Ganzendries's legs and then rounded on Uncle Désiré. The man was staring red-faced at the orthopaedic shoes he had just kicked to the other side of the room. Laetitia did not know whether she found the combination of the words 'horny' and 'Uncle Désiré' ludicrous or depressing. The choice became irrelevant when she thought of her grandfather. Slowly she let go of Oma Ganzendries's head. It immediately inclined towards the ground in embarrassment.

Uncle Désiré was the first to move. He picked up his shoes and disappeared into the hall with them. Laetitia waited for a reaction from her grandmother. None came. Uncle Désiré returned with a shoehorn and sat down. He laid the arch supports straight, positioned the shoe horn and slid his foot into his shoe with a faint groan. Oma

Ganzendries, like her granddaughter, seemed to be wondering how he could think of a shoehorn at a moment like this.

'Désiré?' she said angrily. 'For goodness' sake say something!'

'Yes,' said Uncle Désiré. He moved his toes under the leather and looked at them.

As Laetitia was about to close the wooden back door, she heard hurried footsteps. She waited.

'Don't say a thing,' said her grandmother, with a fleeting look. 'Don't say a thing to Opa.'

'How long has this been going on?'

'A long time,' she said and for Laetitia there was both pride and menace in what she added: 'Thirty-five years. There's no such thing as love, dear.'

There were lots of other addresses Laetitia could go to. The girlfriend who was busy at work had probably arrived home in the meantime. Her parents would offer her a sofa to crash on without a second thought. Yet her clear preference was for George and Nancy Clooney, for the strange rooms in their house and their remarkable equilibrium. Laetitia had the feeling that the dwarfs were keeping something hidden that would be revealed if she lived at close quarters with them for a longer time. A secret, a way out or a lesson. A motivation. Something like that.

It took her a while to find their place. On the new estate the house fronts closely resembled each other and the same trees had been planted in every street. Her eyes scanned the front gardens, looking for the plaster statue of a gnome. When she finally found it, it seemed to be waiting for her. Its eyes, almost washed away by the rain, looked longingly in her direction.

She rang five times. Since no one came to the door she parked her behind on the front step. She wondered whether George Clooney was poring over insurance policies upstairs, or amusing a group of children. Was his wife standing on a stepladder painting someone or just out shopping?

Three-quarters of an hour later she came up the drive with a plastic bag full of provisions and a pack of kitchen roll. She tried to hide her astonishment at Laetitia's return with a cordial smile.

'Hey, we thought we'd never see you again. You sneaked off so quietly.'

Although she would probably have asked her in anyway, Laetitia told her that she would have to spend tonight in the street too. She had to admit that that her story was not free of emotional blackmail. The slight frown on Nancy's forehead made her suspect that the woman also realised that.

Laetitia felt a short but intense surge of rage. What gave that gnome woman the right to judge her so obviously without a word? Did she feel, despite her short stature, Laetitia's superior? Her better? Laetitia drifted off into a new playground meditation that paralysed her with an equal measure of fear and calm. A red plastic mushroom loomed up in front of her like a glorious atom bomb. She remembered the object, which supported a see-saw. At the age of six Laetitia had sat down on one of the seats of the see-saw. She had waited there for someone to sit on the other side. Finally Opa Ganzendries had prised her heaving little body off the attraction and taken her home.

When Laetitia finally managed to suck herself laboriously back to reality, Nancy was looking at her in a non-committal way.

'Come in,' she finally said.

Laetitia looked at the crooked parting in the hair on Nancy's head. Surely her hostess had looked less small the previous evening. Less fragile, above all.

'I saw George today and he said I could spend the night here,' said Laetitia.

Nancy put the shopping on the floor and leant forward for a moment.

'Where did you see him?' she asked.

'In a pub,' said Laetitia. Her face no longer flushed when she lied.

'What pub?'

'Near his office.'

Without a word Nancy put the pack of kitchen roll in a cupboard. Then she took a couple of tins of peeled tomatoes to a storeroom behind the house. It was a long time before she came back. Laetitia sat straight on the sofa.

When George came home, she could see that her presence confused him, although he greeted her warmly. He asked what she wanted to drink and in the kitchen exchanged a few inaudible words with Nancy, who was preparing an evening meal. Nancy's rising intonation betrayed a question. 'Did you see her?' guessed Laetitia, or: 'Does she really have to spend the night here?'

George came back and sat next to her with two glasses of red wine.

'Love's vicissitudes sadly still not sorted out?' he asked in his solemn tone. Laetitia sobbed suddenly but uncontrollably and shook her head. In one great sweep one of her tear-stained cheeks landed on his shoulder.

'It's all over,' she screamed. 'I might just as well be dead!'

She buried her head deeper into the wool of George's sweater, which gave off quite a feminine perfume. She looked at some stray cat hair at close range.

'Come, come,' he said soothingly.

He was stroking the back of her head when Nancy came into the room with an oven dish. Laetitia couldn't see her look, but suspected it was her eyes that made George's hand freeze.

During the meal he tried to make eye contact with his wife while he told a story about a man who had set his own house on fire in order to pocket the insurance money. Her eyes remained focused on her plate, although she left half of her lasagna. Laetitia ate scarcely anything either. Out of politeness she said it was delicious.

While she sat in front of the television only washing-up noises came from the kitchen, no voices. She put her head in and found George with a tea towel and a serious frown. Nancy stood next to him with her back to Laetitia.

'Good night,' said Laetitia.

George nodded distantly. Nancy's back didn't move a muscle.

Less than ten minutes later the parquet was vibrating beneath Laetitia's bed with their excited shouting. The high-pitched questions mounted and the apologetic grunting turned to brusque, angry roaring. They were familiar noises that she could not understand, but that made her grin. If there was no such thing as love, as Oma Ganzendries had confided to her, then as far as Laetitia was concerned that absence could be extended to its logical conclusion. Then no one should love. And if anyone wanted to try it anyway, she would soon put them straight. She enticed the tomcat away from her feet, nestled against him and stroked him at length. He didn't purr.

Her sleep had been dreamless. The music did not intertwine with anything, but simply woke her. Laetitia sat up in bed and listened to the slow notes. She was quickly convinced it was 'The Time Of My Life'. As a child she had played the cassette of the soundtrack of *Dirty Dancing* until the recorder had swallowed the tape like a lunatic. She hated the song because of its corniness and because she had once danced wildly to it with Ben, a year ago, in their living room. She wondered if he still remembered. In answer the ventricles of her heart contracted convulsively.

She pushed the tomcat off the bed, ignoring his claws and hurried into the hall. It didn't matter if she made a noise. George and Nancy Clooney were singing along loudly and off key. They sounded drunk.

"*Cause I've had the time of my life. And I've searched through every open door till I found the truth. And I owe it all to you.*'

They had probably deliberately left the door open, in order to throw their truth in her face. Laetitia watched shamelessly as the little couple hopped and twisted round enthusiastically and now and then discarded an item of clothing. There would undoubtedly be a pillow fight to follow.

George noticed her first. He stopped the arm movement that was helping Nancy spin on her axis. Still panting, with her back

276

against his belly, she followed his gaze. They looked up at her pale face and a smile played around their lips. A gentle one, since they forgave everyone everything.

'You must go tomorrow,' said George, like a proud father about to send his child out into the world.

She nodded briefly. She noticed she was suddenly suffering from night blindness. She groped her way back to the guest room.

George and Nancy Clooney didn't try to hide the fact that they concluded their dance session with hard porn. These things could happen, Laetitia knew.

Fortunately she now had brand-new plans to blow away the musty illusions from her past. The plastic mushroom was a temple, the playground her kingdom. George and Nancy Clooney urgently needed to be shown who was right, who was boss.

Laetitia just need to be patient a little longer. Half an hour after the sounds had finally died away, she tripped downstairs. This time she did her best to be quiet. She hunted through the storeroom. Beside a pile of floor cloths she found a bottle of ether. One of the cloths absorbed the stuff eagerly. She thought it was bound to work.

She was right. Both George and Nancy moved restlessly in their sleep when she pressed the cloth against their mouth and nose, but after that they went even limper than before.

'You two are pretty heavy,' said Laetitia to George Clooney via the rear-view mirror. He had just regained consciousness. In a panic he looked at his wife, who had slid down the seat and was resting against his hip with her upper body. He shouted something to her from under the silver-coloured tape over his mouth. Then he made a furious attempt to struggle free. Laetitia gave him the thumbs up sign. It hadn't been easy to pack their naked, tough little bodies with the blankets and ropes.

'We're almost there,' she said, winking at the garden gnome, which she had secured in the passenger seat with the safety belt.

The playground hadn't improved since she had last been there. That had its advantages: it was empty. As quickly as she could she dragged George to the piece of equipment that had been indicated to her in a vision as his destiny. On the big plastic mushroom rested a long metal plank with a rusty seat at either end. It occurred to Laetitia that 'see-saw' was a word she'd used a lot for a while to mean 'have sex', but after that only sporadically.

But it was still needed to describe a piece of equipment for playing on.

'It has to be done,' she said a few times, when George tried to kick at her as he was being tied up. 'There's no such thing as love. You two are an exception, an aberration. I've got to split you up. George spluttered a few inaudible reproaches.

When she had managed to attach Nancy's body too, awake and violently resisting, to one of the seats, Laetitia retreated backwards from them. She waved, thought of Ben and could not take her eyes off the dwarfs.

Moving slower and slower the see-saw sought a perfectly horizontal line. When it had found it, it came to a complete standstill. George hummed something that made Nancy lift her head up to him. Despite the silver-coloured tape over their mouths Laetitia could see that they were smiling. At each other. They didn't look once in her direction as she ran out of the playground.

Swarm

10

Peter Verhelst

33

The lift doors slide open. The cameras follow Angel. He's holding Pearl in his arms. She's covered in blood. As he runs out into the street, he shouts to the alarmed passers-by that someone must call an ambulance. They all reach for their mobiles. Pearl is bleeding heavily. She's so pale, so fragile, so... light. He carefully sinks to the pavement. It's a radiant morning. When Angel hears a siren, he dials the emergency number on his own mobile and summons all available ambulances. 'Hundreds,' he shouts, 'thousands of men and women!' He sends off a message to the forest – **MISSION ACCOMPLISHED COMING ASAP.** He's dog-tired. He strokes her hair. *Everything will be all right. It will soon be over.* The sun does what it has to do. An ambulance screeches to a halt and Pearl is already being lifted into it. Someone pulls Angel in. Just before the doors slam shut, they hear a voice so shrill that all heads turn towards it. A girl comes running towards them from the Silver Complex. She's naked. She doesn't look you in the eye. Once she has passed the camera zooms in. Her back is burned, the skin has melted. A paramedic gives chase.

In the square there's a bus waiting. At the windows Japanese tourists swing their cameras round to follow the running girl.

Scores of sirens echo among the blocks of flats.

The first ambulance will be found weeks later in the forest. Empty.

The girl with the burned back will identify herself as Phan Thu Kim Phuc. She will be interrogated by the police. She will not be prosecuted. She will not stay on the payroll of the delivery company.

Mister V will not be awarded the Nobel Peace Prize.

32

9

31

The Dedalus Book of Flemish Fantasy

The miniature camera – Russian-made – is as small and unobtrusive as a button on the suit of the man who positions himself in front of the mirror. He sees himself disguised as a tramp. His name is Willard, special agent Willard. The pictures being beamed back to Headquarters are jerky but recognisable.

Willard's hand appears in shot and pushes the door open.

Colonel Schwarzkopf is standing at the window, from where there is a heroic view over the city.

Willard hangs his jacket over a chair.

Without looking at him Schwarzkopf says: 'Hey, Billy. Long time no see. That beard doesn't do you any favours.'

'It's over, Schwarzkopf.'

She shakes her head. 'You've gone soft, Billy.'

'Hands on your head.'

Colonel Schwarzkopf puts one hand on her head.

'Don't do it,' says Willard.

She looks over her shoulder. She smiles. 'At last.'

'Who are you working for, Schwarzkopf?'

She shakes her head. 'Good old Billy. Still believes in the existence of good and evil.'

'All I know is that there's such a thing as a good side and a…'

'How's your wife? What was her name? Cindy? What happened to Cindy, Billy?'

Silence.

'She didn't suffer. The end justifies the sacrifice, doesn't it? Good and evil, Billy?'

He goes in closer, the barrel trained on the back of her head: 'Hands on your head. NOW.'

'We've all lost people,' says Schwarzkopf. 'And what good did it do?'

'I said: hands on your head, Faith.'

'What do you think, Billy?

30

'How's your son? Is he happy? Yesterday I saw my daughter on the computer screen, she was throwing her cuddly toy in the air, Billy, every fucking day and every fucking night I dream she says something to me and comes running towards me as she used to and everything's like it used to be. Know the feeling, Billy?'

That remark gains her the fraction of a second required to dive sideways, draw the gun from its holster, drop onto her side, take aim and … Their bullets cross. They fall at the same time. Schwarzkopf tries to stand, but slips over.

'Who?' says Willard. 'Whose orders were you…'

They will keep looking at each other, with their guns trained on each other, as they bleed to death. Even after they've bled to death. The only pity they show: watching each other die.

Scores of wigs will be found in a cupboard in the room. Strips of sticky tape. Scores of shoes – on the soles a relief pattern will be found, which on closer inspection turns out to be the paw print of… a bear. Finally they will find: the photo of a child, a girl, in the arms of Colonel Schwarzkopf. Her eyes – proud, despite the burst capillaries from the pain she has suffered, filled with melancholy – the eyes of every new mother. On the back is the date of birth and a name in capitals: NAOMI.

No trace of the bodies. In the woods a car is parked at the edge of a lake.
Drops fall from the case. Soon afterwards the car has disappeared beneath the surface of the water. Mr H's telephone vibrates, but in vain.

Mr V is rung up by foreign journalists wanting to talk to him about the Nobel Prize.

29

8

28

Ambulances. Military vehicles. Police cars. Small trucks with TV station logos on their sides.

The evacuation is in full swing. Helicopters hover between the towers. Armed men run up stairways. Armed men slide down a lift shaft, one by one, every second a hand grabs the steel cable. They place explosives on doors, two seconds after the explosion they lob in light grenades and make their way inside. They run into passages carved out of the cliff, closely followed by men armed with cameras. Silvery grey shots of the first corpses lying in the dark are beamed up, and are soon followed by the first tangles of bodies, driven together by panic. They must have run instinctively towards the doors, clambering over each other, crushing each other, desperate to find a breath of air, a loose stone in the massive walls, with their bare hands they tried to prise a gap... *Look at those faces! Whatever you do don't look at the faces! Surely there must be some survivors.* Someone turns on a torch. The camera zooms in on the dark auditorium. It's as if a diver, decades after a shipwreck, hundreds of metres below sea level, is sending back the first pictures of the algae-covered Titanic. But they appear from everywhere, drawn by the light, scores, hundreds of bodies. An unstoppable stampede towards the light. They will find a way out of the Complex. Some are no longer recognisable as human beings, crawling on their hands and knees, stumbling, running, they don't look at you, they look right through you, and when a microphone is thrust in their faces, they produce incoherent sounds that express only the most primitive, most animal fear. They have seen *things*, caught a glimpse of the unspeakable, and now they're running away from it, they're looking for a wall to smash themselves against, in order finally no longer to have to see.

High in the sky helicopters are hovering and one of the

27

pilots looks through his sights, puts his finger on the button, zooms in. At a window bathed in icy white light someone is standing watching. A child with a cuddly toy. The finger on the button relaxes. Everything is OK. The child is pulled away from the window.

In a telephone interview with a female Belgian journalist Mister V maintains: 'What you guys know is just the tip of the iceberg.' The journalist replies: 'I'm coming to see you.'

26

7

25

An aerial view of the Silver Complex. A photo in shades of grey.

The tower expands at lightning speed. It isn't a photo. It's a film transmitted by a camera attached to the warhead of a Cruise missile.

The missile plunges down a chimney stack, like a bullet returning to the barrel – interference in the picture – the missile spins round but doesn't explode, comes to a halt. Impossible to make out how many people are in the auditorium. The camera pans away: it's as if poison gas is being released, the chaos is so great, the tangle so inextricable.

'Scores, perhaps hundreds…' says a voice.

A voice says: 'There are five guards. They are spread around the auditorium in a star formation. One of them has his foot on a detonating device. The principle of the landmine: there are going to be casualties.'

Some hostages are moving their upper bodies to and fro and backwards and forwards. Their heads covered with a veil. Rocking themselves beyond the limit of exhaustion.
> One by one they lose consciousness.
> But the others go on.
> Beneath the billowing veils one catches a glimpse of a singing mouth. They are all *children*. Boys and girls singing songs with Kalashnikovs trained on them.

One by one they slump sideways. On top of each other. Until only one body is left.

The camera zooms in.

24

Every time the body rocks backwards, it throws its arms in the air as if it were throwing up a cuddly toy and the movement lifts the headscarf up to reveal a girl's smiling face. And each time she catches the cuddly toy, throwing it higher each time.

Thousands of children on top of her.

The girl's face, in a trance. That solitary girl's voice still chanting those verses. But they aren't verses. They're words turned inside out, anagrams, impossible new combinations, it's the alphabet itself, distorting, mutating!

The camera pans away.

Men in uniform charge into the auditorium. Shots are fired. Explosions follow. The camera lies there watching. A hand closes its eyes.

At 8 a.m. Mister V's doorbell rings. A woman identifies herself with a press card. Her name is Cindy. Mister V smiles. They chat. They drink tea. Mister V loses consciousness.

23

6

22

Two women are cutting condoms open and mixing the fluid released with human gastric acid. They will see the miracle happen in the microscope.

'What is this?'

'I haven't a clue.'

'Is this regeneration? I remember once seeing something similar in a computer simu…'

'No. Look. This is impossible. What's happening here flouts every law of nature…'

'But it's happening.'

'Holy cow.'

The two women appear on the security screen at one-minute intervals. There's a wall covered in screens. People are working feverishly in every laboratory.

*

'It isn't regeneration. It's *mutation*. It's mutating as we watch. It's impossible.'

'That means…'

'…'

'…'

'… that in a certain sense we're looking into the future.'

'That the future is happening *now*, while *we*…'

'That we're looking at our *own* future?'

'Jesus.'

'I'm scared…'

'Oh my God…'

'I'm afraid that everything we know is no longer…'

'Whose is this smear?'

'But we've already checked that!'

'But that means that one mutation is followed…'

'… by another? But that…'

21

There is a substance that only functions in a human body. Human gastric acid is the fuse of the bomb. That substance – odourless and colourless – can be easily added to water supplies. Not a soul will notice.

*

The same astonishment will hit them when they examine the next smear. The same principle, but differently executed, completely arbitrary. No logic, no pattern of any kind will be found. Exactly the same for the other smears.

'What on earth were they exposed to?'

'How were they infected?'

'It must be highly infectious.'

'In that case...'

'What are you doing now?'

But one of the women has already stuck a needle in her arm, and the blood is dripping into the reservoir. She scarcely allows herself time to stem the blood from the wound. She is shaking so violently that she spills a few drops. 'You focus the microscope. I... if it's true, then...'

The other woman focuses the microscope. They're both thinking of their children.

'What can you see? For Christ's sake, tell me what you...'

The other woman stands up and staggers over to the syringe cupboard. The first woman is worried and takes a step towards her. 'No, don't you dare come any closer.' She holds the hypodermic needle in front of her like a weapon.

*

'If it gets into the ground water, then...'

*

20

In another laboratory they're studying the first results of the experiment that was conducted in the underground Institute. The data that flicker across the screen are impossible to disentangle, dissident variants of the Formula. 'This is a dead end,' says a voice. 'This is pointless. This is a terrible mistake.' Another voice says: 'Perhaps we don't understand it yet and one day we'll…'

*

In the underground auditorium inexplicable holes will be found. When the camera zooms in, you'll feel you can look up to the sky. Through the layers of earth and water. Meltdown.

They will find cavities all over the city.

They don't know what *it* is, but *it* will find its way into the ground water. It will be carried into reservoirs. It will pass through the filtration plants. It will pour invisibly from a tap in the suburbs as a child sticks a toothbrush in its mouth. A woman's voice will say: 'Come on, darling, get a move on.' And the child will nod enthusiastically, with a foaming beard round its mouth.' Rinse your mouth out, darling. You can't go to school like that, can you?' The child will choke on the water.

> The mother sees the camera: 'We've no time for that now, darling. We're late already.' Oh, those men, with their new toys. She pushes the camera away.

*

You'll compare your DNA profile with the one that was made years ago

19

for an identity card and was both impossible to copy and unique, as accurate as an iris scan.

You'll notice that your DNA profile has changed, as if the pattern of your fingerprints has been altered.

It will feel as if someone has been messing about with your *innermost core*.

Everything and everyone has been infected.

No one is any longer who he thought he was.

Nothing is any longer as we thought it was.

Perhaps that's the moment when the *constantly changing thing* – let's call it a virus, for want of a better word – is that the moment when the virus becomes metaphysical?

*

The security screens give an overview of all the laboratories. Soldiers are bursting in everywhere. Not all the soldiers have chemical protective suits

A woman leaves Mister V's house. She has an alibi. She's never been at Mister V's place. She's never heard of Mister V. The authorities will check out her alibi.

18

5

17

Down in the docks a female tramp pushes a child's pram laboriously over mountains of rubbish. She's in a hurry, she's out of breath, but she's stubborn, she has a purpose. She's heard voices that have led her here. Some Africans have given her information in exchange for *services rendered*. The pram falls sideways, but she doesn't give up. She doesn't hear the cars, she doesn't see the revolving lights flashing, the cars surrounding her. She is blinded by the headlights, her pram gets stuck in a mound of sand. One wheel is twisted, but she doesn't give up, why should she, she's on her way to meet her son, she's been on her way to meet her son all her life. Policemen leap from their cars and take aim at the woman. A policeman grabs a megaphone and shouts: 'On the ground! Face down! Hands at the back of your neck!' But she doesn't hear him. She tries to keep pushing the pram, but it veers off course. 'Second warning. If you don't obey instructions, you will be shot.' *My little angel, little angel, little angel*, she whines, she begs as she pushes the pram on two wheels. 'This is the last warning.' Policemen look through their sights, aim for the legs, fingers squeezing the trigger. At the moment they fire, the woman stumbles. Her pram has crashed into one of the supports of the crane. One wheel is spinning in the void. The tramp is lying face down on the ground.

A few metres above her Abel is lying motionless on his back. Arms outstretched. The wind is playing through his clothes. The first birds are circling him. But *is* it Abel?

When the police cars fight their way to the warehouse complex, they will find the bodies of ten men. The complex will be virtually empty. The ship, with a full cargo of cars, will be heading for an unforeseen sandbank.

16

A policeman will lay his hands over the woman's eyes, so that she can finally find peace. The camera in the police car has recorded everything. The tape will be erased.

Mister V wakes in the boot of a car. The car is in the docks. A Mossad agent says: 'Everything you say may be used in evidence against you.' Mister V is arrested on suspicion of attempting to flee to an unspecified country. 'You were in the vicinity of a port.'

15

4

14

The chaos is total. In the square in front of the Silver Complex, in the underground auditorium and in the Complex itself. The residents are being evacuated, floor by floor, block by block. Ambulances are arriving and departing. Journalists are trying to keep on their feet in the commotion. In television studios men and women are having their make-up feverishly retouched during the commercial breaks. For now people are groping in the dark as to the nature of events. Survivors make no sense at all. Some talk about an illegal party, a rave that got completely out of hand. Others mention chemical substances being administered, a nurse talks at length about symptoms she has never before seen in such arbitrary combinations. Symptoms of what? The camera wanders away from the umpteenth body being removed from the scene, but the director intervenes. The police commissioner arrives. Before the first question can be fired at him, a policeman whispers something in his ear. The commissioner is at a loss. In the mêlée the journalist has caught the word *mayor*. The commissioner leaves. The journalist grabs his earpiece and says: 'It's rumoured that there will shortly be an important news announcement on the kidnapping of the mayor of this city.' The director is so astonished that the journalist remains in shot for a number of seconds. A line of screeching children walks behind him. 'Why didn't we know anything about *children* being held hostage?' roars the director.

In the underground auditorium the soldiers have penetrated to the dark heart. They discover a hermetic construction, a smooth, impenetrable cube, so black it seems to absorb all the light. The soldiers have to go round it to gain a clear picture of it. And even then, when they look at each other it's as if their vision is distorted, *curved*. The first soldier falls through the wall, then the second and then there's no stopping it.

13

Ingeniously fitted panels topple and those holes swallow one body after another in a fluid movement. The soldiers switch on their helmet lamps. They have to climb over bodies. Some seem to be clinging to a second wall. And to a third. It is deathly quiet. Completely motionless. Only later, when the building is dismantled, will it become clear that built-in furniture was used that forced the bodies into certain positions. Furniture with strategically placed holes corresponding to the various apertures in the body.

The corridors in the structure narrow towards the centre, like the convolutions of a shell. In the centre itself there is scarcely room for one body. There are two bodies. Welded together. A man and a woman. The woman is on her back, the man on top of her. In her fall she has pulled the leather mask off. It's the man everyone has been hunting for so long, though it takes a while before everyone realises. How could it be otherwise? How can the naked, besmirched, beheaded body be linked to the man you've only ever seen in carefully chosen clothes, a man who has been smiling out at you for years from scores, hundreds of photos in magazines and newspapers, has cropped up every day in newsflashes and during live broadcasts of council meetings, a man who was so at one with his tailor-made suits and ties that his face had become invisible.

The mayor is identified by the missing first section of his index finger.

His secretary Lily is said to have been identified by Max and Lassie, who happened to be going through Polaroids of the victims in the building. Photos that will fill so many walls. The hope that people's grief will be given a direction, a name.

The official report reads: '*At about noon troops found the dead body of our kidnapped mayor. The body of his secretary was found in the*

12

same auditorium. The scene is at present being officially investigated.'
End of message.

The secret report mentions the prototype of an infection device for ritual use. A structure in which young, pure bodies would wilfully allow themselves to become infected, and to be *converted* to the religion of Hepatitis Romanticus. *Barebacking*. The millennial dream of Universal Infection – the dream realised on an industrial scale.

On the abdomen of one of the young men found in the building is the following message in Gothic script: R U HAPPY NOW? On his penis are the letters: **I AM** +. Angel of the Infection. Bridegroom of the Virus. Homo Invictus Viralis.

There's a top secret report containing photos of the decapitated body.

The head is nowhere to be found.

How is it that this of all reports is circulating on the Web?

Mister V is held *in solitary confinement* for an indefinite period. Until national security is guaranteed. A senior civil servant says: 'Mister V is the Bomb. He's the one threatening our security.'

11

3

10

The soldiers penetrate further and further into the Institutes, at the same time as troops swarm over the whole Complex. There seems to be no end to it, a city over a city, Troy beneath Troy, ring after ring, concentric circle after concentric circle.

At the end of a corridor a unit comes face to face with another, unknown unit. Everyone keeps everyone else covered. Everyone waits for an order.

Later a senate committee will conclude that both units received their orders from one and the same officer. The competent authorities will state emphatically that they will investigate everything *exhaustively*. The officer will be struck down by a heart attack on the eve of his trial. The autopsy will not reveal anything suspicious.

Meanwhile one unit has reached the end of a narrow passage. No explosives are needed to open the door. The auditorium is plunged in darkness. Everywhere there are tiny lights, a starry sky that glows in their night-vision binoculars.

On the ground is a man with a chest wound.

On the ground is a second man with a gun barrel in his mouth. The floor is daubed with blood. Part of his face has been blown away.

A man is hanging over a screen, connected to machines by wires. Blood is dripping from his ears, the corners of his eyes and his nose. There is no sign of brain activity on the relevant monitor.

The soldiers take off their night-vision binoculars and look at the big screen which gives a panoramic view of the reception room: bodies hoisting bodies onto stretchers, the battlefield being cleared.

The other screens are dark, but the darkness moves and breathes.

A soldier bends down towards Mr J's mouth, and the soldier's head appears life-size on the screen. The camera focuses.

9

The soldier withdraws his head in alarm. The camera zooms in on the wound again, and tries to focus. The gentle pulsating reappears on the screen.

Meanwhile the two hostile units receive orders to dig in with their backs to each other. Orders are orders. They keep each other under surveillance with mirrors.

Someone shouts: 'This one here's still alive. He's breathing!' Mr J groans. He opens his eyes.

In the food served to Mister V, he finds a razor blade. Deafening music pounds non-stop through his cell: *The Ace of Spades, the Ace of Spades...* Mister V sees no one.

8

2

'You must get as much sleep as possible. Get your strength back. Recuperate.'

Pearl smiles. She pretends to be asleep because that's the only way to look at him undisturbed. He's changed, she has to keep looking at him to recognise her Abel's face under that bald scalp. He's behaving strangely. Just now he was lying outside the tent with his ear to the ground. He has given her medicines to make her sink into a dreamless sleep. Obviously he didn't notice that she didn't swallow everything. She sees him sitting outside the tent for hours, as if his spirit had risen from his body and climbed above the trees to circle around there unimpeded, carried on the wind. But she need only give the slightest groan and he is at her side.

'What happened? And what...' She looks at his bald head.

'Later,' he says, 'later I'll explain everything,' and he doesn't immediately notice her smile, he sees only her tears and when he asks with concern if she's in pain, she asks him to put his hand carefully on her heart. 'Can you hear it beating?' He smiles. She says: 'You said later. That made me happy.'

He takes off his sweater. He takes her hand and holds it to his own wound. Lets her watch as he tends to it. Then he carefully applies the ointment, as if he were caressing her breast, as if he's not aware of the effect this has on her. 'Kiss me,' she says, her voice is hoarse, he bends over her mouth, but she says: 'No, there.' She breathes deeply. Coughing. Pain. His mouth on her breast.

It is the same primeval act that on the roof of the Silver Complex makes Trinity crawl on her back up the wall of the lift shaft. Her right hand on Carlo's head, her left hand searching for a grip. But there is no grip. There are just his fingers unbuttoning what she begs him to unbutton, and his mouth descending over her belly. And while that mouth

6

sets her on fire, and her hands press down imperatively on his head, a telephone starts trilling.

Nestling in each other's arms in the afterglow, they look out over the city. They can take in everything at a glance. 'Your phone,' whispers Carlo. 'Is it your boyfriend?' he says. 'Of course,' she whispers, and she bends backwards so that he can take the telephone out of her trouser pocket. The display reads: **ALLAHU AKBAR.**

'What does that mean?'

'Nothing anymore,' says Trinity. *Just a goodbye*, she thinks.

Carlo keys in: **PEACE**. She laughs. She sends the message. They sink languidly back into an embrace.

Is it possible that her mobile phone can force an aircraft off course? If a laser beam can direct a projectile, so can a telephone.

The aircraft is crammed. They're sitting in a row in business class, Cheryl Ben Tov, her husband and two daughters. Cheryl beckons the stewardess. 'How long are we going to keep circling?'

At that moment the plane swerves and sets a course back to the city it took off from.

Cheryl looks out of the window and sees that they are flying lower and lower, straight towards the heart of town. 'Surely the airport is on the edge of...? Hey, hey what the hell is...'

Mister V hasn't eaten for days. *I and the Razor*, he thinks. He sings: *The Ace of Spades, the Ace of Spades*.

5

1

4

The soldiers have seen so much. They know that a small bullet hole is sometimes more fatal than a bit of the body that has been shot to pulp, but they also know you can't survive with half a head. What else can they offer the man but comfort? The lie of hope. 'Everything will be all right. They'll be coming to get you any minute. Hang on in there.' They hold his hand. 'What's your name? I think he's too far gone. But his mouth is moving.' One of them holds his ear to Mr J's mouth, as if he were hearing his last confession. The soldier hears: '… basically… good thing for the world… radical transformation… project… symbolic value… inextricable knot of complicities… both people and a system, principles and concepts… philosophy of tomorrow… auto-immunity of democracy… very complex secret transactions… changing alliances… trying not to be unjust to one group or another… messianic aspirations without a Messiah… all hope is invested in this appeal… without hope… without teleology… without being part of a particular religion… that unites the weak of the earth… a promise of an independent future for what is to come, one who comes like every Messiah in the shape of peace and justice, a promise independent of religion, that is, universal… messianic aspirations without a Messiah… this expectation without a horizon, expectation of the coming event, with all its contradictions…'

'He's delirious.'

Blood runs off his chin.

His breathing becomes increasingly laboured.

Mr J doesn't look at the soldiers. He seems to be looking at the point *where all rights converge, far beyond the horizon*, but he's looking at the screen. He sees how the camera tries to focus, zooms in, pans out. Zooms in. Deeper and deeper into his own wound. With a final effort he pushes the soldiers away, so forcefully that they look too. The camera goes even further into the wound. Going back in time.

3

The universe contracts. To the size of a heart. Smaller and smaller. As big as an ovum. An atom. And smaller still. Till all that's left is that primeval pixel. Pulsating on the screen. That one second before the explosion. Before that First Fundamental Miracle. The Big Bang.

Is it possible to fathom that one pixel, as one can a single cell?

Is it possible to fish the helix of the world out of that pixel?

It must be possible to excise those *things* from the helix and so change the future.

Mr J starts trembling violently.

'We're losing him.'

Mr J lies motionless.

'No pulse.'

On a radar screen a bright green dot veers off course.

'Mayday mayday, I repeat, mayday mayday.'

Two F16s take off from a nearby airfield.

The bright green dot enters the airspace over the city.

The pilot is no longer answering.

Somewhere men are making a cut in their foreheads and striking it with their hands.

Somewhere men are jumping up and down, up and down.

Somewhere in a wood a man sees a snake sliding out from between his teeth, swaying in front of him, but it isn't a snake, it's his own genetic code chain swaying in front of his eyes, and everywhere black patches are visible, *someone's been messing about with my...*

Somewhere a girl with a cuddly toy in her arms is standing and earnestly scanning the heavens.

Somewhere Pearl is following with her index finger the outlines of the birthmarks on the arm of a familiar warm young male body – marks that form a constellation, *their* constellation.

2

From the highest point of the Silver Complex, Trinity and Carlo see the aircraft approaching.

The soldiers watch the screen. The pixel is pulsating more and more fiercely, as if working itself up to a new Big Bang.

A soldier closes Mr J's eyes.

Trinity covers Carlo's eyes with her hand – a gesture of love.

The camera zooms in at lightning speed on her mouth. The camera slides into her mouth. Into her throat. Deeper. To where the primal scream originates:

.

•

o

o

o

O

Mister V puts the razor blade to his throat. But…

1

0

H MY

GOD!!

The ground splits open and up rises a gigantic silver *crown of a tree.*

But it isn't the crown of a tree. It's a fiery-scaled cobra with jaws wide open that shoots vertically from the ground into the sky and spits at our eyes.

But no... It isn't a snake, it bursts open into a swarm of birds that climbs higher and higher, screeching and swarming up to the stratosphere, millions of birds, millions of beaks open wide.

But no... It's a cloud. A glittering cloud, made up of millions and millions of shards, a cloud that rises up and assumes the form of a skull.

But no... *Christ, it's the mayor's hea...*

But no... It's a Rohrschach test.

-1

Where the Complex once stood, there is now a gaping, smouldering crater, so deep that it seems to be the negative of the Complex itself. *The Void.* Satellite cameras zoom in and show unrecognisable *things* and scenes of devastation for which new words will have to be found if they are ever to be evoked – named in order to be forgotten. Even language must be given a new meaning.

What is that, *forgetting*?

Steel that has been twisted by the heat into the shape of honeycombs, or on second thoughts of sloughed-off snakeskin, or… of an unknown cell structure.

The camera zooms in on details. A child's shoe. That's what triggers the sobs.

We cannot forget the grainy images of people standing at windows waving white cloths. Blurred close-ups of *singing* faces. *Things* are falling out of the top windows. They're not *things*. They're not falling. They're jumping. A man with a briefcase. Two bodies hand in hand.

The camera zooms in on the crater. The heat is so enormous that the images become fluid, unrecognisable, *traumatic*.

Even while the evacuation is still going on photos and eye-witness accounts appear on the Web, words and images that have already taken on a life of their own, that are already detaching themselves from the actual events. They stick in the memory, because why do we start awake weeks later? Things we see or read when we surf the Web infect us. From now on the virtual world is an inextricable part of us. Genetic material.

-2

We all know someone who died in the disaster.

> We all died in it.

> We're all complicit.

> We're all victims.

> We're the ones who took the shot with our mobiles. Shots of people looking at us with their last breath.

> We posted those shots personally on the Web.

> We texted or spoke the accompanying texts in the hope that someone would receive our words.

> We're the ones who stumble dusty-faced out of the Silver Complex, in a snowstorm of fluttering paper and dust.

Where the hell are we?

Some people sit in front of the TV screen day and night, as if entranced by the endless repetition of the collapsing Silver Complex.

> Some don't dare enter their own houses, for fear of a new disaster.

> Huddles.

> Heaps.

> Hope.

Because of the dust situation we haven't seen the sun for days. There are rumours circulating about the composition of the air, saying that the *concentration* per cubic metre is so complex that it cannot be analysed. Surgical masks are distributed to prevent panic.

> Everyone's in shock.

> Firemen descend into the hole and emerge hours or days later, close to exhaustion, and look as if they no longer recognise the world.

-3

For now, astonishment and fear are more powerful than anger.

No one has claimed responsibility for the attack.
There is a flood of phone calls claiming responsibility.

We don't want ambiguous answers. We want the right questions.

The first Chanel-designed surgical masks appear on the streets.

Some women complain of a burning sensation in the cervix after intercourse.

Some people have to be restrained by the forces of law and order from leaping into the crater in search of missing relatives.

Hospitals are stormed.

Men and women stand at the exits to tube stations holding photographs.

Strangers embrace in the street.

A baby has just been recovered alive from under the rubble.

People go on looking, untiringly, day and night.

It will take years before the rubble is cleared away. There are excavations everywhere where holes have been made in the ground. A number of islands are commandeered by the government and ships come and go, loaded with sealed containers.

Families who have lived in the city for generations move away and hole up in the countryside.

-4

Every day crowded trains arrive in the city, carrying young people who think the streets here are paved with gold.

They're predicting a baby boom.

A voice says: 'We're up for it.'

According to the statistics sales of multi-coloured clothing have inexplicably risen. According to statistics firemen and policemen are the sexiest men in town.
V…

A voice says: 'Do you see that spot on the X-ray? You're in a permanent state of recovery.'

A voice says: 'Believe me.'

At night there is a glow visible over the crater, phantom pain trying to become a *thing*, full of meaning and consolation. Silvery blood of the evaporating matrix – zeroes and ones in a huge swarm. We see the glow above the crater. Even we who never believed in… It's not imagination. We're not alone. There are thousands of us. We can't keep our eyes off it. We see a vase in the sky and the vase gives light. So intense that that we can look right through the body in front of us. And it isn't a skeleton that we see: the bones form letters and the letters words, and breathlessly we hold our arms up and add a letter, a V, and another V, everywhere, and…

Your telephone vibrates: ☻

A voice says: 'Cut!'

A voice says: 'Begin at the beginning.'

-5

A voice replies: 'This *is* the beginning.'

Biographical Details

J M H Berckmans (1953-2008) was one of Flanders' most experimental authors and has been termed a "cult author *avant la lettre*". His stories are mostly set around Antwerp where he lived for many years. Influences include Bukowski, Céline, Beckett and de Sade. He worked for a short while as a shoe-salesman in Italy during the time the Red Brigade was active. He had a hatred of conventional literature.

Louis Paul Boon (1912-1979) was the nearest that Flanders ever got to winning the Nobel Prize for Literature. Starting out as a "miserablist" author near to the naturalism of Émile Zola, he became over time Flanders' most accomplished Modernist author, although towards the end of his life his works became less literary and more pornographic. Nevertheless, Boon wrote several novels involving a serious commitment to Socialism including the tale about the Catholic priest who sided with the workers *Pieter Daens*, which has recently been filmed. Three of his most accomplished Modernist novels are available in English translation: *Chapel Road*, its sequel *Summer in Termuren*, and the short novel *Minuet*.

Paul Claes (born 1943) comes originally from Leuven and is a classicist by profession. His novels often have historical settings. He also writes poetry and essays. He is a prolific translator into Dutch of, for instance, Catullus, Sappho, Mallarmé, Rimbaud, and Pound, and has also translated Dutch poetry (Gezelle, Leopold) into English.

Hugo Claus (1929-2008) was one of the most productive and versatile Flemish writers, author of *The Sorrows of Belgium*, as well as being an actor and artist. Claus, like Boon, was considered for the Nobel Prize.

321

Biographical Details

Johan Daisne (1912-1978) was one of the founders of magical realist literature and of Communist sympathies, causing him to study the Russian language. He is perhaps best known internationally as the author of the short-story which was adapted into the 1968 film *Un soir, un train*, with Anouk Aimée and Yves Montand.

Saskia de Coster (born 1976) is an author of contemporary non-realist short-stories, some of which are reminiscent of the works of Jeanette Winterson. She has been writing since an early age. She has published novels, short-stories and newspaper columns and regularly works together with people in the field of fine art and has worked as an experimental artist herself.

Jef Geeraerts (born 1930) started his career as a writer in the 1960s after serving for a while in what was then the Belgian Congo, where he was wounded as a soldier of the colonialist power. By contrast, the present story here is set in Lapland. He often compares societies thought of as primitive with the seeming sophistication of the West. In recent years Geeraerts has re-invented himself as a thriller writer (his "The Public Prosecutor" appeared in English in 2009).

Kristien Hemmerechts (born 1955) is a leading novelist who has also written many short stories that centre on relationships with partners and parents, also involving children and their loss. Her first published work was in English.

Stefan Hertmans (born 1951) is a prize-winning novelist and short-story writer and has also published many essays and poems. He is Professor of Fine Art at Ghent University. He was guest at the London Book Fair in 1999 and 20 of his poems have appeared in English translation in the periodical "Modern Poetry in Translation".

Hubert Lampo (1920-2006) was, alongside Johan Daisne, the leading proponent of magic realism and many of his novels and stories belong to this genre. His novel *The Coming of Joachim*

Stiller was a major landmark in this genre, and has appeared in English translation. Many of his works are set in the Flemish city of Antwerp. Lampo was also interested in the Arthurian legends and British myths.

Rachida Lamrabet (born 1970) is of Moroccan origin and her works often centre around young people of the same origin as herself and their dreams and longings. She has, to date, published three books. She works as a lawyer specialising in equality of opportunity and anti-racism.

Ivo Michiels (born 1923) has written two novel cycles, *The Book Alfa* and *Journal Brut*. The former was inspired by the French *nouveau roman*, while the latter cycle consists of ten experimental novels published between 1983 and 2001. Michiels has lived in Provence since 1979.

Yves Petry (born 1967) studied science and philosophy at Leuven University, then became a writer. Science fiction and anti-utopian elements are evident in the excerpt here of his novel *The Straggler*. He is a frequent contributor to the Flemish literary magazine "De Brakke Hond".

Hugo Raes (born 1929) started out as an experimental poet and novelist and has since then moved to the genres of sci-fi and horror.

Ward Ruyslinck (born 1929) is an anti-establishment author of long standing. His works often reflect the protest of individuals against the Roman Catholic Church, capitalism and the military establishment.

Paul Snoek (1933-1981) made his debut in the 1950s as an experimental writer, although he never became a full-time author, working instead in business. His work moved in an ever more pessimistic direction.

Peter Terrin (born 1968) is regarded as one of the promising new generation of Flemish authors. He published his first novel in 2001. He writes novels and tales involving a measure of morbidity: carjacking, murder, anti-utopia, and the threat of rampant technology. He often produces character studies from the perspective of a disturbed person.

Felix Timmermans (1886-1947) was once one of Flanders' most productive and successful authors. He was an autodidact, and started out by writing rather gloomy tales, such as the story here, but is far better known for his later novels, all written in a quasi-naïve style and celebrate life in the Flemish countryside, with its simple religiosity. Even his examinations of painters and characters from the Bible all exhibit these same traits. The 'folksy' tone of much of his work enjoyed great popularity in interwar Germany.

Walter van den Broeck (born 1941) is a modernist prose author and playwright. He is of German-Flemish-Mexican-Filipino parentage and was brought up in the working-class district of the provincial town of Olen. His multi-layered novels involve a good deal of fantasy, centering on the *cité* (working class housing estate) and by way of contrast, the Belgian royal family, seen from various unusual perspectives. He is best known for his series of novels about a man who is more or less kidnapped and is taken to live in the grounds of the Royal Castle in Brussels.

Karel van de Woestijne (1878-1929) was the leading Flemish Symbolist poet of the early 20th century. He was influenced by Germanic literature and French Symbolism. He was born in Ghent and later on lived with his brother, the painter Gustave van de Woestyne, and others in an artistic collective in Sint-Martens-Latem on the River Leie. His prose often draws on themes from the Ancient World or the Christian religion and are often sensitive examinations of moods and trains of thought in the minds of saints or the dying.

Paul van Ostaijen (1896-1928) was the leading Flemish Dadaist of the early 20th century. Known mostly as a poet, van Ostaijen also wrote satirical short prose, like the text here after his disillusionment with the carnage of WWI. He mixed in Dadaist and Expressionist circles in the Berlin of the 1920s and was among the first Dutch writers to discover Kafka's work.

Annelies Verbeke (born 1976) is one of the most visible young Flemish authors of recent times. She studied Germanic languages, and has written film scenarios and columns in newspapers and periodicals. She specialises in writing about ordinary people in bizarre situations, blending realism with a hint of distorted perception. Her novel *Sleep* has been translated into over a dozen languages.

Peter Verhelst (born 1962) is a versatile poet, novelist and playwright, originally from Brugge (Bruges) and is one of the leading postmodernist Flemish authors. His works circle around catastrophes and a world on the brink of disintegration. He often deals with symbols, artificiality, and intertextuality and avoids politically committed writing.

Dedalus European Anthologies

The Dedalus Book of Greek Fantasy – Connolly   £9.99
The Dedalus Book of Spanish Fantasy – Costa & McDermott   £10.99
The Dedalus Book of Flemish Fantasy – Dickens   £9.99
The Dedalus Book of French Horror – Hale   £10.99
The Dedalus Book of Dutch Fantasy – Huijing   £10.99
The Dedalus Book of Estonian Literature – Kaus   £9.99
The Dedalus Occult Reader – Lachman   £9.99
The Dedalus Book of Portuguese Fantasy – Lisboa & Macedo   £10.99
The Dedalus Book of Austrian Fantasy – Mitchell   £12.99
The Dedalus Book of Medieval Literature – Murdoch   £10.99
The Dedalus Book of Polish Fantasy – Powaga   £10.99
The Dedalus Book of Surrealism – Richardson   £9.99
The Myth of the World: Surrealism 2 – Richardson   £9.99
The Dedalus Book of Finnish Fantasy – Sinisalo   £9.99
The Dedalus Book of British Fantasy – Stableford   £9.99
Tales of the Wandering Jew – Stableford   £9.99

These books can be bought from your local bookshop or online from amazon.
co.uk or direct from Dedalus, either online or by post. Please write to:
**Cash Sales, Dedalus Limited, 24-26, St Judith's Lane, Sawtry, Cambs,
PE28 5XE.**

For further details of the Dedalus list please go to our website:
www.dedalusbooks.com or write to us for a catalogue.

The Dedalus Book of Dutch Fantasy – Richard Huijing

The Dedalus Book of Dutch Fantasy is the most ambitious and wide-ranging anthology of Dutch fiction ever to appear in English, and reads like the Who's Who of Dutch Literature, with stories by undisputed contemporary masters such as Gerard Reve and Harry Mulisch, and classic authors such as Couperus, Van Schendel and Vestdijk, as well as many of the rising stars of the younger generation: Frans Kellendonk, A.F.TH. Van Der Heijden and P. F. Thomese.

The stereotype of the Dutch that most immediately springs to mind is that of a clean, orderly, and down-to-earth people. Richard Huijing reveals the other side of this society: that of a dark netherworld of the macabre, the weird, the perverted, the violent and the fancifully impossible conjured up by a host of the finest writers in the Dutch language of the last hundred years.

"Of all the Dedalus anthologies, the biggest surprise – and the most consistently entertaining as well – is *The Dedalus Book of Dutch Fantasy*. That Huijing could fill his near 400 page anthology with works of such high quality, most of them by writers from this century, seems nothing short of incredible." Gilbert Alter-Gilbert in *Asylum*

£10.99   ISBN 978 0946626 69 4   377p   B. Format

Bruges-la-Morte – Georges Rodenbach

"This is one of the greatest novels ever written about grief, loneliness and isolation; and such subjects are, alas, always relevant these days. (Those suffering similar personal circumstances will find it remarkably consoling.) It is the kind of book, I kept thinking, that should have been turned into an opera by Debussy, along the lines of what he did with Pelléas et Mélisande, by Rodenbach's contemporary and fellow-townsman Maeterlinck. As it turns out, Erich Korngold did such a thing in 1920, but the Nazis banned it, and I'm not sure that he would have had the right musical attitude. If Debussy hadn't done it, Alban Berg would have been ideal.

I keep thinking about music so much because so much music resides in the words, even in (the very able) translation. This is a book which is not only richly, almost oppressively, atmospheric: it is about atmosphere, about how a city can be a state of mind as well as a geographical entity. It has its shocks and its melodrama: but it is a haunting, and a haunted work. Congratulations to Dedalus for reviving it." Nick Lezard's paperback of the week in *The Guardian*

"A widower of five years, Hugues wanders Bruges in mourning. Heavy with a spectral misery, Rodenbach's symbolist novel, first published in France in 1892, is a compelling albeit flawed work. As Alan Hollinghurst remarks in his introduction, it is a novel 'by turns crude and subtle', but although not a classic, it is also significantly more than a curiosity. There is an opiatic quality to the writing which at its best hovers on poetry's border. Hugues's relationship with the dancer who closely resembles his dead wife provides the plot, but the book's real heart lies in the descriptions of Bruges itself, and its 'amalgam of greyish drowsiness'." Chris Power in *The Times*

£7.99 ISBN 978 1 903517 82 6 166p B. Format

The Bells of Bruges – Georges Rodenbach

Shortlisted for The Oxford Weidenfeld Translation Prize for 2008.

The Bells of Bruges is a study of obsessive love which is steeped in the melancholy beauty of Bruges.

There are three loves in the life of Joris Borluut, the town carillonneur of Bruges. He marries the fiery Barbara, whose dark beauty is a reminder of Belgium's Spanish heritage. Repelled by her harshness and violence, he starts an affair with her sister, the gentle, soulful, fair-haired Godelieve. When her sister discovers their affair, Godelieve enters a Beguine convent and Joris devotes himself to his first love, the old city of Bruges. His opposition to a proposal to sacrifice part of the old town to economic advance loses him his position as town architect, and he withdraws to the belfry and his beloved carillon that seems for him to express the soul of Bruges.

"*The Bells of Bruges* is a long and crowded novel that touches on everything from nineteenth-century obsessions with progress and decline, to tourism and town planning... Borluut is caught between two women, the dark, fiery Barbara and the ethereal, pale Godelieve. Between them they represent, on the one hand, the earthy, Latin side of Belgian culture, and its Nordic, mystical side, Rodenbach's obsessive symmetry is such that he provides Borluut with bells that also represent this: a small, clear, tuneful bell and a large, dark bell inlaid with obscene orgiastic images, a 'bronze dress' up which he loses himself. Sex and death are never far away in Rodenbach, either from each other or from the surface of the story. As the novel's extraordinary climax shows, *The Bells of Bruges*, is no exception."

Patrick McGuinness in *The Times Literary Supplement*

£9.99   ISBN 978 1 903517 54 3   244p   B. Format